First Published Worldwide 2021
Copyright © Luke Smitherd 2021

ISBN: 9798511626352

Other Books By Luke Smitherd:

Read on after the end of this novel for a free sample from the beginning of the first book in Luke Smitherd's bestselling series THE STONE MAN.

Dedication:

For Barnett Brettler. Thanks for everything, mate.

Reviewer Acknowledgements:

At the time of writing, the following people wrote a nice Amazon or Audible) review of **THE EMPTY MEN**. Thank you so, so much. I'm a little bit higher up the novelist totem pole these days, but those reviews still mean *everything*. I'm only using the names you put on your reviews, as these will be ones you're happy to have associated with my work (I hope). In alphabetical order they are: 451, 9wt, A Addison, A Sutton, A. Maudsley, AB1701, AJB, Adam de Jesus, Adrian Trickett, Alex Lancaster, Alix Leclerc, Allan, Allmac1, Amanda Evans, AmazonMonster, Andrew Nottingham UK, Andy, Andy P, Ang Wallis, Angewhatever, Angie Hackett, Anne, Anne K Robinson, Anne Mains, Anonymous User, BC Gill, BSM, Barbara Irwin, BigRedMachine, Blanche Padgett, Bnbboy, Bob, Book Thief, Bruce in Suffield, CJ, Canis Major, Carly May, Carol Wootton, Carrotpipe, Charles Dunne, Chris Goulter, Chris Jenkins, Chris Wells, Christopher Ham, Claire Atkinson, Clemmie, Craig G, Craig Melville, DJC, DWFG, Dale, Damien Ryan, Dan Carden, Dan Wright, Daniel, Darren Chantler, Dave Carver, Davey Blie, David Plank, Derek Cooper, Dickamazon, Don, Drac1968, Dragonett, Eddie Clinton, Edwynmccann, Flashheart8, Foilguy, Frederick Catlin, Froggy, G. Walker, Ged Byrne, Gemma Chapman, Gilaine, Grampy Rye-Rye, Hazel, Henry, Iredhanded, J Breckenridge, J Jenkins, J O'Quin, J. Molineaux, JC, JD Bordell, JMM52, Jackie Sosta, Jacqueline, James B., James Bellwood, James Farler, Jameson Skaife, Jamie Greenwood, Jane Eston, Janet Eidys, Jason, Jason Austin, Jaster Girl, Jeff, Jinny, Johnny, Jon Perry, Jonathan Knight, Joolz, Julie Blaskie, Julja, Jullie, Justin Winston, K Young, Kaitlin Pappert, Karajo, Karenr, Katharine, Katof9tails, Katy Costello, Kelly Jane Gill, Kelly Jobes, Kelly Rickard, KendallRN, Kevin Gilmartin, Kevin McGrandles, Kevin Watson, Kia, Kindle Customer, Kindle CustomerMyn, L. Bailey Humphries, L. Sheehan, L. Stenson-Jones, L.J, LMiller, Lacy May, Lady A, Lauren Pollock, Laurie Davenport, Lawrence McClure, Lee Fardoe, Lee Helmore, Lewis, Liam Curran, Liam Hodgson, Linda Cartmell, Linda Urban, Lisa H., Lou DeMarco, LouiseTheFox, Luke, Luke Gittins, M. Rawson, MK1, MM78, MMG, Madalyn King, Marc, Marci, Mariah H, Marion Moore, Mark, Mark Batty, Mark Brennan, Mark Fowler, Mark Ledsom, Mark Say, Mark Terri, Marshe90, Martin McAnaney, Mary J Burke, Matt, Matt de Moraes, Matthew, Me, Melissa Weinberger, Mickey D., Mike, Mike H, Mle, Mr Dog, Mr Johnnie Colquhoun, Mr Keith J Lawrence, Mr North, Mr R A Dean, Mr ris, Mr. D.M. Wood, Mr. J. Clements, Mr. Mark Collins, Mr. S. D. MacMaster, MrMat, Mrs SK de Verenne, NJ Ferris, Neil, Nicola Stamp, Nikunj T., Odeta, P W R Wilcox, P. G., P.S. Stephenson, PC Brickwood, PFJKelly, Pa Broon, Pat Hannigan, Paul, Paul Ashworth, Paul Cox, Paul Roberts, Pauline M, Perks, Peter C, Peter Puzey, Phil A, Puffin Man, R Webb, R. G, R.G, RJL, Ralph Kern, Rich Lambe, Robert Jenkinson, Rowell H, S From East Linton, S Harley, S Kilbourne, S. Andrews, SJ Burns, SJ Stokes, Sally, Sarah, Sarah H, Saultrue, Shadowfire5371, Sharon McLachlan, Shoe Diva, Simon Mills, Simon211175, Smurry, Son of Samhain, Sophie David, Spud, Steve, Steve Blencowe, StevencGlasgow, Stevey G, Stuart, Suzanne S, TAF22, Tammy Stenning, Terri, TerryF, The_Guvnor, Theresa D., This Mum Works, Tim Clark, Todd K. Brooklyn, Tom, Tony Grant, Top Topper, Tracy Collins, Trish Cummings, VOM, Victoria Elizabeth, Voodoogold, Wendy McGregor, William M. Stahura, Winter's Mom, Zidanny, and Zoe Mckechnie. *If you asked for a Smithereen title, check out the list after the afterword to see yours!*

You See the Monster

Monster

By Luke Smitherd

Chapter One:
2002

***

Sam sits in a café. His coffee is now cold, but the taste was disappointing long before that. He wouldn't have chosen this place to meet. Melissa did.

The clientele says everything Sam needs to know about the establishment, in that there are no other customers present; the only other people there are staff. There's a middle-aged, scruffy looking gentleman sitting behind the counter reading a paper. There's a woman somewhere, possibly his wife, who wanders in and out occasionally from the back room, saying nothing. There's a large mirror on the wall to the right of the counter, presumably mounted in an attempt to make the place look bigger. It doesn't work, perhaps because the edges of the glass have been plastered over the years with now-faded stickers. The floor is tiled, the walls are tiled, and sounds from a tinny radio echo unpleasantly off both ageing yet impervious surfaces. Sam possesses one out of those two qualities.

Melissa is late—very late—hence the cold coffee, and even though Sam expected that, he's worried that he's already angry. This was always going to be a difficult conversation, but going in with a hot head certainly wouldn't help. He'd told Leslie to stay at home. It took a three-hour argument to get her to listen. Sam has a decades-long history of saying *yes dear* to his wife, but this was one issue on which he was adamant: Melissa had hurt Leslie enough, and she wasn't going to be present for this. Sam realises he's gripping the handle of his cup way too tight. As long as she doesn't bring that piece of shit with her. Even Melissa wouldn't be that difficult, surely? She knows not to wave a red rag like—

The café door pings as it opens. Sam looks up and for a second thinks that Melissa has no-showed and *oh she wouldn't,* sent the piece of shit by himself ... but Sam sees he's wrong. The man walking in is long-faced, like the idiot, and unkempt, like the piece of shit, but he's too tall, too stocky, and too well-dressed; a full suit and tie job, shoes clean and shiny. In his late thirties, perhaps. Sam notices details like this. He's police, after all. It's 10:27am. Sam's brain goes into processes so automatic he doesn't even consciously know they're happening:

Too early for lunch, but anyhow he eats at nice places. A salesman, maybe, needing a coffee to keep him going—

Sam's eyes go back to the door.

"Hello," he hears the man behind the counter say, a slight sigh in his voice as if two customers in the room at once constitutes an early rush. The newcomer mumbles something in response. "Sorry?" the man behind the counter repeats.

"Just a... can of coke please." The suited man is audible this time.

"Right." Again, a slight sigh. Some people are never happy. Sam looks at his watch again. Doesn't Melissa realise this is her last chance? He hears a chair scrape out as the newcomer sits down, followed by a faint rustling of paper. Sam's eyes move in that direction of their own accord; the man has pulled a folded piece of yellow-looking paper out of his pocket and is now staring at it intensely. Even though his mind is elsewhere, some instinct in Sam keeps his eyes on what the man is doing. He fumbles with the outer corner of the paper, eyes dark and serious, fingers lightly playing with it... and then he slowly tears the very corner off.

He keeps the torn-off piece in his hand, looking between it and the paper still held in his opposite grip. The piece he's torn off is tiny, slightly bigger than a postage stamp. It's mildly weird behavior, but Sam's bad-guy radar isn't going off. In fact, this fellow barely seems to register in his awareness at all, for some reason. It's almost as if the reason Sam keeps looking at him is to remind himself that the man is still even there.

The door pings again and Sam jumps a little in his seat, but quickly comes back to himself as he sees it's Melissa. He mentally winces as he spots two things: she's skinnier than ever, and she's brought the piece of shit with her. Sam's immediate anger switches to a sudden, deep sadness as he sees a faint smile appear on Melissa's face. She saw Sam's expression as the piece of shit walked in. Sam realises this and understands exactly how the conversation will end. He did the right thing not letting Leslie come.

Sam stands up. Melissa reaches the table, her grey jeans, black cardigan and T-shirt creased and unkempt-looking. The POS stands behind her, shifty as ever, gaze darting anywhere around the room except at Sam. Sam still doesn't know how old this man is. Thirty? Thirty-five? Melissa won't tell him and, despite all his contacts and skills, Sam hasn't been able to find out. *Jake's off-grid*, Melissa had proudly parroted, clearly believing that the piece of shit is some kind of shaman, and not a waster from Binley. That said, the off-grid thing may be why Sam can't even get a surname. Leslie wouldn't let him have them tailed. She's always been too soft, too damn *coddling*, and Melissa realised it from the time she was three. Sam knew he was to blame too; if he'd worked less, hadn't always been chasing those promotions, he could have been there to balance it out. By the time he'd realised how bad things had become, so bad that even his weapons-grade denial couldn't curb the truth anymore—when Melissa took the family car for a spin at sixteen, drunk behind the wheel—it was too late. Now she's about to throw her life away with this scumbag.

"Mel," Sam says, trying to keep his voice steady. "I asked for this to be just you and me." He doesn't look at the POS. Melissa makes the face he's seen far too much of in recent years; the one she's *always* ready to pull. She's always waiting for somebody to say something, it seems.

"And I told you, Dad, that Jake is part of my life now and you have to *accept* that," she says, deliberately loudly of course, so the guy behind the counter and the suited man look their way. The latter looks away quickly, eyes back on his folded and yellowed paper—Sam notices he has another torn-off piece between his thumb and forefinger, the previous one now discarded on the table. "I'm eighteen." Melissa lowers her voice, much to Sam's amazement. "I'm an adult now. *You can't tell me what to do.* I don't live under 'your roof' anymore. So if I want to bring Jake, I will. You're the one who wanted this meet-and-greet." Eighteen. And shacked up with a weirdo old enough to be her dad.

It takes everything Sam has not to snatch the ashtray from the table and bludgeon Jake over the head with it until he's a bleeding mess on the floor, but he manages to keep at least *that* instinct in check. Other internal safety measures are falling away with terrible speed, however, and although Sam feels this, he is powerless to stop it.

"Maybe I should, uh, go," Jake mumbles, both his hands in his jacket pockets. "This is a family thing, and—"

"No, she's right," Sam says, suddenly wanting Jake to stay. If that's the way Melissa wants to play, Sam can fucking well play it. "I'd actually like to ask you some questions, Jake. I was going to ask Melissa, but, seeing as you're here—"

Leslie would be losing it at him right now. Another good reason why she wasn't here.

"Don't you fucking dare," Melissa hisses, leaning forward. "You aren't at work. You aren't *questioning* him."

"Didn't say I was, I said I'd like to ask questions, there's a difference—"

"What? What about? What do you suddenly want to know about Jake? You've never asked anything before." Super defensive. Melissa always was a terrible liar, despite a staggering amount of practice.

Sam's heart breaks. He hadn't wanted to believe the worst, the final straw, but Melissa's classic *what, what* told him everything he needed. This was it. He couldn't let her hurt Leslie anymore. They'd failed their daughter in the worst way, but it was Melissa who had banged in the final nails. Like she'd said herself: she was an adult now.

"You know what about," Sam says, and as he sniffs back tears he sees Melissa's screwed-up bulldog expression soften, *just for a moment,* and in there is the little girl he'd delighted with a surprise trip to Center Parcs when she was six. Then the gate falls again and Adult Melissa is fully behind the wheel. The liar. The thief.

"Grandma's necklaces."

"What *about* Grandma's necklaces?"

It's utterly unconvincing. With that sentence Sam feels something profound break off inside him and begin to float away. It leaves a hole that will never fully heal over. Shrink a little—maybe even a lot over the years—but never reconstruct.

"Was it for you?" Sam says, addressing the piece of shit as a flood of sadness automatically switches to anger, as so often with men. "Did you put her up to it? How much did you even *get* for them—"

"*Dad!*"

"*I'm talking to* him—"

"I'm gonna go," the POS says, face flushed, already abandoning his girlfriend, of course. "You guys, uh, you—"

"*Dad, what the fuck do you think you—*"

"Hey," says the man behind the counter, finally waking up, "can you take this outside, I have customers here!" Sam isn't listening, he's already rounding the table, heading after the piece of shit, flushed now himself, not thinking, but of course he really knows *exactly* what he's doing. Sam's always-on-the-details eye notices that the suited man still hasn't moved, although even more of the paper has now been torn away and... is he *crying?*—

Sam's hand grabs the piece of shit's retreating shoulder and Melissa screams. Part of Sam knows this will destroy any remaining hope of a reconciliation with his daughter, but perhaps that's exactly why he's doing it. Rubber-stamping the moment. This was the one thing he'd told himself *must not happen* if Jake turned up, and here he was deciding to—

The POS spins round and slaps Sam's hand off him, shoving Sam away as he does, an action that gives Sam's thick fist the instinctive excuse it's so very hungry for. Sam isn't a big man at 5'9", but he's always had big hands, ones he knew how to use once upon a time. His muscle memory is good, it seems; all the anger, the hurt, and of course the thing that's really behind it all—the knowledge that he let this happen to Melissa and how she's become completely alien to him—shoots down Sam's arm and empties beautifully into Jake's nose. *Smack.*

Jake, Melissa, and the man behind the counter all cry out at the impact—Melissa's is a screech so high Sam almost expects the windows to shatter—and Melissa barges past to get to her boyfriend. Jake's already getting up, a shaking backwards lurch intended to get him as far away from Sam as possible, but the red mist is already leaving Sam's brain and he's realizing just what he's done. It was out of his control, it had just taken him over—

No. He knew what he was doing.

"*Fuck you!*" Melissa yells, bundling Jake towards the door as Sam opens his fists, holding them out to her stupidly. "*Fuck you! You aren't my dad! You aren't my dad!*"

Sam opens his mouth to say *Melissa, wait...* and then doesn't say a word. He just stands there, a storm blowing in his brain that blocks out all thoughts. His pulse beats, hard, and he falls back against the nearest table. His hands are shaking. He watches through the fogged-up windows of the café as Melissa and Jake hurry down the street.

Leslie is going to... Sam thinks. *She'll ...*

But how *will* Leslie react? She must have known this was going to happen, or something like it. They both did.

He looks up towards the suited man and now it's Sam's turn to scream.

The suited man is no longer sitting in the chair. There's the detritus he's left on the table, but that isn't what Sam's looking at, even as he hears the man behind the counter make a strangled sound, repeating *ahhk... ahhk... ahhk.* He hears movement as the woman comes out from the back once more.

"What the hell—*OH MY GOD! OH MY GOD!*"

Tables screech as they are flung aside. Sam dives sideways on autopilot, trying to get to a chair that he can swing even as his mind curls up into a ball and gibbers in terror. His big hands grasp two of the nearest chair's legs and he spins round, barely able to hold it, but the attacker has already darted straight to its target: the couple behind the counter.

"*RUN KELLY, RU*—" the man bellows, but it's already too late. The attack is so *fast*, his throat's torn open before he can even finish his sentence. Blood sprays across the room as the man is flung aside and though Sam's legs are telling him to take the man's advice he tries to get to the counter, raising his weapon high, a man wading through water as he attempts to get around the cluster of overturned tables and chairs between him and the woman. She makes a critical mistake, moving out towards Sam—automatically seeking protection, perhaps?—and not towards the back room. Her screams of dismay for her murdered partner—and terror for herself—hit a pitch even higher than Melissa's earlier shriek and Sam knows it's too late. It's a cry of agony as she's torn from crotch to sternum. Bellowing, Sam throws the chair. It misses wildly, shattering the mirror by the counter, and unless Sam can get to another one *right away* he's dead, the speed of the attacker is insane, he probably only has a second or two—

Sam clutches another chair and jerks up with a cry—*AH!*—ready to swing for dear life, thinking only of Leslie now, but he sees he's now alone in the café. The only sound is the tinny, now blood-spattered radio playing away to itself, and Sam's I'm-going-to-start-working-out-this-year breathing. He jumps backwards, eyes frantically sweeping the floor; the attacker's down under the tables!

The attacker is not.

The back room, an exit! While he was looking around for a chair—

He hesitates, light-headed. Spots dance before his eyes. Something shoots down his arm. Wait, is this—

It is. It's really happening. His heart finally rebels after too many steak dinners with a nice red; he drops to one knee as the chair he's holding clatters to the floor. He grunts, trying to stay conscious, fumbling his phone from his pocket. If he doesn't get someone out to him, he's going to die. No-one will ever know what the hell happened here. *Leslie* will never know—

"*Emergency, which service?*"

At that moment, his brain catches up. *Well bloody hell,* it says, like a drunk wandering in after the fight scene. *What on earth did I miss?*

It's not possible. It's just not.

With that, as Sam grunts out the name of the café, holding on—quite literally—for dear life, he's already making a decision, even if he doesn't consciously know it: *all this didn't happen.* He'll give the description of the suited man and how the couple at the counter were butchered, but he'll leave out certain elements. If someone were to know the truth and ask him why he chose this approach, he'd maybe tell them his family had just been shattered, that it was too much to deal with. Or that he had his eyes on promotion and didn't want anything on his record that might jeopardize that. Good, reasonable explanations.

The truth would be that Sam is simply scared out of his mind, and attempting to file the unspeakable away is the only option available to his psyche.

He wouldn't be alone in such thinking. Things have been this way for a very long time after all, and thus mutually beneficial for all parties involved.

Sam will eventually begin to believe his own story, so much so that when the sleepless nights and terrifying dreams come, he and Leslie—and not Melissa, of course—will put it down to job-related stress and get him onto a course of antidepressants. They'll help, a little. Sam will still retire early without ever truly knowing why, and he will never make sergeant.

He will still enjoy his simple pleasures, and a peaceful life.

***

Chapter Two
2019
***

Erin Lafferty roots through her purse for her front door keys, stomach muscles clenched as she desperately suppresses the need to pee. She knew she should have gone when she stopped for petrol.

"Evening, Erin," says Steve from next door, surprising her from behind. She turns her head to see him smiling and waving. Ben and little Hattie, red-faced and sweaty, smiling and waving alongside Steve. Hattie's holding her dad's hand and a frisbee. Ben has a football. They're coming back from the park then, or rather the tiny patch of grass in the middle of the new-build suburban street. It's a nice neighbourhood, a far cry from where she nearly ended up. Despite the intense pressure in her bladder, she smiles, almost genuinely. They're nice kids, a nice family, and her heart is slightly warmed by the sight of them happily returning home as the sun starts to drop... but she's never been comfortable making small talk. Her anxiety creeps up, amplifying the pressure in her bladder.

Fucking keys—

"Hi Steve," Erin gasps, already dropping her head back to her purse. "Hi Ben, hi Hattie. Hope you've had a nice night."

"Good thanks!" shouts Hattie, trying to wipe her sweaty, flyaway hair from her forehead with the frisbee as the trio reaches their front door. Kids... Erin's thirty. She could still do it, *would* have, if things had worked out with Richard—or if he'd managed to keep his dick in his pants around the women in his office—and maybe she'd have a little Ben or Hattie of her own right now. She still had time. And meanwhile, there's Scubby, hairy little shitbag—

GET THE KEYS—

"That's good," Erin says, two more unsuccessful seconds away from tipping the entire purse out onto her doorstep—then *yes* there are the keys, thank *Christ*—

"What's *that* thing, Erin?" Despite the urgency of the moment, Erin looks up automatically. Hattie's pointing at something on the ground by Erin's feet. Steve smiles apologetically in Erin's direction—*kids, ha ha*—before the smile disappears into a look of confusion.

Erin looks down.

There's a small object on the left of her doorstep.

It makes sense that Hattie would see it when Erin didn't. It's so small it only just pokes over the top of the concrete step. For whatever reason, when Erin's eyes fall on it, her desperate need to urinate abates. She can't really see what the object is from her vantage point so she squats to get a closer look. It's made of... metal? Something smooth and solid-looking, at least, but not all of it. Other parts are... fabric?

She reaches down to pick it up.

An instinct tells her, *don't*.

But that makes no sense.

Erin's thoughts flash back to when nothing made sense—the time immediately after Richard was tough, she'd turned to the wrong people and all the wrong substances—and remembers what she'd learned on her way out of it. Which kinds of thoughts to let move through you. Even so, she steps down and crouches, peering at the thing.

"I... don't know, Hattie," she hears herself say, her voice coming out small and squeaky as she sees the object more clearly. She moves around a little, to put her body between the strange delivery and Hattie's sightline. Again, the instinct doesn't make sense—there's nothing overly threatening about it—but as she glances at the trio next door, she sees the thought mirrored in Steve's face. That same, unsettled concern.

"Come on, you two." He scoops his children towards the door with forced jollity. "One of you is going in the shower first." The sounds of dismay carry into the street as the kids enter the house, but Steve steps back outside for a moment. His smile is gone. He feels the same way.

"You okay, Erin?" he asks.

Then she realises what she's doing, where she is. This is the most normal street in the world. It's some teenage nonsense, a gag—

A weird revenge prank? But Richard was years ago; she's only just got her shit back together so there's been no-one else since.

"Yeah. Looks like the teenagers round here are getting creative," she says with a fake chuckle. It's unconvincing, but it's enough for Steve.

"Okay," he says, giving her a thumbs-up. "Gonna get these two terrors into bed. Think I tired them out enough that they'll put up less of a fight than normal."

"Good luck," Erin says, completing the longest exchange she's ever had with her neighbour, and Steve goes inside.

The thing on her doorstep begins with a small, square wooden base. Sticking out of it is a thin, flat-tipped metal spike about seven inches long, and jutting out from that are pieces of slim, battered and bent metal. They're about an inch wide at their thickest point, jutting out at odd angles. They've been wrapped or crushed into very slender tips where they attach to the central spike. Soldered onto it perhaps? Erin doesn't know. They're angled downwards, giving the effect of tree branches, and Erin recognizes parts of logos: they're strips of aluminium taken from cans. Strung between them are what Erin thought at first were pieces of fabric; now she sees small flies crawling along them and understands she's looking at thin strips of meat.

Bacon?

Her hand goes to her mouth as she realises her mistake. Some of the strips have small patches of fur on them. This meat isn't cured; it's been stripped from some kind of animal, washed, and attached to the construction. There's no blood, but there *is* something sticky on the metal strips. She catches a whiff of it: washing up liquid? It's running a little—must have been left recently—but the detergent seems to form some kind of pattern. There's a series of black marks on the wooden base forming similar loops and lines to those made with the liquid.

Glued to the flattened tip of the central spike is a shape made of tightly woven wool, or maybe straw. It's hard to tell; whatever it is has been dipped in tar, the lines of weaving just about visible underneath. The shape is crude, and it takes her a few seconds to figure it out; it's the triangle at the bottom of it that was throwing her off.

That's supposed to be a skirt. That's supposed to be a woman on top of this thing.

Then:

What the fucking hell?

Her skin breaks out in gooseflesh, and at that moment her bladder smashes back into her attention—

She jumps up, keys still in hand, and unlocks the door before flinging it open and plunging down her hallway, ignoring the insistent beeps of the burglar alarm and Scubby's frantic barks of delight as he runs around her ankles. She only just makes it, almost tearing her underwear as she jams it downwards along with her jeans and sits down into blessed relief. For a moment, her mind is empty of anything but bliss as Scubby's delighted-terrier yips come from the other side of the door. Almost as soon as she's finished though, she's thinking again—of course she is—of the creepy-as-hell construction sitting outside.

The insistent beep of the burglar alarm picks up from BEEP...BEEP... into BEEP-BEEP, BEEP-BEEP, letting her know it's approaching a release of its own.

Call the police? Surely that's silly. But she *is* alone.. Well... maybe not quite. But still rebuilding a life, and that means a lack of people watching her back. She'll tell the police. Just in case it happens again.

Erin finishes in the bathroom and races back down the hallway before insistent beeping turns into a deafening blare. She rushes past poor Scubby who still hasn't received the usual fuss and heads straight for the alarm keypad. It's right by the still-open door, and as she punches in the digits—*1982*, Richard's birth year, she's still not changed it—of course she takes another glance at the thing outside.

BEEPBEEPBEEPBEEPBEEPBEEPBEEPBEEPBEEP—

It's still there, the washing up liquid and the crude tar woman on top glistening in the setting sun.

You expected it to be gone, didn't you?

The beeping stops.

... are you going to leave it there?

She's not going to leave it there, but there's no way in *hell* she's bringing it into the house. She decides to throw it in the bin.

Except—it's evidence.

In the shed then.

But she'd still have to touch it.

The tongs from the barbecue, she could grip it with them. She never used them, al fresco dining was Richard's thing. She briefly pauses to stroke a near-hysterical Scubby and then goes to the garden to fetch the tongs, still charred from the last barbecue, three years ago. Scubby obediently trots behind her, but when she heads back out to the front doorstep, she shoos him inside and closes the door. She doesn't want him sniffing around the object, let alone nibbling at the meat on it. She takes a few pictures with her phone. Evidence.

Holding the tongs out at arm's length, she squats down and uses them to grip the thin metal spike as carefully as if it were Chernobyl graphite. She figures that the best spot from which to lift it is near the base, gingerly angling the tongs between the metal strips and the meat like a grotesque game of *Operation*. She grimaces even as she touches it with the tongs and begins to lift.

The spike pops out of the base.

The whole thing collapses with a flat, wet sound as the meat and metal fall to the concrete driveway, all of it separating as if it had been held together by nothing more than child's glue.

Erin cries out in surprise—the word *no*—and staggers slightly in her crouch, gently falling back onto her buttocks, tongs flying from her hands. The only two pieces of the small construction that are still stuck together are the central spike and the tar-straw woman on top of it.

Erin sees with an inexplicable sense of horror that the fallen metal is lying on the concrete in an uneven circle. Inside it is a smaller circle, made by the fallen meat. The marked wooden base is in the centre. The spike has fallen against it. The tar woman on top, held at a forty-five degree angle atop the fallen spike, is almost perfectly aligned with the centre of the base.

Erin looks at this series of uncanny patterns and tries to tell herself it's just a remarkable coincidence. It is, after all, nothing.

But the shadows have lengthened now—the sun's dipped well below the roof of the house opposite—and the tar woman's tiny shadow stretches long and dark and away from the debris.

Pointing towards Erin.

She remembers Hattie's question.

What's that thing, Erin?

The sun continues to sink, and Erin begins to tremble, sitting where she's fallen in her driveway.

***

Part One

Sleeping

Chapter Three
The Monster Stirs
✳✳✳

Guy and Larry and Marianne are drinking in their kitchen-lounge combo and watching *The Chase* repeats and laughing and laughing and none of them has a clue what's really going on in the world. It's *great,* Guy thinks. It's been a long time since they've been like this, all of them loose and fun, especially Marianne. Or rather, Marianne when *Guy's* there. He always wonders if, after everything with him and Nancy, Marianne leapt on the opportunity to take sides. Maybe tonight means she's at least getting back up to lukewarm with him? He'll take it.

He's already in holiday mode anyway, all packed and prepared. Ugly thoughts of the early airport drive have been pushed away by Guy's good buddy Weiser, a trick the beverage seems to perform outstandingly with all concerns... then suddenly, he wishes Nancy was here.

Maybe if the pair of them had taken this trip a year ago, it would have saved things. Not that he didn't try. But Nancy just wouldn't change, and now he's going alone on a trip initially booked for two. Larry checks something on his phone and looks up at Guy.

"Cov One, Sunderland zip, final whistle." He grins, big teeth shining white in his horsey face. Skeleton-thin Larry. The Blonde Zombie, they called him at university, back in the days when he and Guy used to prank each other mercilessly; Larry would always get high and go too far, but that smile always made Guy come back. It made everyone come back. "Accumulator coming on nicely."

"How much if it comes off?" Guy asks, half-interested, thinking that he and Larry did still keep up the pranking now and then. Maybe once every two or three years—*big* pranks, the kind middle-aged men can afford to spend money on—and more importantly, he can't remember whose turn it is. His? Does he owe Larry? When was the last time—

"About fifty quid, not bad," Larry says.

"Ohhhhhh, unlucky," Marianne says as Jenny from Loughborough blows her shot at the money on TV.

"Who else you got?"

"Oxford two-nil at Burton—"

"Ugh, boring, *boring,*" Marianne blurts out, a little too loudly. Guy wonders how many she's had, realizing he's pretty buzzed himself. Larry politely holds up his hands in response. "Talk about something *interesting* before I blow my brains out," she says. "I've heard about nothing but football all day." Marianne stands, her shorter, thicker frame in direct contrast to Larry's rangy one, and crosses to the fridge. An odd couple in appearance but not at all in their relationship. *They're* solid as a rock.

"Actually, I've been meaning to tell you," she says to Larry, opening a beer for herself. "Helen down the road? Have you seen her new car?"

"No?"

"BMW. Brand new."

"What?"

"Mm-hm. Any idea how she's affording that?"

"Oh *shee-it,* the new guy..."

"Mm-*hm.* Accountant. Fella has *money.*"

"But they've only been together a *month,"* and as Guy sees Larry's glee at this backyard gossip, his stomach turns a little. It's too familiar a feeling these days. He thinks about how, once upon a time, there used to be more of them. Nancy, obviously, but Steve and Mary, Clark and—of course—Frank Beckwith providing the weed, and occasionally other treats. Now Guy and Larry don't hear from them, except Beckwith when he calls to see if Larry wants a top-up for his stash. Guy and Larry, keeping the not-square-at-forty flame alive, even if Larry is turning into an old gossip.

"Maybe," replies Marianne, "but those big fake tits of hers do seem to have him enamoured. I don't know if the woman owns a top with a neckline above knee level?"

Larry laughs, and there it is again. Lurking just below the surface. When did this start?

"Marianne *Neilsen,"* says Larry, his tone playful, but Guy can see in his eyes that he's now a little embarrassed. "Easy..."

"I'm kidding, I'm kidding..."

The words are out before Guy can stop them.

"Ray used to say that behind every 'little joke' there's an element of real malice," he says, his tone ironic.

All the air goes out of the room, just as, Guy realises, he intended it to. What the hell did he do that for? It isn't just that he's pulled up Marianne in her own home—there's an unspoken code about that kind of thing.

It's because he mentioned Ray.

Marianne stares at him, blinking. Larry stares at his beer.

Guy had a point, and he's forgotten it. Why are his thoughts so scrambled? He tries to remember how many Buds he's drunk and it hits him: much more than he realised, he's more *drunk* than he realised, and Marianne's stare tells him her temperature towards him has gone right back to *ice bath*. She manages a restaurant, surely she should be used to drunk talk by now... Guy only mentions Ray when he's really drunk, and it's always in mildly-weaponised terms.

They're stuck in Real Talk now, and none of them know what to do with it. The silence is suffocating. Then Guy has it.

"Plus," he says, forcing a smile. "When the HuffPo money comes in I'll buy Larry a set of fake tits if you really want, but I don't think they'd suit him."

The joke hits Larry, and he lets out a laugh that is half-forced, half-real relief.

Marianne simply scoffs a little and shakes her head, letting it go only because of Larry's laughter, but the damage is done. *Ah Marianne, lighten the fuck up*, says the booze in Guy's head, not for the first time. He waits for her to make another remark. Surprisingly, she doesn't.

"Ah, Guy's HuffPo money," Larry says, waving a finger. "Did I tell you about that baby?"

"No, you didn't," Marianne says flatly.

"Guy just sold his *third* piece to HuffPo," Larry says happily, completely misreading the room. "It's about this Mr Unlucky fella. They bought it even though it's not finished. Guy's going *legitimate*." Guy waves Larry's words away. He's not comfortable talking about it as he knows his friend would kill to be in his shoes, but the Blonde Zombie is missing the vibe as usual. "Tell her, Guy. Baby, you'll love this story." Marianne swigs from her beer bottle and says nothing.

"Well it'll be two of us *going legitimate* soon, it's just a matter of Larry finishing with the shanties," Guy says, trying to curry favour by talking highly of Larry. It's probably not true, and they all know it, but it's the effort that counts.

Larry's writing an article about the growing number of shantytowns in Britain. It'll be decent—Larry is a workmanlike writer—but it's not exactly guaranteed to make him an overnight sensation. He'll be in Glasgow doing more research—quite literally slumming it—while Guy is in Miami for two whole all-inclusive weeks.

"No doubt," Marianne says affectionately to her husband.

"Tell her, Guy," Larry says, ignoring Guy's comment. "It's funny. Well, funny and sad."

Guy smiles. That's the Larry he remembers from college: flannel shirt-wearing, earnest, studying art history, bloody well helping Guy pass. He tries to picture that Larry bitching about the neighbour's fake boobs. Guy stands and crosses to the sink to pour himself a glass of water. No more Bud. Nancy would be proud.

"It's about this guy called Peter Nowak," he says, and tells Marianne as best he can, trying not to slur. Larry's right, it *is* funny and sad. Guy is billing Nowak as the *World's Unluckiest Man*, and best of all, Guy's the one who discovered him. It was at a social media conference in Manchester that he'd overheard two guys in a bar talking about Nowak; one of them used to live near Nowak's home in Northampton. Guy interrupted, fascinated to find out more, and the whole thing went from there. He hasn't spoken to Nowak yet—Nowak hasn't responded to any enquiries—but Guy's verified as much of the story as he can. All he's missing is an interview. He'll get it.

Peter Nowak was a small-scale-but-successful landlord with six houses, including the one in which he lived. He'd grown up in a time when dyslexia wasn't properly recognized, and spent his entire school career angry, frustrated and desperate to get out. When he did, the only job he could get was packing fish at a factory, and *that* was because the owner had a Polish father, like Peter. Once it came out during the interview that Peter spoke Polish—that they both did—that was that. Peter started work that day.

He'd hated the job. He was mildly allergic to seafood— being around it turned his stomach—but because the boss loved him, the raises kept coming. With no formal qualifications and a loathing of the education required to get any, the money was just too good to turn down. Nowak stayed there for five stomach-churning years while he saved up enough to buy his first house. Five years after that, he purchased his second. Around this time Nowak met his future wife, a doctor. Two years later he was married, and twenty-five years after buying his first house he owned six, four of them mortgage-free, and became a full-time landlord. He hung up his stinking rubber gloves on his last day with intense relief, although not before an obligatory hours-long drinking binge in his tearful boss' office. Although he and his wife had no kids, life was good.

Two years ago his luck went to total shit and never recovered.

The tenants in his five rental houses—all in separate parts of town—died. On the same night. One tripped and broke their neck falling down the stairs, one choked to death on a piece of lamb, one fell asleep in the bath and drowned, and one hung himself from the banister after discovering that his girlfriend had left him. He'd used one of her old cardigans for the noose. The last house's residents—an elderly couple—died quietly in their armchairs in front of Sky Movies. The neighbours on of each of his houses' streets knew, of course, and somehow they all managed to mention it to anyone intending to move in. (That is not, by the way, the strangest part of this story. Not in the least.)

The houses remained vacant.

A few months later, during an incredibly hot summer, the same five houses—again, all in different parts of town—burnt down overnight. On the *same* night. Peter had no enemies as far as anyone knew, no disgruntled tenants. There were no signs of arson. Though Peter was a thorough and conscientious man, it turned out he'd somehow let the insurance expire too. On all of them.

Still none of this made the news.

His wife made good money, so he didn't need a job immediately, but he wanted to contribute. He was a hard worker. He couldn't face a factory though, so he bought a van and started working as a delivery driver.

Guy has been able to verify all of this, apart from Nowak's feelings about fish packing. That part was courtesy of the former neighbour. From here on in Guy has fewer concrete facts—he'll get them—but some of this he knows to be true. This is how it was told to him:

Peter Nowak spiralled into depression and six months after he sold his houses his wife had enough of trying to get through to him. She left. Peter's depression got worse, but after reaching rock bottom and developing a drinking problem, he managed to start turning things around. His mortgages had all been paid off, including the remaining house in which he lived, and he didn't have any debt. He could start again, though he'd stay away from the property market.

Then one day, a minibus jumped the lights at an intersection, writing off Peter's van and breaking both his legs. The CCTV camera at the scene had happened to malfunction an hour earlier. The system had already registered the fault and dispatched a repairman, but he'd been held up by a traffic jam, caused by a downed power cable that had only been installed a week before.

No CCTV. No record of the minibus other than Peter's own account. The insurance didn't pay out.

He was self-employed, so had no sick pay for the four weeks he couldn't drive. He'd paid for Income Protection Insurance but it turned out a clerical error had stopped the direct debits going out, so it had been cancelled. The letter informing him of the cancellation was lost in the post.

While Peter was at the bank trying to secure a loan for a new van, a gas leak in his house triggered an explosion that destroyed his kitchen and burnt everything but the basic structure of his home. It barely escaped being condemned. Peter had to spend the last of his money rendering it habitable. Due to his behaviour during his drinking period, he had very few friends left with the means to help him. In desperation, he turned back to the job he'd hated: the fish packing factory. His stomach twisted as he'd entered the building for the interview. It was now run by the previous owner's son who, upon hearing how high Peter's wage had been, laughed out loud. He wasn't short on staff but, in a scarce moment of fortune, the son took pity on Peter because he knew that his father would have wanted it. He would only offer minimum wage, however.

Peter went home and tried to commit suicide. He hung a noose, put his neck in it, and stepped off his coffee table.

The noose broke.

He was found unconscious when the neighbour—alerted by the sound of Novak smashing backwards through the coffee table—saw the scene through the window and broke down the front door. The neighbour had agreed to keep it quiet and did... until Guy overheard him drunkenly telling a friend.

As far as Guy knows, Peter Nowak is still living in that house, working at that factory, and God only knows what the fuck has happened to him in the meantime. It's worth noting that, apparently, even though his record is clean of any claims, no insurance company will touch him now either.

"That can't all be true," Marianne says. Guy realises she's leaning forward, face intent, her displeasure forgotten.

"I'm pretty convinced it is," Guy says. "I did my research about the house and the accident, and I don't think the neighbour was lying. I could just tell."

"And it's a great story," Larry says. "That's the main thing."

It is, in a world where content is king and the content cycle runs 24/7. Nobody has time to verify a story anymore, but Guy *tries* to. He thinks that's important. Even when he's desperate to get out of the social media marketing game. Larry too. Writing clickbait might be more time-consuming but Jesus Christ, it's more lucrative if you can just get up a few levels.

"Well I try to be one of the good guys," he says.

"But he asked the neighbour to keep it quiet," Marianne says, completely failing to surprise Guy by finding a reason to be *negative*. "You're going to do the opposite."

"Baby, after two days no one will give a shit," says Larry. "Guy can pay him for his interview, and it sounds like he needs the money. Toast." He holds up his beer. They all toast. "Everyone wins, and you can guarantee some shitweasel will start a GoFundMe appeal for him. He'll deal with being famous for forty-eight hours, then when it dies down he'll be all set."

Guy's not so sure. Yes, the cycle is fast, but if something reaches that golden state—of going viral—it can last. *Momentum,* as Larry always likes to say, *it's everything in our line of work, everything.*

"Getting noticed, going up a level," Larry slurs, wagging a finger at Guy. "It works like comedy. Real success comes after the third hit. They're gonna notice you dude." This is uncharacteristic for Guy and Larry. They're usually sniping at each other—it's how they talk—but Larry's jealous, so maybe he's trying extra hard on this subject. "The Three Times Rule says so dude."

"Let's hope so." Guy doesn't want to get Larry started on his personal philosophies, but he's off anyway.

"And *what's* the Three Times Rule, baby?" Larry says, theatrically cupping his hand to his ear and turning to Marianne. She rolls her eyes, but this time it's amused.

"*First time they only see it, the second time they register it, the third time they act upon it.*"

"That's my fucking *girl*," Larry says, standing up with purpose, crossing to the kitchen drawer and taking out his mini cordless drill. "Guy? You want some?"

Guy knows he shouldn't. It's not like he has a *problem* or anything—Larry is the pothead, not Guy—but he's generally trying to cut back on everything.

Jesus, that's the kind of thing Nancy would say. Plus, isn't he on holiday now? Damn good point.

"Yeah, let's do it."

Larry grins and squats down. Guy hears the drill whirr. Larry's unscrewing his ridiculously over-the-top secret stash panel: a double plug socket above the skirting board hiding a tiny hollowed out section of wall. Whoever said weed doesn't make you paranoid never met Larry—*you never know when somebody might 'grass' you up,* he liked to pun. Never mind that the cops had better things to do than raid homes for thirty quid's worth of cannabis. Larry stands, baggie in hand. In the past, there would have been nine or ten people here, hungrily eyeing it. When did everyone get so boring?

"*Anyway,*" Marianne says, eyes fixing back on Guy's. "Doesn't seem right to me. Outing him like that, the Unlucky Man. If he wants privacy…"

Guilt has a quick joust with Indignance inside the arena of Guy's brain.

There's a pause. Real Talk threatens.

"Did you guys watch that documentary on Netflix about going vegan?" Guy asks quickly, and all three of them leap at the question like drowning people lunging for a raft.

The subject of Nowak—an amusement, a diversion, a story of mere remarkable coincidence—is dropped.

The mood turns comfortable and relaxed once more.

Perfect.

***

Chapter Four
Signs and Portents, Of Course Ignored
✱✱✱

Miami. An outdoor beachfront restaurant, the night sky outside jet-black thanks to the ambient lighting in the canopy above. The music is as smooth as the wine, the conversation around Guy as empty as the chair opposite. He's starting to think this was a bad idea. At first, he'd tried to fill the slot; a free, all-inclusive holiday, who wouldn't want it? He'd rang round the old crew, people he could happily spend two weeks with, seeing who fancied it. The answer, it turned out, was no one. Couldn't even get a pass from their other halves for a *free holiday*. Times change, it seems. But he'd paid for it—two weeks of self-indulgent R and R—what was he gonna do, *not* go?

The reality has been... different. He misses Nancy, no matter how much he tells himself she would have spoiled it, always looking for trouble. He reminds himself that, by the end, there was no talking to her, but it doesn't help. That empty chair is a vortex of silence in this boisterous restaurant. The near-empty bottle of Pinot he's sunk isn't working.

It's not even his kind of holiday. These all-inclusive sloth-a-thon's were always Nancy's idea, not his, but he'd wanted to keep her happy. He'd really tried.

His phone pings. Larry.

WORKIN' HARD?

Guy smiles. It's an olive branch. This message is the first Guy's heard from him. They'd, characteristically, had one of their big blowout fights at the end of that night at their house. It started in the usual way: one of them makes some meaningless, opinionated point, the other politely disagreeing until they end up in a half-shouting war of attrition while Marianne excuses herself with a sigh. They're best friends; it's part of their stupid, endless dance, especially when they're in their cups. This fight had been about Larry telling Guy to chase Frank Beckwith for some weed as it was 'his turn'. Guy had explained he was supposed to be laying off for a while (he really was starting to wonder if the stuff agreed with him after all this time) and of course Larry pointed out that Guy had just smoked his. Regardless, the altercation ended with Guy storming out the door and into his house, which was easy because he lives next door (something for which he doesn't think Marianne will ever forgive him). He and Nancy and had bought it the second it went up for sale, selling their old house in the process.

He WhatsApps Larry back:

HARDLY WORKIN'.

And just like that, they're okay again. That's their schtick.

GONNA EMAIL YOU WORK IN PROGRESS ON THE SHANTY TOWN/GLASGOW. NOWHERE NEAR FINIS-HED YET, BUT I'D LIKE YOUR OPINION ON IT SO FAR, MISTER SUCCESS. IF YOU FEEL LIKE GIVING IT A LOOK, LET ME KNOW YOUR THOUGHTS. *LOTS* OF WEIRD STUFF GOING ON UP HERE, STUFF I DIDN'T EXPECT AT ALL. DON'T WANNA SPOIL IT BUT IT'S *FREAKY.* UNDERSTAND IF YOU'RE IN HOLIDAY MODE THOUGH.

He's talking about his article. Guy doesn't want to read it on holiday—it feels like a proofing job and he left those days behind post-post-university—but he'll read it when he gets home. He doesn't tell Larry that, though.

SEND IT OVER. MAYBE I'll TAKE A LOOK IN BETWEEN LAP DANCES.

The talk of articles makes Guy think of his own. He's not supposed to be working but he takes his phone out and starts writing a final last-ditch email to Nowak. He's so engrossed, he doesn't notice the large man approaching him.

"Excuse me."

Guy pauses, his thumb hovering over the Send button, and looks up. The man is standing by Guy's table, wearing a thick, ragged-looking coat with a filthy white tank top underneath. And fingerless gloves, but that doesn't make sense because the night is muggy and hot. He has unkempt facial hair; red skin. At first glance, Guy thinks he's old, but it's the dirt and beard creating the illusion; the man can't be much older than him. He's swaying slightly; Guy can smell sweat. No booze, though.

"Excuse me, sorry, sorry to bother you this evening," the stranger repeats, his voice overly gentle, a man practised in trying to sound non-threatening. He isn't even looking at Guy, but at the floor. "I'm just wondering if you can help me, if you had any change so I can get something to eat tonight, anything will do."

The humility of it, the sincerity, almost slaps Guy sober. The man's words aren't a begging act. He's genuinely sorry that he has to bother anyone. He *does* need food.

"Oh, yeah, sure, *Jesus,* yeah," Guy says, quickly fumbling for his wallet. He gets asked for *spare change* all the time in town—and he gives it—but it doesn't usually touch him like this. And it's especially unusual because Guy's policy is always to ignore anyone who actually stops him in his tracks, let alone interrupts his dinner. Maybe the booze is making him soft, but there's something in the man's demeanour. Guy looks across the restaurant; no staff have spotted the stranger. Guy wants to give him some money before they do, wanting to spare the poor man's embarrassment. The open-air nature of the restaurant meant the stranger could wander in quietly without anybody noticing. Guy finds twenty dollars.

"Here—"

"Oh thank you sir, thank you—"

Guy hasn't handed him the cash yet; he notices something hanging around the man's neck.

Dog tags.

"Are you ex-forces? I mean, a veteran?" He remembers the American terminology. The man makes eye contact for the first time, brightening slightly.

"Yes, sir. Afghanistan and Iraq, sir. Can you help me, sir? It doesn't have to be much. Very sorry to interrupt your evening." Guy notices a waiter hurrying over. The veteran has been spotted.

"It's alright." Guy pulls out an extra ten. He must be drunk. "Here, here. Be safe, get yourself something to eat." The vet's eyes widen, the cash vanishes into the coat, and Guy sees the delight in the vet's face as he reaches to shake Guy's hand. He didn't expect ten, let alone thirty. Should it have been more? Now Guy feels bad. He suddenly wants this wrapped up, so he raises his phone as if there's a message requiring his attention. Onscreen is his email to Nowak, still unsent. He hits Send and the *swoosh* sound confirms its departure; his Inbox appears, with Larry's unfinished article already arrived. He continues looking at the screen, expecting the man to move away, but his new dinner guest doesn't seem to take the hint. Guy looks up again and is shocked by the new expression on the veteran's face.

His eyes are wide, and staring at Guy with great intensity. Is he... shaking? The waiter arrives, an older, thin man with a gleaming bald head.

"I'm so sorry about this sir," he says to Guy, then addresses the veteran. "You can't bother our customers, you have to—"

"It's alright, he was just leaving, it's no trouble," Guy says, but he notices that the veteran hasn't moved an inch during this exchange.

He's still staring at Guy. Still holding his hand.

"You'd maybe better go before they get upset," Guy says kindly, a little unnerved. The veteran doesn't turn around, his eyes still locked on Guy's. There's a pause.

"Can you *leave*, please." The waiter's face is red. No response. The waiter turns to Guy. "I'm *so* sorry sir, let me get my colleagues." Guy wants to tell him not to, that it's okay, but now it *isn't* okay. The man's staring is unsettling, and he's still holding Guy's hand. The waiter hurries away for assistance, and Guy decides to make this end. There's a little resistance from the veteran as Guy tries to pull his hand free, but then the vet lets go, blinking as if remembering where he was. He looks at Guy nervously. His tongue darts out, moistening his lips.

"You'd better go, buddy," Guy repeats softly, giving a smile. *And I think I should wash this hand,* Guy thinks. "They're going to cause a scene to get you out, and I don't want that to happen. Take care of your—"

"Bad things for you."

The sentence is so quiet Guy almost doesn't hear it.

"What?"

The veteran looks away from Guy, out into the darkness, then crouches down, face level with the table. His eyes are wide, and he's trembling. "Bad things for you. Not certain, not inevitable, but *possible.*"

"Okay," Guy says, realising he shouldn't have given the man money if it meant being latched onto. "Thanks for the heads up, but—"

"What you just did. They won't like that. I see it. That's what they *gave* me you see, what they *did* to me, I can feel..." The vet screws his face up; resets. "Bad things are coming. *Could* be coming... stop now, stop what you're doing— *all* the things you're doing—and it *might not.* Please?" Guy has no idea what the vet's talking about, but now their faces are close enough that he can smell the man's breath. "I see the bad things when…" He pauses. Squints. "They're coming your way now. They're *circling*. Watching. They're not *sure*."

"Hey," Guy says, uncertain. "I tried to help you out, man… I'm just trying to—" The waiter is coming back, flanked by two younger, bigger guys. This is a relief. Even so, Guy doesn't want this man to get distressed.

"I'm trying to help *you*," the veteran says. He looks terrified. "Listen, they *started* with people like me. Don't you see how that makes sense? *No one sees us.* That's how they got strong, changed things. *They realised they didn't need to follow the rules with us,* we're different. We're not in the ecosystem, in the air! No one sees us, like *them*—"

"Sir?" the bald waiter says testily. "Sir, I need you to leave this man alone so he can finish his dinner. Come on now." Guy realises that other diners are now staring. Of course they are. This scene is cutting through the noise. The veteran ignores the waiter.

"Whatever it is, *stop what you're doing*," he whispers to Guy, and for a moment Guy is actually considering this; wondering what it is he's doing … then realises he's letting a lunatic affect him. He says nothing; simply folds his arms. The veteran's head drops. He stands up, mouth open, holding a hand half-out to Guy as if wanting to touch him.

"Thank you, *sir*," the bald waiter spits. "This way." The veteran's shoulders slump, and he begins to turn in the direction the waiter's pointing.

"It's not too late," he mutters. Then after a moment he adds, "Thank you for the mon—" He looks up suddenly. Looks around himself. At the waiters. At Guy. Fresh horror in his eyes. "*AH!*" he suddenly gasps, and then he's barging away through all three of the waiters and hurtling between the tables. The zipper of his waving coat catches a male diner in the eye, their cry of pain mingling with the gasps of the other patrons as the homeless veteran flees. At the edge of the restaurant's bright canopy, he turns and yells over his shoulder just before he reaches the street.

"*WAKE UP!*" he screams, and then points at the diners, screaming the same words: "*WAKE! UP!*"

A little electric shiver runs through Guy.

"Fuck…*me*," he whispers. He reaches for the bottle, feeling shaken, watching the veteran go. Later, he'll wish he'd looked at the wine instead. Then he wouldn't have seen the speeding truck that appears out of nowhere, hitting the fleeing veteran broadside.

It's so quick that the driver doesn't even have time to sound his horn. He stamps on the brakes, but it's far too late. They screech loud enough to drown out the screams of the witnesses and the thud of the crunching impact. Guy sees the veteran disappearing under the speeding metal, like nothing more than a bundle of rags.

Guy cries out, leaping from his seat to run over, but people are already clustered around the front of the truck. He hears someone saying *I'm a doctor, I'm a doctor* and someone calling an ambulance; it might be the driver. If this were a movie Guy would push his way to the front of the crowd to hear the veteran's dying message, but it isn't; a professional is dealing with it, an ambulance is on its way, and Guy doesn't know CPR or anything that could help this man right now. He feels eyes upon him; the other diners by his table. He realises a lot of them will be wondering what he said to the poor man. He wants to shout *fuck you, I gave him thirty dollars, what did* you *do for him?*

He staggers back into the hotel, leaving the chaos behind, needing the quiet of his room.

After an hour he's still wired—perhaps in a strange kind of shock—and so of course he heads downstairs to the hotel bar. He won't remember what time it is when he leaves.

***

Chapter Five
Escalation, Noticed
✳✳✳

Guy can't wait to go home. The hotel feels poisoned. He can't step outside without seeing the man falling under the screaming truck. He also discovers, surprisingly, that he's uncomfortable by the pool. He's put on some pounds in the last few years—contentment and complacency will slowly get you like that—and once he's noticed the way his stomach spills a little over the band of his trunks, he feels self-conscious, which is new for him. Instead, he spends the time in his room, working on his article—Nowak still hasn't replied, but after the incident with the veteran Guy feels weird about chasing him—and watching two TV channels that seem to only show endless episodes of two shows: *Forensic Files* and *Bar Rescue*. The latter is the damn same every time and it's *so* contrived, but Guy could watch it for hours. Keep it coming, and the margaritas. He hasn't read Larry's unfinished article. The rest of the week passes.

On day one of the second week Guy decides to abandon holiday mode altogether and knuckle down to work. Larry messages to say he's finished *his* first draft; has Guy read the first unfinished article yet, and if not, would he read the complete one instead? Guy says yes—he doesn't want to, but he will—then two days pass and Larry still hasn't sent it over. Guy messages him asking if he's emailed it but gets no reply. By the time Guy has three days of his trip left, he's mildly concerned.

DUDE, he texts. DID YOU SEND IT OR WHAT?

Still no answer. Screw him. With two days to go he turns off the TV, switches off his phone (a *big* deal) and sets up a writing space on the balcony. By the time the last evening rolls around, he's happy with the article. He's discovered the angle he wants—adversity, suffering, breaking points and finding meaning in 'the struggle', real Viktor Frankl stuff from his university philosophy society days—though maybe he's gone too heavy with it.

He looks at the clock. Six pm. Flight home's at seven am tomorrow. He knows he'd better pack... but first, he has an itch he badly needs to scratch. His phone's been off for *two days,* after all. He can just check texts and emails; not go down any rabbit holes. Get the packing done, then maybe go off-site, find a good restaurant. An *indoor* one.

He intends to do exactly that, just as he knows he'll actually end up fucking around on his phone for two hours, *then* packing, by which time it'll be late and he'll not bother going anywhere. But as he switches the device on, his well-practised doublethink is working perfectly.

Guy's phone pings. He gets the message from Larry.

All the messages from Larry.

***

Guy calls Nancy. He wants to speak to her before he responds to any of this. It's too bloody *weird.*

They still talk, now and then. It's only been a year, after all. There are logistical things to discuss occasionally. The divorce hasn't even gone through yet, though it will soon. Guy thinks they're lucky it isn't so acrimonious they have to get the courts involved. There's no hate, even if there's... distaste. But when two people know each other better than anyone else in the world—even if they don't like each other so much now—that remains a resource that sometimes needs to be tapped.

She picks up.

"*Mmh?*"

"Nance?"

"Guy..."

"Did I wake you up or something?" Guy realises he's made a mistake with the time difference; it's not nine pm back home, but eleven. "*Shit,* sorry Nance, I didn't—"

"S'ok..." She's coming around. "I fell asleep on the sofa, long day. I wouldn't normally be—"

"Yeah, I know, I know." Nancy always was a night owl. "Hey, I'd normally hang up here and let you get back to sleep, but I think this might be important. Do you have a minute?"

"Yeah..." she sighs. Guy can't tell if it's tiredness or resignation: *here he is again.* And there she goes already, deciding what Guy's going to say before he says it, *Jesus.* "Go for it."

"Have you spoken to Marianne lately? Like in the last few days?"

Nancy and Marianne were close. Guy had always felt lucky that his wife and his best friend's wife also became genuine best friends. Though it couldn't have been a hard choice for Marianne. *She'd have buddied up with Ted Bundy if it meant siding against yours truly,* he thinks bitterly.

"Uh, no, actually... I've called a few times, but she hasn't picked up. Why?"

The unease in Guy's stomach becomes a growling concern.

"It might be nothing. Larry might have just made some edibles again and gone too far, stoner panic talk." Guy would believe what he was saying if not for the fact that the texts were sent over the last two days, not all in one potentially-intoxicated evening.

"What? Is Marianne okay? Is Larry?" She's fully awake now.

"Ah... geez, Nance, look, I don't wanna worry you—"

"*Guy.*"

He hears it; that *tone.* Guy might miss her, despite his best intentions, but he doesn't miss *that.*

"Fine, fine. Larry sent me some pretty weird messages."

"Saying...?"

He pulls his phone from his ear and puts it onto speaker so he can see Larry's messages. Thirteen of them.

"Well a lot of them say pretty much the same thing at first: *will you text or call me as soon as you get this please? Thanks.*"

"Okay..."

"And then it's like *call me please, text back please,* then he tries me *by* text as the first few were all WhatsApp, *are you getting these, text me please...*"

"Okay, now I'm worried. He doesn't say what it's about?"

"Not really, but..."

The *last* message. That's the one that really freaked Guy out.

"What?"

Guy sighs as he reads it out to Nancy. It's fucking *weird:*

PLEASE PLEASE CALL ME AND DON'T TELL NANCY EITHER DON'T TELL ANYONE. DON'T CONTACT MARIANNE UNDER ANY CIRCUMSTANCES. CONTACT ME. I DON'T KNOW IF SENDING THESE IS SAFE. I DON'T KNOW IF IT UNDERSTANDS TECHNOLOGY. I DON'T KNOW WHAT ELSE TO DO PLEASE CALL ME

"...what the *fuck*..." Nancy says.

"Mm."

"What's the bit about technology, *if it understands?* What the hell? It sounds like he's having an episode. *Don't contact Marianne? Have* you contacted Marianne?"

"That's why I called you. I was going to but... I don't know. If there's a reason I shouldn't contact her then maybe I thought you could, just to check she's okay. Larry doesn't sound good and the fact he's saying to *not* contact her—"

"Yeah, I was thinking the same thing."

They always had that shared brain; this awareness briefly resonates in Guy's mind before it snaps back to the task.

"Will you call her again? Ask about Larry too?"

"Yeah—"

"But *don't* mention anything about the text—"

"Of *course*, Guy." Jesus, he didn't *think* she would mention the text to Marianne, he was only making doubly sure. He waits for her to make another testy remark, his old reflexes ready to spring, but it doesn't come. Nancy Autumn—soon to be Nancy Long again, the late Peter Long's little princess—is maybe growing up. Guy hopes so, for her sake.

"Okay, okay. Are you gonna call Marianne now? I know it's late, but I think this might be serious."

"Yeah. I'll think of an excuse." She pauses. "Look at you, worrying about Marianne."

Guy nearly bites but realises it's a joke.

"Heh. Yeah, I guess."

A pause.

"Okay," she says. "I'll call her now. I'll call you back afterwards."

"Thanks, Nancy."

She hangs up. Guy tries to put it out of his mind. He packs, plays music over his Bluetooth speaker and even sings along, but it isn't working. He can't get that weird message out of his mind. *I don't know if it understands technology.*

His phone rings. It's Nancy.

"Hey. Marianne's fine, absolutely fine."

Guy's surprised how much of a relief that is.

"Did you ask about Larry—"

"Of *course.*" There it is again. "I did it casually, and she was totally normal, like *yeah, all good.* Said Larry got back from Scotland and he's working on some article?"

"Yeah. What excuse did you make for calling?"

"Ah, doesn't matter."

"...what?"

"I just... I just made something up."

"Why are you being weird?" Anger, building.

"Look, I pretended I found some old photos of us and got upset, okay? Like I needed to talk urgently."

"Oh." Anger, vanishing. Embarrassment, rising. "Sorry. That's... that was smart."

"Indeed."

A pause.

"So what the hell do you think these messages are about?"

"Maybe one of Larry's 'jokes'? Those stupid pranks you two do?"

"No... I thought about that, but... too much." Larry wouldn't pretend to ask for help. Would he? "Ah, you know what, you don't think it *is* a prank, do you?"

"Well, hey, they sound fine. Just text him back and say you'll talk to him tomorrow or something?"

"Yeah. Yeah. Bloody hell... this is one of his fucking wind-ups, isn't it? I thought it was my turn to—"

"It probably is. I don't think he expected you to call me. Did you have one of your fallouts?"

The question needles him, but she's right.

"A little one."

"Were you both smoking weed?"

"Actually, *no,*" Guy lies. "He was, I wasn't."

"Oh. Well, that's good. How's the holiday?"

"I haven't been doing much." He doesn't know why he's lying. "Just *working on my painting,* and all that."

"Is that what they call it now?"

"I don't know. Been a while since I was going to be the next Damien Hirst."

"Hey, I was gonna be the new Tracey Emin, and I don't see her schilling half-page space to Swarovski."

"Hey, it paid the bills," Guy says, unintentionally ruining the moment by bringing up *that* bone of contention. Nancy managing the advertising team at *Glamorous* magazine covered Guy's backside while he tried to make a name for himself writing content for the clickbait boom, taking SEO clients where he could get them. Her patience would eventually pay off, but only for Guy. For *them*, it would be too late. She never complained once, and maybe it would have been a little different if she had. Guy couldn't blame her. There are only so many mornings you can get up at 6:30 while your husband snores and so many evenings you can come home to find him in his jogging bottoms.

That and the never talking about *lil' albatrosses* as he called them, because—

Guy cuts *that* piece of thinking right off. *That ship has sailed with Nancy; what's done is done.* It's a mantra that always keeps the lid tight on that potential box of hornets in his brain.

His mood has soured, and it's a shame. He was starting to enjoy that exchange. Maybe just as well; nothing to be gained.

"I'm gonna get to sleep anyway. Let me know what Larry says when you speak to him, but I wouldn't worry about this. I think it's an old stoner's idea of a joke."

"Fucking weirdo."

"Yep. Goodnight."

She hangs up.

Should I... Guy wonders. *Yeah. Fuck it.*

He calls Larry.

It rings out and goes to answerphone.

"Hi bud, I..." Guy says, and to his surprise, pauses before the words *I got your messages* leave his lips. In this momentary hesitation he's reluctant, for some reason, to admit he's read Larry's texts. To be on record stating that he knows something's wrong, as if he were involving himself in danger. The thought is ridiculous but he's feeling very unnerved. "I'm just checking in to say... uh, I fly back in the morning. Gonna be up for a few hours here still so if you're awake, call me back, it'd be good to catch up. Cheers. "

He hangs up and can't stop himself thumbing through Larry's weird, vague texts, drawn back to them like a tongue exploring a loose tooth. His phone pings. It's Larry.

DID YOU TELL NANCY? SHE CALLED

He tries calling.
Larry declines the call. Angry now, Guy texts him back.

NO. WHAT ARE YOU DOING HANGING UP? WHAT'S HAPPENING? IS THIS A WIND-UP? ARE YOU OKAY? YOU'RE FREAKING ME OUT

There's a pause, then to Guy's relief the app shows that Larry is typing.

SORRY I'M SORRY. CAN'T TALK NOW. I'M OKAY. CAN WE MEET TOMORROW NIGHT? I KNOW YOU'LL BE TIRED FROM THE JOURNEY BUT I NEED TO TALK. IT'S URGENT.

Guy doesn't know what the hell to say.

DUDE. IF THIS IS A WIND-UP I'M GOING TO BE SERIOUSLY PISSED OFF. JUST TELL ME WHAT'S GOING ON.

Larry's typing.

DON'T COME TO THE HOUSE. MEET ME AT BARRINGTON'S. 10PM. YOU'LL BE HOME BY THEN RIGHT? DON'T SAY ANYTHING TO MARIANNE.

Guy replies, honestly.

OKAY MAN. BUT YOU'RE SCARING ME. YOU CAN'T JUST TALK NOW?

Larry's reply, straightaway:

NOT NOW. I'LL TELL YOU EVERYTHING TOMORROW. THANK YOU GUY, YOU'RE A GOOD FRIEND.

Guy:

SHIT MAN, NOW I HOPE THIS *IS* A WIND UP. CALL ME WHEN YOU CAN.

No response. After a few minutes, Guy tries calling again. The call cuts off each time. He doesn't know what the hell to think.

Sleep doesn't come easy that night.

Larry doesn't respond to anything in the morning and Guy can't relax during the flight. Unusually, his mind refuses to become distracted by the movie on the headrest screen, or the game on his phone's screen, or the book on his Kindle's screen. There's a funny moment just after take-off: before they get up above the clouds he looks out of the window and sees America stretching away beneath him. The just-risen sun is bright, so bright that the clouds are casting a wide, dark shadow that he can see moving slowly across the landscape, and for a second it looks as if as it were growing.

He goes back to the screens.

By the time his cab gets to Coventry and pulls up outside his house he's exhausted and grumpy and jetlagged. As he walks up his driveway it's nine p.m: just enough time to get a shower and drive to bloody Barrington's. He tries to catch a glimpse of Larry or Marianne through the windows of their house. The lights are all off, the curtains are closed, but both their cars are still in the driveway. Larry's home, then. Why not just knock on the door? He stares at the dead-looking house and considers doing precisely that.

But if Larry's having some sort of a breakdown—one Moron-ianne hasn't picked up on—then he'd better play it Larry's way for now. Guy listens out, though, as he turns the key in his front door lock.

There's no sound from Larry's house.

***

Chapter Six
First Glimpses
✳✳✳

It's almost exactly ten p.m. when Larry walks into Barrington's, where Guy is waiting for him. Except Larry doesn't walk. He hobbles. Larry is on a set of crutches. An accident? Maybe a head injury? That could explain it.

Guy raises his hand—he's got them both a bottle of Bud already, small enough to drive on, but a little something to loosen the lips—and Larry just nods. Crutches aside, even from a distance it's clear Larry's in a bad way. No; Larry looks like *shit.* His face is drawn, cheeks thin, and the skin under his eyes looks dark. Barrington's is a big bar—originally a bank—and Larry takes a while to reach the table. Guy stands to help, but Larry shakes his head.

Guy is frightened.

Larry forces a smile as he reaches his friend, one which collapses as quickly as he does. The crutches clatter noisily to the floor as he falls into Guy's arms, and the few people in the bar—it's not the weekend—turn to look. Guy glares at them, holding a trembling Larry tight until they look away. Larry sniffs as he straightens up, but he won't meet Guy's gaze.

"Thanks for coming," he says. "Thanks, man. I know you only just got back. I'm sorry." Guy helps Larry into a chair and then sits opposite, feeling lightheaded.

"That's fine, that's fine," Guy babbles, leaning forward. "Larry, Jesus... what's happened? Did you have an accident?"

"Nuh," Larry says, restless. His gaze darts around the bar, behind himself, hands working in his lap. "No, not like that. Uh. Um." He keeps swallowing. Trembling, like he's fighting back tears. "Guy. *Guy.* I don't... I don't know what's..."

This is *not* a joke. It's even more serious than Guy had feared.

"Okay, man, just take some deep breaths, nice and slow," Guy says, putting his hand on Larry's leg, a rare intimacy even between them, and they're close. "Start at the beginning. I'm here to help you." Larry shakes his head, looking utterly miserable.

"I don't think you can. No one can. I just have to tell someone, that's all."

"Well... we'll see, right? Can you start at the beginning?"

Larry shifts uncomfortably. Guy thinks of possibilities. The crutches. No accident, but an injury, and he's frightened.

"Do you owe someone money?" Guy offers. "Do you need money?" Larry shakes his head. His lips are tight, colourless lines in his face. He *wants* to tell Guy. "Did someone hurt you?" Larry freezes... but he doesn't shake his head. Guy isn't *entirely* wrong then. What could be—

Oh, shit.

"Did... someone hurt Marianne?"

Larry freezes again, but now the tears are coming. Guy has never seen Larry this broken. It's awful.

"Marianne is hurt?"

Larry wipes his face and mumbles something. The words are so muffled, it sounds like he said *it ate her.*

"What was that, Larry?"

"It's *in my house,*" he whispers, not repeating what he just said. "It's there right now. It's asleep."

The skin crawls on Guy's neck. This is way beyond anything he expected. He needs to text Nancy to tell her to get in touch with Marianne immediately, but first he has to calm Larry down.

"Larry... have you been taking anything, you know... heavy?" Guy asks quietly. Larry looks up sharply.

"*No,* Guy," he says, and now his eyes are pleading. "I'm going to tell you something, and I just need you to listen. I don't even care if you think I'm crazy, *I just have to tell someone.* Something terrible has happened. It's asleep now so I can tell you, it always sleeps around this time, usually for three or four hours but I never know for sure. That's why I haven't left the house before now but... I just had to! *I'm not allowed to tell you all this,* but maybe when it's asleep... I don't have long. I can't... " He pauses, chewing his lip, hard.

Guy doesn't know what to say. He doesn't recognize this Larry.

"Okay man," Guy says, trying to rally and show Larry he's safe. "Tell me everything, you're safe here."

Larry swallows.

"There's a monster in my house, Guy. It came just after I got back from Glasgow. It's been there ever since. It... ate Marianne. It can look and talk just like her too. It can *become her.* When anyone comes to the house, it pretends to *be* her. They'd never know it wasn't."

He pauses, scanning his friend's face. Guy's ears are ringing as he tries to keep a poker face. Once Larry's finished, Guy can get to the men's room and call Marianne—call the *police*—without Larry knowing. He's disturbed, having a psychotic episode—

"It can look like *me*," Larry says, wiping his mouth with the back of his hand. "It can make me *invisible* and then *look like me.* It's been keeping me around ever since it ate my wife, and it's been hurting me for fun. It told me it can make *itself* invisible to people if it wants to. It's told me..." Larry pauses again, looking overwhelmed. "... *it's told me a lot of things.* Guy, it's *horrible.* It looks... just the way it *moves,* I've never seen anything so awful. It's big too, like the size of a cow. But it's *careful,* it covers its tracks. It's *really* clever."

"Larry..."

Guy has nothing. He's stunned. Logic, then. Just to keep Larry talking long enough that excusing himself won't raise suspicion. *Marianne,* shit, what if he's hurt her—

"Larry," Guy repeats, "why is it clever? Why would it need to hide its tracks? Why would it need to be secret if it can be invisi—"

"Because *if they don't cover their tracks then people will know they exist,*" Larry hisses, sneering. "That's why it came in the first place. I'm not allowed to tell anyone about it. It's been with me long enough now that it can read my *mind* a little, Guy. You could come round to the house and think you're talking to me, but I'd be standing beside you invisible and screaming while that thing acts *exactly* as I would act."

"But you're telling me now—"

"I told you, *it's asleep.* If it were awake I could feel it, we're *connected* now. I can feel when it tries to read my mind, it's like spiders in my brain when it reaches out for me. It's hard to stop it." Larry leans forward, his eyes wet and pleading and insane. "If it hears me telling you—if it *knows*—it'll be allowed to kill me. See? I don't *think* it's allowed to kill me otherwise. It's very hard to know, there are rules, a lot of rules, that's the whole nature of these things, of curses, but they're finding ways round them ... we're fucked Guy, I think we're *all fucked.*" The image of the homeless veteran pops up in Guy's brain from nowhere.

They started with people like me, he'd said. *No one sees us. That's how they got strong.*

WAKE UP!

The truck, the screech of brakes—

Guy catches himself. Crazy people are supposed to be endlessly charismatic, convincing. It would be worryingly easy for him to put two and two together—the horrible incident in Miami and Larry's psychotic break—and get a ridiculous five.

Larry leans further forward still, eyes bulging, making his friendly horsey face look like a death mask. "I brought it *home* with me, Guy! It's my fault!"

"You brought a monster home? How could you—"

Larry's shaking his head, waving his hand.

"*No,* the object, the, the trinket thing, they gave it to me. I brought it home! It was ugly as hell but I didn't want to be rude so *I took the fucker home!* I gave it to Marianne as a joke! Elias Heinrich, *Jesus,* he was *warning* me, but I just thought he was a meth head! He even *told* me about the Other Folk, and about Sam's bloody *true stories!* Well now I fucking do too, don't I?!*" His hands are claws in front of his face. Guy mentally files the names *Elias Heinrich, Other Folk,* and *Sam* just in case. He imagines needing to repeat this to a professional in future, maybe even to Larry once this episode has passed. The word *curses* gets reluctantly added too. Crazy, but maybe important.

"Wow," Guy says, trying to sound convincing. "This is some intense stuff, man. I need a minute to process it. I'm gonna go piss, but wait here. I want to talk more about this."

"Leave your phone," Larry gasps, jabbing the table and scanning the room. "Put it on the table until you come back."

Dammit.

"Why?" Guy asks.

"You know why. You don't need a phone to go and have a piss."

"... you don't trust me?"

"It was the *article,* Guy," Larry whispers. "That's why they sent the monster to me, because of the shantytown article. They didn't want me writing it."

"But... Larry," Guy says, trying logic again in a vain attempt to reach a madman. Marianne could be tied up and starving in Larry's basement right now because her husband has decided a monster is impersonating her... but if Larry freaks out in this bar, Guy doesn't know what will happen. "Why didn't the monster kill *you* and not Marianne if *you're* the problem? Think about what you're saying. It doesn't make any sense."

"It's the *rules*, Guy," Larry says, screwing his eyes up in frustration and shaking his head. "Curses. *I gave her the thing, I brought it home and*—shit, look I don't think it can kill me unless—Guy, you should hear the thing talk about *rules!*" His voice carries once more. "I mean *we* have lawyers and contracts but Guy... that's *nothing* compared to these old, old rules—"

"Larry, why would anyone curse *you?*" Guy snaps. "You're writing about shanty towns? Who gives a shit?"

"Didn't you read about the—" He breaks off and quickly looks around himself before whispering: "All the urban voodoo stuff I found there?" Guy hasn't; he didn't read the unfinished article and Larry never sent him the finished one. "That kind of thing was making cultural inroads via the *sub*cultures," Larry babbles. "Local pets going missing. Animal sacrifice. I just thought this was all *good content*, it didn't even occur to me that it was real! The shanty town people didn't like it when I went down to talk to them, told me to keep it quiet but Guy, *they talked like they didn't want to be doing it.* Like they *had* to do this shit, but no one would tell me why. Then Mother Shawna came to talk to me, this old lady and I mean *old,* man." Guy hears all this and wonders where his friend has gone. "Didn't speak a word of English, talked to me through her granddaughter. She'd only come to apologise, that she hadn't had a choice. I didn't know what she was talking about. Then she gave me the thing, the trinket, and I thought it was part of the *apology! Fucking idiot! I* took it! I gave it to Marianne for a laugh and then was gonna throw it in the bin but we got drunk, I left it in the kitchen... maybe if I'd done that, *rejected* it... but maybe it was over the moment I interacted with it, I *don't know...*" Larry's scattergun stream of consciousness has lost Guy again. "Then the next morning there was another one on my doorstep. Another *thing.*" Larry's fingers intertwine, loosen, intertwine. "Then I was scared shitless and binned it before Marianne could see it, but by then, of course, the damage was done."

"What? What *thing?*" Guy cries. His head is spinning. Larry has paused, his eyes far away.

"I think a lot of it... " he says slowly, "is also the fact that they might just enjoy it. I've been trying to figure out what their objective is, but maybe they don't always have one. I think they like to play with us. Maybe they shut me down as a precaution, but maybe it's also because they could and they just *wanted to.* That thing's voice, Guy..." Something dark crosses Larry's eyes and he shivers. "It's *wet.* It's wet and deep and *old* and it sounds so... *gleeful.*"

It talks? Guy catches himself again.

"Larry. You said a *thing* on your doorstep," he asks, trying a different tack. If he can get Larry to trip himself up and be inconsistent, it might unravel his delusion. "What *thing?*"

"A few things. There would be a different one each day. I hid them from Marianne. I stayed up through the third night after the first two, literally sitting and waiting on my front doorstep, and nothing came." He chuckles darkly. "Then I found they left it round the *back.*"

"*Please,* Larry. Left what?"

"The first thing I took home was like this..." He shapes an invisible object about the size of a frying pan in the air. "Like a badly-blown glass bottle covered in this, I don't know, swirls of some kind of hardened resin. But the first one they *left* was just a rotting grapefruit with this shard of old-looking ornate clay pottery stuck in it, looked like an Inca, Mayan design. But I don't know, I just... I knew who'd sent it. I knew. Then the next night they left a mask, like a Greek theatrical mask, but it had been burned. The final one was this little construction made of sticks and thread. It *stank,* I've never smelt anything like it. I was going to go to the police after that but I thought they'd just laugh at me. Then the next night..."

He doesn't finish his sentence. That was clearly the night *the monster came.*

Something strikes Guy.

"You said before the third... *thing* that turned up at your house," Guy says. "You watched and waited all night?"

"Yes. I was so unsettled by them. There was something *about* them."

"But you didn't go back to see the shanty people?"

Larry scowls bitterly.

"I flew back up to Scotland on the fourth morning, I was so freaked out. But the whole fucking shanty had moved on. Gone. They'd been there over *six months* and they leave after I poke around?"

"That was after the third night? You flew there and back the same day?"

Larry nods. It's plausible he could have flown back there, checked the place out, and flown home the same day. The flight is probably an hour and a half.

"Then the fourth night... it came?"

Nods again.

"... and it ate Marianne?"

He looks down, trembling harder than ever.

"So… if I left here now. If *we* left here now," Guys adds hurriedly as Larry's face jerks up, looking terrified. "And we went to your house, I'd see Marianne? And she'd be normal?"

"You wouldn't see *her*," Larry whispers quickly, eyes wide. "You would see *it, being her*. No one would ever know they were talking to the monster. Once it ate her, it knew everything she knew, all the ways she would talk." Tears run down his cheeks, unnoticed. "It's *awful*. To watch it wearing her, *being* her, and she's gone and yet my wife is *right there*… her friend Mary came around the other day. It answered the door to her. It hid me so I was *right there*, screaming, and Mary didn't see or hear a thing. I watched them talk. It was flawless. *Flawless*. And when she left, it… hurt me again. For trying to tell Mary. It enjoys it, Guy." Suddenly he's rolling up the sleeve of his creased shirt. As he moves it triggers the release of some stale odour and Guy realises Larry hasn't washed in at least a few days. If Larry's shirt wasn't black, Guy thinks there would be visible stains on it. "Look."

Guy jerks bolt upright in his seat when he sees Larry's exposed arm.

There are four freshly healed cuts. Ragged lines, evenly spaced out. It is impossible for Guy to see them as anything other than claw marks. Larry is tracking the room again, meerkat-like, to see if anyone is watching. Guy stares at Larry's arm, open-mouthed, trying to think how Larry could have done that to himself. Guy can't. But what Larry is saying is *total bullshit*—

"And the…" Guy's throat is dry. "The crutches," he continues, as Larry quickly pulls his shirt back down to re-cover his arm. "What happened? Why do you need those?"

"It did that to me," Larry says quietly. "Right after it ate Marianne. I'd tried to stop it. It was like punching a boulder made of leather. It didn't even feel me. And then when it was done it grabbed me and it was *laughing* as it ate my foot."

Guy just doesn't know what to say to this.

"You're on crutches because… it ate your foot?"

Larry nods.

"You're missing a foot?" Guy repeats, feeling stupid. Larry nods again. Okay then. "Can you show me?" Guy knows there will be an excuse.

"No," Larry says. "I'm wearing a temporary prosthetic."

"…what?"

"A fake foot."

"I know what prosthetic m—"

"This is still very new, a temporary one until the proper one is finished. It hurts the stump a *lot* if I move it, even though I'm full of painkillers."

"You were allowed to go and see about getting a—"

"It *sleeps*, I told you. How do you think I'm here? If I stay away it can find me anyway, like *that*." He snaps his fingers but the sweat takes away the sound. "It sleeps for several hours and if I dare leave I have to be back before..."

"What did you tell the manufac—"

"That my foot was torn off in an accident."

This has gone beyond the ridiculous.

"Larry... *Larry*..." Where the hell to begin? Logic strikes again. "If it ate your foot you would have bled to death—"

"No. It can breathe fire. It cauterized it."

That does it. Guy loses control.

"Larry... can you fucking *hear yourself?*"

"I can, I *can,* and I know you don't believe me but I just need... I just need..."

Wait.

Larry's story about a mimicking monster is the perfect way to explain away a significant hole in his story, i.e. his supposedly-eaten wife still happily strutting around his house? Maybe Larry's kept his delusions secret from Marianne? She might be safe then, but only until Larry decides he has to try and take out the 'monster' in his home...

That does it. If they're against the clock—and Larry really believes he needs those crutches—then Guy is pretty sure he can run to his car before Larry can get a cab, after all, Larry can't drive on his 'stump'. Guy can beat him home and get Marianne out of there first. He makes one last attempt to reach his broken friend:

"Larry... if what you're saying is true... how do I know who I'm talking to right now? You could be the monster. It knows how to be you, right? How would I know you're the real Larry? See what you've done? You've covered all the angles. There's no way I can prove you wrong, is there?"

"You *couldn't* know," Larry says, his expression suddenly one of sad warmth. He *does* know how he sounds. He sees that he can't even convince his best friend. That he is lost. "You couldn't know at all—"

He bolts upright in his seat, his face a mask of terror and as pale as the grave. Guy has seen this sudden, listening panic before, in an outdoor restaurant on the other side of the Atlantic.

"Larry—"

"*Ssshh!*" Larry hisses, spit flying from his lips. The veins in his eyes bulge red and thick, thrumming with tension. He strains to listen.

"It's okay Larry. Let's go to my house," Guy says, kicking himself for not suggesting this sooner. He wasn't prepared for *any* of this. "We can—"

"*SSH!*" Larry hisses, screwing up his face and hands before jumping to his feet without thinking; he screams as he puts too much weight on his 'stump', falling to the floor. Now people in the bar are standing up, the staff are looking Guy and Larry's way, but Guy is already down beside his fallen friend and Larry's clutching at Guy's jacket, his neck, pulling Guy's face close to his. "*It's awake, oh shit Guy, it's awake, oh fuck, oh FUCK!*"

"I'm not going to let anything happen, Larry," Guy babbles, holding Larry's face still. Larry's pulse beats in his neck under Guy fingers. He thinks of an injured and frightened bird. "Okay, you're safe—"

"It's *already on its way!*" Larry hisses, thrashing around and trying to get his good foot under him. "It's *already galloping, oh it's so* fast! *I think it knows! Oh, Guy, it knows I spoke to you! It's coming to stop me! It'll be here any minute!*"

"Okay, okay, then we'll face it together okay, I'm going to help you, we'll face it together—"

"*You won't be able to stop it! No one can, I have to go, I have to* go, *if I'm here when it arrives it'll be even worse, it will—it will—*" Larry realises that Guy is holding him down. "*Ah! Ah! Guy! Jesus! Please! Let me go!*"

"Call an ambulance!" Guy screams to the barman, who nods, looking almost as terrified as Larry.

"*Let me go! Please, Guy, you don't understand—*"

"Hold on, just hold on buddy, it's okay—"

"*Let me go!*"

Larry's hand finds the previously-fallen crutch and he swings it, catching Guy beautifully above the eye. Guy cries out—mainly in surprise—and stumbles backwards. He hits his chair and falls over it, landing hard on the floor. Winded, it takes him a moment to get his legs under him as he hears the sounds of scrabbling shoes, clattering metal and skittering rubber. By the time he's upright Larry has covered the short distance to the door. Guy is still faster though; he can catch Larry in seconds. He sees the barman pausing with the phone pressed to his chest.

"*Call it!*" Guy yells. "*Still call it!*"

He runs down the central aisle between the chairs and tables, all eyes in the bar fixed on him. Larry disappears through the door to the outside world, passing beyond the frosted glass and out of sight. Two seconds later Guy plunges through them himself and out into the darkened evening street, frantically trying to see which way—

Larry is leaning against the wall to Guy's left, crutches on the floor. His head is held back, holding his stomach as his chest pitches rapidly up and down.

The son of a bitch is laughing hysterically.

Guy stands there for a moment, stunned. What is this?

No. No way.

There's no way this was a prank.

No *way*.

"Larry?"

Larry looks at Guy and his face breaks into a smile of pure delight as the giggles take him all over again.

"Are you kidding me?" Guy says, his anger rising, the blood rushing into his temples. He's *furious*... yet also deeply relieved. "Are you fucking *kidding* me?"

"Oh *shit*, oh *shit*, oh *shit*," Larry gasps, deliriously pleased with himself. "Oh, that was good, that was *good*, I didn't even plan to say half of that, oh *shit*—"

"You stupid bastard!" Guy yells, striding up to Larry and then remembering something. He barges back through the doors and yells to the barman. "Cancel the ambulance, he's fine, he's fine!" He steps back out and rounds on his so-called friend. "That guy was calling an *ambulance!* I thought you'd gone crazy, I was scared to death! For you *and* Marianne! You think that's *funny?*" He knows Larry has been smoking a lot of weed lately, but even by their past elaborate pranking standards this is just... just...

"I know it's... been a while... but you do remember you got me *last* time... right?!" Larry gasps, his laughter slowing down now. "It was your turn! Come on now... fair's fair. Now let's shake and say we're even." He holds his arm out and just before Guy slaps it away, he notices Larry's still-unbuttoned cuff. He yanks Larry's sleeve back to reveal the claw marks beneath; as he does so, the cuff's button snags a little bit of the scab. It peels away from the skin, revealing the unmarked flesh underneath before settling back down.

"No fucking way," Guy mutters. Larry's smile is a little less sure as he continues to peel back the rest of the fake scabbed-over wound off. Guy is ready to kill him. He puts a hand to his mouth to stop himself saying something he shouldn't. Larry rubs under his eyes, smearing the eyeshadow he's used to darken his expression.

"You have to admit, that's some good work," he says.

"What... what's..." Guy paces back and forth, speechless. "Where did you come up with... this?"

"The Peter Nowak thing," Larry says, and now his smile looks forced, ashamed. "I know your mind was away with the fairies with it and it just got me thinking... look, I just wanted to see if I could get you to believe me. And you did a little bit, right? Just a little? I wasn't sure about the prosthetic foot thing, I thought that would be a bit too much, but..."

"This... is..." Guy gives up. "...*really* disappointing," he finishes, making the understatement of the year sound ice cold. He's seeing a petty, mean-spirited side to Larry for the first time.

"Oh come on," Larry says, straightening up. "You always said it yourself, *the best gags are always big,* I had to really sell—"

"Nah," Guy says, turning away. He's starting to lose control. He needs to leave. "I'm not interested. I'll see you later."

"Ah come *onnn,* Guy," Larry calls after him, using an old friendly catchphrase of theirs. Tonight, it just pisses Guy off. "Fair's fair! I didn't think you'd be this much of a dick about it..."

Walking away was the right thing to do. If he'd still been standing there when Larry had said that he might have taken the little prick's head—or foot—off himself. He gets back to his car five minutes later, still furious. Despite everything, he texts Marianne. It's going to be weird and, if she knows nothing about this, she'll ask why he's asking. Good. Then he can tell her *exactly* how much of a dick her husband has been.

I'M JUST CHECKING. ARE YOU OKAY MARIANNE?

Guy sits and breathes. He half expects the windscreen to fog up thanks to the steam he imagines coming off his head. About a minute later, he receives a reply:

YEP, ALL GOOD. WHY? WHAT DID LARRY SAY?

He doesn't want to get into it after all, but he can't send a strange text like that without letting her know Larry was fine. He replies:

THANKS. HE'LL TELL YOU WHY, I'M SURE. HE'S ON HIS WAY
HOME NOW.

Let *him* explain to her what he's done. Unless she was in on it. Guy doesn't think so, though. He texts Nancy as a courtesy to say Marianne's fine. He drives home, anger thundering all the way, and by the time he's back at the house Nancy hasn't responded. Once inside, he pours himself a solid slug of bourbon and paces the living room, listening to Metallica. He remembers his body clock thinks it's six p.m. Sleep will be an issue tonight.

Has irreparable damage been done? He thinks it has when he finds he's still steaming over it the next morning. He brushes his teeth, has his breakfast, and drinks his morning coffee while consuming his morning clickbait, the dopamine receptors in his brain becoming that little bit greedier in the process than they were the day before. He tries to push angry thoughts away as he sits in his home office and starts with emails from his SEO clients—he always starts that way—and then he gets a text from Larry.

HELP ME

"Son of a fucking *bitch!*" Guy yells, suddenly glad he put a spare bed in his office; it gives him somewhere to safely throw his phone in anger. Unfortunately, the Samsung bounces off the bed and hits the wall with force, corner first. He hears a faint crunch, and his rage hits a level so high he feels like he might—if he really tries—be able to strangle Larry from there using his mind.

He walks into the back garden and begins to pace there. He used to do this at the old house after particularly bad arguments with Nancy, the ones where she got really angry with him and deliberately pushed his buttons. She was good at it. She always was smarter than him. He angrily glances at Larry's place next door and notices the piece of paper stuck to the inside of Larry's upstairs bathroom window.

He does an actual double-take—surely he's seeing it wrong somehow, a strange reflection or a trick of the light—but no, it's really there. He squints and realises there's writing on it.

Larry, he thinks. *Please don't take this further. I want to forgive you.*

He walks closer to the fence between their two houses. The window is frosted for privacy, but it's the only one on his side of the house. The message was meant for him, then. He makes out the words:

CAN YOU SEE THIS

He stands there for a minute. He just doesn't need this crap.

A drive. That will clear his head.

From the car, he calls Nancy, the only person who'll understand. He gets her answerphone—she's at work—so he vents into that. For once, she might have a point about his temper. Guy drives around for an hour, and just as he's calming down, Nancy calls him back. She sounds like she's driving, but it's lunchtime; she can't be doing that nightmare hour-long commute then?

"Trouble in paradise..." she says. She sounds like she's amused. Guy nearly starts on *her* for a change, but doesn't. She sat through that answerphone message after all.

"... yes. Trouble." He sighs. "Sorry, Nance. I shouldn't have called—"

"It's okay. I was having a slow day and, truth be told, it's nice to have a reminder of the bullshit I don't have to deal with anymore."

"*Okay,* thanks for your time then Nance," Guy hisses, "but I have to—"

"Go and talk to your friend."

"What? I'll kill him."

"No, you won't. You need to forget about revenge and point-scoring and instead calmly tell your friend how much he's upset you and why."

"Aha, *then* I kill him, I like it, good plan, get him to let his guard down—"

"Guy. I'm serious. The reason you're this upset is because you were worried about him—genuinely worried for your friend—and that isn't funny. He took advantage of your love for him—yes, *he did,*" she adds quickly, "so make him see that. If he still doesn't understand then you leave him alone for a while until he does, or until he completes this apparent dickhead transformation he's undergoing."

Guy is surprised.

"When did you become..." He fails to think of a famous psychologist. "... so zen?"

She sighs.

"Guy... if you'd tried *listening*—" She cuts herself off. "Doesn't matter. You asked for my advice. There it is."

"Okay. *Ah,* sorry Nance, he just got me—"

"Don't worry. Your rant added a little entertainment on the drive."

"Where are you going?" he asks, out of mild curiosity.

"Oh..." She sounds surprised. "Just to Light and Shade. Face to face with the new head of marketing."

"Good, good. Face to face, they must be important then."

"Uh, yeah, yeah I guess. I'm nearly there anyway, I'd better go."

"Okay. Thanks Nance. *Like you.*"

"Mm. *Like you too.*" It's a little joke that's crept in as things have become slightly more cordial. Guy doesn't think they'll ever truly be close again though. As he hangs up, the phone pings.

OKAY, THE PIECE OF PAPER WAS THE LAST ONE, I PROMISE
:D CAN WE BE FRIENDS AGAIN NOW?

Oh, Guy has to go and talk to Larry *right now.*

***

Chapter Seven
Guy Sees the Monster
✳✳✳

Guy knocks on Larry's door.

He sees a shape moving behind the front door's frosted glass panel and hopes it's Marianne. That would be an easier start, but no, the figure is too tall. It has to be Larry. Guy isn't short but Larry's bony body is taller than his. Larry opens the door on the chain—that's unusual and Guy is a little surprised—and peeks around it. He grins sheepishly.

"Are we friends now? Is it safe to take this chain off?"

Guy had arrived calm but the second he sees that fucking grin he wants to slap it right off Larry's face.

Easy, boy.

"Larry... you knew I was really pissed off about this and then you did the thing with the paper—"

"Actually, I meant to take the paper down. That's been there for a few days you know, didn't you notice?"

"No."

"That was the original plan, that was supposed to kinda sow the seeds—"

"That was up before yesterday? Marianne knew about this?"

"Eh? Oh, no, she never uses that bathroom, she uses the en suite. That's *my* bathroom, she wouldn't have seen it—"

"*Either way,*" Guy interrupts, "you went, way, way too far. The fact you even thought that crazy shit up—" His temper is rising. "Look: *this isn't like you.* At all. What's going on?"

"Ah, come on man—"

"Dude." Guy closes his eyes and clenches his fists by his sides. "I'm really doing my best here. Listen to what I'm saying."

"Seriously? It bothered you that much?"

"*Yes!* What did you expect?"

Larry stares at him for a moment.

"Well, shit... I thought you'd be pissed off but then you'd calm down and see the funny side," he says, playing with the door latch, his eyes lowered.

"No."

"Mm. Well. Sorry, then, I guess?"

"Christ..." Guy breathes out, shakes his head, "If you say so, but *yes,* apology accepted."

"Okay. Okay. How was Miami?"

Larry takes the door off the chain but remains standing in the doorway.

"Good thanks, good. Some crazy stuff happened, though."

"Crazy? Like what?"

Guy realises that he hasn't been invited in, either.

"Well can I possibly, maybe, fucking come *in* so I can tell you?"

Larry laughs and nods.

"Two seconds, I'm busting for a piss and you caught me on the way to the loo..." Larry shuts the door before Guy can reply. Larry's outline walks away. Guy doesn't know why Larry didn't let him in before using the toilet, but okay. More unusual is that, a few minutes later, Larry's frosted outline shuffles back towards the door but then simply undoes the latch. *Pop.* The door remains shut.

Larry hurries away quickly without opening the door. Did he go to do something else and *now* he's dashing off for a piss? Either way Guy thinks he should let himself in, so he does, but now he's anxious. Larry is *off.* Nancy was right, payback isn't important here. Larry wouldn't have carried out such a ridiculously stupid joke if he was in his right mind. Guy pushes the door open.

The hallway inside is almost as familiar as Guy's own—and normally as welcoming—but not today. None of the electric lights are on and their hallway doesn't get a lot of sun; in fact right now it's gloomy as hell. Marianne's diminutive form steps through the kitchen-diner door at the end of the hallway. Guy knows that Larry must have gone up the stairs to his right to use their bathroom. The house's lack of a downstairs toilet has been lamented during many a football game.

"Guy," she says, her smile seeming genuine for once. She doesn't *hate* him, after all, and he's been away for two weeks.

"Mama-Marianne," Guy replies, an ironic nickname that comes from Marianne's dislike of children. They hug. "Don't worry about me," he tells her, "we just made up, I think. Did you know we fell out—" Guy stops as she quickly steps back.

"Yeah, I was going to text you," she says. "He told me when he got back from the bar. I wondered why the heck he was meeting you that late, guess he couldn't wait to see you." There's that eye-roll again. "What was it over? I can't get much sense out of him about it but I wanted to try before I spoke to you... didn't want to feel like I was going behind his back."

"Eh?"

"What you were texting me about the other day... he wouldn't tell me."

"Oh... he played this... 'poorly-judged' practical joke." Guy is genuinely surprised Marianne isn't in on it. "Seriously? He didn't tell you about it?" Marianne shakes her head.

"Not a word," she says. "I told him you messaged me and he got all pissy and said that you were being a baby. I assumed you were just having another one of your fallouts."

"He just... " No. He's accepted Larry's apology. "He went a bit too far, that's all." Marianne's eyes flick to the stairs, as if... checking? She then squints conspiratorially and beckons for Guy to follow her into the lounge. Confused, he does. As they enter the room Guy notices that the mirror on the wall has a large crack in it. Marianne sees him looking and waves it away.

"Aerobics weights," she whispers. *Whispers?* They're having a conversation that she doesn't want Larry to hear? "My hands always get slippy and those things are so damn light I never hold onto them properly. Just lucky it wasn't the TV—*ugh*, look, never mind that shit, sorry for the secrecy."

"Is something wrong?" A cold thought strikes him. "Is... he okay?

Worry flashes across Marianne's face.

"I wanted to ask *you*," she says. "I'm sure you boys talk about things that he doesn't tell me, I mean he doesn't want me to worry, but... let's put it this way, when you messaged me? I was confused but not surprised. He hasn't been right for weeks. Didn't you notice?"

No. Guy hadn't until now. He'd been all wrapped up in his own little world and assuming everything was okay around him.

"Not really, no," he says. "I know he might have been... well, a little bit jealous about the HuffPo thing and I would have been too but shit..." Marianne bites at her lip, nodding, worry etched all over her forehead. "What's he been saying?" he asks her.

"I... I don't want to... I don't want you to think he's crazy," she whispers, looking upward again. She listens.

What?

"Crazy how?"

She wraps her arms tightly around herself.

"Ahhhh...."

"Did he... did he bring something home from Scotland?"

She didn't expect that.

"You mean the ugly glass thing?"

He didn't expect *that.* It was real, then. Maybe that's just what gave Larry the idea?

"Yes."

"It's not here anymore, he threw it out the day after he got back. Guy, what did he tell you?"

Then Guy spots the thing sitting on the floor at the far end of the room, parked in front of the recently-installed patio doors.

"Marianne... where did *that* thing come from, then?"

It's about the size of a footstool; whatever it's made of is white—plaster?—and shaped into a kind of haphazard honeycomb design, warped and angling sharply to the right about halfway up. It doesn't seem to have a specific shape as such, but Guy feels deeply unpleasant when he looks at it.

"That?" Marianne says, almost dismissively. "Larry said he made it, it's a joke present for Frank Beckwith?" Then she twigs. "You think it's not for a present?"

Guy can't take his eyes off the thing. It's inoffensive and at the same time just *horrible.* Is that soil on the top of it—

"Guy?"

"Sorry... so he didn't say anything about some strange deliveries turning up?" Guy asks, pointing at the object by the patio doors... but keeping his hand low. He doesn't want to point fully at it, for some reason. "Things like that?"

"No..." Marianne says, her hand going to her mouth. "What else has he been saying to you?"

Neither of them wants to go first, her not wanting to make Larry sound bad and Guy not wanting to say *monsters.*

"Has he said something... really out-there?" Guy asks, testing the water. "Like *really* out-there?"

"He might have." Her face says that Larry definitely has. "He keeps asking me these... *questions* and I can't tell if he's joking. He always says he is afterwards but when he asks he seems..."

"What kind of questions?"

"Tests. Little tests. Like *do I remember this*, and *what's my favourite this*. I know those sound like normal things to ask," she adds hurriedly, wincing, and now Guy sees how she has been holding this in. "But he doesn't ask in that way, not like *hey, let's reminisce*. Like... well yeah, like a test."

"Like he's trying to catch you out?"

"Exactly. Like he's checking who I am or something. And he keeps reading all these books..."

"Like horror books?" The guess is instinctive but the way Marianne's face immediately goes slack confirms that Guy is bang on the money.

"How do you know that?" she asks. "Guy... what's going on?"

Guy's very worried now, too.

"Shit, I don't know Mar," Guy tells her. "He just played this really sick joke yesterday... had make up on and everything."

"What the hell? Make up?"

"Didn't you see it?"

"I ended up helping the on the late shift yesterday as we were short staffed, Clint closed up but I still didn't get home until gone ten... Guy, *make up?*" She screws her face up at him, reddening a little, moving from foot to foot.

"It was... weird," Guy sighs, feeling stupid even saying it. "It was this bullshit joke about monsters, and one was in the house and had..." He can't say *eaten you*. That's too much. "It was keeping him captive and... I was supposed to think he'd gone crazy, I think." She's put her hands over her mouth at the word *monsters* and Guy knows it isn't the first time she's heard it recently. "It was supposed to be a prank, one of our really big ones, but this was *way* too far and—hey, *hey...*" Tears are coming to her eyes and Guy puts his hands on her shoulders, a rare moment of reality between them. "Hey, okay, so it's more than a joke then, something's been going on, yeah? It's okay Marianne, we're talking, right? So now we both know something is wrong and we can figure it out together, help him. It might be nothing. We can deal with it."

"*He keeps talking about monsters,*" she says, her voice muffled and trembling. "Sometimes I think he thinks... he thinks, or half-thinks..."

Guy takes a deep breath and says it for her.

"That you're one?"

She makes a little choking noise behind her hands as Guy confirms her worst fears.

"Then you know... wait, he told you it was a joke...?"

"He... yeah." Marianne's openly crying now and Guy grabs her, hugs her. Jesus Christ, Larry.

"He was testing you," she sobs. "Seeing if you believe it. Then he said it was a joke when you didn't, Guy. Oh my *God.*"

Kind of, Guy wants to say. *It didn't work like that, but—*

"It's okay. We'll get him help."

"So he told you then?" she asks. "He told you about the monster?"

"He did, but—"

Larry will be back coming down again at any second. Guy releases Marianne and steps back, looking towards the door, listening. No sound from upstairs. He turns back to Marianne, wanting to reassure her, but suddenly there's no need.

She now looks completely calm.

Her expression is relaxed, and her unblinking eyes stare right into Guy's.

"I need to talk to my husband," she says, sighing sadly and nodding. "I didn't realise that things had gone this far. I'm so sorry that he did that to you... look, let me handle it." She sounds like she's talking about an issue with one of her glass-collecting staff. "You'd be doing me a favour if you could slip out before he comes back down, I don't want this to be a thing. I'll talk to him tonight and see how it goes... I'll text you in the morning. You don't mind, right? I just want to talk to him by myself first. It'll be better that way."

Guy's surprised by her sudden acceptance of the situation, but he isn't sure if it's really safe for Marianne to talk to Larry alone. If he's having a psychotic breakdown—

"I don't *mind* as such," he says, "but... are you sure you don't want me here when you do? It might not be..." How to say it? "... a good idea."

"No," she says, shaking her head solemnly. "I'd feel more comfortable this way and I know he'd never do a thing to hurt me, I mean Jesus, Guy..."

"I don't want to be out of line Marianne but... I have to insist." Guy holds his hands up quickly. "Hey, say no, *you can say no,* but... don't you think two of us would be better than one—"

"No, I don't actually, Guy," she says a little testily, "and I need you to respect me on this. I'm glad you came over, and I know you mean well, but I want to be able to conduct things my way in my own marriage, if you don't mind. He's not a dangerous man, for God's sake."

Guy feels a little stunned. He and Marianne have only had openly cross words about five times in all the years he's known her, both of them observing the rules when it comes to best friends' partners: *you* can talk to your best friend like they're an utter pile of shit, but you never say a damn word sideways to the other half. Even so, common sense—or maybe instinct—tells him to stand his ground, yelling at him *DON'T LEAVE, DON'T LEAVE.*

"Marianne... uh..." She just folds her arms. *Dammit.* Nancy was the skilled operator, not him. "I'm not sure he *isn't* dangerous right now."

"Jesus, Guy. What do you think he is?"

"He's my best friend, of course, but right now it sounds like—"

"And he's *my husband.* And this is *my house,* Guy."

Guy gapes. He doesn't know what the hell to say.

"Marianne... hey... listen, I'm not attacking you, I'm just trying—"

"I don't like what you're implying Guy."

"I'm not implying anything!"

"Keep your voice down please—"

"Marianne... what the fuck?"

"Okay, you need to go." She points over Guy's shoulder. He can't believe what's happening.

"Whatever you say Marianne, I'm just looking out for you," he says, doing his *absolute best* to stay calm. "I'm... I'll slip out quick then. Can you just text me to let me know it's gone okay? What was said?"

"We'll see."

We'll see? Guy heads towards the door, feeling like this is some kind of bad dream. He hesitates.

"Marianne... are *you* okay—"

"Jesus Christ, Guy, please just *go*—"

"Fine, whatever. Fuck *me*—"

Now he *needs* to go. This is almost a carbon copy of his late-marriage arguments with Nancy, her escalating no matter what he said. Fists clenched, he stomps down the hallway—he doesn't care if Larry hears him—and on his way out notices that the small hallway mirror behind the door also has a crack in it. He's too angry and hyped-up to care about any of this though as he petulantly slams the front door behind him. He stands on their front porch, fingers clutching at his hair as he listens. He may be furious with Marianne right now—she and Larry now hold the top spots on the Shit List—but his worry for her hasn't lessened. He'll wait out here a minute. He really wants a fucking drink.

He doesn't hear footsteps coming down the stairs. He doesn't hear anything at all, strangely. He steps back a little so he's out of direct sight through the front door's frosted glass—he doesn't want Marianne charging out saying *what are you still doing here* or any bullshit like that—but he watches for blurry shadows on the inner wall beyond to see if anyone is moving around: Marianne coming back down the hall, Larry coming back down the stairs. Nothing. Guy waits.

After about a minute he hears something coming from the other side of the door. From upstairs. The sound is so muffled that Guy can't make out what it is. A TV playing? Music? The ordinary sounds of a household and him just being paranoid thinking it might be—

The muffled effect suddenly lifts. Guy hears the noise clearly.

Screaming.

He instinctively darts forward but the latch has now snapped to again and the door is locked. Panic shoots through him and he screams as he fumbles out his spare key and jams it home—

"Larry! Marianne!"

He throws the door open and charges towards the stairs but as he does so movement at the other end of the hallway catches his eye: one of the now-open patio doors to the garden is slowly swinging closed. He pauses for a moment, torn, and then chooses the stairs, the sound *came* from upstairs, and Guy is yelling again—*Larry, Marianne*—as he charges upwards. The layout of the house is almost identical to his, three bedrooms, one master bathroom, and he yanks open three of the doors to find nothing. He's badly out of breath—out of shape—as he throws open the fourth—the master bedroom—and finds Larry sitting on the floor. He's gasping and staring up at Guy with wide eyes, slumped between the bed and the wall.

"Larry, holy shit—"

Guy scans the room. No Marianne. Did she go out the patio door? As he crouches down, Guy sees blood on Larry. He panics, thinking it's Marianne's, but then sees it's coming out of a fresh, deep cut on Larry's arm. He takes Larry's shoulders to ask if he's okay and sees that the healing wounds on Larry's other arm—the claw-like cuts from the other day—are back. Larry's eyes are dark again, his face looking even thinner than the last time Guy saw him and up close Guy can see that now it's not makeup.

One of Larry's feet is missing. His leg ends in a recently-stitched stump.

"Guy..." Larry gasps. "Guy... you shouldn't... you shouldn't..."

Guy's mind is useless. His eyes are locked on the place where Larry's foot should have been.

"Marianne... where's Marianne—" he babbles, and Larry just screws up his face.

"I told you, I told you, Guy you have to *go,* you can't... interfere or you're *involved* and once that happens..." Larry's head starts to loll sideways, eyes rolling, but Guy shakes him and he comes to.

"Larry, I just *spoke* to her, just now, who did this—"

"... Marianne ..."

"Where is she? Did she go out the back? The back door? Someone went out the back—"

Larry shakes his head, weakly rolling his skull against the wall.

"No... it's just ... it's playing, messing with you... it *plays...*"

The new cut on Larry's arm is even deeper than Guy thought; he notices with horror that blood is beginning to pool on the floor underneath his backside, soaking into the shag carpet. Larry needs bandages or he's going to bleed out—

"*Shit,* bandages, where are your bandages?"

"Bandages..."

"*Larry!*"

"... Guy... important... don't interfere..."

The world is screaming in Guy's ears.

"... Larry, you're going to bleed to death if I don't—"

"Too late, *it knows I talked.* It's... gonna end its game, let it ... please ..."

"*Larry where are your fucking bandages?*"

Larry's crying.

Guy jumps up and runs downstairs, frantic. *Heavy bleeding in wounds,* what the fuck are you supposed to do, a tourniquet right, but doesn't that mean you lose your limb because you're cutting off blood flow—

Larry's pained voice floats down to him from upstairs.

"*Let it... do its job, Guy... if you interfere I don't know...*"

Guy flings open drawers and throws their contents out behind himself like a dog digging in the dirt. The first aid box is in the fifth drawer he checks, buried in there after years without use. Guy's shaking hands pop it open: bandages. He runs back to the stairs, lungs feeling like they're made of rusty iron, and when he reaches the bedroom he realises he should have called an *ambulance,* reaching for his phone—

He stops dead in the doorway, frozen.

Larry is looking up at him from the floor, grinning. The cut on his arm has stopped bleeding entirely, but it's the look on his face that really hits Guy. There is no trace of his friend in Larry's expression and Guy suddenly understands: Larry has become someone else and Guy doesn't think even *Larry* knows it.

Neither speaks. Guy is scared out of his mind. This can't be real. When did Larry develop this alternate personality? Did something send him over the edge to bring it out? Guy realises that he's not frightened for himself; he's frightened for Larry. And for Marianne who might be bleeding out somewhere in this house.

"Do..." Guy's throat is so dry that the word cracks. He swallows. "Do you have a name?" Larry's cadaver-grin doesn't change, his eyes red-rimmed and bulging. He doesn't reply.

What the hell do I—

Guy remembers movies.

"Can I speak to Larry? I have a question for *Larry.* Can Larry answer?"

Very slowly—it's the creepiest fucking thing Guy has ever seen—Larry slowly shakes his head back and forth, the movement barely perceptible.

"I... need to find Marianne," Guy tells him. "Can Larry... tell me? It's very important."

"She's gone."

Guy flinches at the sound, gasping out loud and dropping his phone. That isn't Larry's voice. Guy knows such things are possible; the man that gets hit on the head and speaks with a strange accent the rest of his life, the woman who develops a second personality that speaks fluent Portuguese even though she's never left Kentucky. Larry speaking with someone else's voice is shocking enough, but the sound is *horrible.* It's deep, makes-Barry-White-sound-like-a-soprano deep, with a terrible *gurgle.* Larry was right. It sounds *wet.* Eager. Mischievous.

"Gone... gone where?" Guy manages. "Did she go out the back? Through the patio doors?" The monster—better not to think of it as Larry—chuckles deeply.

"I ate her, Guy. I ate her last week. She *screeeeeeeeamed.*"

She can't have gone far. Guy gets out his phone and calls the police. The monster watches. Listens as Guy explains that his neighbour is out in the streets somewhere, that he thinks she's hurt and that his other friend has a deep wound and was bleeding badly but it might have stopped, what should he do? *Put pressure on the wound.* They're on their way. All the while the monster doesn't stop smiling. Guy hangs up the phone. He doesn't want them hearing anything Larry might say while he's in his 'other' state, certainly nothing Larry would want recorded. Guy runs to the bathroom and gets a towel, rushes back to Larry and squats by his side. He's reluctant to be so close to that terrible rictus, but Guy presses the towel against Larry's unbleeding wound. He doesn't know what else to do. Larry doesn't speak. Guy plays psychologist while he wraps the bandage tight around the towel to keep it in place.

"Why are you here, Monster?" Guy stammers. "What do you want?"

"It's not what *I* want," the monster says. "I'm fulfilling a task. I was put upon this man. I can execute my duty in any way I see fit. I'm allowed to enjoy it. To play." That awful voice is so loud from this close distance and his *breath...* Guy has never smelt anything like it. "I like the games. I'd like to play with you."

Guy freezes.

"That's not going to happen, Larry."

The monster chuckles. It shrugs.

"Rules and rules and rules. You're not supposed to know about any of this... but, *aah,* I can't *do* anything with *you* unless you interfere. I'm under obligation to advise you of this. *Ruuuuules...* very, very hard to obey them sometimes. Very hard. Sometimes I come so close to *jusssttt...*" The monster's eyes suddenly roll back in their sockets and his head trembles but the lips remain as tightly pulled back as ever. Larry's striking blue eyes roll forward and lock onto Guy, but it is the monster looking through them. Guy thinks he can hear distant sirens.

"So you will leave?" Guy asks it. "Now this is done?"

The monster stares at him, then slightly angles its head as if a thought was occurring to it.

"You have a wife, Guy Autumn. A pretty wife."

Guy's blood turns into ice.

"Don't even talk about her." Then, feeling stupid, he adds: "We're separated."

"But still married!" the Monster cries. "*His* wife was joined to him by oath. *She* could be food. *Rules!* The best games have rules, Guy Autumn. Part of the game is finding the power in them... and all the ways to bend them. We've had thousands of years to do *that.*" Guy can hear what Larry was talking about: the monster is *old,* or believes it is. Its age drips off every syllable of speech.

"Larry," Guy says, almost pleading. "Are you in there? Can you talk to me?"

The monster's grin briefly turns to the other end of the room, as if seeing something Guy can't. Or someone.

"He's asking me to kill him," it says. Its voice becomes wheedling, mocking. "Can't you hear him? *Listen.* Listen *closely.*" Guy does, despite himself.

Horribly, he believes that he *can* hear a faint sound, one somehow *behind* the silence, and it sounds like Larry screaming at him—

There's a heavy knock on the door downstairs and Guy's head snaps towards it, feeling as if he's just woken up. How long has he been squatting like this? His knees are suddenly barking, as if he's been sitting there for ten minutes rather than just a few seconds, and when he turns back to the monster he sees that its face is now just millimetres away, its jaws spread wide.

Guy yells and leaps backwards across the bedroom floor, landing hard on his backside, and the Monster roars with laughter. Guy's limbs are tissue paper as he leaps to his feet, wondering what the hell the monster did to him, *how* it did it. He watches the monster pointing at the tourniquet around its arm. Its laughter abruptly stops.

"Guy," it says, tapping the tourniquet with its finger. *"You interfered."*

But Guy is already running down the stairs, hearing the monster begin to yell hysterically behind him:

"LALLO-HO! LALLO-HO! AH-SHAM CARRA TEE, LALLO-HO! LALLO-HO!"

Guy yanks the front door open to see two paramedics—a white man and a Hispanic looking woman—and two cops standing outside, two black guys, one older, one younger.

"He's upstairs!" Guy gasps. The paramedics hurry past him, one of the cops following. The older one remains downstairs. His partner presumably wants to question Larry about Marianne so they can find her. "Listen," Guy babbles, "he's having an episode, he's talking crazy so—"

"Could you step outside with me please sir?" the older cop asks. "I need to ask you a few questions."

A voice is yelling from upstairs and its *Larry*, he's himself again and he's screaming at them, begging them not to *interfere*. Guy moves to run up the stairs, but the cop stops him.

"Sir? I need you to stay with me and let them work, you're going to be in the way."

Guy resists for a moment but then stops. What can he do that the professionals can't?

"Marianne," Guy gasps, "his wife, she's outside I think, she might be hurt—"

"We know sir, we have two patrol cars outside right now, they're driving around and we're going to find her. Okay?" His voice is calm, relaxed, and sincere. This is a cop who's been in the business for a while. Two days to retirement, all that. Guy relaxes a little, finally finding something reassuring.

"Yes, but my friend, he's… he's…"

"They're dealing with him now, sir," the cop says. "Let's step outside."

"I live… I live next door," Guy tells him in a daze, sounding like a child.

Larry's frantic, lunatic yells echo down the stairs. There's some thumping and Guy imagines the paramedics are either trying to hold Larry down or sedate him.

"Then let's go next door and you can help by talking to me," the cop says.

"… okay."

The cop nods and looks up the stairs.

"*Mike?*" he calls.

"We're okay, we're okay," someone calls down over the chaos, presumably Mike.

"Let's go,' the cop says. "Get you some water and we'll talk." He's already gently guiding Guy towards the door, seasoned in the ways of shepherding stunned people through explosions of chaos. "It's okay," the cop says softly, "let's go, let's go." The cop shepherds Guy out, snapping the door latch open, and leads Guy down around the fence and onto his driveway. Guy opens the door and heads into the kitchen, collapsing onto a stool at his breakfast bar before his legs give way.

"Did you hear any commotion?" The cop has his notepad out. "Before you went round? Or did the incident happen while you were there?"

"No," Guy says, sitting down. "I went around to—"

They both hear the faint sound of fresh screaming through Guy's open kitchen window.

Several people screaming.

The cop is already running out of Guy's house, shouting something into his radio, and Guy moves to follow but the cop turns and shouts at him.

"*Stay here!*"

He waits for a second so the cop thinks he's obeying, and then quietly follows at a run. The muffled screams are louder outside, incongruent with the calm sunny street around them. As the cop rounds the fence back towards Larry's he sees Guy behind him and turns on the spot.

"*SIR! STAY INSIDE YOUR HOUSE!*"

Now Guy *does* stop. Half a second later the cop runs towards Larry's.

Guy counts three seconds this time—long enough to hear the front door being flung open—and begins to run once more, but then he hears it. The *new* sound rolling out of the now-open front door. He freezes for two reasons:

One, a mere front door shouldn't have stopped a sound like that, especially one so loud. He could hear Larry's screams previously but not *this*. The moment Larry's front door opened the extra sound switched on, as if some sort of sonic seal had been broken, but that's impossible.

Two, the sound itself is like a lion's roar, only louder. Worse. The sound hits Guy in some low, forgotten part of his psyche; a piece of him that understands the truth about shadows. The piece of him that knows the deep, dark truth behind fairy stories and myths. The piece that has lain asleep for most of his life, now awake and ready to run for the hills at the terrible sound of that roar. He forces himself forward all the same, staggering around the fence. The screams become frantic—pained—as he reaches the front door. The roar stops for a moment but then the screeching hits a new pitch; there is a series of loud *crunching* noises and a sound like someone throwing a bucket of water against a wall. As Guy runs into the house—the normal-looking house— he hears thick, wet, chewing noises as if the world's largest cow were working on the world's largest cud. There are thuds and crashes and a fresh scream that collapses into a bubbling, gurgling moan as he reaches the top of the stairs. He runs along the upstairs hallway and sees through the partially open doorway into the bedroom: one wall streaked with running splashes of blood, the dead paramedic woman staring up at him from the floor. It looks darker in there, as if something big was now blocking most of the light from the window, making it hard to see clearly. The shadows on the wall dance in time with the chewing sounds, the crunching, the snorts.

Guy collides with the bedroom door, barging it all the way open.

Larry's upper torso lies on the bed, his legs and most of his stomach now missing, and the bed is streaked with gore. One side of it is charred black, as if it had been torched with a flamethrower. On the left, the paramedic woman's body lies angled sharply against the wall, as if flung, and on the right-hand side is the body of her male colleague, lying in the gap that Larry had occupied earlier between the bed and the wall. Marianne's dressing table is to the left of the en suite doorway and there should be large stretch of empty floor space leading to the attached bathroom, but this space is now filled by something unspeakable.

Guy screams and falls back against the wall.

He sees the monster.

He sees the monster.

He sees the monster.

It looks—

The older cop is on the floor, his left leg missing. He's looking around himself in shock, speechless, not even staring at the monster. The carpet—*everywhere*—is unrecognisable, coloured various shades of red and obscured by globs of viscera. The monster is finishing eating the other, younger cop, gulping him back, and the younger cop's head is the last thing to disappear. His wide eyes are upside down as he hangs from its mouth. Guy doesn't know if he's still alive. Blood runs in rivers from either side of the monster's jaws.

It sees Guy. It moves towards him, still eating, still roaring, but now the sound is more guttural because the thing's throat is full of flesh and liquid. The cop's nightstick lies on the floor.

Guy doesn't run for the doorway, responding with terrified fight instead of terrified flight; somehow he lunges for the nightstick, instinctively choosing *weapon* over *running* even though it looks as if it would be useless against this creature. He hears himself gibbering hysterically as he snatches up the stick, but the monster is feet away from him. It steps over the downed cop and blocks out the light as it moves, huge and dark as it fully swallows the head and torso of the cop inside its mouth. It crunches down, crushing his skull and collarbones and ribcage as if they were made of meringue. Too late, Guys instincts finally switch to the smart decision and he gets up to run but the monster swats him, toying with him, catching him in his side and neck and Guy's entire body flies into the wall and something wet sprays across his face and he knows its claws have actually opened his neck, his *neck*, and he falls to the floor, stunned. He desperately tries to clear his vision and he can't, he's hit his head and he can't see properly, and then his sight is suddenly back but it's *fractured*. His brain yells *concussion* as his vision goes double, *quintuple* and he sees five blurry figures before him now, all of them broken and unclear, but he knows they're all the monster as he hears it laughing and Guy blindly and pointlessly flings the nightstick at it. The nightstick bounces away with a strange *cracking* sound—a tinkling? *What—*

The monster vanishes.

The walls ring for a moment with its booming laughter... and something else, like it was hurt—

There is silence except for the choked moans of the dying, older cop, who is surely bleeding out. Guy tries to see Larry's body on the bed. He can't. His vision is still shot. He blinks, putting a hand to his neck as he heads towards the sound of the cop's wailing; he's cut badly in several places but none of the wounds are *pumping* the way an artery would.

Where did it go, where did it go—

His vision starts to clear as he crawls over to the cop, the word *tourniquet* coming to mind again as he operates on autopilot. The cop's leg is missing above the knee—Guy thinks that maybe he can stop the bleeding—but his hands are shaking so much that he can't get them to undo his belt buckle. His breath is coming in ragged little gasps—*Larry is dead, Larry is dead,* his brain screams, *he was telling the truth, MARIANNE is dead too then, eaten by a monster, that was a MONSTER, THAT WAS A REAL MONSTER*—but he gets the belt off and ties it around the cop's leg as tight as he can. The cop's eyes are bulging but now his eyelids are starting to flutter. He's going into shock and Guy's shaking hand finds the cop's and grips it hard as Guy kneels beside him and calls for an ambulance for the second time that day.

"Hold... on," he says, his knuckles white, and the cop grips Guy's hand back, still hanging on. "Help is coming, help is coming." As the person on a switchboard somewhere answers and asks what Guy's emergency is, he sees it; the big mirror on Marianne's dressing table, cracked like the two downstairs. He realises that, through his previously-blurred vision, he'd seen his own fractured reflection in the broken mirror, monstrous and distorted, and in his stunned confusion he'd flung the nightstick at that by mistake.

He'd missed... and hit the smaller, previously-unbroken vanity mirror sitting below it.

That's how lucky he was.

But... how does that work... what is it about breaking mirrors...

He should be dead. But then, it had time to kill him.

And was it even advancing—

Someone answers the phone, interrupting the next thought that fills Guy with ice:

You interfered.

"Officer... officer down," he says, and gives the address. "Please... please hurry." The cop is tugging at Guy's hand, trying to get his attention. Guy looks at him. The cop is mouthing words, Guy can't quite make them out. He bends down, puts his left ear to the cop's, and regrets choosing that side because this way he's facing the bed, seeing the bloody mess that used to be his best friend. He suddenly remembers his brother Ray, and can't help but think, in a moment of utterly selfish despair, *oh God, I have to go through this again.*

"Did... you ... see ... it?" the cop asks. Guy looks down into the man's eyes and nods frantically. He asks the most important and stupidly obvious question of his life because he absolutely has to hear the cop's answer:

"Did... did you?"

You See The Monster

***

Chapter Eight
Disbelief
✱✱✱

Guy is in a holding cell by himself at the police station. He wouldn't be getting out of there—no chance of bail—if it wasn't for, he's told, the testimony of the older cop. The injured man had been ranting and raving but one thing they could ascertain, apparently, is that Guy didn't kill anyone. The older cop has died since—blood loss, they couldn't save him—and Guy is the only surviving witness. They'd taken him to hospital to fix his neck—it wasn't as bad as he'd feared—and right in the middle of being discharged the cops turned up and took Guy downtown. That was hours ago, and Guy still can't stop shaking. It must be dark outside by now.

Detective Munsen has come to tell Guy he's going home, that his wife is here, and that Guy shouldn't leave town for a while. Munsen's demeanour has changed from when he and his partner were interrogating Guy—not questioning, *interrogating,* two of their own are dead after all—so Guy thinks the detective now believes he's innocent. Which even *Guy* doesn't fully believe, as his story makes no sense, even with whatever the cop said to back it up. He'd been hysterical when the ambulance arrived but whatever sedative they gave him at the hospital sure felt good. His time there was a blur—he remembers Nancy coming, he's sure of that, but they made her leave when the cops arrived—and he's not one hundred percent sure now of what he said in the interrogation room. Guy knows he didn't say anything about what Larry said before he died. He *knows* that. There was a *creature* in the house, that's all he could say. *Can you describe it?* It was big, is all he told them. *Like a bear?* Yes. A really big one though. *How could it have been in the house?* Guy said he didn't know.

Larry is dead. Guy's best friend—and most likely his best friend's wife as well—are dead.

Detective Munsen is only a little older than Guy, in his mid-forties, but his prematurely-white hair gives him the illusion of being more senior, even with his eighties-newsreader-thick thatch. His blue shirt has dark patches under his arms. It's been a long day for him. Even longer for Guy. He doesn't know if he'll ever sleep again. Then Munsen inadvertently offers him a way to understand the world once more.

"A word, before you go, Mister Autumn," Detective Munsen says, his Coventry accent so thick he could probably chew on the words as they leave his mouth.

"I have a few things I want to ask you too," Guy says. The tape from the dressing on Guy's neck is irritating his skin but that doesn't concern him too much as his back and neck have been stiff as a board since he left the hospital. His jaw aches from the constant clenching. What he saw was impossible. He killed a monster, or more likely sent it away. It happened in the house next door to his. He's frightened to go home tonight, maybe ever; he's checking into a hotel the second he gets out of here.

Detective Munsen looks mildly surprised. He holds his hand up to show Guy he can go first.

"One... any news on Marianne?"

Munsen lowers his head, nodding.

"That was one of the things I wanted to talk to you about."

Guy stares at him, frozen with worry.

"We found some... body parts in Mister Neilsen's basement," Munsen says gently, but he examines Guy's face closely as he talks. "Including a segment of jawbone. We're waiting on confirmation of dental records but, given the size of them and the items of clothing found nearby, it's very likely that they belonged to Mrs Neilsen."

Marianne—

The room goes grey and Guy thinks he's going to throw up. Munsen stands but Guy holds up a hand.

"Take a moment," Munsen tells him, but jumps in surprise when Guy slaps himself across the face, hard. "*Hey,*" he says, "easy, now."

Guy ignores the detective; he needs to remember this conversation. He has to be clearheaded.

"But the back door... the back door was open..." he says.

"I don't know, Mister Autumn. That might well have been part of Mister Neilsen's delusion, part of his mind games."

"But work, *her* work, why didn't they report her—"

"Mister Neilsen had been calling in sick on his wife's behalf. She hadn't been in for several days."

Was that Larry, Guy wonders. *Or the monster covering its tracks, like he said—*

"Okay, second... question," Guy asks Munsen, sniffing. "What exactly did the cop say? You said his story corroborated mine."

A pause.

"It did." No more information comes than that.

"And what have you written in your report?"

"You aren't a suspect, Mister Autumn. You're free to go. Would you like to stay longer?"

Guy doesn't know what to say. He wants to know what the hell the pros make of all this—how they've explained it away or even better how he can convince himself that he hasn't gone crazy and/or there aren't monsters in the houses of the human race—but he also can't believe he's being allowed to leave.

"No."

"Then answer me this and you're gone. Did Mister Neilsen ever offer you drugs, or take drugs in your presence?"

"No... never," Guy lies. "I mean, he drank..."

"Would you agree to a blood test as part of our investigation?"

Guy quickly thinks back to when he last had a blaze. He knows it's detectable for around forty-five days with a urine test, but that's for a regular user. Is it different if you haven't done it for a while? He's been pretty good in that regard lately, apart from that blip before the holiday. See, Nancy? Shows what you know.

"...why?"

"We found stashes of hallucinogenic drugs in the house, Mister Autumn. It's possible that he somehow got you to ingest it or laced your food when he was at *your* house. You wouldn't have even known he was doing it."

Hallucinogens? Larry on hard drugs? Larry with a *stash* of hard drugs?

"But... the cop..."

"We're checking the air conditioning in the house to see if Mister Neilsen was putting anything into the circulating..." He pauses, trying to think of a new word. He can't. "... air."

Surely the cop wasn't in there long enough, even if Larry had that kind of shit?

"But the wound on my neck..."

He'd heard the doctor in the hospital. He remembers that lucid snippet clearly. *Consistent with an animal attack.*

"Mm. The working theory is that we think Mister Neilsen was keeping an animal of some sort in his basement, Mister Autumn, and that Mrs Neilsen didn't know about it. Perhaps an adolescent bear." Again, he watches Guy's face, who doesn't know what Munsen sees because Guy suddenly has to stop himself from bursting out laughing. A fucking *what*? This day couldn't get any more insane— "Or a full grown wolverine, even," Munsen finishes.

Guy's jaw hits the floor.

The detective, it seems, is serious. It's Guy's turn to examine the other man closely. Munsen is actually managing to keep a straight face.

"... a *what*?"

Munsen shrugs, and sighs.

"It must have escaped. Delusional people, Mister Autumn," misinterpreting Guy's *what* as *wow, I can't believe Larry would do such a crazy thing as keep a wild bear* instead of *what, are you fucking kidding me, where the hell would he get an adolescent bear or a bloody wolverine? This is the West Midlands!* "I learned a long time ago to not try and apply rational logic to their thinking. Although I dread to think what it would have been like to be high and experiencing a dangerous animal up close."

Munsen shakes his head and Guy hears the tone in the detective's voice, that this is somehow a simple open-and-shut case of *crazy guy keeps adolescent bear in basement.* It hits him then: Munsen truly is serious. To the detective— outwardly, at least—this is an acceptable explanation.

Something is seriously wrong... but Guy doesn't want to jeopardise his chances of getting out of there. And should a detective even be telling him all this? Munsen could be testing Guy's reactions but... all *this*?

"What... do you think..." Guy asks, picking his words very carefully, "do you think happened to the other cop on the scene ...?"

"We're still looking for him," Detective Munsen says, sadly. "We're pretty sure he'll show up. Perhaps injured, concussed." It takes an effort for Guy not to gasp. Does this cop even hear himself? *We're pretty sure he'll turn up?*

"Mister Autumn? Are you alright? Would you like some water?"

Guy isn't alright. He's even more scared than he was before this conversation began. He doesn't expect the police to believe a story about monsters but he does expect them to be massively confused by all the elements of the 'rational' story: a missing cop, a magically disappearing bear-slash-wolverine, drugs in the air that start you tripping the second you walk into a house? It makes absolutely no sense and Guy wants to scream *what the fuck is wrong with you* but he needs to keep calm and get out of there so he can figure all this out.

Something is wrong—

"I'm... I'm just..."

"I understand. Your wife is waiting outside and she's going to take you home. We'll be in touch about counselling services, you've had an incredible ordeal. We might need to talk to you again soon though so, just to reiterate: don't leave town for a while, okay?" Amazing they're letting him out at all. "On another note, Mister Autumn," Munsen continues, "in case we didn't say it before: we know you tried to save Officer Boothby. That was heroic."

"Thanks..."

A cop was eaten. Was that allowed because they were *interfering?* Guy stops, tries to think rationally. Everything the cop said could be reasonable. Unlikely? Yes. But less likely than a giant fucking monster eating your neighbours?

Something creaks its way out of Guy's memory and stops him all over again, something previously flippant that now feels very, very relevant. An old rule that even *he* knows.

He asked Larry—or the monster—to let him in.

And Larry had stood there for a long time *until* Guy asked to come in, hadn't he? As if Larry were waiting for him to walk in. And even then, when Guy asked to come in, Larry didn't say yes. Guy just walked in. *Larry didn't invite him in.*

You lose all power over a vampire if you invite them in. But what if that was a bastardisation of a real, existing rule? What if *you're* the one that loses all protection if you enter without being invited? And there's no question that, by the time Guy got there, that house was the *monster's* house. Its lair.

"Mister Autumn?"

The cops and the paramedics. They didn't get invited in either. He just told them where Larry was and they entered.

"Mister Autumn..."

Rules and rules and rules. Larry was right.

"Are you alright?"

Guy looks at the cop and the monster's words come back to him as clearly as if its deep, wet voice was speaking directly into his ear:

We've been working on that for thousands of years, it had said.

Guy thinks about rules and why they would need to be in place. Like Larry said: old, *old* rules, designed long ago to keep things fair. But, as with any law, if loopholes are found, those rules then become sources of power to those who know what they're doing...

Then he tries to think it was just a load of drugs and a frightened bear.

His hands start to shake.

This isn't over, and he knows it.

"I'd...like to go now, Detective."

The detective does a well-practised sombre nod.

"Of course. Let me take you to your wife."

Guy doesn't correct him and say *ex-wife* because, technically, Munsen is right. The detective leads Guy to her; he sees his wife sitting there, looking small—and Nancy was never small at 5'9"—her tied-up red hair refusing to stay in place, her hands pulling anxiously at her light winter coat. She's still wearing a smart blouse and trousers; she came straight from work, then. She sees Guy and leaps out of her seat, looking exhausted. She has red circles around her eyes that remind Guy of something terrible; another day when he saw her pretty, high-cheekboned face riddled with sorrow.

Larry's party, he thinks, the memory like a piece of jagged glass in his mind. *That was when—*

LARRY'S party—

He collapses into her arms in the reception of the police station and as they both bawl for their lost friends Guy realises something disgusting; unlike Nancy, he's not only thinking about Larry and Marianne. A selfish thought is beginning to shriek in his head and he can't ignore it.

What if he's next?

He holds Nancy tight, feeling her chest heaving against his. What if he's brought this onto Nancy too? He can't tell her what he's thinking. He can't do that to her. He doesn't even know if—

How the fuck can he find out?

He doesn't know. He doesn't know. He doesn't even know if any of this is real, so how could he start to—

Then he remembers. He *does* have a starting point. The names Larry said.

Elias Heinrich. Sam. The Other Folk.

That's something. It's enough to take him back into the present. No matter the cause, their best friends are dead. The two of them must grieve.

He holds his wife as if she still were.

***

Part Two

Nightmares

Chapter Nine
Belief
✳✳✳

Something I didn't expect to find is not only the creation of trinkets (NOTE: GUY, NEXT PART IS NICE BUT HAVEN'T FOUND THE WORDS YET FOR THE SHANTY ITSELF, NEEDS WORK. FUCKED-UP PEOPLE, METAL SHACKS... EYES-IN-THE-BACK-OF-YOUR-HEAD-TIME, FUCKING WEIRDNESSSS... WASHING LINES BETWEEN CORRUGATED IRON WALLS, FLOOR COVERED WITH ENDLESS GARBAGE YADA YADA YADAAA, IT'S A W.I.P. DON'T FORGET! THIS IS JUST THE STRUCTURE STAGE) *but genuine street craft that wouldn't look out of place amongst the reclaimed furniture and bric-a-brac of an East Village hipster's apartment.*

Guy is waiting in Coffee #1 by Coventry train station and rereading Larry's unfinished article for the sixth or seventh time. It's heartbreaking to see Larry's constant apologetic notes all the way through; Guy had no idea how highly his friend regarded his opinion.

He hasn't been home in four days. He's staying at the Premier Inn. Nancy had offered him a room at her place but he didn't take it; he's pretty sure that she was secretly relieved, and that's fine.

Three women whose names I have to get from Dylan and his brother (the women refuse to even talk to me) are Sally, Abigail, and Shona. They're a mix of backgrounds and ages, so much so that they look unusual hanging around together, if not working together. A genuine Ad Man's dream of a multigenerational and multi-ethnic sisterhood. I ask what they're making, and I'm met with stony silence. Shona in particular is noticeable by her attempts to ignore me; her eyes screw up and she lowers her head. I can't really describe the thing she's working on, or at least not in terms of what I think its intended purpose might be.

Guy had pored over the article, hoping to find whatever it was they'd wanted to silence but also any indicators of how Larry confirmed his way into what he'd called his *curse*; but then what other word could be used to describe having a monster set upon you?

Could being cursed be as simple as accepting the object—the *trinket*, to again use Larry's word—that he was offered? Larry's article reads well enough but it isn't the kind of viral clickbait that his friend had been hoping for, something to get middle America worried and clicking their tongues. This is more of a descriptive, light human interest story, but there's no angle, no hook. It's very upsetting that Larry died over something that just wasn't, unfortunately, ready for primetime.

A piece of decoration? Larry writes. *Some kind of sundial? It may just be incomplete. Either way it's angular, constructed of a strange mix of tin and what appears to be rags. The other two are each working on something completely different, Sally putting sharp-looking things into what I think is a bar of soap and Shona making something out of small animal bones. Shona looks my way when I try to enquire about the purpose of the objects and I'm reminded of some of the expressions I saw in the* Smoke Shack n' Sweat Lodge; *eyes open and the whites nearly totally exposed, the pupils rolled firmly back into her head. (NOTE: I SAW KIDS DOING THIS AS WELL MORE THAN ONCE BUT THEN THEY WERE OKAY. SHOULD I INCLUDE THIS? TOO MUCH? OR DO I NEED MORE OF THIS KIND OF THING? IT WAS CREEPY AS FUCK) She seems to come around, realises I'm talking to her, then goes about the business of ignoring me. She was working in a trance.*

There's enough in there to confirm what Larry had already told Guy; how he'd came across some weird supernatural-looking stuff. Signs of voodoo and the spread of its use amongst the community, which is unusual, to say the least, in the UK. Guy wonders how it crossed over here. It sounds like the practices going on were crossing traditional ethnic lines as well; voodoo, to the best of Guy's knowledge, comes from Afro-Carribean and Hispanic culture, but here the whites and the Asians were getting involved as well. But the key part, for Guy, is about the 'trinkets'.

More voodoo-like behavior, Larry writes. *I wonder if these trinkets are the kind of thing Shaunessy had been talking about finding around his home? Not being a superstitious man—if I spill salt, I'm only concerned if it ruins my meal—I try to take a photo, but even before the girls can complain Dylan's brother is my face, telling me in no uncertain terms to put my camera away. Of all of the things I expected to find in abundance here—unexpected industry, relationships and yes, drugs—I didn't expect to see such widespread and fervent religious behaviour.*

There were old women sitting around, not doing much, but all dressed so identically that I couldn't say for certain that it wasn't some kind of uniform: grey dress under white cardigan. No one would confirm this for me. People there were busy... if not afflicted by a level of deep malaise. This is to be expected, one would think, but this level of depression would usually be associated with a lack *of drive. Quite the opposite was in effect, somehow, glum-faced people hurrying here and there with pieces of wood, metal, string. I saw more fitting here and there a few times, usually when visitors like me were around—there were a few—but I could never seem to ascertain what the cause was. After a while I believed it was a sham routine.*

The trinkets had to be that which Larry was given and found outside his house. He writes that he saw similar weird objects both in the shanty dwellings and there's a part in the article's intro about a stop he made on his drive over on his first day, trying to make personal inroads into the shanties. Larry had spoken to one Perry Shaunessy at a local petrol station, who'd explained how he'd found a trinket in his car park and he'd *just known* it was to do with *those weirdos from the other side of town.* He'd told Larry that he'd picked the object up—*"Like a shitty Oscar statue only made out of chicken still on the bone"*—with a shovel—*"Who knows what the terrorists are using, right?"*—and thrown it into the industrial bins around the back of his petrol station.

Larry talks more about what the residents called *a Smoke Shack n' Sweat Lodge* earlier in the article, though not much. Quite tellingly there is a brief mention of Larry being invited to sit in on a session in the lodge, or in fact a load of canvas wrapped around four poles with a sheet of rubber for a roof. Guy knows of sweat lodges from Native American tradition: a heavy night on the peyote where everyone gets spiritual. Larry says he went in and that he just observed. Maybe that was enough, without taking the fucking trinket home? Guy can picture Larry doing that, clear as day: Larry trying to keep a straight face as they gave it to him. Larry who could never, *ever* understand any kind of religious fervour and who straight up laughed at horror films. *They're just so stupid,* he would say. *How can you get scared by this?*

Guy winces at his table.

Larry's dead—

He cuts the thought off. He has a job to do.

He finds the part of Larry's article he keeps going back to like a tongue finding a loose tooth:

There's one residence (NOTE: I HOPE THIS COMES ACROSS AS FREAKY AS IT LOOKED BECAUSE THIS WAS WEIRDEST BIT) that they wouldn't let me anywhere near. It was treated with near-sacred reverence by the people there, something precious in this community of dirt and chaos: an old hessian-looking tent. Initially I thought it to perhaps be a prayer hut or place of contemplation, placed right at the back of the shanty. There was an ornate symbol daubed on both sides of it in orange paint. It couldn't be someone's shelter, least of all because of the tiny moth-holes dotted around it but because people were coming and going into it all day long, laden with the all-important trinkets. I asked if I could go in but was aggressively warned off. I think, in hindsight, my initial impression was wrong; I thought their reluctance to let me inside stemmed from some kind of religious element, and that may have been some of it. But I think the real reason was this: they didn't want me to see the animal sacrifices going on in there.

Then the kicker:

I never saw it, but I heard them. Large pigs, maybe even hogtied bulls; whatever the species, they were animals large enough to be heard grunting and bellowing all over the camp.

Guy wipes sweat from his forehead. He doesn't believe that it was animals inside that tent.

A middle-aged man enters the coffee shop. He's dressed in a brown suit and shoes and looks like a younger Bob Newhart, and even as Guy recognises the man from his website photo the first thing Guy notices is the pronounced limp. As Guy stands he can't stop his eyes from dropping towards it. The man sees this and, to Guy's embarrassment, acknowledges it as they shake hands.

"Excuse the walking pace," the man says good-naturedly, his voice only slightly gruff. A smoker? "People often end up standing a while before I get to them. It's not like I enjoy making a grand entrance or anything."

"Sorry," Guy says, "I didn't mean to—"

"*Ah,* no, no," he says, smiling as he waves Guy off and sits. "People notice, people notice. It's a normal thing to do. Hell, it's how I make a living. Noticing things." He waves a hand lazily around himself, meaning all the things in the coffee shop. "Besides, it's my one good war story."

"You got shot?"

Guy knows this man is an ex-cop but, given that this is Britain and he said *shot,* Guy assumes this particular ex-cop might have once been a soldier too. Either way, Sam is now a private detective.

"No... sorry, poor turn of phrase," Sam says with a sad smile. "I meant my most *interesting* story. My gardener backed his car into me accidentally when I was standing behind it. Happened about six months ago. It's fine but some days it plays up. Hasn't happened for a while." He shrugs. "It's more of a funny story when I tell it properly."

"One for the family reunion, eh?" Guy says, just trying to make conversation, but immediately regrets it. This is because, even though he'd scoured Larry's article for any mention of *Other Folk* and *Elias Heinrich,* or *Sam,* he couldn't find one. But he *could* find an open Facebook page—one with a depressingly low number of members—for a memorial service in Glasgow last week, one for an Elias Heinrich. Even with the polite language on the page— *fallen upon hard times*—and given that Larry met Elias in the shantytown, it's safe to guess Elias was homeless. As uncommon as that name would be in Scotland, it would be even more so for the deceased to coincidentally *also* have a brother called Sam. Especially one with a *temporarily closed due to bereavement* header on his website's home page; a website with a picture of Sam that looks, yes, like a younger Bob Newhart. Either way, comments about *family reunion* are incredibly fucking dumb, although Sam's genial poker face doesn't change. Guy hopes it still doesn't when he tells Sam the *other* reason he's been asked here, this one being in a professional capacity: he's going to ask Sam to help him to find Larry's shantytown.

"Thanks for agreeing to meet me, uh, Mr Heinrich," Guy babbles, reddening. "I'll, uh, get us some drinks. What would you like?"

"Americano please, black, with a little ice."

Guy goes to the counter to order. He appreciates Sam coming out here; the man is only based in Leicester, but even a half hour's drive to Coventry for what he thinks is a consultation would be an inconvenience. Guy feels bad; Sam must need the money. His outdated website would suggest so.

Guy's phone vibrates. A text.

ANY NEWS?

That's Nancy, again. Guy texts back:

I MIGHT BE ABOUT TO GET SOME. I'LL LET YOU KNOW.

Nancy has been amazing, staying in touch and checking in even though she and Guy's communication has been mildly hostile for a long time. He doesn't know if Nancy truly believes his account, and she's grieving herself, but *any news*—she asks it regularly—seems to be her way of engaging with this as much as she can. *Any news* means *any developments,* but also subtly asks *the* question, the one Guy desperately hopes he never has an answer for:

Have you seen anything else?

She hadn't asked him for his version of events during the car ride from the police station on that first night after... after what happened at Larry's house. Instead she drove him to the hotel in silence, with a brief stop en route at IKEA—she hadn't asked why—holding his hand whenever they were on a straight road. Her patience was impressive, especially for her. Guy was unbelievably glad she was there, and even more glad when she asked if he wanted a drink before he went to his room. Guy wondered if she would have come if she were dating anybody right now. He wondered, in a particularly bleak moment, who else would do this for him now that Larry was gone. They'd sat in silence for ten minutes with a whisky each, taking it in turns to cry. Then Guy, sounding like a man recently brought back from the dead, told her his story. Then the police's story. Throughout the whole thing she'd listened quietly, her hand almost glued to her mouth—because Guy had asked her not to interrupt until he was done—and by the end of it she was out of her seat and pacing.

Guy hadn't used the word *monster*. He'd used the word *creature*. And of course, he left out the part about interfering, about rules. He didn't want to worry her about that, although the freestanding mirrors he'd bought at IKEA were probably cause enough. It took him six trips through the hotel reception to get all of them up to the room, along with the baseball bat that he would keep in the bed with him for the next few sleepless nights. When his story was finished, she said:

"So which story do you believe? Your own, or that you were drugged and imagined it?"

Does Guy believe in monsters? Amazingly, he still doesn't fucking know. Drugs in the house and the power of suggestion? A lot more feasible than the alternative. And right now, the only inroad he has is whatever Sam can tell him. Worst case, that turns out to be nothing, but it couldn't hurt having an ex-copper onside when he's trying to find Larry's shantytown.

They won't let you find them, he thinks.

Guy takes the coffees back to the table by the window. They have the choice of seats; it's nine am. In two hours this place will be full of office workers and students and freelancers on laptops. The weather outside is cold and grey.

A private detective with the first name Sam? Guy would have expected the man to be wearing a trench coat. Instead Sam is bald and cheery-faced, not the tallest fellow at around five foot seven, and overweight; extra pounds gained, presumably, *since* his retirement from the force (his website lists his credentials). His cheeks are a little red but his genial demeanour already suggests a personality far removed from that of the clichéd, embittered and haunted ex-cop. Guy sits, handing Sam his coffee.

"So," Sam says. "You wanted me to find some people, is my understanding? Glasgow? Like I told you, that's not a problem if you're prepared to cover expenses, but why not hire someone over there?"

Sam's bloody true stories, Larry had said, quoting Elias Heinrich. Guy is hoping to hear some of them.

"You came recommended," Guy says.

"Oh," Sam says, brightening. "Nice to hear. Who by?"

"Friend of mine," Guy says. "Larry Neilsen. You know him?"

Guy doesn't expect Sam to—he thinks Larry only knew Elias by the sound of it—but Sam blinks a little too immediately and rapidly at Larry's name.

"Hmm," Sam says, scratching his cheek. "Not sure I know the name." Guy's pulse quickens, a faint chill shooting down his back. Sam is lying, and that means he has a reason to do so. He's already looking out of the window and picking up his mug. Guy is impressed. Sam's good. "Forgive me for asking, Mister Autumn," Sam continues, "but... how are *you* doing?"

"Sorry?"

He's diverting, but smiles that gentle smile again, the one Guy thinks must have opened doors with Joe Public his entire career. He's *very* good.

"Most people don't come to see me because everything is just fine, so I never expect to see somebody who is over the moon, don't get me wrong, but... you don't look well."

Guy knows he doesn't. He hasn't recognized himself in the mirror ever since that day at Larry's.

"No, I understand. I've... not been sleeping well." That's a huge understatement. He's barely slept in days, despite the prescription-strength sleep meds Nancy has given him. He wakes up constantly, screaming every time. Nancy—God bless her—stayed in another room in the hotel the first night and insisted on coming with him the next day when he went back to his house to get his things. The house *next door* to Larry's place. He couldn't stop her. Guy will be selling that house as soon as he can. Not just because of monsters, but because he simply can't live next to Larry's house anymore. He thought the place would be crawling with reporters too but that's the *other* strange thing on top of the cops just letting him go: Larry's story never made the local news. All that was at the house were a few officers watching over the place, tape around the building. It was awful to see.

"Well, the consultation is always free, as you know," Sam says, shrugging, "and you certainly wouldn't be the first person that didn't want to *go into it on the phone,* as it were. So shoot, I'm all yours."

"Mr Heinrich..." Guy doesn't know how to begin. "I'm afraid I'm not being entirely honest with you. I'm going to pay you for your time today, free consultation or not, and it's entirely possible that I may well need your professional services after all... but I came here today to talk to you about Larry Neilsen." Guy watches Sam carefully; this time the older man is ready. He doesn't even blink. "I think you *do* know the name. I also understand that there may be a very good reason why you're telling me otherwise." He leaves the statement out there.

"Alright," Sam says, not sounding offended or annoyed. "Why would that be?"

"Did you know Larry Neilsen is dead?"

Sam breathes out gently, considering his mug.

"Alright. Yes, I do," he says, and his brilliant blue eyes hold Guy's.

"Why did you say you didn't know the name?"

"Because I don't know who you are, Mister Autumn. I find it rather pays to be careful in playing one's hand."

"Please, call me Guy. And I understand. But *how* do you know his name?" Guy notices his hands shaking and puts them in his lap.

"Then you please call me Sam," Heinrich says, "and I'm afraid it's nothing particularly revelatory." He shakes his head sadly. "You're an Internet guy, uh... Mister Autumn," Sam says, tripping up in his sentence. Guy winces a little; everyone stumbles the same way when they use the word *guy* and then try and say his first name next. "I'm sure your profession has online forums where you discuss matters pertaining to your business?"

"Sure."

"So do private investigators. I do still have a lot of friends in the force. We talk, I go on the private forums. I'm not someone who takes in delight the more grisly or salubrious tales nor do I particularly seek them out, but some of them are hard to miss. So I heard about it. *Larry Neilsen* isn't exactly a common name, either."

"Forums?" Something occurs to Guy. "Sam, if I had to guess, I would say that the thread you read about Larry Neilsen's death has since been taken down?

Sam doesn't answer and his face becomes unreadable. Guy doesn't know how to proceed. Sam could get up and leave at any time—after all, he knows he was brought there on false pretences—so caution is in order. Elias was right; Sam knows something.

"I wouldn't know about that," he says eventually.

"Okay." Guy leans back in his chair and tries his best to appear casual, even though he feels anything but. "What's your opinion about the case? A house full of drugs that somehow makes people hallucinate and the police blaming a room full of dead bodies on kidnapped bear that eats people? Kind of amazing that isn't being pursued further, let alone that it isn't all over the news, surely?"

Sam nods in an agreeable manner, sipping at his coffee, and Guy can picture Sam telling families that their loved ones are dead. He'd be great at it, gentle but professional.

"I wish you'd called me to explain a little before you came to see me, Mister Autumn," he says, shrugging sadly. "I don't like to waste people's time."

"Waste... how so?" Never mind that technically, Guy is the one wasting his. "And I told you, it's Guy."

"I can think of, off the top of my head, at least ten other colleagues in my career that have looked into similar things. Similar cases to Neilsen's." He can't mean monsters. Guy hasn't even mentioned them yet. "Incidentally, I'm assuming that the late Mister Neilsen didn't actually recommend me?"

"No."

"Then, respectfully: what do I have to do with this?"

It's time to drop the bomb and hope for the best.

"Larry... he went to Glasgow, before he died," Guy says. "While he was there, I believe he met your brother. There was some creepy stuff going on up there, and I have reason to believe that's what led to Larry being killed. He was highly disturbed when he came home, and he briefly told me about a conversation he had with your brother, Elias." He pauses. Sam's expression hasn't changed, but is the man's skin suddenly a little bit more pale? "I heard about your brother's death, and I'm very sorry for your loss. But I think your brother's death and Larry's death were related in some way, and apparently Elias said that you know about this kind of thing... the kind of thing they were involved with. I contacted you because I desperately need insight as to what's going on, and other than a half-finished article that Larry was writing I don't know where to start. I'm sorry I was deceptive in my explanation for wanting to meet you, but I wasn't sure you would come if I told you all of this."

Sam blinks a few times.

"Why do you desperately need insight?" he asks.

His voice is quiet but steady.

"Because I want to find out what happened to my friend."

"No, you don't," Sam says. "Please remember that I've made a career out of hearing people's stories for several decades, Guy. I'm sure you want to find out what happened, that's normal. But I can tell that's not your *real* reason."

"What's that then?" Guy asks, too quickly, too forcefully. *How dare he*, Guy thinks, anger flaring. *I'm trying to get answers for—*

"You're scared. You're scared out of your mind," Sam says. He points at Guy, gesturing to the bandage on Guy's neck. The dressing is being changed tomorrow. Just one more night in the hotel to get through. "Your injury, there. Do you mind me asking how you got it?"

Guy can't.

"...yes. Sorry."

"Alright. Then you were there?" Sam asks. Guy can only blink. "The night your friend died. You were, weren't you?"

"... yes."

"Then I think I know why you're not sleeping, Guy. I understand." He picks up his coffee mug—his shoulders relaxing a little now—and sips at it, talking to the cup. "I'll be blunt: there's some truth to what you're saying. Over the years, I *have* seen one or two things on the job—I won't be the only one—and I've also *heard* about some things. Like I say, I talk with other professionals, very, *very* privately. For a little while, I even took a major interest after experiencing something particularly..." He tries to find the word. "... dark." He shrugs, sips, looks around himself, smiling sadly. "But the point is this, Guy. After everything I've seen and heard and from stories people told me—that never made it into one single report—I soon learned that it's in your best interests to leave it well alone. Do you understand what I'm saying?" Those blue eyes find Guy again, perfectly timed for maximum impact. "That's what I did. I left it alone. I did that because it was smart, and because frankly, I was a married man and you have to protect the things most precious to you. I don't have answers for you I'm afraid Guy, and even if I did, I wouldn't share them with you as they wouldn't lead you to a happy place. I made the mistake, as a younger man—not a *young* man, but a *younger* man—of telling my little brother about some of the stories I'd heard. I'll always regret that. Always. Young minds are very keen. I think he'd be alive today if I'd—" The mask breaks for a second and Sam sips at his mug again. Guy sees the older man's hand shaking. The mug goes back to the table. "I have to ask," Sam says, "did you do anything, involve yourself in any way, before your friend met with his trouble? Did you go to Glasgow? Did you poke around? Agree to anything unusual?"

Guy sees the monster's smile, pointing at the bandage wrapped around its arm.

You interfered, it said.

"Well... no..."

Larry said it played games. That could be all it was.

"Then I think," Sam says, "in my uneducated opinion—whatever the opinion of an overweight ex-copper means to you—I don't think you have anything to worry about. I don't know how it all works—like I say, I decided it was best not to pursue it—but in all the stories there always seemed to be some necessary element of agreement, of being complicit in some way. I think it's over. I think you're safe. I hope that's of some consolation to you."

Guy leans forward, eager, anger forgotten. He needs Sam to say it.

"Safe from *what*, Sam?"

Sam leans forward too.

"Whatever you're imagining. Retribution, perhaps. You're on the outside, and that *kind of thing,*" he says, his voice deadpan beyond belief, "doesn't happen on the outside."

"I'm not sure I am, Sam," Guy tells him, feeling like crying because he wishes he was on the outside *so much.* The room suddenly feels dreamlike, and that isn't surprising given that, ever since Larry died, he's been drugged up to the eyeballs on antidepressants and prescription sleeping pills that barely work.

"How do you mean?"

Guy's hand goes to his bandage and he says nothing. He can't talk to a stranger about what really happened, not yet.

"How many people know about this *kind of thing,* Sam?" he asks instead.

"No one truly knows, Guy, including me. That's the whole point."

No one sees us, the veteran had said. *That's how they got strong. That's how things changed. They discovered that they don't need to follow the rules with us.*

"I think... it's spreading, Sam. It's worse. I think they found a way in."

Sam's hand pauses mid-mug raise. Guy seizes the moment and puts his cards at least partly on the table.

"Have you *seen* them?" Guy whispers.

Sam looks around himself in a relaxed stretching motion that doesn't fool Guy at all.

"Yes," he says, surprising Guy by not saying *I don't know what you're talking about.* "Actually *seeing* them, yes. Once. The few other times I've been close have been after the fact things—near misses—back when I was actively trying follow leads for a little while. I've known one or two people, just one or two—good, sane people in higher positions of power than you'd be comfortable knowing about—that have told me things too. The truth is in the eyes. It sounds like a cliché but its damn true. They were telling the truth. But that was nearly two decades ago Guy, and those leads, if ever they were anything, are now ice cold. I'm going to tell you this as a courtesy because with the utmost respect and sympathy I don't want to be involved, *but,*"—he holds up a hand as Guy opens his mouth to protest— "you need to know that side of things is *over.* It's done. You are safe, your family are safe. Let this rest. If you have money to spend on a private investigator—if you actually do—then I would strongly recommend that you instead spend your money preparing to go to trial."

"What makes you think I'm going to trial?" Guy asks him.

"Well, I doubt there were many other survivors?" Sam nods at Guy's neck. "Though I'm glad to see it, I'm surprised that there was even one. Witnesses are very, very rare. I should know." Guy bleaches at the word *rare.*

"I'm the only survivor..."

"Then you have to be suspect number one—"

"I'm not a suspect," Guy tells him.

Sam freezes.

"What?"

"They let me go. Blamed it on an animal attack, all that. They've wrapped it all up already. If there's a trial or whatever I'll be a witness at most."

Sam stares at Guy. Then his brow furrows.

"Are you fucking with me?"

The F bomb coming from this genial middle-aged man is somehow stunning.

"No!" Guy whispers sharply, leaning in again. "The police have been compromised to some degree. I don't know... I've been thinking about this and I don't think Munsen—the detective who dealt with me—*knows* he a part of it. I think it's infiltrated the cops somehow—" He throws up his hands in frustration. "Sam, I told you, *this is spreading.* They found a way in. Let's just cut the shit and say what's going on here." He's suddenly getting angry. "Larry was *eaten,* his wife was *eaten—*"

"There was a fellow I knew about in London," Sam says, cutting Guy off. "Said the same about his brother and his brother's wife and children. *Devoured,* he said, except they lived in a central apartment and you don't exactly find grizzly bears hanging around King's Cross. Never went to trial either." Sam's eyes are burning. "You wouldn't have heard about it because *nobody* did. Detective friend of mine knew that family, interviewed the fella, heard his account of what was left of the bodies, *how* they were left. He retired a month after taking that interview. You understand? And the brother in question—the only surviving witness—disappeared shortly after that."

"You said I had nothing to worry about..."

"You didn't let me finish. He disappeared and they found *his* body a month later."

"... eaten?"

"No. There were remains, sure, but remains of the kind you get when someone puts a shotgun in their own mouth and pulls the trigger."

"I won't do that."

"Maybe not yet, and that's why I'm telling you this," Sam says, and now he openly looks around himself, leaning back in his seat for a moment. "There's no justice here. Just a different circle of life that neither you nor I know enough about. Let it die. Mourn your friends. Move on. Get *well.*" Then Sam surprises Guy by reaching across the table and taking his hand. "Let it end." He lets Guy go. "Thank you for the coffee. I'm genuinely sorry I can't help you, but I *am* glad we talked. You needed to hear this—"

"I lied earlier, Sam." Guy blurts. "I interfered."

"What do you—"

"I... saw the thing. I saw it happen and was doing all sorts of things that got in the way. I thought I sent it away at the end, that I interrupted its attack, but when I think about it... it was just standing there and laughing like I'd done exactly what it wanted me to do." Sam's hand goes to his mouth. The genial uncle façade truly slips for a moment and again Guy wonders: *what has this man really seen?* "I think I'm in trouble, Sam," Guy says. "Big trouble. And if Larry's involvement somehow put something onto me, I don't want to put this onto anyone else." That's a lie. Guy doesn't *want* to put this on anyone else, but that certainly isn't his main concern. "Larry talked about curses. I don't know about their rules but... maybe I'm cursed too. I *interfered*—"

"I have cancer, Guy."

That's unexpected.

"I'm... sorry... uh..."

Sam politely waves away Guy's awkwardness.

"Prognosis isn't good. As in... the worst. It went away a while ago, but I found out this week that it came back. Lost my brother and regained the Big C all in the space of a few days. "

Guy feels bad for Sam and disgust for himself as he thinks *that's bad, but let's get back to the fact that monsters are after me?*

"How come you... you know..." Guy points at the table.

"I never like to cancel an appointment," Sam says, shrugging. "I have maybe a year. I could sell the house and go and spend it on a beach somewhere, but... not my style. I've never stopped working, not since Leslie died. Retirement scares the hell out of me."

Silence. Guy assumes Leslie was Sam's wife.

"Why are you telling me this, Sam?" Guy asks.

"Because I'm thinking," Sam says, and he is, his eyes focused on the table. After nearly thirty seconds of silence Guy has to break it.

"How did your brother die?" he asks.

"How did yours?"

Something rises quickly behind Guy's eyes and he stamps it down hard.

"How did you know... about that?"

"I like to check who I'm meeting. That kind of information isn't hard to find out."

"I'd rather not talk about that," Guy says... but realises that he'd started it. "Sorry. I didn't mean to—"

"It's okay," Sam says. "He was close?"

"Pretty close."

"Mm. Mine wasn't."

That shuts down Guy's next question of *don't you want to get payback for him?*

"... I need to find the shantytown, Sam."

"You won't. It will have separated. Dispersed." Sam's eyes are still on the table. "There's a pattern. I asked around last week after..." The hand wave again. *My brother.* He thinks for another second. "You said your friend was working on an article?"

"Yes. It isn't finished, though."

"Is there a finished version?"

This is good.

"Larry told me there was, but..." It hits Guy fresh, just as it's been doing for days. *Larry.* "... uh, he, uh, by the end he was..."

"It's alright," Sam says. "Do you have the unfinished version, at least?"

"Yes, oh yes," Guy babbles. "You'll help me, then?"

Sam sighs heavily.

"You *definitely* interfered?" he asks.

"Yes. Ninety percent sure."

Sam sighs again.

"Bloody *hell...* look, I'm an old man, Guy," Sam says, and his tone says *look at me.* "I don't know how much help I *can* be. I'm out of date, out of touch."

"I don't care—"

"—and if you *are* 'on the inside' now, and I help you, there is of course every possibility that I would end up on the inside too."

"...yes."

Sam wipes his face again and puts both hands on the table.

"I'm probably too old for a last hurrah, Guy." He cocks his head, looks out the window. There's something else to this; not just Sam's brother or the fact that Guy's on the inside and needs help, but something else Sam's not telling. "But I don't have long left anyway, right?" Sam says, that grim gallows-humour smile creeping back onto his face. "And like I told you: I'm a workaholic, and the phone hasn't exactly been ringing off the hook lately." He wags a finger at Guy. "But I would very much like to give these things a bloody nose for what they did."

Does he means Elias? Guy nearly asks *what did they do* but keeps his mouth shut. Sam just got on board!

"Send me the article you have," Sam says. "I'll have a read. See if anything snags."

"Great, great—"

"Do you remember that business with the Macarthur Quintuplets? The kidnapping?"

"Uh-huh."

"I was involved with that, you know." Guy's eyebrows raise. That was an international-headline-level case. "There was talk of a lot more sinister, grisly, and downright *sadistic* stuff attached to that. That was some of the worst stuff—the worst *human* stuff, at least—that I could be involved with." Guy suddenly can't take his eyes off Heinrich. "I thought I might have to quit over it. But then I learned that I had a whole extra layer, deep down, of... steel, for want of a less pompous word. I could handle it, God help me." He points that finger at Guy again. "This will be worse, I think. For you especially. Being *very* straightforward: I'm dead anyway, Guy. What's the worst they can do? But before we go any further forward, you have to ask yourself: do you have the steel for this?"

Ice runs down Guy's back.

"I don't think I have much choice, Sam."

"That's not the same thing."

"I can do this," Guy says. He'll tell the man anything he wants right now.

Then Sam nods, and the spell is broken; he's just a late-middle-aged man standing and groaning as his knees take his body weight, outwardly ordinary.

"Okay," Sam says, as if this were a normal meeting. "Email me the article. I'll be in touch."

"Oh, yes, yes," Guy says hurriedly, standing too. "Thank you, Sam. Thank you so much." They shake hands.

"Actually... thank *you*, Guy," Sam says, nodding, and there it is again, that hidden something. He's suddenly on the team, this stranger? An ally... Guy feels a sense of a burden being passed, if only temporarily; this is the start of something. Maybe he'll be able to sleep tonight.

"Speak soon," Sam says, then turns and walks awkwardly out of the shop, and as he passes a patron near the door—a willowy woman with her dark hair tied up in a half-up, half-down style—Sam's body creates a change in shadow on the woman's blue blouse that plays tricks with Guy's eyes. It must be the stress and fatigue he's experiencing, but for a brief moment Guy thinks he sees a squat, kind of see-through little black figure sitting on her shoulders, latched onto her like a limpet; the light refracting through the window makes Guy think—just for half a second—he sees its eyes *glitter*, a horrible pinpoint flash of brightness in the middle of its shadowy head. He blinks... and realises it's just the down half of the woman's hair lying on the back of her neck. *Jesus,* he needs another coffee. He's getting delirious. If he starts seeing things he's screwed.

He orders an Americano to go and thinks—not for the first time—about hallucinogenic drugs and dangerous animals kept indoors and tries to tell himself that he might, after all, be crazy.

It doesn't work.

***

Chapter Ten
Proof
✱✱✱

Doctor Cheng isn't much of a talker. Guy assumes it's because the man is so young; a lack of confidence, or time to develop a good bedside manner. Guy is sitting in a chair in a small, sparsely decorated and brightly strip-lit hospital room. He's so tired he can barely sit up straight. He passed out in the hotel room for most of yesterday, exhaustion finally getting the best of him, and when he woke up, it was 9 p.m. The sleeping pills made even less of a dent in the night time as a result. He feels as if he's losing his mind.

He'd missed calls from Nancy and Sam yesterday. Neither left a message. He called Sam first, but no answer. Same this morning. Nancy picked up though. He's meeting her later. She's coming to check he's okay and won't be swayed from doing so.

"Okay Mister Autumn, let's take a look at this," Cheng says, donning his surgical gloves. "You're lucky. The attack was very close to the artery."

"Uh-huh." As Cheng starts to work at the dressing, Guy winces slightly; one thing that's *definitely* real is the damage to his neck. It stings like a motherfucker.

"Mm," Cheng says, sounding mildly confused.

"Everything okay?"

"Mister Autumn..." Cheng replies, peeling away the last of the dressing. "Have you been putting anything on this?"

"No."

"And this is the same dressing that we applied when you were admitted? You haven't redressed this yourself?"

"No," Guy says, starting to get worried. "Why?"

Cheng shakes his head a little in disbelief.

"You're a *very* fast healer," he says.

"What do you mean?" Guys says, hearing the defensiveness in his own voice. Maybe Nancy was right and he *is* argumentative. "Are you saying there was never any..." He's doubting his own sanity. Again.

"What? No, no," Cheng says, a confused smile on his face. He holds up the dressing, shows Guy the coating of dried blood and scabbed-over tissue on the inside. "Like I said, you've had a close call." His brow furrows for a moment. "Why would there not have been..." His brain finishes the dance between what doesn't make sense and what needs to be let go, then continues to function. Guy suddenly pictures it like Tinkerbell in reverse; rather than a fairy dying every time someone says they don't believe in them, something dark is born every time someone pushes an inconvenient reality away. "It's only barely healed, that much is obvious, but even so, I'd still expect there to be a much higher amount of scabbing."

"Oh. Well, that's, that's good..."

"Here, let me get you a mirror," he says, grabbing a small one from the counter. He shows Guy his own neck. Guy screams and falls sideways out of his seat.

"Mister—are you—" Cheng babbles, moving round to help Guy up, but Guy's ignoring him and grabbing for Cheng's mirror, not getting up. He doesn't think his legs would support him. He looks at the glass and moans out loud, the awful truth undeniable.

On the large patch of skin previously covered by the dressing, Guy's neck has developed a coating of white scales.

They're smallish—each one of them is around a centimetre square—and they look fresh, the way pinkish new tissue does after a wound has healed. To Guy's disgust they *glisten* in the light as he turns his neck back and forth. Is that—

He draws the mirror closer, squinting even as his mind reels. *Yes.* At the outer edge of where the dressing would have been, new scales are starting to form. Are they working their way outwards?

"Mister Autumn!" Cheng cries, hovering nearby, hands working helplessly as he just doesn't know what to do. A more experienced doctor may have done, perhaps. "It's fine, look, your wound is fine—"

"What the fuck are you talking about?" Guy yells, feeling what used to be his own skin under his fingertips; it's alien, reptilian. He feels the segmented surface move as he presses it, reminding him of when he held a python once at a zoo as a child. The room spins. "Look at it! Look at it!"

"I *am*," Cheng snaps, but trying to keep his professional front. "That's healthy skin, that's *excellent* healing, let me get—" He's moving towards the door now and Guy knows he's going to call for assistance and even in his panic he realises that he just can't have that, can't have more *attention* and he's seen enough horror movies for his subconscious to put two and two together on autopilot and—

"Wait!" Guy snaps, getting hurriedly to his feet. "Look... look at my neck again! Look *closely*. You don't see anything unusual? Nothing?"

"I don't *need* to, Mister Autumn!" Cheng says, but he stops moving towards the door. That's good. "There's nothing wrong with that at all!" Guy's heart pounds and his brain screams *this is proof, this is proof,* but he still needs to hear Cheng say it. "Look," Cheng says, breathing out as he mentally changes down a gear or two. "I know you've had a traumatic experience..."

Guy lifts the mirror as Cheng talks, expecting the old oh-it-was-just-a-trick-of-the—

No. The scales are still there, coating his neck with white and his soul with disbelieving terror.

This means its real—

No. If Cheng can't see it then Guy *might* still be crazy.

"... and sometimes stress can make us see things that aren't there," Cheng continues, remembering his training. It shouldn't be difficult; Cheng looks like he only graduated med school last week. "Looking through your notes I see you've been prescribed—"

"You're right, you're right," Guy says, dragging his eyes away from the mirror. He tries to keep his voice even. "Sorry, I'm sorry. Can we—"

"Please sit, would you like me to—"

"No, I'm sorry, it's uh, it's been a rough few days. Can we get this redressed please? I need to get going."

He needs it covered up. He doesn't want to get halfway out of the hospital and find out that Cheng isn't the only one who can't see it, prompting *questions.* He needs to get out of here and figure out what's going on.

Cheng looks at Guy, weighing him up.

"Did you drive here yourself?"

"No," Guy lies. "My wife is waiting for me, so..."

Cheng hesitates. His eyes glance briefly at the clock behind Guy's head.

A few more questions and ten minutes later Guy's heading for the car park. Cheng was right about one thing: Guy shouldn't be driving. He completes the twenty-five minute drive to the hotel in seventeen.

**

There is a knock at the hotel room door. Guy yanks it open so quickly, grabbing Nancy's wrist without thinking, that she lets out a scream of fright. Her handbag falls to the floor.

"*Nancy—*"

"*Jesus!*"

"Sorrysorrysorry..."

He bends, quickly picking up her purse. She's dressed smartly—work clothes—and he's been wearing the same t shirt, jeans and underwear for two days straight now. Guy knows he must stink. Nancy stares at him, red-faced, outraged at the physical contact, but sees the worry in Guy's eyes and the automatic anger vanishes... but not entirely, of course. Guy knows that's to be expected.

"It's alright, it's okay," she says, but her jaw is tense. She's treating him with kid gloves, or at least by her standards, keeping her snappier responses in check.

Makes a nice change, part of him snaps.

Shut up, the conscious part responds.

"Nancy, I need you to look at something for me. It's really important."

"Okay, okay," she says gently. "Guy, are you okay, have you seen any—"

The dressing is still on his neck. He couldn't bring himself to take it off in case he kept catching sight of it in the mirror before Nancy got here. Something strikes him for a moment.

"Thanks for coming, Nancy. It... means a lot." He's shaking.

"It's alright," she says, rubbing his arm—like a friend, he notices—and then she sees his face up close.

"Guy, you look awful—"

"I need you to look at my neck and tell me what you s—"

"Medical dressing—"

"Not fucking *yet*—" He catches his own snapping. "Yes, *dressing*, but I'm going to take it off and I want you to tell me what's underneath. Okay?"

"You just had it changed? It's fresh." She sees the mirrors he's placed in a circle around the bed. They were in boxes when she last saw them.

"I like the décor."

"Not funny, Nancy."

"Sorry. *Sorry.* This is all just fucked up beyond belief. I'm trying to make light of..."

"Then don't."

"Look, why don't you check out of this shithole and—"

"Well I know it's not the kind of all-inclusive bullshit places you made us go to," he snaps, the unbearable tension of the last few days thrumming in his veins.

"You know it was *you* who started us doing that," she snaps back, her own dam breaking. "*You* that picked that place in—" She stops herself. Guy almost feels disappointed. "Can we not do this?" she asks. "We're both strung out. I haven't been sleeping either, you know. Can we...?"

She's being the adult. Even though Guy *knows* what's she saying about the holidays is bullshit, he follows her lead.

"Sorry," he says to the floor, then crosses to the bathroom. He talks to her through the open door. "Bear with me a sec." He runs water over his fingers, preparing to wet the surgical tape. "This will—" He sees her expression as he catches her looking. If she was a doubtful but still-willing believer before, it's clear she's now beginning to think he might be going over the edge. This is where, in the past, he would get angry and start stamping around because she doesn't believe *him*, her former husband, convincing her only further that he's gone mad. But she'd be crazy if she *didn't* have doubts. "It's alright," he tells her, and means it. "It all sounds crazy and I don't know what's real anymore, but if you just look at this and tell me what you see, it'll help, okay?" He soaks the thin paper tape with water.

"What did the PI say?" she asks from the bedroom.

"Sam? It was interesting," he says, the tape beginning to come away under his fingers. "I think he knows about... what I saw."

"He believed you?"

The anger threatens to come up again—he's so goddamm *tired,* and he thinks he could be forgiven—but he doesn't say a word, instead just continuing to fiddle with the tape. He doesn't want to look in the mirror, but he has to see it's still there before he goes and checks with her. The white pad comes away revealing an infinitely more horrible whiteness beneath it, one that catches the bathroom strip-light like a freshly-caught fish shining under the sun. He walks into the bedroom sideways, his neck turned away from her.

"I don't think you're going to see anything," he tells her, talking to the wall. "The doctor couldn't, so don't worry if you just see a normal, freshly-healed wound."

"Freshly healed? They said you should be wearing that dressing for two—
"

Guy turns around and shows her his neck. He keeps his eyes closed.

"Jesus…"

If she'd seen the scales, she would have screamed it. It's a *Jesus* of surprise at the healing.

"What do you see?" he asks. She reaches for his neck, but he takes her wrist to stop her, incredibly gently this time. She stiffens briefly, and not in a good way. "Nance…"

"Your neck, its healed already—"

"Describe it—"

"Like… a healed wound, pink skin—"

"Nothing white?"

"No… nothing." She steps back. "What do you think I should see?" She pauses. "What do *you* see?"

"Scales. White scales."

"… what?"

Guy walks into the bathroom and looks in the mirror. Nancy follows him, stands next to him. The scales shine just as horribly as before.

"Scales from here," he says, touching his finger to the bottom edge of them, "up to here." He touches the top. "You don't see them." Her hand is on his back.

"I'm sorry," she says. "I don't."

There's no history of mental illness in Guy's family that he knows of. But this—

"I'll take a photo," she says. "Let's take a photo on my phone and see if you see them on there."

"Okay," he says. She fetches her phone and holds it up to take a picture.

"Turn so I can—"

She screams, a blood-curdling yell of a kind that Guy has never heard her produce before. The phone flies across the room and bounces off the opposite wall as Nancy recoils.

"Nancy!" Guy goes to her and to his dismay she holds out her hands to keep him back. "What, what?!" She pulls her hands back immediately, realizing what she's doing. "You can see them?" Guy barks. "You saw them on the phone?"

"I can see them," she says, starting to cry out of sheer shock.

"The camera?" he asks, his voice breaking too. "You saw them on the screen?"

The tears are flowing openly now as she nods her head, holding her hands out to Guy once more.

"But I can see them *now* too," she sobs. "With my eyes, I can see them *without the camera now.*" Her face is pleading. "*What are they?*"

The terror Guy sees in her sets something off: his chest starts to constrict and he can't breathe. Little white lights dance over his eyes. Is this what PTSD is? The walls are closing in.

It's over, Sam had tried to say. He was wrong. *Dead* wrong. Guy is inside the circle. He curls up into a ball as he tries to breathe.

Larry warned you, his brain hisses, *but you still interfered.*

Nancy is on his back with her arms around him but even as he tries to find air he's dimly aware that they've embraced more in the past week than they have for the last two years. Her head is pulled far away from his neck though.

I'm on the inside, his mind babbles. *I'm on the inside.*

But he knows that's not the right phrase. He needs to use Larry's word.

I'm cursed.

That isn't the worst of it. He catches half of his reflection in one of the mirrors and gains a terrible confirmation. His hunch in the hospital was right: the scales have spread a little. They've moved outwards around his neck.

He's not just cursed. He's running out of time.

***

There's a park a few blocks away from the hotel with a pack of pre-teens on it, playing football. Nancy and Guy sit on a nearby bench in the weak sun and watch the game. They're not talking. Guy just breathes steadily, deliberately. The happy, energetic scene in front of them is completely at odds with the darkness going on inside, that he feels all around them.

"It feels like a dream," Nancy says, as if reading his thoughts. "Well... a nightmare, of course," she adds. Guy doesn't say anything. "I mean, all this stuff about rules, but it *killed those cops too—*"

"They directly interfered..." He knows it doesn't sound quite right, but doesn't throw in his theory about them—about everyone who entered Larry's house on that terrible day—not being invited in.

"What are you going to *do*, Guy?"

"I think I have a little time. A week or so, at least."

"Do you think you can stop it spreading?"

"I don't fucking know, do I—" He catches himself and pats her hand, his eyes closed. "I'm sorry, I'm just barely holding it together—"

"That's okay," she says, but her now-stiff body says otherwise, even if she means what she said. "Let's try and stay on the same team. Okay? We're the good guys. We're not beaten yet. Let's try..." She's trying to be positive in the face of doom. Normally such things don't work on Guy, but right now he's hanging on every word of this pep talk. "Listen, you're not beaten yet, okay? Those things have to operate in darkness for a reason, right? All their rules. That has to mean there are things *they* are afraid of."

Guy's sees Nancy's eyes and something forgotten washes over him.

"I think you need to stay away from me now, Nancy."

"Oh, *no* chance—"

"I don't want you near me when... this completes, Nancy. I think it's like a virus or something."

"I am *not* going to—

"—if somehow I get *you* sucked in then they'll have something they can use to stop me. Forget the angry I'm-no-damsel-in-distress routine, I *know* you're not, you've always been stronger than me." The words are out before he knew he was going to say them, but he doesn't stop. "You're my wife on paper, we said vows that haven't yet been broken, and I think that's *exactly* the kind of rules they'll understand. You'll already be on their radar. I don't want you showing up anymore."

"*No chance—*"

He goes to grab her arms but instead closes his hands in the air nearby.

"Who are always the easiest people to be manipulated when it comes to, to, I don't know, using the *pain* of their loved ones against them?" Guy hisses. "Men and women of conscience—"

"And that's you, is it?"

The words are a slap. He suddenly remembers the *other* worst moment of his life again, after that fucking party at Larry's, Nancy sitting and crying at the foot of their bed, a defeated child's sob, her arms wrapped around herself, and him knowing somehow that this is it, that *this is over,* and wondering how the hell it had happened. A kid's excited scream from the football pitch cuts through an uncomfortable moment.

"Sorry," she says softly.

He lets it go for once.

"It's okay."

Silence.

"Sitting here like this," she says, almost to herself. "It makes it all seem unreal."

"I know." He gestures at the kids. "Hearing all the lil'—" He catches himself before he says *lil' albatrosses* out of habit, knowing it's probably the worst thing he could say right now. "Uh, the little kids laughing..."

"Mm," she says, pretending not to have heard. "Sunlight, too. Makes it hard to imagine anything like..."

"Yeah. Yeah."

She's right. The lack of shadows makes it—

Something strikes him.

"Guy—"

"Hold... hold on a sec," he says. He waits, tense but letting the cogs turn.

"Guy. *Guy*," Nancy repeats. "What are you thinking—"

There it is. An inkling, a thought. A *starting point*, at least.

"They have to operate in *darkness*..." he says, turning to Nancy. The fear is there, but something else is creeping in; it's desperate and shaky but it's there. There's *something*. There's hope. And something else... "So I have to try and make that as difficult as possible. I have to try and drag them into the *light*."

She brightens but its brief.

"You want to... expose them or something? That's crazy, how would you even... they wouldn't want that Guy, they could make things worse—"

"It *is* risky but it's the only thing I can start with right now, Nance," he says, half of his brain talking to her but the other half already running desperately to ideas, to execution of concept. "I don't have a lot of choice, do I? This isn't some straight-to-video B-movie where everything stays secret until the third act, or the monster or the ghost disappears for no reason every time someone who isn't involved with things walks into the room. This shit on my neck is growing. What happens when it reaches my eyes?"

She grabs his hand at this and he regrets saying it.

"Your neck, then," she says. "What if it gets worse, what if the speed of it is something they can affect, and they *make* it worse because you start poking around? What can happen to you?"

It's a question Guy has no answer to.

"I still have to try, Nancy," he says, and there it is again, that excitement behind the fear, and he realises it for what it is: the thrill of the hunt. Waking up.

Middle class life, man, he thinks. *It's soft and it's safe but it puts you to sleep.*

"And think about it," he says. "If they don't want to be brought into the light, doesn't what I do for a living make me pretty well placed to do that? Social bloody *media?* Don't you think that makes me dangerous to them?" He nearly believes it, but she clearly doesn't, folding her arms. "My *job* is to draw attention to things online," he tries, feeling that excitement still building. Yes, *there's something else too,* but he's letting a plan form.

"No one will believe you," Nancy says. "And as soon as you start, those things are going to close in on you."

"I don't think they can just do what they like. We know there are rules. I'll keep my eyes open. They're going to try to scare me, to convince me they *can* do whatever they want, but I don't think it works that way."

"No. No, no, no." She holds her forehead with both hands, an action Guy knows very well. He stands and tries to embrace her but of course she won't have it, pushing him away. She looks at him, shocked and furious. Of *course* she is. Guy knows that the last thing he should be trying to do is hold her. It's different if she starts it.

"Nancy, look at it *this* way then, if you won't listen to me because I want to protect you: it's about me maximizing my chances to, I don't know, operate against them. If they get to you, then they have influence over me. If I keep quiet to keep us safe then I think that's exactly what they *want.* The only way to protect us—"

"But you don't *know!*" Nancy cries, standing up. "Something this big? You think you can stop this? You don't even know how!"

He decides to go for broke. It would be a cheap shot if he didn't mean every single word.

"Imagine it. Remember when we talked about... you know." He points at the kids, choosing his words very carefully by not using any. Nancy looks hurt and shocked but he's genuinely not trying to hurt her; he's just trying to get her to *listen.*

"This..." She pauses, giving him the benefit of the doubt. "This better be good."

"Think about how you used to picture that," he says.

"It's hard to picture the way I *used to think about it* because you would always be—"

"I know, I know," he tells her, hit for the first time—in his darkness—by the idea of the light that children would bring. *Too fucking late now, buddy,* he thinks bitterly. "But picture yourself with those kids. Then picture introducing them to a world where this thing has become even bigger, influencing everything and getting..." Guy can't imagine what the world would become if things like the creature he saw in Larry's house held more sway. "Imagine we'd done nothing about it? It *is* growing Nancy, and imagine I let that happen *because they used you to stop me.*" She doesn't reply. "I might be able to get this so far into the public eye that the only way to discredit me is for them to *stop* what is happening to me. Don't you see? *That might be how I stop what's happening to me.*"

Her eyes are red, but she isn't crying.

"That was a really shitty shot to take," she mutters, and she's right... but he can see she knows why he did it.

"I can't think of anyone else I would rather have with me in this," Guy tells her. "No one." Something inside him turns over, something buried.

"You fucking Autumn boys," she says, turning her face away. "Ray wouldn't listen. You're exactly the same." Guy closes his eyes. He knows Nancy can't help it. This is how she backs down. "I grieved twice already for Ray."

"Nancy..."

"First for him, and then for us. For what it *did* to us. To you. And now you're... you're going off alone again..." Guy wants to reach for her. He doesn't. "*Fuck,*" she sniffs. "Fine. That's how you operate best anyway." The wall is going up again, and for once that's good. "Where will you start?" Acceptance.

"I don't know," Guy lies, because he already does. The less she knows, the better. His body is thrumming, and as he moves away from thoughts of Ray and Nancy, he finally understands *why* he's shaking like that, what's coming through. "I need to talk to Sam again. We're going to plan."

"Oh, so it's okay to put him in danger—"

"Frankly, yes," Guy says, shocking himself as he realises he means it. "He's already a dying man, and I think he has a little payback in mind, no matter what he might say."

"Dying—"

"Don't worry about it Nancy. Go home," Guy says, not looking at her. Whatever bridge had been rebuilt between them, he thinks they've just destroyed it. Right now that's fine because it's helping that *something else* come through and now he recognizes it, for once can *bathe* in it. It's almost joyous, embracing this enemy that is now his shield and armour.

"Call me later," Nancy sniffs, her face like iron; once Nancy is set, she's set for good. Guy learned that in the hardest way. She turns away and Guy lets her go. She shouldn't be there now. Guy knows he needs to soak this in. They *cursed* him. *How dare they.* He watches her go, his brain firing on all cylinders. *Curses.* That's where he's starting.

Because who does he know of that *sounds* cursed? He kicks himself for not thinking of it the second he heard Larry use the C word, but that was in another lifetime.

Peter Nowak, the World's Unluckiest Man.

There it is again, the *something else*. Those fuckers *cursed* him. It's anger, and Guy realises that he has so much, so much.

***

Chapter Eleven
Learning
✳✳✳

Sam opens his front door and Guy almost pushes past him in his haste to get inside, apologizing as he does so. Sam's home is typical of any middle-class Midlands residential street; three-bedroom-size, detached. Bought, perhaps, in more financially secure times for him. The 52 plate Volvo in the driveway would seem to support that.

"Come in, come in," Sam says, lightly sarcastic. He's lost the tie but he's still wearing a shirt and trousers combo at home. The hallway is dark, the wallpaper a little faded. Patches on the walls where pictures once hung. An astonishingly old, grey-haired spaniel shuffles out of the living room and makes its wheezing way over to Guy's feet, tail wagging. "Leave him alone, Rufus," Sam chastises gently, but Rufus ignores him completely, nose to Guy's shoes.

"Sorry Sam, I need your Wi-Fi," Guy babbles. "Uh, is the living room through here..." Sam holds out a hand towards a door.

"Be my guest," he says, and that's exactly what Guy's going to be; he's brought his overnight bag. When Guy finally spoke to Sam last night, he'd said that Guy needed to move into his place.

"Better than you being in that hotel," he'd said, "but we shouldn't talk about the other reasons on the phone. It sounds like they have people inside the police system—you'd be in jail if they didn't want this to go away quickly— which means we don't know who they have on the phone lines. Plus, if we're going to do this, we need to do it properly, and *I* need to be able to stop you from doing or agreeing to anything that can put someone else in the same mess. They might want you to spread this somehow." Guy's questions could wait; he was just glad to have Sam on board. But right now, in Sam's house, Guy has an appointment to make, and he's late. A crash on the M69 held him up for an hour and a half, and none of his apology texts were being replied to. He thought he'd be there with time to talk to Sam before getting set up.

"Wi-Fi code is foxes3869," Sam says as Guy enters a living room that would have been modern in the 90s. More signs of a life that is... quitting? Sam heads to the kitchenette at one end of the room to make them some tea. Away to his right, Rufus has already tired himself out and is heading for a threadbare old dog basket in the corner. He curls up but keeps his shiny black eyes on Guy, who places his laptop on Sam's dining table and opens the device. He fiddles with his dressing while it boots up. He'd made a new one yesterday with a first aid kit. To the naked eye the scales might look like normal skin but Guy's keeping them covered just in case. Cameras and kids with phones everywhere.

Plus, the scales have spread even further now. They're covering nearly all of his neck and have started to reach south past his collarbone. The only blessing is that they don't seem to be moving towards his face. He doesn't want to think what might happen once that is covered.

Guy's MacBook gives its familiar chime and, as the desktop is revealed for the first time in days, he hooks it up to Sam's wifi. The Mail app opens up automatically and here comes the swarm of messages, a shit ton of them, the daily dose of distraction. This isn't anything unusual, the backlog of several days arriving all together, enquiries from clients, responses from tweets and posts, invoices. Guy's seen and ignored them all already on his phone, only using it for occasionally communicating with Nancy and searching the internet for information. He'd spent last night looking up disappearances and phenomena, Googling things like *weird disappearances Britain* and *strange murders America* and *unusual objects*, following each spin-off link and forum comment deeper down the rabbit hole. He couldn't see any patterns. Just crazy, crazy shit. Nothing about ways to defend himself. He has the breaking-a-mirror thing, but that might just be coincidence... although all the mirrors in Larry's house just happened to be broken. A pre-emptive security measure by a certain big fucking monster?

He looks for the email chain that he needs, the one that went back and forth from his phone last night. He sees the email he sent that finally got him a reply:

SUBJECT: RE: THE SUPERNATURAL.

To: NOWAK, PETER

Dear Mr Nowak,

I know I have been attempting to contact you for some time and that you are wary of the press. I can assure you now that matters have changed, and my enquiry is entirely personal. If this sounds like madness, then please do forgive me.

I have become involved with forces way beyond my understanding, hence the title of this email. I also believe that your desire to avoid talking to people may be more than a desire for privacy; silence may be a matter of life and death to you. At the same time, I believe the option of remaining silent has passed for me, and I need information so that I can do something to protect myself and my loved ones. I enclose a photo of what is happening to me. I can assure you that it is real and that anything we discuss is private and confidential. I enclose a signed NDA form regarding our possible conversation in advance. This way you know that your name and privacy will be respected and that I will say nothing about you in public.

Sincerely,

Guy Autumn.

PS: we could talk online as I believe seeing each other would be better. If you wanted to use this option I would recommend, for safety's sake, getting a VPN for your computer or phone. The link below provides a free trial version.

PPS: I am begging you for your time. I'm desperate and fear that I am running out of my own. I don't know what is happening to me.

There's Nowak's email reply, containing the FaceTime ID Guy needs:

I'll talk to you if I can see you. Do you have FaceTime? 10am EST.

Facetime ID: playupskybluespnowak@hotmail.com

He looks at Sam's clock. 10:13. *Fuck.* If he had an iPhone he could have Facetimed Nowak on the drive over. Guy enters the Facetime ID on his MacBook and hits call. Sam follows him into the room.

"Is this something I should see?" he asks.

"Yeah," Guy says, not taking his eyes off the screen. "If I'm right about him."

"Do you take milk and sugar?" Sam asks.

"Oh… milk no sugar, thanks."

Sam shuffles over to the kitchenette. Guy's own frantic face fills the screen as he waits for Nowak to pick up. Guy looks away.

The ringing stops. The call is connecting. The video image of Guy quickly shrinks to a little inset in the main feed. He pulls out his wallet and places it against the screen, covering that part of it.

The main window fills with an image of a stubbly-faced man, lit by the light of his laptop screen. The stream isn't good; the image is badly pixelated. Guy knows Nowak is in his late forties, but the man looks much older. His blonde hair is thinning and his jowly cheeks are covered with thread veins as red as his nose, making it instantly clear how he chooses to deal with his troubled life. The room behind Nowak is dark—his curtains must be drawn—but Guy realises the actual walls are blackened. Fire damage? But why hasn't Nowak repaired it?

Then the answer is obvious. After all, how does Guy even know Nowak's name?

The sunken, haunted expression in Nowak's eyes is all too familiar. Guy knows that his guess about Nowak and curses was absolutely right. *No*, wait. It's more than that. He looks at Nowak onscreen and gets a strange feeling way down in his gut; a little nauseous, like the feeling one gets when starting to realise the chicken à la King one just ate might mean an evening talking to the toilet bowl.

Nowak is a part of this. Guy can feel it almost physically. How is that possible?

"Can you see me?" Nowak asks.

"Yes. It's not very clear though."

"Mm. Probably my end. I'm tethered to a phone signal."

Of course; he wouldn't have WiFi. The electrics in his house must be unreliable at best.

"I don't mind if you don't?"

"No."

"Thanks for taking my call, Mister Nowak. My name's Guy."

"I know. And you're welcome. Peter. I don't…" Nowak pauses again, looks away from the screen. "I don't talk to people much. Sorry if I seem… you know." He does a little hand wave near his head. He means *weird.*

"Don't worry, don't worry," Guy babbles, "I'm just glad we're talking." Sam is still making tea. *Hurry up—*

"I used to speak to a few people over the years, people that were *involved.* Back when I still... well, talked."

"What did you talk with them about, Peter?"

Nowak shrugs.

"You said this was personal, so I'm assuming you're involved too." He points at the camera. "I know that look. It's coming off you in waves. So I guess you're safe to talk to about this, but I need you to start us off." His tone is flat, quiet. He sounds the way Guy imagined him: a blue collar guy. But he just looks... *beaten.*

"I understand, Peter," Guy tells him. Sam finally comes back with two mugs of tea and Guy takes a deep breath. He hasn't briefed Sam on Nowak at all. "I think you—and I—are victims of curses of some sort."

"Why do you think *you're* cursed?" Nowak asks.

"Maybe because I was writing an article about you," Guy guesses, shrugging. "Maybe I was next in line after my best friend was cursed. Maybe—"

"No," Nowak says, interrupting gently. "I mean why do you think you're right? What happened to you?" He points at the now-larger dressing on Guy's neck. "Something to do with that?" Sam puts the mugs on the table and sits in the chair opposite Guy. "Who's that?" Nowak asks quickly.

"That's Sam, he's..." Guy trails off. "He's going to be helping me with this." Sam nods in response, shrugs, and sips from his mug. Nowak nods.

"So tell me," he says. "Did you actually physically *see* something? You were touched by something?"

This will be the first time Sam hears the whole story. He's politely listening.

"Okay," Guy says, and begins with the incident in Miami—it occurs to him that the veteran's vision would make him a goddamn *soothsayer* or something—and Larry's shanty trip. When Guy gets to the incident at Larry's he freezes, almost physically unable to talk about it. Nowak helps him out.

"You don't have to describe the... thing," he says. "Just tell me what happened."

Guy does. It's extremely difficult. He doesn't look at Sam during the telling.

"After that," Guy says, finishing, "this started." He reaches up and peels the bandages away, wincing slightly at the feel of those awful scales beneath his fingers. He removes it halfway and touches the outside edge of them. "This was *here* a day or two ago," he says, moving his finger two inches inside the edge. The dressing is only to cover the visible part of his neck. The rest is now expanding well below the neckline of his sweater, out of sight, growing. His neck and shoulder and most of his pectoral on that side are now covered, reminding Guy of those single-shoulder armour things roman gladiators sometimes wore.

Sam looks slightly confused.

"Come round here Sam," Guy says, sighing. "Look at the screen."

Sam does. When he sees it—sees *them*—there is no cry of dismay... but Guy catches a slight intake of breath as Sam looks back at Guy's neck in the flesh, now seeing its true appearance off-screen as well. Nowak hears it too.

"Your friend couldn't see it? Until he saw it on camera?"

Sam shakes his head and sits down without a word.

"No, he couldn't."

Nowak nods.

"From your emails I'm assuming you know a lot of my life story, right?" he asks.

"Yeah."

"You know how this started, though?" He gestures at the room around him. "This?"

"I'd very much like to know."

"Started with a bloody flyer through the letterbox," Nowak says, leaning back and lacing his fingers over his belly, getting as comfortable as he can. "A flyer. I don't think those... things own a printing press but they must have connections or control over people that do... even so I don't think the seance was an event they created. I don't think they work that way. Not yet anyway."

Just like that, he's there, lost in the memory of a life that is long gone.

"It was a simple looking thing," he says. "Like something your grandmother might knock up to send to the W.I., like an invite to a flower arranging day or something? Printed on normal printer paper as well, not like, glossy flyer paper... really basic. The edges looked hand-guillotined. It was for a local medium doing séances. Not very common in Cov. Other than the subject matter, it looked normal, no *mystical things* nonsense, just like *do you want answers or peace of mind, come see Joanne Berkeley*—Joanne Berkeley, not even *Madame Rose* or any crap like that—and I of course threw the bloody thing in the bin. What do I want to go to a séance for, unless it's to talk to Cov's chances of promotion and ask what the hell happened."

Guy is leaning forward in his chair.

"Then the flyer turned up again," Nowak says softly. "In the middle of a pile of magazines I was clearing away. I was certain I'd thrown it out, but I just threw it out again, no big deal, must have been mistaken. Then the next day I was pulling a box down from the top cupboard shelf and the thing flutters down to the floor. That one freaked me out a little, but I thought hey, maybe I didn't bin it after all and Claire put it there."

Guy knows Claire is the former Mrs Nowak.

"But you know when you've noticed something a few times and it finally registers?" Nowak says. "So this time I made *sure* I screwed that thing up tight and put it in the bin. The *outside* bin. Again, no big deal, but I made a point of it. It was early and the bin men came about half an hour later and collected our rubbish."

He holds his hands out in front of him, looking at the space in between them.

"Then I open up my drawer at work the next day *and the fucking thing is in there,* unfolded but still with the creases where I screwed it up. I know it's the same one because it had the same little snaggle-toothed piece missing from the corner. I freak out a bit and call Claire to see if she's winding me up and she hasn't got a clue. And I manage to accept that somehow it... just... happened. Do you know what I mean?"

"Actually... yeah I do."

"So, a few weeks later some friends come round for a barbecue on a weeknight, early, like five-thirty, straight from work. Getting the last of the sun, you know? And we end up getting drunk and the conversation turns to our parents and the booze has made us all a bit emotional. None of our parents are still with us. Sometimes you talk about these things and it hits you."

Guy nods even though he wasn't close to either of his parents, now deceased. Nancy would constantly tell him it affected him more than he realised, but Nancy is Nancy.

"And Claire brings up this séance woman and I remember that the flyer— I'd seen it enough times—made a big deal about being open late, *Open Until 10pm,* huge text. It's only about eight thirty at this point. I go and get the flyer because of course now I've kept the fucking thing and I call the number. She sounds as ordinary as her name, and about my age. I ask if she can see us now and yes, she can, and I find myself asking who designed and posted her flyers. She'd paid some local kids to do it. She's *normal,* apart from her job. We call a cab and we bundle round, five of us. Me, Claire, this couple we know and another friend. Normal people, old friends, as normal as the house we end up at."

"So we go in and she's all smiles in a big baggy jumper and glasses, earth mother type. We go in her living room and I could tell she's really *tried* to do it up for the right vibe but it feels cheap. We've sobered up a little and we're all thinking *this is a bit stupid* but it's a laugh, a story to tell, the night we got drunk and went to a séance over in bloody Wyken. Right?"

"Right."

He nods, pauses for a moment.

"The board kept spelling out my name."

He chews his lip.

"I was shitting myself a little because I hadn't *told* her my name. That had been deliberate, we'd all said on the way over that we wouldn't say them, but hey, Peter isn't an uncommon name, right? Could be a Barnum statement, that kind of thing."

Finally, something Guy *does* understand. A Barnum statement: a general sentence that's vague enough to be said to nearly anyone, yet carefully worded so that any person hearing it would still think the sentence was specific to them. *You can be emotional sometimes.* The term doesn't quite apply here but Guy understands what Nowak means. *I'm getting 'Peter...?'* There could be no Peter in the room but there would be a very good chance someone would say something like *my dead Grandad is called Peter* and then you're off to the races.

"So I 'fess up and she starts addressing me, asking if I have any questions. I can't bring myself to address my parents or anything—I don't know why, I think I was embarrassed—and so I ask a general question instead. *Is there life after death?* It's kind of a joke question really. Then the pointer starts going around the board, going for ages. It's spelling out a question of its own." He holds up a hand, seeing the words. "*Do... you... want... to... understand... the... world?*"

The hairs are up on Guy's neck.

"I say yeah, sure. Then it asks another question: *are you giving confirmation?*" Nowak shakes his head sadly. "Giving confirmation... bastards. Fucking bastards."

That's all it took? He was inside the circle with *that?*

"And you did?" Guy asks.

"Yes."

"What did it tell you?"

Nowak leans forward, his face deadly serious, the pixelated image filling the camera.

"Absolutely... *nothing,*" he says, and then bursts into hysterical laughter that goes on for a full thirty seconds. Guy forces a smile, but that was unsettling. Sure, it was a joke, but a: it wasn't that funny, and b: this sudden burst of mischief comes out of nowhere. Is Nowak playing with a full deck? He's been living this life a long time. "Sorry, sorry, couldn't help it," Nowak says, wiping his eyes, coughing. "Sorry." *Ping,* back to quiet. "No, nothing. After I gave confirmation, Joanne couldn't get *anything.* We left an awkward, slow twenty minutes later and walked to the nearest pub. The mood was spoiled by then. We lasted another half an hour and we took separate cabs home. Or rather we would have done if the cab Claire and I took hadn't broken down. We ordered another one. That broke down. That's how it started."

"But why did you end up on their radar in the first place, Peter?" Guy asks. "What do they gain from... I mean, if this is a curse then what's the point?"

Nowak falls silent for several moments.

"I thought about this a lot, as you can imagine," he finally says. "And I keep coming back to the same thing, the only thing that makes sense. *Suffering.* It has a particularly unique energy. It never stops. And I think they feed on it."

Suddenly, Peter is brandishing a sawn-off shotgun on camera.

Guy recoils in his chair. Sam stands up quickly, rushing round to see.

"And I'm *very* done with it," Nowak says, his voice calm.

"Peter... what's that for..."

"As bad as things are for me—and they're bad—they were even worse for those around me," he says, staring into the camera now, not at his screen. "I think that's part of it too, picking someone with a conscience. That makes it worse. Plus it means I'm more likely to be compliant, to stay quiet, avoid more pain to those around me. Clever little bastards."

"Peter, *listen to me—*"

"It's like..." Nowak sighs, tries to think. "It's never things that would majorly torture *me* or kill *me.* It's never *constant* either; as ridiculously coincidental as things are, they're always far apart enough that people can just say *wow, that man is crazily unlucky.* Even Claire didn't believe me for a while. Then her mother slipped on a patch of ice outside our house and broke her neck. *In summer.* You can imagine the rest. Loved ones. Friends. You won't know about those. And even strangers..."

Guy is frozen. Should he let Nowak talk? Is he about to watch a man kill himself?

"Listen to me, Peter," Sam says, his voice calm but firm. A professional. "I'm Sam—"

"Depending on your definition," Nowak says, completely ignoring him, "there have been between three and ten mass murders, terrorist attacks... instances of public death in this country during the last decade. I've been within a square mile of all of them, each time."

"Peter," Sam continues, still trying, leaning closer, "let's keep talking, but—"

"So much so that MI5 have me on a watchlist even though I'm not a suspect. You didn't know *that*."

Guy is sweating. He tries to help Sam.

"I want to hear all this Peter, but please put the gun—"

"Why do you think I still live here?" Nowak cries, gesturing to the room around him. "I can't *afford* to buy somewhere away from people. Not anymore. This is the best I can do. At least the houses either side of me are derelict now. There's no one immediately around. *I can't do any harm.* But I've had enough anyway. I'm so tired."

He's turning the gun in his hands, angling the tip of the barrel towards his face. How the hell did he get a shotgun in England—

"*Peter!*" This time it's Guy and Sam together.

"I don't think they'll know about this conversation though, Guy," Nowak says. "I don't think they know much about computers—technology in general—even though they've been doing this a loooong time. Since before the Internet. Before computers. Before we'd even learned how to talk and the only light we had to keep them at bay was daylight and fire."

His words echo Larry's—*I don't think it understands technology*—and something cold runs across Guy's skin. Horribly, it's strongest in the ever-growing scales on his neck. Nowak's eyes are far away. The barrel, however, is directly in front of his face.

"*Please* Peter, please—"

"This," Nowak says, patting the gun, "Is overdue. I read your email and it made me realise... I'm done."

"*Peter, for fuck's sake—*"

Sam puts a hand on his shoulder but Guy keeps screaming because suddenly he's not just trying to save Nowak's life but his own, for he can see how he would go exactly the same way, not wanting to live as whatever the hell he's becoming. Even Rufus is standing, giving off little choked, raspy barks, alarmed at the sudden chaos.

"Thank you for listening, Guy." Peter wraps his mouth around the end of the shortened shotgun's barrel.

"*NO!*"

He pulls the trigger.

Click.

The hammers come down on empty chambers and Peter drops the shotgun, laughing uproariously and as relief turns into rage Guy realises that Peter has gone insane some time ago.

"*Jesus! Jesus!*" Guy is up out of his seat and there's Sam's hand again, firmly pressing on Guy's shoulder. His eyes are intensely on Guy's, telling him not to lose his shit.

"Oh, oh, oh *shit*," Nowak says onscreen, wiping his eyes. He looks at Guy for a moment, at Sam. "Didn't you... it was a joke, like a prank..." He suddenly looks embarrassed, that rapid shift again. He looks at the gun like he's forgotten what it is. "... sorry, I don't get many... I didn't think it mattered if I was alright in the end..." He looks like a scolded little boy.

"That's alright, Peter," Sam says. "We get it—shut *up*, Rufus—we get it."

"Sorry," Nowak says. "Thought you'd be okay afterwards once you saw—"

"Yeah..." Guy breathes, forcing himself down. *Don't judge him,* he thinks. *You're next.*

Rufus goes back to his basket and gives off a wheezing, annoyed sigh.

"I was actually trying to prove a *point,*" Nowak says. "There's a reason for it. Here." He cocks the shotgun and shows the chambers. They're full, the cartridges still sitting unfired and unmarked.

"How is that possible?" Guy gasps. "The hammers came down, I saw it, I heard—"

"*I can't kill myself,*" Nowak says, eyes swimming, energy ramping straight back up again. "Whatever they managed to put on me extends to everything I try and use. The only one I haven't tried yet is jumping off something really high, but I worry that I'd survive and be broken. Then I'd have to live an even worse life."

"But the only thing they gain from all this is your suffering...?"

"That has to at least be half the reason. In my case at least, there's another half. A practical one."

Guys nerves are shot. Nowak might be crazy but Guy knows what's being said is the truth. Once you're *on the inside,* it seems, you know these things. Sam moves his chair round next to Guys, in front of the screen.

"I was after some land in Northampton," Nowak says. "Done deal. Wanted to build houses on it. You know my history with property, I'm sure, and this was after *this business* had started, but before I lost the houses. Anyway, it was all set and then guess what, the seller dies. After a delay his son takes over the deal and then gets into a thoroughly unlikely legal dispute himself, freezing his assets indefinitely. I'm sure you can see where this is going."

"A series of unfortunate events prevent the deal going forward..."

"Yes. And what happens in the meantime with that land?"

Guy has it.

"A shantytown springs up."

Nowak points at the camera—*bingo*—and then shrugs.

"Kind of. They weren't travellers and I don't know if you'd call it a shantytown either, but a bunch of tents and boxes sprung up... yeah, you could call it a shantytown. Not a term we use a lot here. By the time the deal would have even stood a chance of happening, it was the last of my concerns, for obvious reasons."

"What was the point though? What benefit would they get from the shantytown?"

"Who knows?" Nowak asks. "There must be one." Guy thinks about trinkets but doesn't say anything. Nowak didn't get one; he just signed up unwittingly by agreeing to something in a séance. It's becoming a minefield, one Guy will have to somehow navigate if he wants to stand a chance. "A breeding ground for more stuff like this? I don't know and we probably never *will* know. All that matters is that they wanted it there." Nowak scratches at his cheek. "I visited it, you know."

"You did?" Guy asks. "What did you see?"

"Apart from tents and a load of miserable people?" Nowak says. "Hippy stuff. Lots of like..." He waves a hand around. "I'd say they were all on drugs but that wouldn't be true. They were talking clearly, but they were just... *slowed down*. Old women chanting a bit. Saw one fella like—" Nowak breaks off and rolls his eyes back. Guy has read about this. "Dressed normally, if a bit dirty. It was weird, weird. And they were *making* things, these... I don't know. Sculptures. But when I got close they got angry so I left. I didn't expect to find much by going there." He sighs. "Curses... I think they're difficult to land, or the circumstances have to be right, *just the right person*—based on whatever rules they have—and getting them on the *inside* of the rules. They can't just say *poof, you're cursed.* Hence all that business with the flyer and the séance and me saying *I confirm*."

"Peter," Guy says quietly. "You said people in my position talked to you. What did you mean, *my position?* I didn't agree to anything. How could I be on the inside? I mean I have this on my neck but the thing *touched* me... I mean it was..." He begins to say *accident,* or *an attack,* but it doesn't feel right.

"Take it from me," Nowak says. "It takes one to know one, right? I've spoken with enough people that have... entered this *world* if you will, to varying degrees. You get to recognise it. There's an aura, a feeling those people give off. You're *in* now. It's not heavy on you, but it's there. I knew it the second you appeared on my screen. You could have covered your neck and I'd still know. How else would I know you're safe to talk to?" He points at Sam. "Him too."

Guy is startled.

"What?"

"Yeah. Can feel it," Nowak says. Guy looks at Sam's poker face and again wonders why the hell Sam's helping. "Maybe it's because he's helping you? Either way, he's in."

It isn't the time talk to Sam about this.

"My neck is getting worse, Peter," Guy says. "What do you think will happen when it...?"

Nowak lowers his eyes.

"I don't like to say, Guy. This one time..." He pauses.

"What? What time?"

"I don't like to *say,* it might be very different—"

"Tell me!"

"A woman got in touch once, before she disappeared. Claimed to have had something similar happen to you. Close encounter. We talked on the phone, and then Skyped like this. Hers had been going on a while longer. She could even take her top off to show me the progression. There wasn't anything, you know, revealing about it. Her torso was... it had changed. Hers had started at her hip, she said. She'd had four or five scratches or whatever, like yours."

"She was growing white scales? Like mine?"

"Not the same, but it was a transformation. It had come upon her very quickly. She said her *thoughts* were starting to change. She didn't see people as people anymore. She'd find herself waking up in her neighbours' gardens in the night, or with her face pressed against their windows. Said she was becoming something. She'd stopped leaving the house once the change reached her hands and neck, even though it couldn't be seen with the naked eye. We spoke on Skype twice. The first time, she said she was going to kill herself. Not having any luck issues, that was an option for her. The second time, her voice kept changing."

"What did she say... the second time?"

Nowak sighs heavily.

"Her mind was different. She was nearly fully changed physically and she... she said she was starting to want to know what it would be like to... well. Complete. She looked happy about it."

Her thoughts were starting to change.

"She waited too long," Nowak finished. "I think there's two kinds of curses, Guy. Ones that create suffering... and ones that swell their ranks. I think those are a little harder to set up; I don't think they're allowed to just go and claw people and start their change. I think you were played."

Could this be true? Two birds with one stone; silence Larry and his article, silence Guy's by... he can't finish the thought. Did he walk right into something—

But he sent the monster away. And he only has one cut—maybe he stopped things early enough, interrupted the process?

"I never heard from her after that," Nowak says. "When I called her number, it didn't exist anymore. *She waited too long.*"

He stares at Guy for a while until his point is understood.

"*No—*" Guy gasps, outraged.

"There's a greater good here, Guy. You have serious thinking to do about how to handle your situation—"

"Get fucked!"

"I'm only being—"

A tiny spark leaps across Nowak's face. He looks down slightly.

"Goddamn it," he says.

"What? What?"

"I think our conversation is about to end," he says, sounding defeated. Another tiny spark fizzes across his face. "Maybe this isn't them directly but as you can probably guess, I don't have a lot of luck with tech—"

The call ends suddenly.

"I suppose his Internet provider got really strict on bandwidth..." Sam says quietly, breaking the silence. Guy glares at him. "Sorry," Sam says. "Gallows humour. Part of the old job. Hard habit to break."

"He implied I need to—"

"He did," Sam interrupts. "Let's not start thinking about that until we know everything, okay? Take a minute to calm down, too, that was stressful for you."

"Stress has become rather common at the moment, Sam."

"I believe you," Sam says. "Your neck... I couldn't see the way it really looked until..."

"I know."

Silence again.

Then Sam slaps his thighs in that very British *right then* manner. "Do you want to put your stuff in the spare room?" he asks. It strikes Guy how, a week ago, this would have been weird indeed: staying in the house of a dying stranger. Guy suddenly wonders where else he would actually go. Who else does he know these days that would have him?

"Uh... yeah. Sam... is there something you're not telling me?" Sam becomes, of course, instantly unreadable. "Nowak said that *you're* on the inside. Could be because you're helping me, but that doesn't sound right. Look..." There isn't room to be polite, even in Sam's home. "Can I trust you? You said you wanted to give them a bloody nose for *what they did,* which, by the way, you still haven't told me. You've asked me to move in so we can work together on this, but I have no idea what your stake *is* in this. You weren't close to your brother, so it can't be that. They've infiltrated the police by the looks of it, which means they have people working for them, so cards on the table: how do I know that you're not one of them?"

"It's a fair question," Sam says, folding his arms. "I'd ask it myself. And really, there's no way you *can* know; you're going to have to trust me. Although... hmm. Sounds like those things treat matters like *giving your word* and *agreements* and *rules* as sacred. Right? They're bound by it."

"Seems that way."

"Then I can give you this," Sam says, holding both his hands in the air, palms out. "I swear to you, on my late wife's soul, that I am not working for them, or with them, or have any plans to harm you or anyone you love, directly or indirectly. Don't think I'd be allowed or able to say that if I was batting for the other team." He drops his hands back to his sides. "That's the best I can do, I'm afraid."

"Was it your wife?" Guy suddenly blurts out.

"What?"

"Did they... you said your wife died. Leslie. Did they..."

"No, no. I'm afraid that was nothing more supernatural than a twenty-a-day habit and a stubborn attitude." He smiles sadly. "Might have been a little different if Melissa had still been around—uh, our daughter, Melissa, long story, we don't speak—anyway. I couldn't talk Leslie out of it on my own."

"Sorry. I shouldn't have asked," Guy says, rubbing his forehead. "I feel so…"

"It's alright. If you want me to tell you what they did to me, I will," Sam says. "I want you to feel better. And yes, no matter how our relationship may have been at the end, Elias was *my* brother. They got to him. He was family."

Something grinds faintly inside Guy again, and of course, it's Ray.

"I understand," he says.

"Then you're doing better than me," Sam says, moving to the table to pick up his mug. "I've actually got something to show you. Go put your bag in your room—top of the stairs, on the left—and I'll tell you all about it, including what I saw."

Guy is halfway out of the door but stops sharply.

"What you saw?" he asks Sam "You mean in the past?"

"Well, yes," Sam says. "But also last night."

Guy almost runs up the stairs, managing to smash his big toe in his haste.

***

Chapter Twelve
More Learning, and Plans are Made
✳✳✳

"I told you I have terminal cancer, right?" Sam says, taking a small box down from a bookcase with no books on it. Along with a few certificates and small awards—presumably for service in his former job—the shelves are instead filled with picture frames of varying sizes. Each contains an image of Sam and the same small, curly haired woman, taken in various locations around the globe, smiling from ear to ear. There's only one picture of somebody else: a black-haired teenage girl, skinny, frowning at the camera. Surely Melissa, the daughter, the centerpiece of the incredible story Sam has just finished telling Guy. The one set in a Coventry café back in the noughts. Guy is stunned, of course, but Sam is already moving on to the next tale.

"You did tell me, Sam," Guy's left leg can't stop jiggling.

"Thing is, I didn't tell you what kind," Sam says, opening the box and removing a cigar the size of a roll of carpet. Guy's eyebrows raise.

"I thought you said that you tried to get Leslie to quit smoking?"

"Oh, I did, I did," Sam says, sincere. "A filthy habit. I only allow myself one of these a year, at Christmas." He produces a silver cigar cutter and expertly snips the cigar's tip. "I think that now, however, I'm rather going to fill my boots, to use the common parlance. Would you...?"

"No, but thanks."

Sam nods, places the cigar to his lips, and strikes a match. He heats the cigar's tip expertly high above the naked flame until it blackens, then draws and exhales smoke with a deeply contented sigh, eyes closed.

"Goodness *me*," he says, savouring the new flavour of the words in his mouth. "That *is* the stuff. The cancer I have, ironically to this moment, is lung cancer. I believe regular—*regular*—cigar smokers tend to get mouth cancer."

"Lung cancer? But you didn't smoke cigarettes—"

"No," he says, speaking around the cigar as he draws again, the words muffled. "*Hfunny 'at, in'nit?*"

"Wait, you think it's a *curse?* Sam, I know there's some weird stuff going on, but—"

"Uh-huh," Sam says, smiling that sad smile again. "Weird as a lifelong non-smoker—well, a once-a-year *cigar* smoker—who never went to social clubs or rarely even *pubs* back in the less-enlightened days before the smoking ban, more strange than him getting lung cancer?" He catches Guy's expression. "Well, actually, *yes,* I suppose the existence of monsters is rather more unusual than that, but even so..."

"But how would you have even been cursed?" Guy asks. "Yes, you're involved with me, but you didn't find out about the cancer situation *today,* right? You said you got the result recently, but that means you looked into this a while ago, at least a few weeks—" The penny falls further. "...you read Larry's unfinished article. The one I sent you." Sam nods. "You read about the trinkets..." The penny bounces. "Wait, *they sent you one?*"

"Worse than that," Sam says, pulling on the cigar and staring at the table. "My brother sent it to me. It actually came via the post; I recognized his handwriting on the packaging. I'd know it anywhere."

"Jesus..."

"He was an addict, a real mess," Sam continues, his voice faraway. "And painfully jealous of me. We'd have moments where I'd think we'd got past all that nonsense, and then it would all start up again, all the jibes and *excuses* and..." He sighs, waving his free hand. "Doesn't matter. My point: I hope he somehow didn't know what he was doing when he sent that thing to me, or maybe they had leverage on him... I hope to God that he didn't do it because he hated me. But the note he included tells me otherwise. He killed himself not too long after, so..." He shrugs, the cigar smoke kinking in the air with the gesture. "*Ahhhh*... yeah, he definitely knew what he was doing." Sam's eyes drop again.

"What did the note say?"

"*I'm sorry,*" Sam says. The cigar suddenly jabs in Guy's direction, Sam back to all-business mode. An ability learned in his old career, changing state on a dime whenever necessary. "Regardless, they used him. I come from a big family, Guy, and even though only my parents came over here from the old country, we'd still make sure to see the others once or twice a year. They'd come here or we'd fly to the continent. Family... that, for me, is a line that you never cross." That sad shrug again. "They're all dead now, though, kids scattered everywhere. I don't have any connection with the youngsters. Just me left now. And Melissa, of course, but *I* might as well be dead, in her eyes." Guy suddenly, horribly realises that he's the same. It was Nancy who picked him up from the station. His *ex-wife*. Again: where else could he go? Where have all the others gone? And why is he making this about himself while a lonely widower is talking about all his family being dead—

"So I did mean it," Sam continues, "about giving them a bloody nose. I really did. They made the last contact my brother ever had with me into be an act of... well..." His fingers make air quotes, cigar suspended between two of them. "*Evil.*"

"But how do you connect it to your cancer, Sam?"

"Actually..." Sam cocks his head as an idea strikes him. "Do you want to see it?"

"You still *have* it?"

"Uh-huh."

"Why?"

He shrugs.

"I didn't know what it was until I read your friend's unfinished article. After that I wondered if it might be useful to your situation somehow."

"Okay, but *what makes you think*—"

"*Do you want to see it?*"

"Yes." Guy is surprised at his answer. "I don't want to get close to it though."

"Me neither. I'll wear gloves. It's in the shed. Back in a second."

Sam stands with an old-man grunt, still holding the cigar, and heads towards the back door.

"Do you need a hand—"

"No," Sam says. "It isn't heavy."

He leaves. Guy checks his phone. There's a text from Nancy.

YOU OKAY?

YEAH, Guy writes back. I'M OKAY. I'M AT SAM'S.

I DON'T LIKE THIS. I DON'T LIKE YOU DOING IT ALONE. I DON'T KNOW HOW YOU TALKED ME INTO LETTING YOU DO THAT.

I'M NOT, Guy texts back. I TOLD YOU, I'M WITH SAM.

CHECK IN WITH ME IN TWO HOURS' TIME, she writes. LET ME KNOW YOU'RE OKAY.

For a moment it's there again, the anger, she's *nagging*, and then Guy realises she's just worried and *what the fuck is wrong with him?*

But he knows the answer. It's the same thing that happened to the woman Nowak knew. He grips his phone so hard it creaks, but simply writes:

YOU GOT IT.

He makes an addition, trying to believe it:

I'M GOING TO WIN, NANCY.

I HOPE SO, she writes.

Sam returns, cigar in his mouth, trailing smoke with his gloved hands carrying an object covered in a plastic garden refuse sack. He walks slowly, holding the sack as if it were an unexploded bomb.

"Can you move your laptop?" he says. Guy quickly does so. The bag makes a metallic *clunk* sound as it touches down. Sam pulls the plastic down around the object inside, unveiling it as if he were removing someone's dress from their shoulders.

The construction is about the size of a large toaster, and of a vaguely similar shape. It *is* metallic, but of a cheap material; tin, perhaps? Thin, light, and whoever bent it into shape clearly wasn't a craftsman. The dull-silver-coloured metal looks like it was kicked down a flight of stairs after construction, dented and scratched to hell; the impression of each surface is almost one of lightly crumpled tinfoil. It was clearly intended to be roughly cuboid, but each side is completely uneven in length and width; the overall cube shape sacrificed to ensure that the metal sides actually meet. It's crudely soldered together, with drawings on each side that Guy can see, rendered in... correction fluid? The thick texture and thin brush strokes make Guy think it's not white paint. The pictures on the two visible sides—and one on the top—are even more haphazard than the object's construction, as if a child painted them. Each messy image has a painted-on border made up of what might be lettering—Guy doesn't recognise it, looking like a cross between the Korean alphabet and old Nordic runes—that runs in an uneven streak around each picture. One is a human face. The other a stick figure of a man. The one on top is harder to make out, a Rorschach test-esque mirrored image, both halves joined in the centre by a thin line.

The thing makes Guy feel creeped out to hell. Just looking at it makes him squint, and his head has begun to ache. It's as if those markings are resonating with something way, way down inside his brain, something dimly remembered and instinctive. He's much closer to it than he was to the one in Larry's house, and the feeling is stronger as a result. It's *disgusting.*

Did Elias only send *this,* Guy wonders, *or did he* make *it?*

"Can you turn it?" Guy asks. Sam obliges with his gloved hands; Guy sees a strange shape that looks almost like a logo, and what appears to be, at first glance, a very basic picture of an animal. A picture of a horse, perhaps, drawn by a simpleton.

Then Guy notices the six legs. The pointed ears that look less like ears and more like horns.

"It's… can you cover it up again, please?" Guy asks, pinching the bridge of his nose. He can't stomach any more. The plastic rustles as Sam covers the metal trinket.

"I'll put it back in the shed," he says quietly, the words mangled around the cigar in his mouth. He carries the thing out of the room.

Sam accepted it. Is that all it takes?

"So how did you connect that to your cancer, Sam?" Guy asks once Sam has returned. "You sound pretty certain. Okay, it sounds like an unlikely diagnosis, and that thing definitely came out of the shanty towns—"

"You can feel it, can't you?" Sam says, interrupting. "When you look at it. I had such a visceral reaction to it when I first saw it I thought I was going crazy. I put it down to the emotion of receiving a handmade gift from my brother, even if it was weird. It just meant…" He trails off. "Never mind. Carry on."

"You said something happened last night, you saw something."

"Yes. Very much so, very much so."

Sam's face is deadly serious.

"Go on."

"I don't want you to worry any more than you already are, okay?"

Guy is instantly more worried.

"Why do you say that?"

"It happened outside this house. The night I was trying to call you back. It's perhaps good I couldn't get hold of you because I wasn't at *my* best, to say the least."

"Sam. What the fuck happened?"

"I'd gone to the supermarket to get some Nytol," Sam says. "I was very wired after reading your friend's article and needed to sleep. It was dark and I wasn't really thinking about anything *but* the article and the thing my brother sent me."

"Of course."

"So when I first caught a glimpse, I thought I was imagining it. Like I say: it was *dark*, and my eyes were also caught by the object on my doorstep, but I thought I'd seen movement in my peripheral—"

"Wait, object? Another—"

"Yes," says Sam impatiently, his cigar hand waving away the interruption. "They'd sent another one, maybe an insurance policy. That one's in the bin out front, I smashed it up later once I'd calmed down. I wasn't going to have two on the property."

"What did it look like?"

"It was mainly made of meat, but that really isn't the important part of the story. Can I possibly...?"

"Sorry, sorry. Sorry, Sam," Guy repeats.

Those things came back, they were here just last night—

Sam continues his story.

***

There's something hiding in the dark, away to Sam's left, just outside of the cone of light from his front porch. In the shrubs by the path.

Could he have imag—

No. There it was again, about five feet away. That... glimmer, reminding him of a dog's eye catching the light, the tapetum lucidum *behind the canine lens, but this was more silvery. There! Two of those little glittery points in the dark by his shrubs.*

Sam is looking at a pair of eyes.

He backs up a step, leaving his breath hanging in the cold night air. Even in his thick coat and hat, Sam suddenly feels cold as the rest of the shape comes into view around those glittering points of darkness; it's like a Magic Eye picture becoming clear. It's a little human-like figure, watching him from the darkness at the side of his front path.

Sam freezes.

It's a squat little figure maybe only a foot high. It's hunched and rounded; he can't make out its face though, or any other details because it's so damn hard to see, even though it's standing very still. Does it know Sam can see it? Maybe he wouldn't be able to if he hadn't accepted the first trinket?

Sam takes a step towards it, blood pulsing. It still doesn't move. He nearly manages to tell himself he's imagining it but then those eyes glitter again in the dark and he knows it's there. He takes another step forward. Is it going to dart forward and attack him, perhaps latching onto his leg and then running up onto his face—

Talk to it, *he thinks.*

"I..." He coughs. "I can see you."

It doesn't move.

Light.

Very slowly, very carefully, Sam pulls his phone out of his pocket. Only later will he agonize over his mistake: he never thought to take a photo. Sam turns his phone light on, shining it on the creature—

It scuttles a little further back into the shrubs, causing Sam to jump. It moved before the light even hit it and is in the shadows cast by Sam's phone. The thing is almost like a shadow itself, like seeing something out of the corner of your eye, except this was in the centre of his vision.

It's still once more. Sam listens to his frantic breathing as they watch each other. It keeps blinking in and out of Sam's sight, but he can see it's there.

Two minutes pass.

What is he going to do? Are these things going to keep coming? First the trinket—

Elias.

The thing is part of that which—

The shopping bag. He'd bought things other than Nytol, household items. And Sam gets this idea, a crazy one, and he can't believe what he's doing but he's crouching down to his bag.

"I can see you," Sam says again, swallowing. His hands are feeling blindly and frantically around in the bag, his eyes on the thing under the bush, and the blood pumping in his ears is so loud he wonders if he might have a heart attack on his driveway—

The thing starts to walk forward. Little shuffling steps, as if it were a bag of flesh being operated by worms from the inside. It doesn't step clear out of the shadows but moves forward enough that Sam can make out its shape a little better, when he can focus on it that is. He can't believe what he's seeing.

If it has clothes, Sam can't make them out. It's a gnome-like thing from someone's nightmares. A barrel with arms and legs, it shoulders practically meeting in the middle behind its head. Its glittery eyes are shiny buttons in the dark.

It starts hitching.

Wait. Is it miming laughter? It is. It's holding its belly.

Then the creature balls up a fist, clear for a moment, and puts it to its mouth, jerking its head forward—

It's miming coughing. Then the laughing again.

Sam knows what its making fun of. And it knows that because—

Yes. How else could he have a lung cancer diagnosis?

Sam's anger becomes rage with perfect timing as his hands finally find the two things he's been looking for: the can of deodorant and one of the three disposable lighters he'd bought on a whim off the shop counter. They're only a pound, *he'd thought.* Might come in useful. He hadn't expected *this use.*

He grabs them and yanks them out of the bag in a single motion, managing to pop the deodorant's twist lock with one hand while frantically flicking the lighter's wheel with the other. He doesn't want to give the little shit a chance to—

The flame ignites the spray with a tinny, breathy roar and becomes mini-napalm. Sam lunges forward with his impromptu blowtorch and thrusts the burning jet towards his interloper.

"I see you!" he yells, and the creature cries out (did he manage to touch it? Burn it? Only scare it? Sam will never know) as it vanishes. Later, Sam will think of how surprisingly low the sound was, akin to the woof of a medium-sized dog.

Sam drops the can and the lighter immediately, his hands shaking so violently that he has to clasp them together before putting them to his face, his wet breathing coating his fingers.

***

As soon as Sam had begun to describe the creature he'd seen, Guy's memory had been triggered. To his credit he'd bitten his lip and waited for Sam to finish, managing to pay attention even as his mind yammered away about the frightening connection it had just made.

The fleeting glimpse he'd had in the coffee shop the other day, as he was leaving after meeting Sam for the first time. The thing he thought he saw on the woman's shoulders, the little black figure with the glittery eyes.

Sam has finished his story. Should Guy tell him what he'd seen? He doesn't want to worry—

Wait, of *course* he fucking should.

"Tell me," Guy says. "Was it about *yae* big?" he asks, holding his hands about a foot or so apart. "A little thing like..." He ducks his head down and raises his shoulders as high as they'll go.

"Yes!" Sam cries. "Exactly that!"

"I've seen one too."

"When?"

"Just a glimpse, I thought I'd imagined—it was in the coffee shop the other day, after you left. Saw one sitting on a woman's neck. The eyes glittered, like you said. I thought it was a shadow, I mean I was exhausted—"

"Good lord."

"Yeah." Guy thinks a moment. "Fuck me, Sam You realise that you attacking is probably classed as an *interference*, right? That maybe it wanted you to attack it? To put you on the map? Cursing you with cancer is one thing, but a direct attack...?"

Sam sighs, shrugs.

"Well... *hell*," he says, slumping a little in his chair. "We're damned if we do something, we're damned if we don't."

"So it had a physical presence, right? Because if it was scared of fire, that means it could be burnt."

"Not necessarily," Sam says. "If they don't like the light, fire could be an *instinctive* fear. Same way humans are still motivated by instincts left over from our caveman days."

Guy realises two things: they're psychoanalysing monsters, and he really needs a drink.

"Sam, I hate to ask, but do you have any strong booze?"

For a moment—just the briefest flash—Sam's eyes dart up and away, behind Guy's head. Guy knows there's a clock on the wall there, and he opens his mouth to explain—*this is some heavy stuff, I know it's not even five o'clock yet but*—but Sam's already nodding.

"Of course, of course, of course," he says, crossing to a small cabinet on the other side of the room. "Scotch?"

"Perfect."

He pours a generous measure and hands it over.

"Thanks." Guy is nearly self-conscious about drinking it now, but a sip turns into a full swig that turns into him putting the whole thing away in one go; he needed it. He gasps as it disappears, eyes watering. "Jesus, that hit the spot."

"Quite," Sam says.

"Sam..." Guy pauses. "I'm really sorry this has happened to you."

Sam waves him away, cigar smoke swirling.

"Don't think about it like that. I'm ready to go." He shrugs sadly. "I'm tired, my hips ache, and this world is leaving me behind." He points at Rufus, fast asleep now in his basket and snoring quietly. "Sad to say, but that little shit is the main thing keeping me here, and he's not long for this world either. I get him checked out and the vet says it's up to me... he doesn't seem to have any major pain, although I think he hides it. I even have to put CBD ointment on his joints or he gets ever so stiff." He smiles with great affection. "But he'll surprise you with his tank. If you tell him, he'll run for a minute, although then he's out of it for the day. He's sixteen, you know."

"Jesus," Guy says.

"Two old dogs together," Sam says. "Past it. I'm not very good with technology, like our man Nowak said about our adversaries, and in today's world that means I'm right in the shadows too, albeit different ones. I'm sure you noticed my website isn't exactly cutting edge. The PI thing is really just something to keep me busy, and it doesn't. Besides, without Leslie..." He smiles gently, shrugging. "I told you before, though." He wags a finger, sincere. "I want to give these bastards a bloody nose. They need to pay for this. And I meant what I said about a last hurrah. Even if I'm actually scared, pardon my French, *shitless*. Yes, my previous incident was a lot more dangerous, but once in a lifetime was already bad enough. And you know what really gets me? Since I finally started looking into this and asking questions about your friend..." He waves the cigar in the air in a little circle. "*Poof.* Just like that, all the contacts I have about *that kind of thing* have clammed up, watertight. No replies. That unnerves me no end. I know some of these people well. These are not easily unsettled individuals. These are professionals. I thought I knew something about all this but it turns out I had no idea. Its worse than I thought." The words are heavy with weariness and self-recrimination.

"Did you notice something?" Guy asks. "About the video call with Nowak?"

"You mean your neck changing after I'd seen it onscreen?" Sam says. "I *was* going to mention that to you..."

"No, but I'll come to that in a second," Guy replies. "*He* didn't mention a trinket, did he?

"He did not. But he *did* agree to something at the séance."

"But his curse is different than mine, even than yours. I'm sure they're all different but the ones we have are changing us, right? Nowak's is ongoing. Ours are..." Guy trails off, not wanting to say *permanent changes*. His might be unpleasant but Sam's is permanent in the most permanent way possible. "So maybe some curses need trinkets, some need verbal agreement, and some require getting clawed by a massive bastard monster."

"So?"

"Well even Nowak said it; he reckons there are two kinds of curses, right? Ones that cause suffering, changing the world by existing, and ones that swell their ranks. But I think there's more to it than that. Look at y—" He catches himself.

"It's okay," Sam says. "*Safe space,* as I believe the youth say."

"Well I think that even if there are only two kinds," Guy continues, a little red-faced now, "they're not above using them to straight up silence people or influence things. Any suffering side-effects—cancer tends to bring that—is a bonus."

"Probably more to it than that, too," Sam says. "I can buy into the mere presence of successful curses slowly changing the, I don't know, *spiritual ecosystem* or what have you, and having the bonus of effectively running a monstrous protection racket... but there's got to be another element to it."

"Like what?"

"Killing me with cancer wouldn't be the most efficient way to shut me up," Sam says, chewing thoughtfully on his stogie. Guy can see him going away, turning the issue over in his mind, and wonders if this is how Sam looked when on the job, working on a case. "I'm sure they understand poison or knives just fine."

"I don't think they're allowed to just kill without—"

"Mm, mm. Even so, mine would more likely be in the causing-suffering-by-curse camp. But cancer seems... well, a little pedestrian for them, no? I just think there's something else coming." He nods at his own words. "I think... I think this is a setup for another stage in this process."

"Again... like what?"

"No idea," he says thoughtfully. "Yet."

Silence again. Guy feels awkward, and *really* wants more scotch—

"Okay," Sam says finally. "What leads do we have?"

"Leads?"

"Yes. Leads. Where do we start? We're trying to expose these things, right?"

Guy pauses for a moment, thinking briefly of only trying to save his own scaly skin. Then he remembers his last conversation with Nancy. What he'd said about bringing them into the light.

"I don't know if you'd call this a lead," he says slowly, figuring it out as he goes, "but I think I need to start going public with this as soon as possible." Sam whistles softly in response. "I know," Guy tells him, "but we need to draw them out a little. We can't learn about them unless we get them to expose themselves. *We* don't know what *they* know *I* know. I don't think they're omnipotent. Let's stir the sludge and see what rises to the surface."

"Well 'going public' might get their attention, but I don't know how effective that will be. You'll be dismissed as a crackpot."

Guy taps his neck.

"We have this."

"They'll say it's make-up."

"We get a 4K camera—my phone's a piece of shit and I'm guessing yours won't be much better—and we get really close up, press it, make the scales move. It'll be super clear and there'll be makeup experts that know the difference, surely?"

"Worth a try," Sam says, scratching at his chin, "and there's an audio-visual place down the way that we can go for the camera. We can go now if you like. But I think we also have two other starting points, one more likely, the other a bit of a long shot."

"Okay. What's the short shot?"

"We get your friend's article out,' Sam says. "They didn't like him poking around, did they?"

"I thought about that already," Guy tells him. "But the only way that's going to have any impact is if it's published on a notable site, not some blog. And it's not *finished*. I could maybe write up an ending for it—" *Because Larry died.* "Uh... I could do that, but I don't know if there's enough as it is to make it work."

"Do you think he might have had a finished version somewhere?"

Guy prickles at the question. He's annoyed he didn't remember this.

"Yes, he told me he'd finished it," Guy says sharply. "But if he did I'm assuming the police have it. They'd have taken his PC to check the hard drive, right?"

"They'd certainly have taken it but that doesn't always mean they can access the files inside."

"Well Larry didn't use cloud backups either, he was always too much of a conspiracy type, so we can't even try to get his files via that route. So unless you can pull some strings, we're screwed." He hears the tone that's crept into his voice; he and Larry would snap at each other like a couple of New York cab drivers. He has to remember that normal people don't talk to each other like that.

"He was a conspiracy type?"

"Yes."

"So he was extra careful about storing his work, you mean."

"Yes, *obviously*," Guy says, and this time the snap needs an apology. "*Sorry, Jesus—*"

"So where did he back up his files, then?" Sam asks, ignoring it. "You said he didn't use cloud backups, by that you mean..." Sam flitters his fingers above his head. "Data in the ether, right? He didn't use those."

"No, he..." Guy doesn't know. Where *did* Larry back up his files?

"What about an external hard drive for backups then?" Sam asks. Guy raises his eyebrows, surprised. Sam frowns. "I'm not a *complete* luddite, you know," he says.

"Even if he had them," Guy replies, "they would have been seized—" Holy shit. Maybe not. "Sam... you are *good* at this."

"I rather believe so, yes."

"Guy had a little secret stash hole in his house," Guy says, sitting up. "He kept his weed in it, I mean he was *really* paranoid about that being found. I mean who would be rooting around in his house for drugs anyway, right?"

"Well I believe the cannabis itself might have explained the paranoia—"

"So he *had this panel in his house*," Guy continues. "Did you ever see those fake plug sockets? Those ones that pull out to show a hidden storage space in the wall?

"Yes. I've seen them. They're easy to spot if you know what you're looking for."

"Maybe, but Larry went a step further for that reason and made his own. He hollowed out a section of the wall and put an actual socket cover over it. The only way to get it off would be to take out the screws. He even kept a drill in a drawer nearby so he could unscrew it and rescrew it super quickly, he used it all the time. Well, he smoked a lot of weed."

"Do you think that would be somewhere he kept a backup?"

"Not ordinarily, but if he'd started to think he was uncovering something with his article..." Guy realises what Sam is talking about: going into Larry's house. Back into that place. His face flushes. "Uh, but there's a police presence there at the moment so we wouldn't be able to—"

"Actually, I was going to mention this to you anyway," Sam says, eyeballing Guy, "The on-site police presence left this morning. I've been keeping tabs, called in a few favours to keep me abreast of what was going on at the scene. I don't know the situation with your friend's estate, but I *do* know that right now his house is locked up, and empty. I assume you still have a key?"

Empty, he says. Is it?

"I do, but really, is there any point to this?" Guy blusters. "We get the finished article, sure, but then even if its usable, or if it's even *there*, we'd have to get a decent site to run it if we actually want anyone to see it. I'm sorry, but this is stupid, it's fucking stupid. Think of something else." Sam eyeballs him again, and this time Guy's not backing down. "No, I'm sorry but it just is. Waste of fucking time."

"Do you always talk to people like this?"

The question cuts, but of course Guy keeps going. He can't stop.

"Yes, when they want to waste time," he snaps. "Sorry for swearing, but let's be serious—"

"So... you *do* talk to your friends like this."

Now Guy does stop.

"*Jeeeeesus,*" he breathes, sitting back and pulling at his hair. "I did it again... everything's been... me and Larry were always very harsh together. It was our schtick, we knew the other could take it. I'm really sorry. I'll keep it in check. The stress—"

"You're frightened to go back in the house," Sam says quietly, not taking the apology. "I understand. It's very understandable. But someone has to go back in because we have practically zero leads and if there's anything in that finished article that we don't currently know, we *need* to know it. I can go, if you give me the key. There's no reason to think anything unpleasant would still be there. Coppers have been in and around that house for days and no one has told me anything."

"Yeah," Guy says, "but they weren't *on the inside*, were they? You are. I *definitely* am. And what if its different if their *intention* was to find Larry's article? These were cops investigating a murder. That isn't interfering with monster business as they don't *know* they were really looking for monsters, unlike the cops who burst in on the one eating Larry. So if someone went in specifically intending to find Larry's article—"

Guy hears himself. Playing a game where he doesn't know the rules is unbelievably maddening. And terrifying.

"Maybe," Sam says. "We could pay someone to go for us, if you like, or to come accompany me."

Guy feels like a total coward. Was that Sam's intention? Guy is beginning to realise how shrewd an operator he's dealing with.

"No," he says. "I'll go."

"Do you want to go now?"

"We'd be seen."

"The alternative is going in the dark."

"If the neighbours see me going in—especially after the curtain twitchers saw me leaving in an ambulance after a murder—then they're going to call the cops and we might have major problems. Whatever strings were pulled to get me off will surely only have so much influence. It's gonna have to be after dark." He feels sick.

"I don't think it will be allowed to come back, Guy," Sam says gently. "It did its job, right?" Sam tenses, realizing what he just said, but Guy ignores it, thinking about going inside that house again. If that thing turned up, Guy thinks he would go mad on the spot. He remembers his theory about not being invited into the house and how that might have removed all protection.

"Wait," he says. "You said there was a long shot?"

"Ah yes," Sam says. "It doesn't quite fit the shanty town description, but it might be worth checking out, just in case."

"What?"

"I asked around," Sam says. "There's a small community that's recently set up on a field out in Stretton-on-Dunsmore. I have the road name."

"That's a rural area, Sam," Guy says. "Shanty towns are near cities, not in the West Midlands countryside. Homeless people need to be near urban areas. That'll be a traveller community or something."

"Uh-huh," Sam says, nodding. "Exactly. There aren't any caravans or trailers there. It's all tents."

"A campsite then?" Guy asks, but he knows what Sam is getting at.

"Nope. That field is privately owned apparently, but no one has been able to get hold of the owner. Funny that, eh? And didn't our friend Mister Nowak just say something about owning some land that a load of tents turned up on...?"

Guy considers it.

"You're right. It *is* a long shot."

"But still worth checking, surely?"

"Yes. Okay. Let's go get the camera," Guy says. "By the time we've been out to this bloody field, found nothing, gone and picked out a camera, come back, filmed something and got it uploaded... it'll almost certainly be dark." Guy sighs at his own words. Sam stubs out his nearly-finished cigar, pointing at the cupboard under his kitchen sink.

"There's a cordless drill under there," he says. "For unscrewing the socket cover quickly. We'll take our own just in case. It should have plenty of juice but put it on charge for a few hours anyway, we don't want to be faffing around with screwdrivers in the dark in that house." Guy walks to the cupboard, saving Sam's back and knees. The man has been up and down a lot and doesn't look physically comfortable.

"Hey..." Guy says, something occurring to him as he squats down and rummages for the drill. "Larry mentioned the *Other Folk* to me. Ring a bell?" Sam shakes his head.

"No," he says. "We'll look into that. So: we're definitely doing this?" Guy turns his head to look at Sam only to be caught by the older man's gaze; he doesn't know how Sam keeps doing it. "We're in?"

"Yeah," Guy tells him. "We're both on the inside, right? Nothing to lose."

Sam chuckles bitterly.

"Nothing like expendable backup."

"We're both expendable now, Sam," Guy says, forcing a smile as he feels the sickening fear begin to grow in his stomach. They're going back into that house. After dark... a thought occurs to him all the same.

"But maybe that makes us dangerous."

***

Chapter Thirteen
Field Work

***

The approach towards the alleged shanty was, thankfully, down a high hill; from their elevated vantage point, the shanty is easy to spot. The high wall of hedgerows lining either side of the road would have made it hard to know which was the shanty-field otherwise.

"There," Sam says unnecessarily, taking a hand from the wheel to point.

"Uh-huh."

Guy is already beginning to doubt that the endeavour will bear any monstrous fruit; what he sees ahead of him is barely even large enough to be called a camp—let alone a town—but that's what it is. The field is small, and the tents within don't even fill it.

Even so, he thinks. *They're out in the countryside, and they're not travellers. Travellers use caravans, not tents. Nowak said the shanty on his land was tents, too. And this isn't a campsite—*

He cuts that thinking off. One monster and suddenly something as simple as tents take on supernatural meaning. Plus, even at a distance, Guy can see that these tents are all fairly modern. No weird old hessian tent with symbols on it like the one in Larry's article.

Sam pulls over and parks with two wheels on the kerb, turning on the hazard lights. The road—the lane, more accurately—is quiet. They can even hear birds singing in the trees that occasionally pop up along the endless hedgerow, keeping it interesting. The car shouldn't be a problem here, about a seven- or eight-minute walk downhill to the camp. Sam said he believes in being over-cautious; they can't be seen having arrived in it. Their excuse to look around means they have to have appeared on foot.

Sam opens the back door.

"Come on, Roof," he says. A few moments later, Rufus has completed his stretching-to-stand routine and has gingerly exited the car on his aching knees.

As soon as his paws hit the floor, the dog's eyes become alive. His tail wags with a happiness Guy hasn't seen in him before. Looks like Sam was right about Rufus still having something in the tank.

They leave the car and begin to head towards the camp, Rufus wheezing alongside them.

***

"Max!" Sam yells as Rufus streaks towards the cluster of tents. The nearest of them is about sixty feet away from the gate leading from the road into the field.

Rufus hasn't walked anywhere but exactly at Sam's heel as the two men made their way down the hill, but as Sam cracked back the gate's bolt and faintly muttered *guu-won* under his breath, Rufus' ears had perked upright. His head snapped around to look at his master, pausing for a nanosecond to read Sam's body languge. *Are you sure?* The dog had then dashed away.

For a moment Guy is stunned; Rufus is *old* and, in the short time Guy has known the dog, Rufus has constantly looked like he was one sleep away from a peaceful death. All of a sudden instinct is overriding arthritic joints and bagpipe lungs and Rufus has disappeared amongst the tents, ignoring Sam calling a name that isn't his.

"Sorry!" Sam calls to the few people that are standing up from deckchairs or poking their heads out of the entrance flaps to tents. "I shouldn't have taken him off the lead yet!" He and Guy fall into step, heading towards the camp, but already Guy thinks their canine ruse is a waste of time.

This isn't the kind of place they're looking for.

The shanty town described in Larry's article wouldn't have looked out of place in Sierra Leone, a mix of corrugated iron, wooden construction, and street culture; it sounded as if there were, as desperate as the residents' situation was, *things going on there.* Life. Nowak had talked about what looked like a hippy commune, people working away on trinkets and chanting. This just looks like a load of drug addicts hanging out in field.

The tents are all modern, nearly all of them having gas cooking stoves outside. Guy spots a mattress here and there, some with people lying on them, others strewn with things like magazines and mugs. The air is thick with smoke, both cigarette and cannabis. There seems to be little to no conversation though; that's unusual. What else would these people have to do? The faces Guy can see look blank, although some now look at him and Sam. One of them, a man around Guy's age who was standing next to a woman in a black gypsy skirt with a blue Nike T-shirt on top, breaks away from her and begins to stroll over, half-holding up a hand. Guy looks for Rufus but can't see him; he begins to worry but then he hears the laughter of children—it rings out in this place like a song in a morgue—and a corresponding bark. That's good but... there are kids here?

"What do you reckon?" Guy mutters to Sam, who is holding up a hand to the approaching man. They walk towards him.

"Honestly? Camp Crackhead," Sam mutters back. "It's a bit weird that they're out here, but look at the back of the camp." Guy chances a glance; there are three cars parked there. They can get into town, then. How many people are here? Thirty at most? Larry's article estimated nearly two hundred in that shanty. "It can't hurt to double check though."

"You do the talking," Guy mutters back.

"Of course," Sam says.

"There are kids here," Guy mutters. "They can't be living here. We need to report that. Unless they're travellers."

"These aren't travellers."

"Ayup," says the approaching man, drawing on the cigarette in his mouth. His face is thin. He looks very tired. "Everything alright?"

"Just my dog," Sam says. "He'll come back in a second, I just didn't want him to bother anyone."

The man holds out a hand.

"Rich," he says quietly, and even Guy's non-police instincts can see that Rich is mildly suspicious. It isn't surprising.

"I'm Sam," Sam says, shaking Rich's admittedly dirty hand. Guy detects his inner snob rising and offers his hand too. Rich takes it, and if he glances at the dressing on Guy's neck as he does so, Guy can't say for sure. Either way, there is no terror like that in the eyes of the veteran in Miami... but then Rich pauses. Guy tenses up.

There's something here after all.

"You two Old Bill?" he asks, and Guy breathes out.

"Not police, no," Sam chuckles. "Not anymore, anyway. Retired. Full disclosure." His honesty is totally disarming; Rich snorts and then turns back towards the camp for a moment. Three kids run out into the open area of the field, Rufus trying to keep up, but he's already losing steam, hobbling along, tongue out. The mind is strong but at Rufus' advanced age that can only mean so much. Guy looks at some of the other campers; about fifteen or so of them are staring his way now, all of them with that same blank, dull expression.

"Max!" Sam calls again, but Rufus of course doesn't even glance over. Sam fakes another chuckle and turns to Rich. "He'll come back in a second when he's tired. Don't worry, we're not going to poke around, we'll just wait here."

"S'alright, s'alright," Rich says, but waves at a few men and women of varying ages that are now watching. They relax and turn away, going back onto mattresses and deckchairs, into tents. The atmosphere here isn't *weird* as Larry and Nowak described it, but it is deeply depressing. "Some of them get a bit, y'know... 'cos of the kids."

"I get it," Sam says. Rich nods. He watches Rufus forty feet away, now lying on his back as he's stroked by one of the children, a little girl in a tracksuit.

"Alright, well, maybe like, wait here," Rich says. "It's not just the kids, some of the lads are, y'know—" he takes his cigarette out of his mouth to mime a super-thin roll up, moving it rapidly back and forth near his lips. "And they, y'know, don't like people seein'—"

"I can smell it," Sam says, again with the fake chuckle. "Reminds me of the seventies, smoking a joint in a field." Guy realises he doesn't actually know how old Sam is, but his bigger concern is wasting time; there's nothing *here.* These people have transport and it's probably only a ten minute drive into an urban area; why *wouldn't* you camp out somewhere you aren't going to be bothered, where drunks aren't going to smash up your tent when they find it in an alleyway? Where you can at least have a community?

On top of all of that... he's detecting nothing. He sensed a presence in Nowak and that was over a WiFi connection. He's not even getting a whiff of it here. Even so, maybe if he got closer—

Their faces, though. *Slowed down,* Nowak had said. But these are surely just the lost faces of the dispossessed, of addicts—

"I won't hassle you," Sam says reassuringly. "Does the farmer hassle you? For being here?"

Rich pauses for a second, sizing Sam up, and then shakes his head.

"Dunno, never seen him," he says. "No one has even said anything. No police." Rich considers something. "You, uh... you actually retired Old Bill?"

"I am."

Rich nods again.

"Can you explain something?"

"Sure."

YOU SEE THE MONSTER

Guy looks at Rufus; the dog is in canine paradise as all three children rub at his belly and scratch his ears.

"What's the deal with, y'know, squatters rights?" Rich asks. "We can't get kicked off here, right?"

"It's a good question," says Sam, "and the answer is: it depends. Why?"

"Well, because—hang on a second," Rich says, turning back to the camp. "*Nige!*" A skinny man of about forty, wearing double-denim and a face that looks built to scowl, turns away from a group of three men having a conversation. "*Come here a second, you wanna hear this!*" He turns back to Sam as Nige starts to head over. "Tell him too," Rich says.

"No problem. Michael," Sam says to Guy, using a fake name because Guy, ever over-cautious, had asked him to, "go and grab Max, will you? My knee is playing up." Somehow Sam's ever-inexpressive-but-totally-expressive eyes convey exactly what he's thinking: *yeah, I think this is a waste of time too, but just have a closer look at the place as you go to get the dog, just in case.*

Guy gives him a thumbs-up, Sam hands him the detached lead, and Guy begins to head over to the three children and the now-coughing dog. They look up as he approaches, as do a few people in the camp over to his left, but they glance at Sam talking comfortably to Rich and Nige and decide nothing is up. Guy reaches the three lil' albatrosses and squats down, smiling at the kids but looking over their heads at the camp. Even now he's forty feet closer, there's nothing to report. He notices a very small trench in the grass, dug a half-inch deep and about an inch wide, that runs around the outside of the camp. *Conscientious*, Guy thinks. *To stop any fires that might spread. That's good.*

"Hi kids," he says, feeling awkward as the children smile at him. They all look around the same age, maybe six or seven. The boys are wearing shorts and T-shirts, clothing that is pushing it for this time of year—camping itself will soon be madness—and the girl is in jeans and a brown sweater, her frizzy red hair sticking out in all directions. Guy risks a closer look at the camp: Tents. Dazed-looking people smoking, staring at the sky. Two-litre bottles of water here and there. An instant barbecue with some unspecified meat cooking on it. The cars. A Portaloo—

That isn't a Portaloo. It's a shed.

The beautifully-twinned concepts of *field* and *drugs* had dimly created *festival* in his brain, and the barely-noticed shed—partially hidden by people and rising smoke—had blended with that and become *Portaloo*. The wooden shed isn't an old one, either, not some old and rotting hay store inherited along with these people's new digs. It's brand new, untreated for the elements by the looks of it. Its pointed felt roof reaches around seven feet.

Storage? They brought this with them?

He isn't feeling anything here. He'll take a look at the shed, then leave. He bends down towards Rufus. He realises the kids are watching. He gives them a smile.

"Watch this," he says. *"Roof."* The dog's head snaps up. *"Guu-won."*

Rufus thrashes weakly on the spot, his body arching and straightening like an accordion as he tries to get back to his feet, but he's had a rest and so is immediately off, streaking—thankfully—towards the cars. Close enough to get near to that shed.

"Max, you little shit!" Guy yells, hoping its convincing, and runs after Rufus' furry grey form. The dog is already starting to tire and Guy glances over his shoulder at Sam and the slouched people surrounding him. All of them look Guy's way, as do the people now sitting up on dirty mattresses and knackered deck chairs. He holds up a hand as he runs. *"Sorry! I don't know what's got into him today!"* He expects them to shout, to pursue him, to scream *get away from there* but nobody does. They all turn away.

There's nothing going on here. Even so, Guy has reached the cars. Rufus is sniffing around the tires, wheezing like an old steam train, tail wagging. Guy checks the camp again; still no one is paying attention. The shed is ten feet away to his left. It really is new, Guy notices, apart from the—

There's a complex orange symbol daubed on the right-hand side of the shed. A mix of uneven circles and jagged lines.

Oh. Oh, shit.

He couldn't see it until he was this side of it.

It can't mean anything though. Larry said the tent in his shanty was guarded, that they wouldn't let him anywhere near it. No one is even watching him here. He waits, standing in the shade that the shed is creating. He isn't feeling a *thing.* But they're definitely part of it, the orange symbol thing isn't just a fucking coincidence—

He gets closer, checking the camp all the time. Sam, he notices, is pointing away to the opposite direction to the shed as he talks; the campers look where he points. Is he deliberately creating a distraction? Has he seen Guy?

Guy darts over to the shed, crouching a little, heart beating hard as he preps excuses in his head for getting caught. *I thought it was an outhouse. I really needed to go.* The shed door doesn't even have a padlock on it, the clasp simply resting in place. Guy pauses; no one is looking. He reaches out with a shaking hand and cracks open the shed door. He looks inside. The glimpse is only brief, but it's enough.

The shed is empty.

He quickly closes the door and glances at the camp; Sam has fully turned around now and is pointing at the other hedge. Yes, definitely a distraction. Guy quickly moves away from the shed towards Rufus, whispering to the dog by his real name, who slowly trots over on stiff limbs.

If these people are connected then why isn't he feeling—

The answer comes.

Maybe they're just not up and running yet. Maybe they're just getting started.

Guy clips on Rufus' lead at the third try—his hands are shaking—and starts to walk back to Sam. He needs to talk to his—friend? Colleague?—but sees that the kids have headed over to where he is. They're smiling.

"This your dog?" the little girl asks him.

"No, no," Guy says, still walking and forcing a smile in return. "This is my friend's dog."

"What's he called?"

"Ru—Max. He's called Max."

All three kids start cooing *Max, Max* as the little grey dog painfully totters towards them. He's going to suffer for that headlong charge tonight, that much is obvious, but his wheezing panting suggests it was worth it. Sam's gesturing has slowed down now, Guy sees; distraction over. Guy decides to give him a minute; let the pro get his information. He wants to be out of here. Empty shed or not, he's creeped out by the fact it has that symbol on it.

"What kind of a dog is he?" one of the little boys asks, sweeping his sweaty uncut brown hair out of his eyes, and all of sudden he reminds Guy so much of Ray as a kid that for a moment Guy can't breathe. He just stands there with his mouth open. "Is he... a terrier?" Kid Ray asks helpfully, and Guy blinks his way out of the past.

"No, he's a... he's a spaniel," Guy coughs.

"Ah!" the kid says, beaming and revealing missing baby teeth. "Kevin Barley at school, he has a spaniel. It's only got one ear." They go to school, then. How does that work? Not his business, Guy thinks. He'll report this but he's going to let the professionals deal with it.

"Really," Guy says, trying to put Kid Ray out of his mind as he looks back at Sam. Rich is hailing someone else and a woman starts to head over to them, around fifty with a shock of red hair that can only be related to the little girl at

Guy's feet. She walks slowly, as if she's in pain, but she's much too young for arthiritis, Guy thinks. She looks half asleep.

"Do you want to see a picture of him?" the kid asks.

"Huh? Of who?"

"Kevin Barley's dog."

"Oh." He looks at Sam, shaking the woman's hand and smiling. "Yeah. Yeah, why not."

"Do you have a phone?" the kid asks.

"Yes."

"He's on Instagram. They made an account for the dog."

"Great," he says. Sam is still talking. *Fuck it,* Guy can stall five more minutes. "Show me."

The kid shrugs.

"I don't have a phone."

"Ah well," Guy says. "Another time."

"*At barkleybarley,*" the kid says. "That's the Instagram. It's cool."

"Okay."

"Can we see?" the girl asks, and now all three of them are standing up, beaming.

"Well... you can look on your phones—"

"We don't *have any,*" the other little boy says, chubby and short for his age. "I wanna see the dog..."

"Me too," the girl says, and there's a whine in her voice as they all start to talk at once. Guy needs to shut them up. He takes his phone out of his pocket as he watches the red-haired woman explaining something to Sam, swaying slightly as she does so. He can't tell if Sam is interested or just pretending to be. Guy punches in *barkleybarley* into the search bar. They want to see a dog picture on a phone when there's one right by their feet? Well, living in a field or not, at least these kids are being kept away from phones—

Barkley only has 178 followers but the dog is cute. Certainly better looking than poor Rufus anyway, which isn't hard. Guy squats down again and shows the phone's screen to the kids. They all immediately coo.

"He's funny, isn't he," laughs Kid Ray, telling the other two who laugh and agree. Guy, one eye on Sam, swipes the feed up to show another picture—this time of Barkley jumping through a lawn sprinkler, his one remaining ear flying in the air—and the kids laugh. They're relaxed; maybe they trust him enough to answer questions?

"What does everyone do here all day?" Guy asks, trying to sound light. "When you're not at school?"

"Mummy says they make us help *change the air*," the red-haired girl says happily.

Something shivers down Guy's neck.

We're not in the ecosystem, Guy hears the veteran say.

"What do..." Guy stammers. "Who—"

"Hey," a woman's voice says, and Guy jumps to his feet. The grass had muffled her footsteps. She's the spit of Kid Ray, right down to the shorts and T-shirt. Clearly his mother. "Don't talk to my son." Guy immediately turns red, realising he's been caught showing a kid something on a phone... but then notices the woman's face.

She's not angry. She's scared.

"Sorry, sorry," Guy babbles, "we were walking the dog and your friends started talking to my friend—"

"What are you showing my son?" she asks. *Show her the phone,* Guy's brain hisses, *at least then she knows you weren't showing them anything weird!* "Your, uh, your son wanted me to see his friend's dog—" He turns the phone's screen round to show her.

Oh, shit, he thinks, realisation hitting him as the woman's face whitens and her jaw drops. *I was showing these kids pictures of puppies. Oh, fuck.*

"Barkley Barley, Mum," the kid says, relieving Guy by backing up his story, "Kevin Barley's dog, from school." The boy's voice is small, though; Guy glances down and all of the kids look sheepish. They weren't doing anything wrong though—

The woman's face doesn't change. Is she... she's shaking? And she's not looking at Guy anymore. She's looking at the floor? Guy follows her gaze.

All of them are now standing on the inside of the shallow trench in the earth around the camp.

Her hands go to her mouth, covering it. She slowly looks back at the image onscreen and begins to shake her head from side to side. Tears start to pour from her eyes.

"Kids..." she croaks, "kids... go and... go and..." She's backing away from Guy, her eyes locked on his phone's screen. What the flying fuck? Everything changed as soon as she saw what was onscreen, saw they were inside the trench, but a one-eared dog? *Instagram?*

"Haaa..." Guy hears from below him. Guy's head flips around and he looks down to see Kid Ray's eyes rolling back in his sockets. Spit is already forming at the corners of his mouth.

"Matt!" the woman screams, pushing Guy aside and catching her son in her arms before he falls. The boy's head hangs limply over her arm like a pair of freshly-removed gloves.

Larry was wrong in his article. This is no sham routine.

"He... help!" Guy screams, learning a lesson from Larry's house and already dialling 999 on his phone as the other boy and the red-haired girl begin to sway gently on the spot. Their eyes roll back too and they fall to the floor like sacks of meat. They begin to twitch.

"Hamareth," Matt breathes, his white eyes strobing under flickering eyelids.. *"Tee-sham. Loth—"*

Guy's thumb pauses mid-dial.

"Leffamm," the two pitching children on the floor say in sightless unison, spittle flicking from their mouths as Guy runs around to them. *"Kast. Kast."*

All three children begin to make choking sounds.

Shouts go up from the camp. Guy looks up to see nearly everyone is beginning to run in different directions, leaving Sam standing alone and looking horrified. The mother is whispering something frantically in her son's ear, rocking back and forth on her knees, but the boy continues to babble as Guy realises that everyone in the camp seems to be getting something, why aren't they coming—

Then everyone reappears, walking towards the children now, and all of them are carrying something; a baseball bat, a plank of wood, a glass bottle. Rich and Nige are there, faces dark.

They're not walking towards the children. They're walking towards Guy.

"Woah!" Guy yells, leaping to his feet and beginning to back up towards the gate. Rufus follows. Guy sees Sam hobbling towards him too, quickly making his way between the tents back to Guy, but this means he's technically walking *after* the mob. *"I didn't do anything! I'm calling an ambulance to help!"*

He remembers he didn't dial—

"Ha. Ha. Ha." Guy can hear all three children chanting in unison now—

WHAM.

The noise rings around the field. Everyone there stops.

What the hell—

The advancing mob spins quickly on the spot to look behind them. That noise had been *loud*, as if something were—

WHAM.

—hitting wood.

Sam turns as well. No one is looking at Guy now. Everyone is looking at the shed.

WHAM.

Guy sees it this time. The whole shed rocks violently from the impact inside it.

Rich turns to look at Guy. His eyes are wide, but he isn't angry; his face is fishbelly-white. He's scared out of his mind.

"GET OUUUUUT!!" he screams.

The spell is broken; everyone turns, faces pale, and begins to bellow at Guy, frantically shaking their fists and weapons at him, but not advancing another step. Sam hobble-runs out and around them and reaches Guy.

"Let's go, let's go," he says, snatching Rufus' lead out of Guy's hand and already hobble-running towards the gate. Mouth gaping, Guy turns to follow—*what the absolute blinding fuck was that*—but as he does, he catches a glimpse of the children, each one attended by a parent now. The children are still.

"He's not breathing!" Matt's mother screams.

"Fiona!" one of the men howls. *"Fiona!"*

A bottle smashes near Guy's feet and he runs even faster, pursuing the disappearing Sam. They turn right out of the gate and begin to run back up the hill, the camp hidden from view by the hedgerow.

He can still hear it, though.

WHAM.

WHAM.

By the time they are two thirds of the way back to the car, it's a few minutes later; both men are unfit, the car was parked a long away, and the uphill journey back was slower going. Guy joins Rufus and Sam, who is standing with his hands on his knees, breathing even more heavily than Guy. Guy finally brings himself to turn and look back down the hill. The camp is so far away that from here the people look like toys, but the sight is still unforgettable.

"Oh my God..." Guy whispers.

The tents are ablaze. A handful of people with petrol cans are finishing their task, lighting the remaining few that aren't already burning. They were clearly prepped for whatever situation is occurring. The three mothers are holding their children, but from the way they are rocking around and clawing at the air, Guy thinks something terrible has happened to them.

The rest of the people are standing in a circle around the shed, holding hands and swaying. The shed is now still.

"Let's… go and buy the… camera…" Sam wheezes.

"Are you… kidding?" Guy snaps back. "They're… part of this!"

"Unless you… have backup in your… pocket," Sam says, wiping his forehead and closing his eyes, "they'll tear us to pieces if we go back there. Maybe we can come back when it's dark, I don't… what the hell was in that shed?"

"*Nothing!*"

"What did you… do with the…"

"I didn't do anything!" Guy yells, turning to Sam. "The kids started fitting when the Mum came over and—" What the hell has just happened? How did that escalate so—

Sam's jaw is slowly dropping. Guy spins back and sees why. The adults have now left the area in front of the shed. The mothers move to join them, carrying the limp bodies of their children.

One by one, the camp's members climb into their burning tents.

"*Jesus!*" Guy begins to run again… but stops. It's too late. It's too far away. By the time he runs there, all of the people will be dead. Even if he ran the rest of the way to the car now, he still wouldn't make it. "*Sam! Sam! Oh* shit, *oh* shit, *oh* shit—" He looks up and down the road. No cars. No one to get him down there, or to pull over themselves.

Sam doesn't take his eyes off the scene before him. He's raising his phone.

"I'm going to call some ambulances," he says, voice like steel. He turns to Guy, who has his hands in his hair. "You need to walk in the opposite direction. You shouldn't be here when the police and ambulance arrive. Keep going until you find somewhere to wait and then text me. I'll say I was passing and give—"

"*What the fuck did we do?!*" Guy screams. "*Look what we did!*" He looks down towards the terrible flames. There is no movement at the camp. The shed is still.

"*I'll give a witness statement,*" Sam says firmly, "and I'll be able to keep it quick. I'm one of them after all. There were kids in there, and this needs to be called in. I'll then come and get you and we'll go and get the camera and carry on."

Guy looks at Sam as if he were seeing a lunatic on this country lane.

"*We carry on?*" he yells. "Do you see what we *did?*"

"Did you kill the man in Miami?"

There is no malice in Sam's voice, his face.

"No... no," Guy stammers, stunned. He looks back at the flames, back to Sam.

"And you didn't kill anyone here," Sam says. "This happens, Guy. When you try and do the right thing. When you try and stop something big and bad from happening. The badness consumes people. But it isn't you. And it isn't a reason to stop." He points at Guy's neck. "And you're on the clock. You're in a *war*, Guy. There isn't time to stand around in a war." He dials. "You can deal with this afterwards, but right now, time is of the essence. Okay? Get walking—hello. Ambulance please." Sam stares at the floor. The matter is closed.

Guy is stunned. There's professional and then there's—

He's right.

Guy slowly turns his back on the burning field like a man walking out of a car wreck, listening to Sam calmly talking to the operator. Guy staggers back up the road, eyes focused on the concrete beneath him.

The kids—

He's on the clock.

A little piece of him dies—he feels it and thinks that it will be the first of many—but he keeps walking.

***

Chapter Fourteen
Video Evidence
* * *

It's about two hours since the nightmare in the field when Sam arrives at the country pub where Guy is waiting, still feeling sick. By that time Guy was nursing his second bourbon on the rocks and trying to see the sights around him and not the ones in his head, nausea washing through him with every ignorance-is-bliss laugh from the pub patrons. He'd managed to bring himself to look at Barkley Barley's Instagram page again but couldn't spot anything. What was it about the picture of the dog? What mattered so much?

"Maybe it's not actually the dog itself that set them off," Sam says, seeing what Guy is looking at as he sits at Guy's table, giving his associate time to finish his drink. "I can look into any reports of missing one-earned dogs, but something tells me that it won't turn anything up. But we'll put it on the list of things to work with. That's growing already. That's good."

"Larry said in his article that they wouldn't let him use his camera on-site," Guy says. "Do you think it was something to do with my phone's camera?"

"Did you take pictures?"

"No. But it can't be the phone itself," Guy says. "Those kids said they went to school, so you know they'll be—" His mind flinches as he says it and he stops talking. Sam picks up the thread.

"Around phones all day," Sam finishes. "Maybe. Depends on the school."

"The woman, though," Guy says, remembering. "She only freaked out once she saw I had my phone inside the boundary."

"I spotted that."

"The kids said they were being made to *change the air*," Guy says, his voice monotone. "What do you think that means?"

"I think it's all something to do with the trinkets," Sam says. "That area, that ground... they were making them there."

"They were?"

"When I was talking to them I was just trying to get a look around. They were just asking me questions about land disputes, like I'm a lawyer or something. I didn't have time to get the conversation to go where I wanted… but I saw some trinkets inside one of the tents. As soon as I laid eyes on them, I could *feel* that…" He shudders. "Maybe you have to see them to… I don't know. Either way, maybe *changing the air* is a fancy way of saying *spreading curses.*"

"Fuck…" Guy breathes. "This… it's gotta be all over the news by now?" He hasn't been able to bring himself to check his News app. A mass suicide in the Midlands? That would be national news, let alone regional.

"No," Sam says, sighing. "All the tents were empty once they put the fires out. All of them."

Guy just stares at him.

"Yep," Sam says, nodding. "So if your camera theory is right, then we need to get a good one and use it." He points at Guy's drink. "You done? We need to get going, and I've left Rufus in the car."

Guy opens his mouth to protest, then stops. He doesn't want to hear another *this is a war* speech. He downs his drink in one, and they leave.

They have work to do.

***

As Sam and Guy walk between the endless aisles of the high ceilinged, brightly-lit store, the world almost seems normal for a moment. It's only for a fraction of a second, before Guy looks directly at one of the round, white ceiling lights and an image of a rolled-back eyeball under flickering eyelids jumps into his mind. He looks at the other shoppers, people blissfully unaware of the awful world going on around them, separated from it only by walls of rules whose loopholes are starting to give way. He envies the blissfully ignorant Rufus, sleeping in the car with the window wound down a crack. *It's a cold day,* Sam had said, *so he'll be fine.*

As they head into the camera section Guy sees that there's a camera hooked up to a monitor to display it's high-res capabilities. Sam does too.

"This any good?" he asks, pointing at it. "I have no idea. On-sale though."

Two young boys are standing in front of the camera and goofing around. They're watching themselves on the TV. Guy freezes for a moment but then he sees that these kids are older—a good few years older—than the children in the field.

Here, at what he thinks is the end of his rope—it isn't, not by a long way—Guy's brain shifts, adapts. *Yes*, he thinks. *I can deal with it all later, can't I?*

Feeling dreamlike, and actually believing what he's thinking, Guy looks at the camera Sam is pointing at. *Camera*, he thinks, already shifting greedily into the practical, the normal. *What's it like?*

Both the boys are dressed in tracksuits. One is a young white kid, very white—a redhead—the other black with his hair in cornrows, both probably still pre-teens. They're showing their butts to the camera. Riveting stuff, as their helpless giggles would seem to suggest—

Camera

Yes. The image looks impressive, the price is good, and a quick glance at the info sticker says it has 4K capability. Guy doesn't think they're going to need much more than this.

"Yeah, looks good,' Guy says.

Plus, a voice in his head whispers, *if you do what Nowak said and end up killing yourself, you're not gonna need the money anyway, right?* Guy swallows and looks around for an assistant so they can buy the camera. *Maybe we can stop what's happening,* he tells himself for the thousandth time. *Expose them enough that they leave me and Sam alone, put us back to normal—*

Or maybe you'll end up in a burning tent—

The black kid straightens up and flicks the finger to the camera, setting off the redhead who laughs *Chris!*

An idea occurs to Guy.

"Hey," The two boys immediately freeze. Guy could be a security guard after all. "It's okay. I want to check something. I need an opinion, okay?" They stare at him, still wary.

"Guy?" Sam asks.

"Just checking something," he repeats, not looking at Sam. He makes sure he keeps a good few feet between himself and the kids, not wanting to look dodgy, and his brain tries to make a memory association but Guy stops it. The process is complete, then.

Guy starts to pull at the dressing on his neck. Chris looks even more uncomfortable, the redhead looks more intrigued. "It's okay," Guy says, "it's healed up. I just need you to check something for me, okay?" He finishes removing the dressing and points at the spot underneath. "You see my neck?" The redhead nods. Chris just stares. "How does it look?"

"Pink," Chris says, piping up. "Did you get hurt or something?"

"I did, yeah. Look at that TV a second?"

They do, turning to the monitor hooked up to the camera.

"Guy," Sam says. His expression is one of deep concern. "I'm not sure about this."

"It's okay, it's just a magic trick," Guy says, glaring at him. The boys only see themselves as Guy isn't in the frame yet. Stepping forward as much as he can to get onscreen as well while maintaining a non-pervy distance, Guy crouches down slightly so his neck is fully in shot. He sees it onscreen and immediately looks away. It's an act of almost physical repulsion. "You see the scales?" he asks the boys. They don't reply, squinting at the screen in confusion, trying to figure out what the point of this is. "You *don't* see scales?"

"It's kinda... white?" the Redhead mutters, sounding as if he feels stupid saying it.

"No... yeah!" Chris agrees. "Like a white... blur or something. It's hard to see on—"

Guy looks at Sam, who raises his eyebrows, acknowledging the difference. *This* is gradual, but one glance at the camera during the Nowak call and Sam immediately saw the scales onscreen.

Chris moves around to Guy's side—so he can more clearly see Guy's neck in the flesh—and gasps.

"It's there!" he cries, seeing them in real life now. "Like a, like a *blur* on your neck! How do you do th—"

"Let me see!" the Redhead yelps, moving around Guy. He laughs with delight. "*Shit!* Can I touch it?"

"I don't think that's a good idea," Sam mutters.

"This doesn't make sense," Guy tells him. "Nancy saw it clearly straightaway. You did. They're saying it's a blur..."

"You folks need help with anything?" An assistant has appeared out of nowhere, smiling helpfully. The interruption is not welcome.

"I'll come and ask if we do, won't I?" Guy snaps angrily. "*Thanks!*" The assistant bleaches slightly and hurries away. Guy doesn't look at Sam, knowing he will be staring disapprovingly, but in that moment all Guy cares about is that he hasn't scared the kids away. Their eyes are glued to his neck.

"Boys, do me a favour and look at the TV again," Sam says, calm and authoritative. A pro. "Just come back round, will you?"

The boys do so immediately, thinking perhaps that this is all some kind of David Blaine stunt—if kids today even know who the hell David Blaine is—and stare at the monitor. They squint again.

"So you still just see a white blur on the TV?" Sam asks.

"Yeah," they both say.

"... still?" Sam asks.

"Same."

Then the redhead's face lights up.

"*Wait,*" he says. "Like... a pattern?"

"*Yeah,* like a pattern," Chris confirms, excited. "How *are* you doing this?" His face brightens and he looks at Guy. "Is this a prank? For like a viral video?"

"Are we gonna be Youtubers?" the redhead laughs, a sound so delighted that Guy suddenly feels like crying.

"Is it clear?" Guy asks instead, pointing at the screen. "The pattern. Look closely."

The boys lean towards the TV together. They watch for a few seconds.

"It... is," Chris says. "Oh shit, it *is!*" He runs around Guy again to look at his neck. "Look at it! Ha ha! How are you doing that?"

"It took *them* a few views then," Sam mutters. "It took time, repeated exposure."

He catches Guy's eye, and nods, smiling a little. They're both thinking the same thing.

We can use that to our advantage.

"*How the hell does* that *work, though?*" Guy whispers to Sam. "*Human eyes and camera lenses work the same way, light hitting a lens, right? So what's the difference?*"

"One's mechanical, one's flesh and blood," Sam mutters back. "Could just be that simple?"

"I don't think s—" Guy begins, but then notices the look on the redhead kid's face. The boy's brow is furrowed, looking from Guy to the screen and back.

"Are you... okay?" the kid asks, his voice small.

"Of course. Thanks for asking."

"Like he said, it's a magic trick kids," Sam says, plastering on a perfect fake grin and giving a chuckle. "We're practicing it, got to try it out on unsuspecting people! We can't tell you how it's done though, or that would spoil the secret!

The redhead doesn't return Sam's smile.

"My friend Jake at school said he knew about this other kid from his *old* school," he says. "Said the kid stopped *coming* to school. Said that when he went 'round to call on the kid, the kid's Mum said he couldn't come out." He stares at the TV screen, not meeting Guy's eyes as he says the last part. "Then as Jake was leaving he saw the kid through the window and the kid's eyes had changed."

Guy's jaw nearly drops.

"Are you like... that kid?" the boy asks.

"Nah," Guy says, recovering and answering confidently because he knows what he's saying is true. Whatever is on him couldn't be seen through a window. His is hidden. "I'm just a magician."

The redhead scowls.

"No you're not. Don't lie."

"He's a magician, Dan!" Chris says. "Come and look at his neck—"

"Did it scare you?" Sam asks Dan. "The story the kid told you?" Guy's glad Sam asked. He doesn't want Dan to be afraid, and Sam is better with kids. The boy considers the question.

"Not really, I s'pose," he says finally, shrugging. "It's not happening to anyone I *know*, you know? So it's okay."

Guy and Sam thank the boys and buy the camera, adding a tripod while they're at it.

***

They drive back to Sam's in silence. Guy notices that Sam's turning away from the route home.

"Need petrol," he says. As they pull up at the pumps, Guy sees the church on the other side of the road. It's a relatively modern building by church standards, maybe built in the last few decades or so. It looks like a Pentecostal place made out of grey concrete with an enormous white crucifix covering the front of the building. Guy gets out of the car, feeling restless as Sam fills up the tank. Rufus, exhausted from the walking, is still curled up asleep on the back seat of the car. Guy's looking at the church and thinking about it, thinking about it, and the idea sounds so *stupid*, but...

Sam sees Guy looking and puts two and two together.

"You going to go in?"

Guy shuffles on the spot, embarrassed.

"I don't...believe in it..."

Sam shrugs and moves his hands around him in the air as if to say, *well, shit, I think our beliefs on everything have been challenged a little bit, don't you?*

"It can't hurt, can it?" he says. "I'll go in as well. We both should."

"Do you think they'll have..." Guy feels stupid saying it. "Holy water?"

"I don't know," Sam says, watching the numbers on the pump. "And I'm not even sure this is a religious thing, as stupid as that might sound. But like I say, it can't hurt. Go on over. I'll finish up here and join you." He looks back at the pump as if the matter is settled. Guy feels embarrassed as he turns and begin to cross the street.

As he reaches the opposite kerb he realises he's nervous. He actually hesitates before crossing over the gravel edge of the car park, noticing that his hand has gone unconsciously to the scales on his neck. He pauses.

Can't hurt, Sam had said. That might not be true anymore.

Pointing his toe like a ballerina, Guy moves his foot gingerly over the car park's edge, and slowly touches the gravel with the toe of his shoe, wincing. Nothing happens. He doesn't burst into flames. Okay then. He breathes out, checking that Sam wasn't watching that, but Sam has already gone inside the petrol station to pay. Guy heads inside the church.

It's cheaply-furnished inside, the only ornate decoration being the elaborate glass frieze of Jesus on the cross above the stage—he doesn't know the right name—area. It's large and white and airy and silent other than the occasional cough from one of the twelve or so people present, the sound echoing gently up into the high wooden-slatted ceiling. There's no sermon going on, but Guy guesses this is quiet worship time or something. The people are spread out individually around the large hall, picking their places on the long equally-white benches, other than a pair of old ladies sitting together on the back row.

Something about those two grabs at his attention—he keeps looking back at them—but he ignores it. He doesn't actually know what he's attempting to do here but a holy place *surely* has to give him... what? A drizzling of something? Armour of God? But if Guy doesn't believe in Him—

A place he came to for peace and reassurance is suddenly a mental minefield:

If God exists then he allows monsters to exist.

Well that's nothing new. There's demons in the bible. They're Legion, remember?

Well in that case, better start praying, dickhead!

Marianne was the religious one. Didn't help her.

That was a good one.

Well maybe she practised it but didn't believe *it. Maybe she went through the motions but had no faith. Isn't that what it's all supposed to be about for these guys?*

You don't have any.

It still can't hurt to offer up a prayer, can it? Fuck it. I'll take all the help I can fucking—

"Mm. *Mm.*"

The noise from behind him jerks Guy out of his thoughts. It's the sound he's heard babies make when dealing with something unpleasant and want to be away; that of mild distress. He turns around, looking for the source, then yelps and jumps out of his seat when he discovers that the two old women from the back row are not only sitting right behind him now, but that one is leaning her face so forward that it's right behind Guy's head. He'd turned around and found himself staring right into her heavily-lidded eyes, the same way he had with the monster when it was pretending to be Larry.

He hears creaking and shuffling as everyone else in the silent church turns around at his cry of surprise, but he ignores them. He's too busy looking at the old woman, heart still pounding. This isn't right, he can feel it; there's a sick feeling in his stomach again, but this isn't the same as the one he got when he looked at Nowak onscreen. This is darker, as if his bowels were about to turn to water... and he notices that it's the leaning-forward woman's companion that made the distressed noise. Her eyes are screwed tightly shut and Guy is reminded of the description of one of the women from the shanty in Larry's article. She's overweight and wearing a grey dress under a white cardigan. Her friend—the one leaning in so close she could tell what kind of shower gel Guy used if he'd actually bothered to wash for the last three days—is, Guy realises, dressed in an identical dress minus the cardigan, her bone-thin arms and shoulders on display. Her larger friend then opens her eyes and looks at Guy, her expression neutral.

"That hurts," the skinny one says. "when you use words like those in here. Bad words. They hurt a little. Just a little."

"Uh.. sorry," Guy says, confused. Bad words? What's the crazy bitch on about?

I wasn't even talking, he thinks, *I don't fucking need this kind of—*

"*Mmmmm,*" says the big woman, more loudly this time, screwing up her eyes again. "*Mmm!*"

"*Again,*" the thin woman whispers, and she's smiling now. "Those *words.* It's hard enough for us to even be in here. Difficult. Words like those in a place like this. Create waves. It hurts." She doesn't look like it hurts though, with that thin smile that creeps across her face like a dead worm. She's not that old— mid-sixties perhaps—but something about her suddenly *feels* old—

He wasn't talking, no. But he'd sworn in his head.

Dread slips into Guy's bones and he begins to wonder just how old this woman might really be. She sees realization creep into his face and that horrible thin grin spreads a little wider. Her—*its*—skinny fingers come up and rest on the back of the pew he'd been sitting in—Guy is still standing—and he sees it's wearing green nail polish. A modern, fun grandma's nail polish, at odds with the greyness of her dress, and Guy understands that this is its best attempt to match what a modern-day older woman looks like.

So much so that they both used the same outfit.

"You mean..." Guy catches the word on the way out, his eyes riveted on whatever it is he's currently talking to. "... curse words."

"We have to be so very *neutral* here." The smile disappears, its expression becoming one of worry, and Guy understands that it isn't used to this face, how it should work. It's trying all the facial expressions out. "We hear those words and they are in our *brains* and that upsets everything. It's *unpleasant*."

Guy begins to slowly edge sideways, as if that wouldn't be noticed. The end of the long pew is maybe ten feet away and even then he'd be a good thirty feet from the door. He doesn't know what he's expecting; what is this thing allowed to *do?* It obviously isn't really an old woman. He looks in its eyes and feels like a mouse before a swaying snake as the thing starts moving sideways with him now, keeping perfect pace. Its eyes hold his. He looks at the door. No Sam yet. The worm-smile is back on the old woman-thing's face as if, after trying it on, it now knows a smile is the correct expression for how it's currently feeling. Its fingers walk along the top edge of the pew as if it's typing its way to the left, its nails tapping a light, clickety rhythm that makes Guy's skin crawl.

His heart is beating painfully hard—they're reading his *thoughts*—and his throat is dry and *wait,* how many others—

He manages to tear his eyes away from the awful, bony, hypnotic, sideways-sliding thing in front of him and flashes a glance around the hall. No one seems to be paying attention, deliberately ignoring the audible grunts of the bigger woman-thing now as they would if someone with mental health issues were struggling in a social setting, not wanting to stare or point at someone less fortunate. Just these two then—

No. He sees it, and this time it lasts longer before it disappears. Another one of those little dark, hunched things, sitting on the neck of an old man in a brown sweater, seated away to Guy's right. It looks like its head is bent to the old man's ear, its pudgy, shadowy arms buried in his hair, its legs hanging over the old man's shoulders as it sits. Then, once again, it's gone from Guy's sight as if it were a station he'd passed on an ancient antenna TV.

Guy swallows and looks back at the old woman-thing in front of him. It remains hunched and blinking, that expression frozen. He wants to run but a desperation of a different kind cuts through the fear. If they were waiting for him *then this is a lead—*

Its face. Something behind that face that Guy can't see with his eyes—

But it's not attacking him. Guy makes himself stand up straight.

"You... can read my thoughts?"

The fat one laughs. Spit is now running out of one side of its mouth. The laughter has made it lose control of its unaccustomed face.

"No," the skinny one says. "But I could be lying." That smile cracks a little more, exposing her teeth. Guy expects to see fangs, or crooked yellow bone at least, but instead what's revealed is a row of teeth so perfectly shaped and so brilliantly white that they look as if they're made of plastic. Something rushes through him, an almost irresistible urge to take shelter—

He resists. The old woman-thing perhaps looks a little smaller as result, but still a dangerous, cunning snake, albeit a coiled one.

"Then how can you hear—"

"Anything like that—*bad words*—speaks to us," it chuckles, amused. "We feel it. It stands out like a beacon. Curse words... they belong to us. *Mm.* But in here..." It twitches its head slightly, done with the sentence. It continues to stare at Guy and he realises that its body isn't moving at all. No expansion and contraction of the ribcage. It's something he would never notice until it wasn't there, but realizing that a still-talking person isn't breathing is freaky as fuck.

"What... what are those little things doing?" he asks, pointing at the old man across the church. Even though Guy can't see the squat passenger on the old man's shoulders anymore he's sure it's still there. "Sitting on the shoulders of... what are they *doing?*"

The old woman-thing's head twitches. Its mouth twists dramatically as if it had just sucked an extra-sour lemon before the thin smile reappears. It's as if her face were glitching.

"Whispering. *Very* quietly," it says, finally. "Influencing."

"Influencing how—" That can wait. There are bigger questions. He has to push this. "What do you want? You can't touch me. Neither of you can."

"Can't we?"

He opens his mouth to say *no* and freezes, thinking of Nowak. The thing has asked him a question. Any answer might be a confirmation, a way into some kind of trap and then they have him. What was that bullshit line an old university friend told him to use with cops? *I don't answer questions.* That has to be his new mantra.

"You... tell me," Guy says.

"We're just *looking* at you," the thing says, and its expression suddenly becomes one of surprise. It isn't surprised, Guy knows. Another attempt at appropriate humanity. "Our purpose this day is not to hurt you. Our purpose today is nothing to do with you at all."

"You're not here for me?"

The pair look at each other and then back at Guy.

"No. We just wait for the bad words. This place brings the *smell* out of them... it's revealing. A good place to begin." The fat one chuckles again. The spit is now dripping from underneath the left hand side of its chin. "You must understand this now, I think?" The skinny one sways its head back and forth. "You can smell things yourself a little, no? You are talking to us. That does not normally happen." Guy doesn't know what it means about smelling things but he knows he's certainly seeing them now, sensing them. He felt something in Nowak, in these two. He's changing, alright.

I don't answer questions.

"But you're interesting," the thing says. "You smell different to the others. What's your name?"

"Nice try."

Its eyebrows stay raised.

"Yes. Interesting," it says. "Perhaps we will visit you."

Guy shivers.

"I'd rather you didn't."

"I don't know if we would be allowed yet," it says. "I will see. I've smelled you now. I can find you anywhere if I need to. You knew us and yet..." It suddenly inhales through its nose, deeply, but keeps its eyes open and its brows raised, still bent at the waist and clutching the top of the pew. The image is bizarre. It considers Guy. "You're... *changing*. Aren't you?"

Guy starts to feel as if he may be standing on the edge of the abyss... but not going to fall in after all. Not now, at least.

"You can't touch me," he repeats, his voice shaking as anger starts to beat fear. "Not yet anyway, *you can't fucking touch me—*"

Both of them wince and the big one makes that *Mm!* sound again, wincing and screwing up its face.

"Not necessary," the skinny one says, its misplaced expression now turning into one of joy, looking as if its grandchild had just taken its first step. "You hurt us on purpose. We're only *interested* in you."

"You're going to be hearing about me really soon," Guy hisses, leaning down into the thing's face as close as he dares. He raises a shaking finger. "Someone is going to tell you my name because I'm going to be causing you some *big* problems."

"Guy?"

It's Sam. Guy didn't hear him approach but sees how this looks from Sam's point of view: Guy right up in the grill of some old dear. Sam looks shocked, red-faced again and clearly thinking Guy's finally snapped. His car keys are still gripped tightly in his right hand. Neither of the things in front of Guy turn to look at Sam. Guy looks around the church quickly, checking to see if anyone else is misreading the situation, but they aren't.

"It's alright Sam," Guy whispers, holding out a hand. "These are—"

"What are you *doing?*" Sam hisses back, mortified.

The old woman-creature blinks up at Guy, still with that *yes, walk to gramma, you can do it Timmy* expression plastered onto its not-quite-right face.

"Come here, Sam," Guy says. "You'll see. Get close."

Both the old women-things chuckle, deep and gurgling, as Sam hurries quietly over like a maitre'd trying to hide a scene from other diners. He grabs Guy's arm.

"Come *on,*" he begins say... and then stops. His brow furrows and he turns to look at the two pretend women in front of him, confused. "Uh..." Guy sees understanding dawn on Sam's face as the blood leaves it. He glances at Guy for confirmation, who nods quickly. Sam's hand leaves Guy's arm as he backs up half a step, but now it's Guy's turn to grab *him.*

"With me, Sam. With me."

Sam's eyes dart from Guy to the old women, Guy to the old women. Then he nods, his pulse visibly thrumming in his neck. Guy pauses and Sam sees him checking. Sam angrily nods again, pulling his arm free, embarrassed.

Answers, Guy thinks.

"You really don't know who I am, do you?" he asks them.

"Not yet, other than the first name your friend just said," it says. "Should we?"

"How long do I have?" Guy asks, pointing at his neck and bracing himself for the answer. "Can you tell?"

The old bitch just grins at him, chuckling.

"Larry, then," Sam says, and the tremor in his voice makes Guy feel less ashamed. "Larry Neilsen. What did *he* do?"

"*Aah.* We know this name," the thing says, its eyes still on Guy even as it addresses Sam. "Did you know him?"

"N—" Sam catches himself. "I mean, what can you tell us about him?"

"Nothing to tell. He was dealt with," it says with a grin, its hands coming away from the top of the pew. It sits back in its seat, its eyes releasing Guy as they close. Its associate does the same, chin still glistening. Guy's fear evaporates under the rage that roars up at her words. Larry was *dealt with?* Shaking, he leans closer to them both, trembling with anger now, and whispers:

"*Fuck you, fuck you, fuck you—*"

"*Mm!*"

The skinny one's eyes snap open and immediately it's up once more and in Guy's face. Its eyes blaze and something behind them buckles Guy's knees, the near-full force of whatever it is, whatever is hidden, leaping straight from its being into Guy's brain and he stumbles with the sudden shock. Sam half-catches him, pushing him fully back upright.

"You smell of trouble," the thing says, its voice monotone but deeply intense. "Of mischief. We will find a way to visit you. *Before* you become one of the *Other Folk.*" It sounds deeply satisfied as it says the name.

"The Other Folk? Who *are* the Other Folk?" Sam asks, before Guy can. The old woman-thing only cocks its head in response, ignoring Sam, and inhales. "Yes..." it says. "I think we will find a way to visit you. Sleep well." It sits back quickly and closes its eyes once more. The pair of them look as if they're asleep.

Sam's breathing rapidly. This just got very real for him. Last night was one thing, this is another.

Guy and Sam don't move.

Neither do the creatures.

After a few more seconds Guy tries sidling sideways by a foot.

They still don't move.

Guy looks at Sam and jerks his head towards the door. Sam, jaw clenched, gives a lightly shaking thumbs up. Keeping his eyes on them all the way, Guy fully slides out of the row and he and Sam begin to make their way towards the exit. By the time they're halfway out they're having to walk backwards so they can keep their eyes on the pair in the pew. From here, the creatures' two hunched backs—one clad in grey, the other in white—look like two gargoyles squatting together. They look harmless and somehow full of malice at the same time.

It's a matter of time, Guy thinks, one hand going to his neck, the other hand fumbling for the edge of the open door, his eyes still on the pair. *They might visit you. Poor Sam.*

He tries to remember how he beat the fear just moments ago—despite everything, he knows that anger is often a gift—but he can't quite find it. He needs to come out of this with *something*—

FUCKYOUFUCKYOUFUCKYOU he thinks and then he's turning and running out of the door as quickly as possible, grabbing a bewildered Sam's jacket as he does and dragging the older man outside with him. Neither of them say a word until they're back inside the car with the door locked and the wheels moving at speed, both men shaking wildly. Guy already regrets his childish impulse. They were in a church; that means they're everywhere, and he's just pissed them off. In the back seat, Rufus hasn't even raised his hairy head, but his eyes are watching the two men in the front.

"Are you okay?" Guy asks Sam. "I know that was the first time you've... actually talked to them..." He decides to say it. "You don't have to do this, Sam. I wouldn't blame you at all. You can just let nature take its course. It's a little different once you've been that close to it—"

"I'm in," Sam breathes. "I'm in. And I wouldn't be making that offer so easily if I were you." He's looking out of the window as he talks, and his tone is angry. "You need backup you don't care about, the kind they *can't* leverage. I'm the cannon fodder here, if need be. There aren't going to be many volunteers for that job, so take what you have." He breathes out heavily and rubs his eyes with his free hand. "Look, I'm a bit shaken," he says, "and thinking about, you know... back in the day, how I could have... I mean my head is spinning. Do you mind if we don't talk?"

Now? Guy wonders. *Innocent children dying in a field and it's all* let's go to war *but when it happens to you, it's different?*

He doesn't say it.

"That's fine, that's completely fine."

"Thanks," Sam says. "I'm going to have a lie down when we get back, okay? I need to lie down for an hour. Maybe two. It's nearly three pm now. That way it will be dark by the time we go to Larry's. Do you need me to help you film the video?"

"No, I can do it myself. Sam, are you—"

"I told you, *yes.*"

Guy can't help it.

"Did you hear what she said? That I'm going to become one of the Other Folk?" He shivers. "I'm going to be *joining* her."

"We don't... *know* that's what she meant," Sam says carefully.

"She was pretty fucking clear, Sam."

"Well... " Sam sighs. "That isn't news, is it? Like I said: can we not talk?"

"*Fine,* fine."

Guy is furious now too, but things are already really fucking shit. They drive back to Sam's and neither of them says a word until Guy is sitting in Sam's living room, staring at the wall, and Sam sticks his head around the door.

"Help yourself to the drinks cabinet," he says, before disappearing. Guy doesn't know if that was a jibe and if it is he doesn't know what the hell Sam's angry with *him* about. He hears the upstairs door close and wonders yet again what he's doing in this man's house. He glances at his phone and realises it's time to check in with Nancy just as the battery dies. *Fuck.* He goes to his bag to get his charger and through the window he notices the sun beginning to peek out from behind a cloud in the grey sky above. He tries to feel happy about seeing it but it's impossible.

He's waiting for it to set, after all.

***

Chapter Fifteen
Checking Sources
✳✳✳

"My name is Guy Autumn and I want to show you something."

He found a spare key in the kitchen drawer earlier, let himself out, and drove to B and Q to buy several lamps for the filming. All the lighting, as well as the camera lens, is turned his way, set up in Sam's living room. He wants to be as brightly lit as possible. The metaphor isn't lost on him. He's glad of it though; the sun has nearly set outside and the now-intense illumination indoors makes him feel better. Sam is still upstairs, presumably sleeping, a fact that frankly blows Guy's mind. Rufus is in his basket, doing the same; Sam wasn't lying about the dog sleeping off his brief runs.

"I'll get right to the point." He pulls his T-shirt off. He doesn't want to start the video shirtless in case that put people off or gave them the wrong impression. The worrying thing is that, by now, he *has* to be shirtless to expose all of the scales. "I'd like to draw your attention to my neck... I mean my neck and chest." He forces himself to look at his image on the laptop for the briefest glance—he has the tripod-mounted camera hooked up to it—to make sure the money shot is *in* shot. It is, but even with the quickest look possible he can't miss the fact that the scales have actually spread a little further in the last few hours. Before they were covering his neck and shoulder but only some of his pectoral. Now the whole pec is covered too. They must be saving the face for last. "Some of you may see white scales, like that of a fish or a reptile," he says, looking back into the lens only now, with notable relief. "Some of you may possibly see nothing but regular, freshly-healed skin; I don't *think* you'll see that but I don't know how this works yet. Some of you—the ones I want to speak to the most—will only see perhaps a blur."

He's practised the speech about fifty times before he hits record—in between going back to Barkley Barley's Instagram page—but he still has to pause to remember what comes next. He's trimmed it to be as short as he can make it. If there's one thing he knows about the current online culture it's that popcorn is the most popular thing to consume, not steak.

"The reason I want to address those people the most is because you—if you're one of them—" He's tripping up but just continues—"are the people I think will believe me. This is because you will hopefully be able to see the change over time and that will let you know that what I'm saying is real."

He hopes desperately that the gradual-reveal effect isn't one that only happens with kids. Sam and he realised the same thing in the store when they saw that: if there are enough people that have the same experience, this video could be dynamite.

"Let me explain," he continues. "I would like you to restart this video and rewatch it. It will be the same clip, obviously, and there's no way therefore that I could tamper with the footage mid-viewing. Hopefully you will see a blurred image on my neck, chest and shoulder before it visibly changes into *white scales*. You may dismiss this as hypnotic suggestion but I think you would have to agree this goes far beyond that kind of thing. In the description below I have added a link to a website."

That had been easy to set up. One Squarespace subscription and twenty minutes later he'd made a website featuring nothing but an online storage link.

"If this video has intrigued you in any way, please visit this website and click on the Dropbox link. It will take you to a folder containing the original video file that I have uploaded here. The reasons for this are twofold: one, so any of you that know anything about special effects or CGI or even makeup can analyse this as closely as possible, and two, I don't know how long this video will be allowed to stay up on YouTube, if I manage to get it posted at all. I have reason to believe that it may be taken down extremely quickly, as there are influencing..." What was the word he wrote again? *Dammit,* it was good, and this was going well. "... *forces* out there that don't want me talking about this kind of thing. I don't think they directly understand tech very well but they perhaps have people that do. Please reupload this video to YouTube with my permission. The more people talking about it the better and the more uploads out there means the more versions there will be of it to have taken down. I would like you to share this video with two of your friends to see if you all experience the visual effect of my changing neck more *clearly*, if showing it to other people means *you* see it better. If it does, please let me know in the comments below."

He takes a deep breath before he goes for the headline.

"Something supernatural has happened to me. I want to get people talking about it before I go any further. That's it for now. Thank you."

He'd deliberately left an air of mystery in there. Nothing gets people talking more than a story where there can be wild speculation. He leans over and pauses just before he turns the camera off. He remembers, for some reason, the words the homeless man yelled out in the restaurant before he died. Guy thinks that they're actually quite appropriate. He leans back. "Please... *wake up,*" he adds. He turns the camera off.

He can't imagine how people—the ones who see the blur—could watch this and *not* be intrigued. A video that changes the more you watch it? He's seen optical illusion videos before but nothing like this. Surely anyone that sees it would have to share? His worry is the way the cops let his case slide on such a flimsy resolution. Was that a physical, real world thing—someone at the top telling them to quash it—or, daresay... magic at work? Clouding the minds of the police involved? If so, could viewers' amazement be—

He's thinking too much. Hell, one of the cops even said *not this fella.* The good news is Guy knows he has an advantage over most first-time wannabe Youtubers; a network of people in the social media and clickbait field that owe him a few favors. He starts the upload on YouTube and titles the video MAGIC NECK. Short and sweet; says what it is and easy to repeat over the water cooler. He submits the completed upload and after a few moments—while he expects it to say *there's a problem with your upload* or something along those lines—it tells him it's been submitted for processing. It gives him the pre-published sharing link. Guy copies it and puts together a mass email to his hopefully-helpful guys and girls. If it's going to pass processing it should do so shortly, and if it doesn't and the link mysteriously ends up being dead then they won't give a shit, they'll just move onto the next piece of popcorn.

He sent Nancy a text earlier, as requested. He wrote a long, honest message out, explaining everything that just happened in the church and what those creatures had said. Then he'd deleted it all, and instead sent:

TWO HOUR CHECK IN. ALL IS WELL.

He hated the lying but until *he* knows a little more there's no point adding to her worry. *We will find a way to visit you,* they'd said. He told himself it's a bluff. They can't just do that. There are rules.

Nancy had replied almost immediately:

THANKS. WHAT'S YOUR NEXT MOVE?

I'M WORKING ON SOMETHING RIGHT NOW, he'd texted back. I'LL GIVE YOU A CALL WHEN I'M DONE.

He's done now. He calls her. She picks up almost straight away—she's answering from her office—and Guy tells her all about the YouTube video idea. He thought she might react with anger born of worry; he hadn't told her about it beforehand because he didn't want her to talk him out of putting a flag in the ground like that. By the time he's finished though her voice is, astonishingly, still calm.

"You should have told me you were going to do that," she says.

"I know. You're not mad?"

"Not really. Guy... I can't imagine what you're going through and I can't apply normal logic to it, I can't judge your decisions. I just hope they're the right ones." She sighs. "You are *such* an infuriating man, though—" Her sentence cuts off and Guy knows she's bitten her lip. She'd started doing that towards the end of their relationship, giving up before things even became conflicts. Guy suddenly misses *their* popcorn. The good kind, the kind that matters.

"I'm sorry I didn't tell you," he says.

"It's okay."

Something horrible occurs to him. Why the hell didn't he think of this sooner?

He doesn't want to frighten her but he needs to warn her.

"Nance, if you find anything unusual near the house... don't touch it, okay? And certainly don't bring it indoors."

"Riiight..." she says. "There's absolutely no fucking way you aren't explaining why you just said that. Tell me."

Dammit.

He tells her, explaining about the trinkets Larry saw in the shanties, the one he'd seen at Larry's house and the object Sam had shown him.

"Okay... Jesus," she says when he's done. "Understood. Anything I find like that, I'll either smash it or burn it."

"No, don't do anything. Just leave it be until I know more about all this."

"Whatever you say. Look, you're being pretty honest with me right now, so is there anything you need to tell me about? Don't *protect* me, Guy. I want to know what's going on. I do still care about you, you know."

He pauses, wondering if it's worth mentioning it. Then he remembers all those moments in *Lost* where one character has seen something incredible and then someone else turns up, asks why the previous character looks so freaked out, and is infuriatingly told *oh... nothing.*

"It might just be the stress of all this, Nance, but... I feel like my thoughts are changing."

"How?" She sounds immediately frightened.

"Look, don't get—"

"*How?*"

"Short-tempered. Aggressive, ready to go all the time."

"Have you been drinking?"

The question is so immediate that it hurts, and even more so that the answer is *yes.* Sam had said Guy could help himself to the drinks cabinet after all, but he hasn't taken the piss with it.

"Yes, but this was before that. I might be imagining it but I..." Guy nearly mentions Nowak's story but thinks better of it. "... worry, is all," he finishes. Nancy sighs a little bit and doesn't answer. "What?" he asks.

"Guy..." she says, awkwardly, "haven't you always... you know..."

He tenses up, *waiting* for her to say it. Even now, she can't let it go, the usual bullshit: *you're so argumentative,* completely missing her own part in things as usual, as if he were somehow capable of having a fucking argument by himself, but before she finishes he hears movement upstairs and leaps out of his seat, dropping the phone. Then he hears a bedroom door close and sees Rufus stand up painfully to stretch. It's only Sam, coming downstairs. Guy breathes out heavily, putting his hands to his face. He doesn't know how much more he can take of this constantly being wired.

"*Guy? Guy, what's happened?*" Nancy's frantic but tinny voice floats up to him from the floor. He snatches up the phone.

"It's okay, it's okay. Sam slammed a door upstairs and made me jump," he lies. "I'd better go anyway, he's coming down."

"What are you doing next?" She asks, nervously.

"We're working with Larry's article," he says. It's kind of the truth. "We're going to get it out there."

She sighs again.

"Alright. Keep me posted. Another two hours maximum."

She really is worried. Warmth breaks through Guy's irritation for a moment.

"Okay. Two hours."

"And Guy?"

"Yes?"

"Remember: this is bigger than you. You're doing great and you're incredibly brave. Bye."

She hangs up. Guy feels a little stunned. Sam enters, looking sheepish and holding up his hands. Rufus slowly trots over for some fuss and Sam obliges.

"Sorry about earlier," he says, eyes on the floor. "Can we leave it at that?"

"Of course."

"Not angry with you."

"Okay."

It's awkward.

"So we're okay?" Sam asks. Guy's touched that he wanted to clarify it.

"Yes, yes."

"Okay. I couldn't actually sleep," Sam says, scratching his ear. "Was on my laptop and sending a few messages. Trying to turn something up about the *Other Folk* and chasing up—pardon the pun—leads on one-eared dogs, or families called Barley in the local area."

"Anything interesting?"

"Nope. Not yet, anyway." With that, he crosses to the drinks cabinet, pulls out the bottle of scotch and, to Guy's astonishment, takes a large pull on it. Sam coughs.

"Right," he says, slapping gently at his chest. "Right." He looks out of the window at the darkened sky. "I think that's good enough, don't you?"

"If not now, it definitely will be by the time we get there."

"Indeed. Do you want to drive?"

Guy knows Sam's had less than him, even with that big slug.

"Probably best if you do."

"Okay. Let's go."

As they turn to the door, Guy's phone pings. A notification from YouTube. His video has processed and is live. He's gone public.

Soon they will know about this.

There's no turning back now.

***

Never, in any of his weirdest dreams, could Guy ever have imagined being so nervous to be on his own street. To be pulling up near his own house; *near* and not *outside* because both he and Sam agreed that it's not a good idea to be parking on Guy's drive. They don't want to draw attention and vehicles at the house of the briefly-accused might be noteworthy to curtain-twitching eyes.

They pull up on the opposite side of the road, about fifty feet back from Larry and Guy's houses.

"Curtains are drawn," Sam says, scanning the houses that are close enough to see Larry's. "I think we're okay. You ready?"

"No."

"You saw a monster eating people inside that house, Guy," Sam says kindly, surprising Guy with both his psychic powers and his tenderness. "There's absolutely no shame in being nervous."

"Do you think it's safe in there?"

"I have absolutely no idea."

"We're interfering again. And putting the video up might mean all bets are off. And we'll be going in without being invited—"

"We'll find out," Sam says kindly, interrupting. If he's scared, he's hiding it well. "And don't forget, even if we do..." He holds up the pocket mirror and hammer. Both men have them. "We have the insurance policy." Guy isn't reassured. It's hard to believe in an *insurance policy* when you have zero clue about the rules. "I *can* go in by myself, Guy."

"No. Plus you don't know exactly where the fake socket is."

"You can tell me—"

"Let's just go." They exit the car.

Larry's house *looks* haunted now, compared to the others; it's not just that it's the only building on the block without a single light on inside, but it's the only one without a porch light on *out*side. Its dark exterior looks like a missing tooth in an otherwise perfect row. Guy fishes the key out of his pocket as they approach the front door. They haven't brought any weapons other than the mirrors. They've both seen the larger monsters. Anything other than a machine gun isn't going to slow them down, and Guy doubts even Sam's contacts could produce something like that.

Guy puts his ear to the cold plastic door, straining to listen. The inside of the house is as quiet as the street in which it stands. Guy, shaking, glances at Sam as he turns the key in the lock. Sam gives an encouraging nod and Guy takes a deep breath as he opens the door a crack. The hallway beyond is jet blackness. They can't turn the torches on until they're inside, as lighting them up out here might draw attention.

An idea strikes him.

FUCK YOU FUCK YOU FUCK YOU, he thinks. He listens for any grunts, any movement from inside. If they're going to wake anything up, he'd rather do it out here, where they can run. Nothing happens.

"*Is everything okay?*" Sam whispers.

But it isn't a church, Guy thinks. *Hearing swearing in Larry's house wouldn't bother them—*

"Yeah," he says, and steps over the threshold into the darkened hallway, squinting hard, heart tapdancing. "*Get in here, come on, I want to get the fucking torches on,*" he snaps. Sam joins him and Guy can't close the door quick enough so he can turn on the torch.

"*Hands,*" Sam whispers.

"*I fucking know,*" Guy hisses, snapping for the third time in thirty seconds but not giving a fuck. He covers the torchlight a little with his hands. This is to make sure they aren't as visible from the outside. They could just turn the lights on, but they'd agreed that was riskier, even if onlooker-spotted torchlight would be more suspicious. Plus, if the porch light was off... ? Guy flicks the nearest light switch to check. No electricity.

"*That's unusual,*" Sam whispers.

"*What?*"

"*Police don't normally cut the power at a crime scene,*" he whispers, "*even when the police presence has left. That's for the families to deal with, and that's not exactly at the forefront of their minds so soon after the event.*"

They stare at each other in the dark.

"*Let's... keep quiet,*" Guy says.

"*Okay. Which way?*" Sam asks, and Guy responds by heading straight down the hallway to the kitchen, listening with bat-like intensity all the way. The torchlight in the dark makes the place feel as if it's been abandoned for years, by humans at least. There's something else in the air, though; a residue. It became that thing's home for a while, after all. The place is tainted. Guy's skin is crawling.

"*This feels wrong,*" Sam says, a quiet worry in his voice that Guy hasn't heard before.

"*I know,*" Guy says and then has to bite down a scream of surprise as Sam grabs at his arm. "*Fuck* me, *Sam!*" he hisses, but Sam shines the torch into his own face so Guy can see him. Sam's gone from nervous to terrified in a space of seconds.

"*Listen to me,*" he says, blinking quickly. "*You know how many crime scenes I've been to?*"

"*No!*"

"*None of them ever felt like this,*" he says. "*This place is bad now. Very bad.*"

Guy freezes.

"*I know,*" he says again.

"*We should come back in the daylight,*" Sam says. "*I was wrong. We shouldn't be here now. It's dangerous. Sod the neighbours—*"

"*I can't come back,*" Guy tells him, and it's the truth. It's taking everything he has just to stand inside this house now and he knows he will never be able to get himself across that threshold again, daytime or nightime, now he's felt what it's like inside. His chest is constricting and it feels like the very walls themselves could reach out and pull him inside them at any second. It's getting worse the longer he stands here. "*We don't have long,*" Guy tells Sam, and his own brow furrows as he wonders why he said that, but Sam nods quickly. Sam clearly knows *exactly* what Guy means.

They *don't* have long. They're being watched.

"*Okay. Okay,*" Sam sputters. "*Let's go, let's be quick.*" He releases Guy's arm and they continue down the hallway. Guy's sweating as they enter the kitchen. He knows that Larry's socket-stash hole is at floor level, just beside the last set of cupboards in the kitchen worktop, and he goes straight to it, squatting down and expecting it to have been removed by the cops, its contents taken away for evidence. It's still there though, looking exactly as an ordinary double power socket should. Sam stands behind Guy, shining his light where Guy is looking.

"*Pass me the drill,*" Guy tells him, his voice breathless and shaky, "*and keep your eyes open. I can see what I'm doing, you just...*" He doesn't want to say *watch my back*. Instead he just puts the thin barrel of his own mini-torch between his teeth and holds his hand out for the drill. Sam passes it to him, Guy slots the drill's screwdriver head into the screw, and pulls the trigger.

Nothing happens.

Guy quickly checks the drill's body to see if there isn't some kind of safety switch on the thing, but there isn't one. He looks up at Sam, who is shining his torch into the darkness beyond the kitchen door through which they just passed.

"*Sam!*" Guy whispers, and when Sam looks his way Guy rapidly pulls the drill's trigger, clicking it over and over, showing that it isn't working.

"*It should be charged!*" Sam hisses. "*You said you charged it!*"

"*I fucking did!*"

He did. He put in on charge before they even left to buy the camera. Even if the fucker was totally flat it's had several hours, easily enough to spin out two screws—

"*Wait... which socket did you use at my place?*"

"*The kitchen one, the one by the sink!*"

"Oh..." Even in the dark Guy can see Sam looking sheepish. *"That one doesn't work."*

"Then why the fuck didn't you—" There's no time for this, even as fear pushes Guy's anger into rage. He jumps up and fumbles for the kitchen drawer containing Larry's own cordless drill, yanking it open. To his great relief, the drill is still there. He grabs it. To his total dismay, nothing happens when he pulls the trigger.

The battery is dead on this one too.

"Fuck!"

He squats back down and jams the drill's bit back into the screw, planning on manually turning the drill around like an awkward screwdriver—why the *fuck* didn't they bring a normal screwdriver, he'd been only thinking about speed, speed—but the drill's barrel just turns independently of its body.

"Fuck!!"

His blood is rising as panic begins to set in. He tries to tell himself that it's just a screw, he can get it out, if he was calm he'd have had it out already, but a louder voice is telling him he really should be panicking a great deal indeed. The air now feels thicker, more *sludgy*, as if it's sliding in and out of his lungs like thin syrup. He smells something and a shiver runs down his back. *"Sam... can you smell ammonia?"* The torch between Guy's teeth lights up Sam's face. Sam's nose twitches. His eyes widen.

"Yes—" he begins, and then they hear the scratching sound.

It's coming from upstairs.

Skri.

Skri-skri.

Skri-skri-skri—

It begins like the tiny skittering of a rodent in-between the floorboards in the ceiling above them and slightly away to the left. For the briefest moment Guy thinks that's all it is, a mouse with a lousy sense of timing, but then the small, single scratching sound doubles, then triples, and quickly it sounds as if fifteen or twenty mice are going to town on the plaster. If it *were* a sudden cluster of mice they would be covering an area about ten feet in diameter, from the sound of it. Guy and Sam are frozen as those myriad scratches quickly go from a tickling of tiny teeth on wood to a clawing, scraping sound, knives scoring a granite carving block. They multiply again and now the noise is deafening. Guy and Sam shine torches on the ceiling, expecting it to give way and reveal something terrible, but it does not.

Skri-skri, ski-skri-skri, ski, ski-ski-skri-skri—

"We have to go," Sam says, staring above him and beginning to back away. Guy begins to stand, agreeing, but to his amazement something inside himself makes him stop.

"We have to get it—"

He twists the drill's barrel open with a yank, pulling the short screwdriver bit free, and his fumbling hands nearly drop it in his haste. His breath is coming in rapid pants and he's scared out of his mind but *if something is coming there's a reason and that means they have to get what they came for—*

"Guy!"

The scratches are slowly but surely starting to come together as one, no longer random razors-as-raindrops-on-wood but becoming a gouging, tearing blade, cutting to a steady rhythm.

SKRIIIIIIIII— SKRIIIIIIIII— SKRIIIIIIIII—

"Go, Sam!" Guy yells, spit flying around the torch barrel in his mouth. *"It's okay, it's okay—"* He can barely get the words out as he squats down once more and slots the tiny drill-screwdriver-head home again, its short stem held between his gloved fingers.

"Don't be fucking stupid!" Sam snaps, frantic. *"Let's go! Something's coming! Something's coming!"*

Guy knows it is. He can hear it. It's so *loud.*

SKRIIIIIIIII— SKRIIIIIIIII— SKRIIIIIIIII—

"You go, you go!"

"Come on! Come on!"

The bit twists in Guy's fingers and it falls to the floor. He desperately pans the torch around, trying to see it. He finds it, snatches it up.

SKRIIIIIIIIIIIIIIIIIIIIIIIIT.

The scratching stops.

THUD.

Something very large hits the ceiling above so hard that the plates rattle in the kitchen cupboards. Guy and Sam exchange a glance, wide-eyed and frozen in place.

Then the sliding sound begins.

It sounds as if someone's dragging a sleeping bag full of lead across the floor above, one so heavy that they have to stop every second or so. Something rustles as it moves, making Guy think crazily of crusty silk. Whatever it is, it's moved from above and to the left to being directly overhead.

It's heading for the stairs.

Sam looks at Guy, eyes wide with terror and sweat beading on his forehead, but he mouths:

Get it.

Guy's amazed that Sam agrees, and the stairs are maybe only ten feet away from where the thing above is but it's moving slowly and if Guy can just get these fucking *screws out—*

The *slumphing* continues above, now several feet away to Guy's right. It's coming.

The first screw starts to spin, the initial turn cracked, and quickly it's out enough that Guy can get the rest of it with his sweaty fingers; he spins it open, pulls it free and goes to throw it away, almost moaning with a combination of relief and frustration, but pauses mid-throw. It might make a noise if he flings it. Then he realises that there's no point in being quiet, as the thing knows they're here, and hurls the screw away.

It pings loudly off something. The *slumphing* stops.

Guy freezes, looking at Sam, who grits his teeth and turns his hand over in the air like a spinning top, his face screwed tight. *Hurry up, fucking hurry up—*

The slumphing begins again and now it's faster.

If it wasn't certain they were here before, it is now. It sounds *eager.*

Slumph—thud, slumph—thud, slumph—thud—

Guy's fingers yank stupidly on the unscrewed edge of the fake socket cover, hoping he can tear the whole thing free, but he can't. He picks up the screwdriver head again, hearing himself gibbering quietly as he slots it into the remaining screw, and begins to hear the thing both through the ceiling and through the kitchen door, its hungry movements echoing down the stairs—

"It's on the stairs!" Sam spits, almost hopping on the spot, his torch trained solely on the open kitchen doorway now, waiting for something unspeakable to lurch into view. *"We have to go, we have to go!"*

"I've nearly got it!" Guy yells, and he nearly has, the screw is coming loose and in a few seconds he's going to have the fake socket cover off, but he can hear that the thing on the stairs is halfway down, the wood is creaking beneath its immense weight. Guy can hear it *breathing.* The sound is low and hitching, like a broken air conditioning unit made of slobbering meat, and Guy realises that if he sees anything like the last time he was here then he will go irretrievably insane but then *yes,* the screw twists free, it's *out* and the cover is falling off and Guy can see inside the hiding-place in Larry's kitchen wall. He snatches the torch out of his mouth and trains it on the hole, the tiny spotlight wavering as his hand trembles.

There's nothing in there except several bags of weed.

"No," Guy gasps, and the dividing wall between them and the creature on the stairs creaks and strains as the thing pushes along it and nears the bottom. He yanks out the cannabis bags, hoping that there will be something hidden behind them, but there isn't. He expects a response from Sam, but Sam has fallen silent. He flings the last bag behind him, tracking the torchlight around the tiny chamber, but there's nothing—

There *is* something. Right at the back, so small and so similar in colour to the aluminium walls around it that Guy nearly didn't see it in his panic.

It's a little silver USB thumbdrive. External storage, just as Sam guessed.

There's no time to marvel at Sam's abilities as Guy jams his fingers into the space, scraping them on the edges of the tiny walls as he almost sobs in relief, and pinches out the thumbdrive. *"I've got it Sam!"* he gasps, slipping the tiny gadget into his pocket and leaping to his feet, but Sam doesn't turn around, perhaps not hearing Guy over the wheezing and creaking cacophony from the stairs. Guy rushes over to him and understands that which Sam already has: the way back out is past the bottom of the stairs. They will have to go past that thing to get outside, if they can.

Guy hears the final wet *THUD* of something reaching the ground floor.

Sam turns to Guy, his face a dispatch of terror.

"We're trapped," he whispers.

Slumph—thud, slumph—thud, slumph—thud. It'll round the doorway in a few seconds. Blind panic tries to seize the wheel of Guy's brain but he catches it just in time, not out of bravery or composure but out of a desperate survival instinct. If he loses it now, they're dead.

"The mirrors!" Guy hisses at Sam. *"Get the mirrors out of the bag!"*

"What if they don't work?!"

"Just fucking—"

But Sam is already slamming the bag down on the counter and rooting through it, and Guy's straining eyes stay on the open doorway, of the rectangle of darkness that is waiting to be filled by—

Sam has stopped and is looking at something behind Guy.

Setting his jaw, Guy slowly turns around to see what other awful thing has arrived, but then sees Sam dart forward to snatch up one of the barstools from the breakfast counter, moving with a speed that can only come from adrenaline in a man of his age and fitness. He runs forward, carrying the stool, and Guy spins around as he gets it. How the *fuck* could he have forgotten? Pants-shitting terror, that's how.

Sam yanks the curtain back, the dark brown ones that in the darkness and fear Guy had forgotten weren't a solid wall, but a covering for the recently-fitted glass patio doors in Larry's kitchen. The new ones, so new Guy forgot they were even there. Sam's desperate guess at what lay behind the floor-to-ceiling curtains was correct as he swings the barstool at one of the glass doors as hard as he can. The noise of one of the double-glazed panels shattering is so loud that it briefly drowns out the approach of the creature in the hallway, but only *one* of the double panes has shattered, so Guy is already snatching up the remaining barstool and running towards Sam before the older man can draw his barstool back for another swing.

"Get out of the way Sam!" Guy screams, and Sam steps back, wheezing hard as Guy hears the thing behind them slap wetly onto the kitchen tiles, finally entering the room. It's breathing hard too, knowing that it's so close to losing its prey at the last gasp. Guy doesn't turn, charging towards the patio and flinging the barstool at the glass with everything he has in him. The stool obliterates the panel, flying straight through and giving them jagged-edged passage into the dark garden beyond. The neighbours have definitely heard *this* but now Guy is far beyond caring. *"Let's go, let's go!"* Guy realises that Sam has frozen in place, the barstool clattering out of his now-limp hands.

He's staring back into the kitchen, at the thing that is bearing down on them.

Guy nearly follows Sam's gaze but he manages to catch himself just in time, the gaping horror of Sam's expression telling Guy that he absolutely should not look. He has nightmares enough already. He yanks on Sam's sleeve, hearing the open kitchen door slam against the wall, a sound followed by a *SHRIIIIP* of something scraping along and a creak as the wooden doorframe is stretched to its limits. Guy hears awful, wet, heavy breathing and a *SLUMPH-SLAP, SLUMPH-SLAP, SLUMPH-SLAP* of terribly large but frantic pursuit. Sam resists Guy's attempts to move him, a dead weight frozen in fear.

"SAM!" Guy slaps him across the face, hard, and the sideways force of the blow tips Sam towards the patio, their feet crunching on huge shards of glass. The two men dash out into the night, their unspeakable-sounding pursuer only feet behind them.

"The car, the car," Sam wheezes, trying to keep up and only just managing. They sprint around the side of the house, back out to the street, and for a moment Guy has a horrible feeling that somehow the creature inside is going to burst through the wall and snatch them back inside, but it doesn't happen.

As they dash breathlessly past the front of the house, they both watch the front door for movement. By the time they reach the car, limbs hollow and chests cramping, they even manage to take a moment to check the houses that are close enough for anyone inside to identify the car or worse, them. Noone is at the front windows. Anyone looking would be peering out the back, towards the source of the noise. Sam collapses against the car, next to Guy. He's clutching at his chest, face pained.

"*Go,*" he gasps, trying to pass Guy the keys but only managing to drop them onto the ground. "*Drive. You... drive.*" Guy bends and grabs them up, swaying badly as he stands up too fast after all the exertion, staggering around the vehicle.

Once inside the car with the doors locked, Guy starts the engine and tries to pull away as quickly as possible without making too much noise. The only sound inside the vehicle is the broken-bellows breathing of two badly out of shape men who have just literally run for their lives. Guy checks his pocket; the thumbdrive is still there.

Sam is trying to say something.

"What?" Guy asks, checking the rearview mirror. He has a horrible moment where he thinks he sees a huge, hunched shadow chasing them down the street; it's just a parked black van.

"It... we heard it *enter,*" Sam wheezes. "It wasn't... there, then it... it *was.* It came *for us.*"

Guy doesn't answer.

"Did you... did you *see* it?" Sam asks him.

***

Chapter Sixteen
More Video Evidence
✳✳✳

Guy and Sam are in a McDonalds. It was the nearest place to stop and sit somewhere that wasn't the car. Neither of them has an appetite but they've ordered a coffee each for two reasons: so they can sit at the corner table and not be disturbed, and so they can discreetly sip some of the bourbon they've poured into their coffee cups. Guy picked some up at the petrol station. Guy's is already finished and Sam is nursing his, looking out of the window. His hands have only just stopped shaking. Guy doesn't think whatever was in that house was the same thing he encountered before. That had legs. The thing that just missed them sounded like it was sliding. Like a worm.

"Why was it allowed to be there?" Sam says quietly, still looking out of the window. "To attack us? Is it because we're involved now? Do you think it knew what we'd come for?"

"Maybe its territorial," Guy offers. "That space is clearly theirs now. There were no incidents with the police there, right? You'd have heard about it. So it *has* to be because we're on the inside of things." Guy drains the last of his spiked coffee and checks no-one's looking before he starts to pour more bourbon into the empty cup. Sam watches him do it. Guy pauses, offering Sam the bottle. Sam nods, offering his cup. Guy tops him up. "We'll leave the car," Guy tells him. "Get a cab, pick it up tomorrow." Sam just grunts. Then:

"Maybe it didn't even know who we were. It was just something sensing others that it *could* attack, that it was allowed to. Like you say: territorial."

"We don't even know if it *was* attacking us, Sam," Guy tells him, voicing an idea he's been bouncing around in his head. "It might have just been coming to see who we were, *what* we were. The old lady-things in the church didn't attack us, after all. They were curious."

"You think?"

- 185 -

"We got out alive, didn't we?"

Sam turns away a little and Guy realises that he shouldn't have said that. The booze is in his bloodstream... but he has to admit to himself that, as disappointed as he is to think it, his opinion of Sam has lessened slightly. Heinrich is supposed to be the professional, but he'd lost it in there. Even though Sam's an old man who looks like a tubbier Anthony Hopkins, he had an air of a John Wayne about him in Guy's mind, a seasoned gunslinger who's been there and seen it. The experience in the house made Guy see that Sam is just as human as he is.

Well, as human as he *was;* Guy has just checked the scales in the McDonald's bathroom mirror, opening his shirt buttons. They've spread even more—nearly all of the other side of his chest is covered as well now—and he thinks the rate is accelerating. He's not sure if he'll even have a week before... what?

The Other Folk. That's what the things in the church said. That's what he'll become. He nearly says it again to Sam but he can already imagine the older man pointlessly saying *you don't know that* in response.

"Okay," Sam says, drumming his fingers on the table. "Let's see if it was worth it. Fire it up."

Guy reluctantly nods. His MacBook is on the table with the thumbdrive inserted, as it has been since they arrived. Neither of them had been in any hurry to open it after what had just happened, and Guy is especially nervous about what he might find.

He opens the USB drive.

Seven folders appear onscreen; five of them are Larry's video diaries for the last few years: 2016 VIDS, 2017 VIDS, all the way to 2020 VIDS. No surprise there. Larry was always getting his phone out, turning the camera to himself, and saying the date and time before documenting what the hell was going on, usually when high. Unfortunately, there are no 2021 VIDS, which would have potentially been very useful. One folder is marked COOK IT which Guy knows is a reference to Larry's tax files. It's the title of the last folder that he's most interested in, however: SHANTIES.

He opens it. Inside are seven Word files, one of which Guy recognises: InProgress4.doc. That's his unfinished article, and Guy knows this because the file Larry sent him has the same name. After that are InProgress5 and InProgress6 but then the motherlode: FinalVersion.doc.

But there's a folder after the word files: Untitled Folder. Guy opens that. There's a video inside, jhsdfjg.mov.

Now there's a title that was written in a hurry.

"Anything?" Sam asks.

"Yeah, hold on." Guy opens the video file.

A frozen image of Larry appears on the screen. He's filmed himself. He looks gaunt and if this is really him then it can't have been recorded that long before he was... before he died. While Guy was on the other side of the world. Larry looks spectral, lit only by his computer screen. Behind him and around him there is only darkness.

Guy has to watch this.

"Sam, uh..."

Guy starts to lose it.

"Are you alright?" Sam asks, that professional tone suddenly in his voice.

"Let me..." Guy sniffs his emotion back and quickly connects the MacBook to the McDonald's wifi. "Let me send the finished article to you. You can get reading it. There's a... there's a video of Larry here. One I haven't seen before. You read, I'm going to..."

"Of course, of course."

The email goes and Sam lifts up his phone to read it. Guy plugs his headphones into the MacBook's headphone jack—he still can't get on with wireless headphones—and braces himself.

He presses play.

Larry's hushed breathing enters Guy's ears. The Blonde Zombie's eyes are up and away, above the camera. He's listening. This goes on for a few minutes. Did he even know that he'd already pressed record?

His eyes dart straight into the camera. Straight into Guy's. This truly *is* Larry, Guy sees it now, and lets out a sigh of relief.

It's not the Monster. It's Guy's best friend.

Just like that, it's suddenly even worse. *This* was how Larry's last days played out.

He looks insane.

"It's asleep," Larry croaks. *"I don't know when I last had any food. I've been..."* He freezes, his eyes darting away again, thinking he's heard something. *"I wanted to leave this recording but I didn't dare, I didn't want to risk... but now its eaten..."* His eyes immediately fill with tears and he covers his face, crying silently. This goes on for a minute and Guy covers his own face too, hoping Sam is focused on the article and not watching. *"I'm alone,"* Larry sobs. *"There's no-one to talk to. I think it's going to eat me anyway. I think it knows if I tell anyone while its awake. I think that's in the rules that it's* allowed *to know. I don't know*

what it wants. I promised not to publish the article, that I'd delete it, but it says it doesn't care what I do. I don't know if anyone will see this. I'm going to put the article in the weed-hole. Maybe the police will find it... after." He looks down, his face threatening to crumble again, but when he looks back up his expression is one of disgusted despair. *"I said I'd join the Other Folk,"* he says, his voice dripping with anger, and as Guy hears the words *Other Folk* again he understands that Larry's anger is directed at himself. *"I gave it that. It didn't even have to ask. I'm so... after I saw what it did to Marianne..."* He suddenly jabs his finger at the screen, defending himself against an accuser inside his own head. *"You'd do the same! You'd do the fucking same!"* His face finally collapses. *"But it just laughed,"* he says. *"It said that isn't an option for me. I think... I think it's going to..."* He pauses. *"We allowed this to happen,"* he says. *"People like me."*

Guy's fingers reach out involuntarily and touch his friend's onscreen face. *Oh, Larry. You didn't know. No-one did.*

"I'm sorry," Larry says. *"I'm sorry. I just want this to end. I hope—"*

He freezes, unbridled terror written all over his face as he looks away. Guy starts to hear the beginning of an all too familiar scratching sound, that awful signal that heralds the arrival of something unspeakable, and then Larry's arm darts above the screen and the camera arcs downward for a split second before the footage ends. He's slapped his laptop closed. Guy does the same, wiping at his face with a trembling hand, and then stands and heads to the Gents once more before Sam can ask any questions. He manages to make it to the cubicle before he throws up into the toilet.

Spitting the last of it out, he drops the seat down and parks himself on it before yanking wads of tissue out of the dispenser. He jams them into his mouth to cover his howls as he sits and bawls it all out. Will he, like Larry, cave in the end, so broken that he will offer to join whatever the fucking *Other Folk* may be? He doesn't even know what that means but the sheer self-hatred in Larry's face tells Guy that its's the worst kind of self-betrayal.

His phone pings. He wipes his eyes clear and pulls the device out of his pocket. It's Nancy:

CHECK IN.

He does, lying:

ALL GOOD.

He'd leave it at that, but now he has his phone in his hand—and isn't that always the way, like an alcoholic saying *I'll just have the one*—he sees he has other notifications and automatically opens his phone.

Then the email title punches out at him:

YOUR VIDEO

The YouTube video. Holy shit. He'd forgotten all about it.

He doesn't bother checking the email and of course goes straight to his YouTube app, excited. A response already means it might have gone viral! Maybe enough people secretly have experienced something similar so—

The results are disappointing.

It's only had 73 views. No comments. He'd been hoping to tap into something immediately; not just people being amazed, either. After what he'd experienced out in the world around him in the last few days—so much in such a relatively small space of time—he'd thought (or hoped) that the video might quickly trigger a wave of shares and comments in the vain of *hey, this is like that time I saw x*, or *that person I heard about who x*. It certainly doesn't look like it has, at least not so far. But then Guy hasn't heard from his social media and SEO buddies and content whores yet, and they should help Guy gain some traction. He needs to give it time… although he knows, as he feels the surface of his chest through his shirt, that's a luxury he doesn't have.

He's also a little relieved though, he has to admit. He'd half expected to find some kind of… he doesn't know, *darkness* in the comments. He quickly opens his Mail app to read the YOUR VIDEO email. Now the initial surprise has calmed down, Guy is half-expecting spam.

The sender's email doesn't give much away—*aliivulgares170@hotmail.com*—and the message inside is brief. It could be a time waster, a conspiracy nut, or one of a thousand other *could bes*, but seeing that it's an actual response from Guy's video sends a tingle up his spine.

He hadn't included any contact details on his website. It felt too risky, somehow. Whoever has sent this has gone out of their way to find out how to contact Guy.

How did this happen to you
Did you agree to something
Did you take something into your home
Did you receive a visit personally directed to you
Did you engage in occult practices

Did you visit eastern Europe recently

Did you get any unusual tattoos that were already designed by someone else

Did you take up a new hobby or interest

Guy thinks about replying. He doesn't. He needs to talk to Sam about it first. He doesn't know who this message is from and he's wary of answering any questions at all at the moment. It looks like whoever sent this knows something about what's going on, as evidenced by the *did you take something into your house* and similar questions... but that could just be a lucky coincidence. All of these questions could just be standard supernatural questions that any ghost hunter or scam-artist medium might ask. Even if they *do* know what's happening, they might not necessarily be on his side.

They don't understand technology very well though, he thinks again. *But they might have people that do.*

He checks the other emails; nothing to do with the video, so he blows his nose and heads back to the table. Sam, to his credit, looks up but doesn't ask questions.

"Sorry about that. It was intense," Guy tells him. Sam waves Guy away kindly.

"Was it... bad?"

"It wasn't fun to watch, no. But Larry mentioned this *Other Folk* again."

"Okay," Sam says, nodding. "I was trying to turn something up about that, but I keep finding dead ends. I've run it up my limited network though so something might shake out yet."

"Good. Are you finished with the article?"

"Nearly," Sam says, sighing and holding up his phone. "I'm into the new stuff now but I have to say... it doesn't look promising."

"No?" Guy's heart sinks.

"No. The part we already read is fairly unchanged, and the only extra part is some moralising about gentrification and his experiences in town talking to locals and what they think of the shanties. Don't judge a book by its cover, yada yada. I'll be done in a few minutes but I don't think there's anything here to go on." Sam sees the expression on Guy's face. "Hey, I didn't know the fellow," he says reassuringly. "There might be some things in here between the lines that you'll notice and I don't. And even if there isn't, it was worth a shot. As you said, maybe you can get it put up somewhere, get it onto a site with some traction, and continue the flushing-out process that we've started, keep stirring things up."

"Speaking of which," Guy says, sitting down and pulling out his phone. "I got an email off the back of the video. Might be nothing, but have a look."

He hands his phone over and as soon as Sam sees the screen, a slow smile creeps onto his face. He breathes in heavily and leans back in his chair, looking satisfied.

"Did you see the email address?" Sam asks, rocking back and forth slightly.

"No?" Guy says, excitement growing.

"*Aliivulgares170@hotmail.com,*" he says. "That's Latin."

"How do you know that?"

"Benefits of a classical education," Sam says. "My appearance may fool you but I was actually somewhat of a scholar back in my day, although I think it's fair to say my parents were horrified when I didn't become a doctor."

Guy is smiling too now, caught by Sam's shift in mood. It feels like they're getting a win. They badly need one.

"So what is it?"

"*Alii Vulgares* roughly translates to... *Other Folk.*"

"No fucking way."

"Uh-huh," Sam grins. "Whoever sent you that email genuinely knows their stuff."

"Or they're working for the bad guys."

"I don't think they send emails, Guy," Sam says. "That email address is a deliberate crumb. They're deliberately using the name of the bad guys as a hidden clue, to see if *you* are the real deal."

"Or it's a trap."

"Email back and say that you'd be prepared to talk on the phone or meet in a public place," Sam says. "See what they say."

"Okay. Now?"

"Hey. It's a lead," Sam says. "Yes, now. I'll finish reading this while you do."

Sam goes back to Larry's article and Guy quickly types up a response:

IT'S COMPLICATED BUT IT SOUNDS TO ME LIKE YOU KNOW A LOT ABOUT THIS. I'D LIKE TO TALK. ARE YOU IN THE UK? WE CAN SPEAK ON THE PHONE OR MEET FACE TO FACE IF YOU PREFER, SOMEWHERE PUBLIC IN THE DAYTIME. LET ME KNOW WHAT YOU THINK. TIME IS OF THE ESSENCE,

HOWEVER, AS I DON'T THINK I HAVE LONG. HERE'S MY NUMBER.

Guy adds his digits but just as he hits send his phone screen changes; Nancy's calling. Guy answers.

"Nancy?"

"Hi," she says. She sounds a little out of breath and Guy is immediately worried.

"Is everything o—"

"I think I might have screwed up," she says, her voice trembling. She's terrified. "I think I might have screwed up really badly."

"What... how have you..." Guy catches himself. Nancy's scared. He needs to stay calm. "It's okay, we'll fix it, don't worry—"

"I don't think... I don't think we can..."

"Tell me what happened, just... tell me."

"My Mum turned up! I was so surprised to see her that I didn't think!"

"Your Mum did something? Why is she—"

"She was on her way back from Birmingham!" Nancy cries. "She'd been to a thing at the bloody NEC and stopped by on her way back to surprise me, and I didn't even think, I just *took* it, and I know you said not to—"

"Stop, stop," Guy says, trying to be as soothing as he can but wanting to scream. *I just took it,* she'd said. *It.* What is *it?* Guy has a horrible feeling that he knows. "What did you take?"

"It was in the middle of her saying hello," Nancy says, voice shaking even more as Guy hears that she is pacing. "So my mind was in two places at once. I *never* would have picked it up myself."

"Nancy, *what is* it?"

"The vase thing."

Oh my God.

"My mum handed it to me!" she cries. "She was on the doorstep with it in her hands and says it looks like the mail's arrived and hands it to me. I was surprised to see her and I didn't think about... it had a tag on with my name on. What do you think this means—"

A gift? It could still be perfectly normal—

"Wait, it came in the post? There might be a return address—"

"She *told* me it came in the post," Nancy says, her voice darkening. "But... I think she just picked it up off the doorstep while she was waiting."

Something obvious finally occurs to Guy.

"So your *mother* brought it in?" he asks her, blood rushing in his temples. "Not you? It might be alright if you didn't—" He hears the eagerness in his voice—he doesn't want to sound relieved at his mother-in-law potentially taking a curse for the team—but in this moment he doesn't care, he would sell Mary to those bastards in a heartbeat if it meant saving Nancy—

Ah, he doesn't mean that, he loves Mary, but if Nancy became a part of this because of Guy—

"Oh my *God,*" Nancy gasps, "you think my mother might be—"

"Not necessarily," Guy says quickly. "I think these things are more personal than that, more targeted." He has no idea if this is true. "Don't panic, don't panic, we don't know what the situation is," he says, standing up and beginning to pace.

"Well my fucking *name* was on it, she said it came in the *post,*" Nancy repeats. "Oh shit..."

"Maybe... maybe—"

"Gimme a second," Nancy says, "Mum's in the other room, this all only just happened a few minutes ago, I'm gonna ask her where it was—" She puts the phone down for a moment, but almost immediately comes back. "We'll figure this out, okay, we'll—"

"I know, go ask, go ask."

She does. She comes back.

"She said it was just sitting on the doorstep. I guess she either assumed it had been posted, or..." She sighs. "It was just left there, I think."

Shit.

"Is it still in the house? Where is it now?"

"In my bedroom, in the cupboard. I mean I say *vase* but it's really small, it's like one of those stem vases you might see a single orchid inside or something."

"Can you take a picture and send—" He stops himself. The picture feels like a bad idea somehow. "Wait, don't. Describe it."

"Okay." This time she takes her phone with her. He hears her walking up the stairs. Her mother asks something muffled in the background. "One second Mum, I just gotta..." Guy hears a door open, and Nancy breathes out as she sounds like she's squatting down to look at the 'vase'. "It's maybe ten inches long, most of it neck. It's made of clay, I think. You can tell its handmade. I mean..." She sighs again. "It's not nice to look at. It's green, like a dark bottle green. There are these patterns all over it. They're... well they're pretty disgusting now I think about it. They're yellow but the way they... they're just not nice to look at. Violent, if that makes any sense. It bulbs out at the bottom which I assumed was for water but maybe this thing isn't actually a vase at all. The top is like... it flattens at the top where it opens..." She sighs. "I don't really wanna say this. I'm not being deliberately gross but if you saw this thing—even my mother insinuated that she thought the same thing—but the hole at the top looks a little bit like a slightly opened vagina. It just does, don't blame me."

"Jesus."

"Yeah."

She accepted it. He's terrified for his wife. But she can't know.

Maybe Mary took the curse—

"Okay. Okay. It could just be a warning," Guy says, trying to convince himself.

"Guy?" She sounds calm, to his surprise.

"Yes?"

"Whatever it is... it shows that what you're doing is already working."

"Well, I suppose that's—"

"I want you to listen to me now. Okay?"

He doesn't respond. He hears her breathing down the phone. It's even, steady.

"Don't stop," she says. "No matter what."

"Nancy..."

"They killed Marianne. Larry too," she says, and there's quiet steel in her voice. "They're doing terrible things. This is bigger than both of us and I'm not scared."

She actually sounds like she means it.

"*I* fucking am!" Guy barks. "Nancy, if they do anything to you—"

"If this delivery has done anything to me, then its already done. We'll wait and see. But you *do not stop*, Guy."

"No way. They're trying to do something to you—"

"And they're *already doing something to you*," she says, interrupting. "You keep going. You expose them. Okay?" Guy has never heard her like this.

"I'll fix it, Nancy," he tells her, talking fast. "I'm gonna make it so they won't have a choice but to stop what's happening to me and anything that might... I'm going to stop it. I'll save us."

"Do you promise? That you won't stop?"

"..."

"*Say yes, I promise I won't stop.*"

"Yes. I promise I won't stop."

"Good. And I don't think this is anything. I think they're just trying to scare you."

"It's working."

"You have to deal with that, Guy."

"How do you feel? Different in any way? Physically? Mentally?"

"No different than usual."

"Your mum?"

"She seems absolutely fine."

"Okay..."

There's nothing Guy can do right now. He just has to keep going, like she says.

"I'm with Sam," Guy says. "We may have uncovered some leads but I'll let you know if anything comes of them. I'm gonna go, but contact me if you notice even the slightest change, okay?"

"Same to you."

"Bye."

"Bye."

He hangs up, feeling numb already, wondering what the hell he was thinking. He thought he had what it takes to go toe to toe with the forces of darkness? Their first counter-move, and he was ready to quit.

This means they know about the video. It means they're starting to go to work.

And maybe... that they're worried?

It could be a bluff; they know he knows what trinkets are. He heads back to the table.

"Everything okay?" Sam asks.

"I'll... I'll tell you later," Guy says, swaying a little as gentle lights dance before his eyes. "I need to take an hour off. Okay? Just... switch off."

"Fine by me," Sam says. "Let's get back. Regroup." He waves a hand at the giant menu that spans the counter. "Eat some food that isn't any of this shit."

***

Guy wishes he could say Sam was right, but he can't. Guy hasn't spotted anything only he might notice in Larry's article. They're back at Sam's place now and Guy is poring over the text for the third time, spotting nothing. The only good news is that the article is, as Sam said, finished. Since they got back Guy has sent it away to a few places, from the long shot—HuffPo, as he has a little inroad there now but certainly nothing that can guarantee acceptance—to the more likely: *weirdly.com*. It's not exactly a heavy hitter but its considerably better than just whacking it on a blog somewhere or worse, just on Facebook. He'll see.

They'd picked up some Chinese food on the way back; their appetites seem to have come on since they left the McDonald's. Guy has hardly been eating since Larry died and perhaps his body was finally protesting. They'd eaten in silence upon arrival and, after Sam moved himself to the sofa to watch TV—they'd both needed to switch off for half an hour or so—Sam actually dozed off and is still out now, Rufus curled up next to him on the sofa. The man certainly can sleep. He'd offered Guy the bottle of bourbon again just before he passed out, who'd gratefully obliged. That, combined with the few shots Guy put away in McDonald's, meant he's now really feeling the booze. He's mildly relaxed—which is a miracle given the last few days—and he can feel that lovely sluggish warm feeling in his neck and face.

He's had his phone and laptop internet switched off since they got back; he had to in order to stop himself from frantically refreshing, waiting for a reply from the mysterious emailer, but there hasn't been one. The frustration became too much and he'd needed to isolate his mind for just a while. Plus, he's been deliberately avoiding checking the YouTube video, knowing how easy it would be to get into the endless dopamine trap of refreshing it. Before he'd disconnected he'd received responses from most of his associates that he'd sent the video link to, saying they are going to be sharing the vid and all asking the same question: how the hell did you do it? Guy doesn't reply but this news is encouraging.

But now curiosity bests him and he opens his YouTube app. He's again surprised and half-relieved to see that the video is actually still up; maybe those things can infiltrate the cops but they can't put a dent in Silicon Valley yet; *not good with technology* and all that. Email notifications start to ping in as the Mail app connects; anything from the *Other Folk* mailer? No, but holy shit...

YouTube comments.

Quite a few of them since they left McD's. Guy's colleagues' shares must have helped. He checks the number of views the video has:

7,365.

Jesus. That's a hell of a jump. Nowhere near viral yet but that's great. The comments:

—HOLY SHIT THIS IS FUCKIN CRAZY DOES ANYONE ELSE GET THIS

—I know how this is done. Derren Brown uses suggestion all the time to make you see things. It's like that. V. cool though, well done.

—Wow!

—This is truly amazing. I don't know how he does this.

Most concerning though is the one at the bottom:

—Am I missing something? Tell me if so. My buddy sent me this and I don't see anything. Apparently I should.

It has a helpful reply underneath from some genius wordsmith:

—u are a fag

Someone couldn't see it? This is a big deal. Of course, Guy assumed from Nancy and the boys in the AV store that everyone could. It never occurred to him that some wouldn't see it at all. This would totally dilute its impact—

Or maybe the debate will help. Guy doesn't know. But it's starting. He gets himself another glass of the brown stuff and browses through other videos, going back to his own every twenty minutes or so, doing exactly what he'd promised himself he wouldn't: refreshing and refreshing.

Not my fault, Guy drunkenly thinks. *System's designed that way. Like they say in tech, if the product is free, you are the product.*

He smirks bitterly. The view count is now at 8,365.

To make matters worse, just like the rats in the early stages of the Skinner Box experiment, he's getting results every time he pushes the lever. Two hours later he's still pushing, the count is up to 11,576, and a considerable amount of Sam's bottle has disappeared down Guy's gullet.

New comments trickling in:

—This is scary as f**k

—This is great, well done sir.

—u suk diks

Guy is shaking a little with excitement. Every time he hits the refresh button he expects to get the message saying *this content has been removed for monstrous copyright violation,* but it doesn't happen. He can't sit still. He gets goosebumps and realises that he will now drive himself insane refreshing the page. He should leave this alone and let it build.

Look how excited you're getting, a sober voice calls to him from another room in his brain, *because for once something is maybe looking like it might go viral. No wonder shit has been happening right under your—*

Sam suddenly stirs on the sofa.

"Mm," he says, wiping his eyes. "Dozed off. What time is it?"

"About ten," Guy tells him, glad of the subject change.

"Spot anything in the article?"

"'Fraid not." Guy hears the slur in his voice.

"Anything from our emailing friend?"

"No, but the video is picking up *fast*, Sam," Guy tells him. "I haven't checked with any of my guys but I think them posting about it wherever has helped."

Sam nods, coughs a little.

"Good, good," he says. "I'm going to make some coffee and try to do some more research into this *Other Folk* business." He stands up, unconsciously scratching Rufus' dozing head.

"Sam, you passed out," Guy says. "If you need to sleep, it's okay to go to bed. Frankly, you're not going to be any good to me if you can't think straight."

"Hm." Sam pauses, looking at Guy. "That, uh… hasn't stopped you though, has it?"

"What?"

"Never mind."

Guy knows Sam is right. He *can't* think straight, he realises. He's not been sleeping the last *few days*, but he hasn't told Sam that.

"Shit," Guy says, suddenly remembering. "I didn't tell you. Nancy got a thing delivered. She took it in the house."

"Nancy—you mean a trinket? She received a trinket?"

"Yeah."

"*What?*"

"Yeah."

"Has anything happened?"

"Not yet," Guy shrugs. "I'm hoping it's a bluff. Those fuckers are *smart*, eh?" He lets out a giggle, a high-pitched noise that he knows is hiding a chasm of fear. Sam breathes out heavily and runs his hands over his head.

"Look, sorry I made the crack about the booze," he says. "You just had even more worries added to your plate. I'd be drinking too in your shoes."

Crack about the booze?

"Can I ask…" Sam says, walking to the kitchenette and turning on the kettle. "Was your divorce amicable? Tell me if I'm being improper by asking. I'm just curious."

"Not divorced yet," Guy mutters, eyeing the bottle once more. "Still married, technically."

"Oh. A trial separation?"

"Oh no. A separation, full separation. I mean... we're *getting* divorced, just isn't finished yet."

"I'm sorry to hear that."

"Yeah. 'S sad," Guy says, leaning back in his chair. "Things just stopped... being the same."

"Did something happen?"

"Like, did I cheat? No. Nothing like that."

"Ah. Just petered out."

"No," Guy says. "There was... it wasn't anything that happened to *us.*"

"How do you mean?"

Guy doesn't want to talk about this.

"*My* brother," Guy says quietly, somehow talking anyway. "Ray. He'd gone through a bad divorce and nobody knew how just how much it affected him. I wasn't..."

He can't admit that ugliest truth: *I was so busy. I kept meaning to call more. I didn't go to see him very much.*

Guy sees it then, sudden and heavily barbed: Ray's body, sitting on his couch. The two empty pill bottles on the floor nearby. Remembering how the words *dude, can you not hear the fucking doorbell* died in his mouth.

Then he's back in Sam's living room, looking at Sam's stupid pudgy face. Why is he talking about this bullshit?

"We lost him," Guy hears himself say. "After that I didn't want... I took it out on Nancy."

"I'm sorry to hear that. Both elements."

Guy shrugs.

"Yeah. After a bit I went to counselling, like a support group thing, but it seemed... I dunno. A bit bollocks. Should have kept going, in hindsight." Guy shrugs again. "Maybe. Things might have different if I—either way. You know. Stuff changed, after that. We had this last big argument... at this party, at Larry's. Came at the worst time. I think that, for her... it was a... you know." Guy can't find the words and settles for drawing his finger across his throat.

"Are you and your wife still close?"

It's a good question. Are they? Kind of, Guy supposes. They care about each other, don't they?

It's more than that for you, isn't it, a voice whispers inside. *She gave up on you though, and rightly so.*

"I guess," Guy replies. "Yeah, I think so... she cares. She's really worried about me right now, at least."

"And you're worried about her, of course."

"Well... yeah." Guy knows it's a case of him having a little blood in his bourbon system right now, but even so, Sam's questions are starting to sound a little weird.

"I see."

Guy suddenly wonders if there's something behind all this. An old familiar feeling starts to stir in Guy's belly as Sam takes the boiled kettle off its mount. Guy begins to wait. He knows something is coming. It always is.

"See what?" Guy asks.

"Nothing," Sam says, and it's a little too quick. "Just... I understand."

"Understand what?"

Now Sam pauses, kettle frozen in the air.

"Is something wrong?" he asks.

"Why are you asking if we're close?"

Sam gives Guy that blank stare for a second, then nods.

"I'm wondering if they can get to you. Via her," he says quietly. "Especially now, if they've done something to her. Are you prepared to see this through?"

"What's that supposed to mean?" Guy's face is getting flush as he feels his anger rising, so strong it surprises him. *Her thoughts were changing,* he thinks. That's what Nowak had said about the cursed woman he knew. The one who became a monster.

"Well... exactly what I'm saying," Sam says, brow furrowing. "I'm not testing you here Guy. I'm wondering if you will finish what you've started if they lean on your wife. It's a relevant question, don't you think?"

"You think I'm going to pussy out?" Guy asks, not answering the question. "Is that it?"

Sams shrugs again.

"Not necessarily, and I wouldn't criticize you if you did," he says. "After this evening, I don't think anyone would, least of all me. But I just want to know where the line is with you."

"Well where is it with *you?*" Guy asks, standing up. His voice is raised and he must have stood up too fast because he's briefly dizzy. "What is this about, is this about *commitment* or something? I don't see you making any videos. I'm the one in the firing line." Sam doesn't say anything. He only stands there holding his fucking kettle like a silly old cunt. "I'm the one putting myself out there to expose these fucking things, to *do* something about it. What are you doing?"

"Guy," Sam says calmly. "You're getting angry about something I'm not saying. I know this has been stressful and you had ways of talking to your friends that they may have been comfortable with, but I'm not okay with being spoken to in that way."

"But you *are* okay with using me to get revenge for your fucking brother?" Guy spits, and Sam's forehead goes suddenly slack. Guy doesn't stop. "At least be *honest*. Don't play the moral card here. I saw you in Larry's house. You absolutely shit yourself, I *saw* it. Big man when it comes to dealing with other people burning to death, but if it's shit that involves you? You *shit* your old man diaper. So don't talk like you'd put yourself out front the way I am."

Silence except for Guy's ragged breathing, he realises. Sam's poker face is back.

"So you're doing this for everyone else, are you?"

"Good question, coming from the guy that does wonderfully altruistic things for a living like tracking down cheating husbands," Guy snaps back.

Sam's eyebrows raise.

"I was a police officer before my... current career," he says. He pauses for a moment, considering something. "*Aah...*" he sighs, nearly letting it go... but then gives it to Guy. "You keep people distracted for a living. Congratulations—" Sam stops himself.

"What? *What?*" Guy barks, sensing a moment to be righteous. "What were you going to say then? *Say it.*"

"Doesn't matter."

"No, no. Say what you were gonna say. I'm waiting."

"Yes," Sam says cooly. "I believe you. You're that kind of person, I think, a kind I have close personal experience with. I recognize it."

"Yeah? What kind of person is that?"

"The kind that's *always* waiting for somebody to *say something.*"

He begins to open the cupboard, presumably to get a mug, and then suddenly slams it shut angrily. "No," he says. "I'm not doing this in my own fucking house. Go to bed, Guy. Sleep it off."

Guy rediscovers his voice, and it's very loud. *Here it is now*, he thinks, *here we are.*

"Don't fucking tell me to sleep it off you old prick!" Sam jumps slightly in surprise. "Go have another fucking *nap* yourself!"

Guy feels it then; it's almost a physical sensation as he crosses a line. This is *Sam's* house, his *home*, and Guy is talking to him like... *wait*, wait. Guy's pulse is throbbing in his temples. He's really drunk, he realises, *really* drunk. He would never—

He just did.

He puts his hand on his face. "*Uhh...* shit. Shit. Sam... that was too much. I'm exhausted, I'm drunk, I'm beyond stressed—"

"And they always have an excuse, too," Sam says to the door as he makes his way towards it. "The booze, the stress. The *curse*, even." He pauses and faces Guy, and what makes Sam's words even worse is look on his face. He isn't even angry. "Did you ever think that the excuses are empty? That maybe this is just *you?*"

Guy feels like he should be exploding with anger at this but for some reason he can't. It's pity he sees in Sam's eyes.

"I'm going to go for a walk," Sam says, turning away. "I need to be away from you. I'm not sure about what I'm saying and I don't think you should be either. You know where the spare room is. Come on, Rufus." He picks up the dog's lead and Rufus, yawning, stretches creakily and shakes his coat.

"Where are you gonna go," Guy asks, and it's concern. "It's late—"

"I'll find a 24 hour place, cab it, whatever," Sam says icily. "Come *on*, Rufus." The dog finally reaches him and the pair disappear into the hallway, Sam's words gently chilling the air behind him. "I'll do some research on the *Other Folk*, like I said. Just not here. I'll be a while." Guy hears the front door open as he feels his head throb. There's a pause before Sam adds: "Don't worry."

Then they're gone.

***

Guy is in bed with his laptop.

He nearly took the bottle with him but—after taking a swig directly from it before putting it back in Sam's cupboard—he left it downstairs.

He has the freestanding mirrors all around the bed, the ones he bought for his hotel room. He brought them here in his car when he first came... when was it? Today?

He has the baseball bat with him and he's also brought Sam's kitchen carving knife for good measure. He also has the five electric lamps he bought on his trip out earlier, blazing away, as well as the main room light. He's taking no chances. Despite the brightness and the fucking *constant fear*, exhaustion and booze is making it so that, for once, he can't keep his eyes open. Sam's been gone about... an hour? Guy didn't check the time when Sam left and it feels like ages since the older man headed out.

He's not, to his amazement, thinking about monsters.

He's not even thinking about the scales on his body, the ones that have spread even more since he was in McDonald's. He had glimpsed them by accident when he undressed for bed—he's surrounded by mirrors, after all— and the upper half of his torso is now entirely changed (*why isn't it on my face yet,* he'd thought, *my eyes—*)

He's not thinking about the argument with Sam.

He's thinking about the party argument with Nancy.

He has Larry's video diary folder open on the laptop. He knows the date he's looking for.

There's only one video file timestamped with it. His finger hovers over the mouse, ready to click.

He's been staring at the file for a while. It's the one from Larry's birthday party.

He remembers Larry showing this video to him about a week later, after the incident.

I think you need to see this mate, he'd said. Just him and Guy, at Guy's place, back when it was his and Nancy's place. She'd been at work.

Larry had shown him. Guy remembers thinking *I'll do something about that. See someone. It's Ray. It's not been the same since Ray. I'll fix it.*

He'd tried. He'd at least been to that hippy therapy group, hadn't he?

The file sits there. Guy's finger still hovers.

He closes the laptop's lid and stares at the ceiling.

Was Sam right?

Was Larry right?

It's not Guy's fault about Nancy. His brother *died.*

It's not his fault about his job. He has to make a *living.*

He's trying to fix it. He's trying to fucking—

—save

Oop. Nearly went there. Didn't even take the sleeping pills...

... and again.

Nearly—

***

There's something in Guy's bedroom with him. He just heard it.

He doesn't know what time it is but something's woken him up and it wasn't the front door. He might have imagined it—

Sobering adrenaline shoots through his skin as he jerks bolt-upright in bed, realising something terrifying:

All the lights in the bedroom are off.

It could be a power cut—

With an accordion for lungs Guy tries to check, squinting to try and make out the red-light standby glow of the TV on the opposite side of the bedroom. If the power is on, the standby light will be—

Could Sam have come in and turned the lights off—

It's difficult to see the little LED dot because the black rectangular shapes of the mirrors around the bed are blocking his view. He leans all the way sideways to see around them, bent double with tension from feeling so *exposed* as the red dot finally appears in his sightline.

This isn't a power cut. That's when Guy finally notices that feeling in his stomach, the same one he had with the things in the church, except now it's much more immediate.

Something is in the room and it's turned off the lights.

Something that made a noise as it moved, waking him up. He's been awake about seven seconds, so that means whatever did it is still here. Close by. Silent. Still.

His breath shivers its way out as Guy listens in the dark. The spare bedroom is large and the only furniture in there is the bed and a chest of drawers with the TV on top of it. Lots of space. Easy for something to move around in the blackness. It could be right by the bed. It could be sitting in between two of the mirrors, even.

He commands his right hand to slide under the pillow and grip the knife. His ears are almost burning as they try to hear any movement. *Breathing—*no. Only his own.

They can't come here, there are rules—

The thing in the church. It said they'd visit.

Guy can't feel the knife. He tries not to panic, feeling for it with greater and greater urgency; his stomach turns over with dread as he understands that the knife is gone. Something has taken it while he slept. His left hand darts for the baseball bat by his side, the movement loud in the darkness as the sheets flap but he's starting to panic and yes, the baseball bat is gone too.

Oh my God. Oh my God. Oh my God—

Guy waits in the darkness, blind and unarmed with something lurking nearby.

A rustling sound comes from the direction of the bedroom door. Guy flinches. The sound is faint and slow but the amount of time it takes implies something big is turning on the spot. Guy wonders if it's *trying* to make noise, to let him know it's there. Then there's a thud— a dull one, as if something very heavy just took a step—and then there's the rustling sound again. This time it sounds closer and Guy kicks his legs free of the sheet, sounds be damned, and he's up on his knees, fists balled, *freeze* giving way to *fight* now that there is nowhere for him to go.

"Fuck off!" he screams. It doesn't sound defiant or brave but at least it's something. *"Fuck off! Get out! You aren't welcome here! You aren't allowed here!"*

If Sam is in his bedroom, then he heard that for sure.

Silence. Guy's breathing is so heavy now that he's straining to hear anything else. There's a bedside lamp on the nightstand but he'd have to put his hand out past the wall of mirrors to reach it. The thought of doing so comes to him clearly: he would put his hand out only to feel something wet and muscular coil around it in the dark, something that would then grow teeth and bite down into his flesh—

That *thud* again and now it's right by the bed. Guy leaps to his feet and for a terrifying moment as the mattress bounces under him he thinks he's going to over balance and topple off the bed, falling through the mirrors into a world of broken glass and unseen horror. He stays upright.

"FUCK OFF!" he repeats impotently. *"GET OUT! GET OUT!"*

"You're frightened. You're alone."

The voice makes every remaining hair on Guy's body rise up. It's supposed to be a man's voice, one without rasp or growl or hiss. What's so awful is that it's *supposed* to be human and yet no human could ever sound this way. It's somewhere between hearing a low bit-rate digital recording or a Zoom conversation over slow internet—like hearing a voice generated by text to speech software, one meant to be soothing but still somehow alien—and a voice that's been slowed down by ten percent. Guy thinks for a second that this is it, the breaking point: he's finally been driven mad.

Then he remembers that whatever it is *wants* him to be frightened.

Something, somewhere very deep inside him, sends up a faint shout:

Come on then.

Yet he can't say it—

"We're going to come back, Guy," it says. "We're going to *keep* coming back."

"Do it," Guy hears someone else say, and to his total amazement he realises it's him. He sounds terrified but the words are suddenly *there! "Fucking do it."* Just saying it is breaking the spell. "You have my knife. You have my bat. I'm defenceless. I bet you're good in the dark too, that's where you like to be, right? So you can see me just fine right now while I'm blind. So do it."

Silence.

"Do it!"

More silence. Then laughter, surprisingly light and high pitched. It sounds like a giggling baby, only with that weird bad-digital filter.

"Laugh all you want!" Guy barks. His heart is galloping but he's starting to feel more confident. "You can't do *shit,* can you? That's probably the only way you're allowed to be in here! You—"

Something lands on the bed with a soft *whump.*

Guy cries out and leaps away so hard that his back hits the wall, but he pushes himself back up—

Fuck this—

He lunges sideways, diving onto his stomach, and grabs the lamp's switches. Four of the five don't respond—has it unplugged them, or broken them—but the fifth comes on, the *shittest* one that only gives off a dim light, one further obscured by the mirror in front of it. The room is still gloomy but at least Guy can see, looking towards where he thinks the voice was last coming from, but as the light blooms there is a sudden sliding, *rushing* sound moving away from the bed. There is a very short hallway from the bedroom door into the bedroom itself—created by the room's internal ensuite bathroom—and that is still fully in shadow. The thing has now moved inside that short hallway, tucked around the wall enough to be hidden in the dim light— *no,* Guy can see the black edge of something standing there. It goes all the way up the wall to the ceiling. He's terrified but... it had moved away *to stay unseen...*

He was right.

It can't do anything.

He looks at the foot of the bed. His knife and baseball bat are lying there, both broken in two. The remains of the bat look charred, as if whatever had gripped it burned upon contact. He doesn't think he needs them though. It's just more mind games.

"Get out," Guy says again, voice still trembling. More laughter in response. "This is *our place*," he says, desperately trying to think of the right language, to talk like the little woman in *Poltergeist.* "You have no power here, no right—"

"You are ours."

"Not yet I'm fucking not! If you can do something, do something! Or get the fuck *out!*"

How did it get in? Guy locked all the doors. Can they just appear? Can they—

"We see what you are doing," it says. "*It... will... not... work.*"

"Bullshit!"

"We have a message for you."

"I'm not interested!"

"I have already delivered it. It's downstairs."

Guy is stunned. What has it done? What message?

"... what message?"

"Go and see for yourself."

"What is it? What is it?" There's no answer. Guy moves closer, trying to see more than that dim outline. "What's the message?" Nothing. "Tell me!"

"Downstairs. *Go and find out.*"

He'd have to enter that darkened archway—have to pass by it—in order to so. It knows he won't.

That laugh again. Where the fuck is Sam?! For a moment there Guy felt like he was winning. Now for every moment he doesn't get off this bed and back up the words *you can't do anything,* he loses.

Show them, he thinks. *Go and see!*

The moment has faded. Guy knows there is no way he's going to pass that thing. It's waiting.

"What did you do to Nancy?" he asks.

No answer. The thing just stands there.

... now what?

Guy sits on the bed. His phone is on the night stand, well within reach, and he is suddenly convinced that the *message* is Nancy's brutalized and slaughtered remains. Not taking his eyes off the outline behind the wall, Guy reaches over and picks the phone up. He frantically thumbs out a text. He doesn't want the thing in the room to hear a verbal conversation.

ARE YOU OKAY?

The reply comes back straightaway even though it's the middle of the night. Guy knows she's left her phone on in case he calls.

YEAH. WHY?

—CAN YOU SEND ME A PHOTO TO PROVE IT?

30 seconds later a bleary-eyed, front-flash-lit picture of Guy's normal-looking wife arrives in his phone, along with a text:

HERE. WHAT'S HAPPENED? I'M WORRIED.

—SORRY. I JUST HAD A REALLY BAD DREAM.

IS THAT THE TRUTH? I DON'T BELIEVE YOU.

What can he tell her? That there's a fucking monster in his room? That would just—
He'd said he was done lying.
He tells her the truth.

—THERE'S SOMETHING HERE. ITS IN THE ROOM WITH ME. IT SAYS ITS LEFT A MESSAGE DOWNSTAIRS. IT CAN'T TOUCH ME THOUGH. I EVEN DARED IT TO AND IT DIDN'T. DON'T CALL AS I DON'T WANT TO MAKE ANY MORE NOISE. IT'S STILL HERE NOW.

HOLY SHIT. ARE YOU SURE YOU'RE OKAY? IT DEFINITELY CAN'T HURT YOU? I WANT TO CALL YOU. CAN YOU TALK?

He sees the curtains are open. The time is just after two am. The sun won't be up for a good five hours. When dawn breaks this room will fill with light. Sam still isn't home?

— IT WOULD PROBABLY BE OK BUT I JUST WANT TO SIT HERE QUIETLY. IT'S TRYING TO SCREW WITH ME AND I'M GOING TO WAIT IT OUT.I'M GOING TO WAIT UNTIL THE SUN COMES UP. DON'T CALL THE POLICE. I DON'T WANT TO RISK STUFF GOING DOWN HERE LIKE IT DID AT LARRY'S HOUSE. I DON'T THINK IT CAN BE HERE WHEN THE SUN COMES UP. IT DOESN'T LIKE LIGHT. I'M ALRIGHT. PLEASE DON'T FREAK OUT.

There's a long pause until she replies:

WHAT DOES IT LOOK LIKE?

—I CAN'T SEE IT PROPERLY BUT IT'S REALLY BIG.

He'd take a photo and send it to her but he'd need to use the flash to make it visible and he doesn't want to push it. All the while the thing remains standing around the corner. The urge to piss begins to build with increasingly brutal force in Guy's bladder.

OH MY GOD, Nancy texts. GUY I'M SO WORRIED.

—*YOU'RE* WORRIED? HANG ON, I HAVE TO FIND OUT WHERE SAM IS. GIVE ME A MINUTE.

He finds Sam's number in his Contacts list.

—SAM. WHERE ARE YOU? IF YOU'RE IN YOUR ROOM, DON'T COME OUT. DON'T CALL, JUST TEXT. IF YOU'RE STILL OUT SOMEWHERE, I DON'T THINK YOU SHOULD COME HOME. THERE'S SOMETHING HERE. IT'S WATCHING ME. I'VE TALKED TO IT. I THINK I'M SAFE, DUE TO THE RULES OR MY MIRRORS OR WHO KNOWS, BUT MAYBE IF YOU COME BACK TO THE HOUSE IT CAN HURT YOU. IT WANTS ME TO GO DOWNSTAIRS AND SEE SOMETHING. IT DOESN'T SEEM TO LIKE THE LIGHT SO WHEN THE SUN COMES UP IT MIGHT LEAVE. I'M OKAY.

The little dots shimmer at the bottom of his Messages app, showing him that Sam's replying immediately.

DON'T MOVE. STAY WHERE YOU ARE. THE SUN WILL BE UP BY 7:30. DID YOU INVITE IT IN?

Guy starts to type OF COURSE I FUCKING DIDN'T but then hazy memories of their argument resurface. Did he really talk to Sam like that inside his own—
Monster in the room, MONSTER IN THE ROOM—
Okay, okay.

—NO. I WOKE UP AND IT WAS HERE. IT HAD TURNED OFF ALL THE LIGHTS AND BROKEN MY WEAPONS WHILE I WAS ASLEEP. ALL IT WILL SAY IS THERE'S A MESSAGE DOWNSTAIRS.

BLOODY HELL. OKAY. STAY CALM. IF IT COULD HURT YOU IT
WOULD HAVE, SURELY.

—WHERE ARE YOU?

I WALKED ALL THE WAY BACK TO THE MCDONALD'S, ONLY
PLACE OPEN. BEEN DOING RESEARCH. DO. NOT. MOVE. MY
CAR IS STILL HERE SO I'LL SLEEP IN IT UNTIL SUN-UP.

—DID YOU FIND ANYTHING?

THE OTHER FOLK STUFF IS A DEAD END. WE NEED TO GET
HOLD OF YOUR MYSTERY EMAILER.

The emailer! Guy thinks. *Check your email, maybe they replied—*
Could that be why this thing has come to pay him a visit? To scare him out
of getting close to the truth? Constantly glancing at the lurking thing in the
shadows—and not really believing he's doing it—Guy checks his email.
There it is! *Aliivulgares170@hotmail.com!* They replied!
... but also a shit ton of emails from YouTube?
One thing at a time. He opens the email—

WHAT'S HAPPENING?

Nancy.

—ONE SECOND

The email reads:

COME AND SEE ME. I WON'T TALK ON THE PHONE. IN
PERSON IS SAFER. I KNOW YOU'VE PROBABLY LEARNED A
THING OR TWO ABOUT QUESTIONS AND ANSWERS AND
CONFIRMATIONS ETC, SO HERE IT IS IN WRITING: I HEREBY
RELEASE YOU FROM ANY OBLIGATION OR DANGER AND
NEITHER I NOR ANY OF MY ASSOCIATES HAVE POWER,
CLAIM OR DOMINION OVER YOU, YOUR FRIENDS, OR YOUR
FAMILY. THAT SHOULD BE GOOD ENOUGH BUT YOU
UNDERSTANDABLY WILL EXPECT A LOOPHOLE. IT'S UP TO
YOU. I THINK I CAN SHOW YOU A WAY OUT, IF YOU WANT IT.
YOU SEEM TO BE COURTING TROUBLE AND TRYING TO BE A
HERO BUT YOU ARE WASTING YOUR TIME. YOU SHOULD
KNOW WHAT YOUR OPTIONS ARE BEFORE YOU GO ANY

FURTHER DOWN THAT ROUTE. HERE IS MY ADDRESS. IF YOU WANT TO DEFINITELY CATCH ME, MAKE SURE YOU VISIT IN THE NEXT 24 HOURS.

There's a timeframe on it? The address follows: 110 Appledore Avenue, Nottingham. Holy shit. Is he going to go? Really? He texts Sam:

—DON'T WORRY ABOUT DOING ANYMORE RESEARCH, THE EMAILER'S REPLIED. THEY WANT ME TO MEET WITH THEM. THEY'VE SENT ME THEIR ADDRESS. GET TO SLEEP, IF YOU CAN.

ROGER THAT, Sam says. BE CAREFUL. DON'T GO BACK TO SLEEP. IT MIGHT NOT BE SAFE.

—DON'T WORRY, THERE'S NO CHANCE OF THAT.

YouTube comment emails—
He goes straight to the YouTube app itself rather than his emails. He can just scroll down them there rather than click through different—
The video is gone.
He looks up at the shape standing in the shadows. It hasn't moved a fraction. Guy goes back to his Mail app and rapidly scrolls through it to try and see—
There. CONTENT VIOLATION is the vague term YouTube have auto-emailed in their takedown notification.
They got it taken down... but he sees how many comments emails he has. Hundreds.
But that won't be—
The Dropbox link. Maybe some other people re-loaded it, like he asked in the video? He quickly types MAGIC NECK into YouTube's search bar.
The thumbnails of five identical videos appear at the top of the list. People have been spreading it. They're already getting hits in the thousands. Guy doesn't know how long they'll be up either but it's a sign, a thin sliver of hope that his plan—that so many people would be reposting that YouTube couldn't keep up with them all without being extremely vigilant—will play out. Plus, especially with a video like this, if they kept taking it down without any real reason—*content violation*—that would raise questions and whoever is making this happen would have to stop. A guy talks about secret monsters in a video and YouTube keeps taking it down? The Tinfoil Hat crew would be all over it like Red Weed on Victorian London.

He continues to read through the comment notification emails that he can no longer reply to now the video is down:

—*Fake fake fake*

—*I want to dismiss this but I can't. This has really freaked me out. I don't know how you could have done this. There was nothing there and then I went back to the start of the video and it was there all along. Who else did this happen to? Anyone? It can't be just me. I don't know what's going on.*

—*I don't get it it's just a guy with something stuck on his neck its there right from the start of the video I dont know what your all talking about*

—*Immigrants did this to you*

—*Can you do my wife while I watch and you turn her into a snake*

There's a lot of comments like the second one. Those are the ones Guy was hoping for, the ones where people couldn't see anything at first and then they could. To everyone else—the people that couldn't see anything and the people that could see the scales right away—the amazement must seem laughable. Either way, Guy's original video is down now and the future of that piece of footage is now in the hands of other people.

One comment email in particular catches his eye:

365,378 views, someone had said. *Can we get this to 400K? This shit needs to be seen.*

It's official. Now Guy has gone viral. *Momentum*, Larry's favourite word. Guy has momentum.

"You can't stop this!" Guy suddenly barks at the partially-hidden thing. "Is this the real reason you're here? We've got you worrying?!"

No answer.

GUY!?

Nancy.

—I'M OKAY. HANG ON, I'M CHECKING SOME STUFF ON MY PHONE.

The websites you sent Larry's article to, he thinks. *A lot of them were in the states, hell, California's eight hours behind us. Maybe they replied?*

Feeling feverish, Guy scrolls through the hundreds of YouTube emails trying to see the message he's looking for: HuffPo. It's a *no* from them even though he said they can have it for free. They say they're not interested in the subject matter, but Guy thinks it's more to do with the fact that Larry, the original author—Guy credited him, of course—was technically a crackhead that got killed by his pet bear. They must have done some background checking, which is surprisingly rare in Guy's field, but he guesses HuffPo doesn't take chances.

But *Weirdly.com*, the relative minnow: turns out that they love what he has to offer. The backstory of the original author was, apparently, a help with getting it accepted. This is another win.

"You're *fucked!*" Guy barks, realizing he's still pretty drunk. Perhaps he'd be losing his mind right now otherwise. "That's why you're here! You might not know shit about computers but you know when you sense a disturbance in the force, don't you? *Ha!*"

Again, no answer. Guy can't hear it breathing. Maybe it doesn't need oxygen.

Ciara's email from *weirdly.com* writes that not only is the article scheduled for posting tomorrow (as with HuffPo, Guy'd told them they could have it for free and waived all his rights) but it seems his additional ploy worked: he hadn't tried it with Huffpo and the rest as it just seemed a little too out-there for them, but Guy knows *weirdly.com*'s content. He'd considered mentioning some theories to them about the existence of monsters when he'd sent the initial contact email about Larry's article (their demographic is more open to that kind of thing) but then decided to go the whole hog. He sent them a link to Larry's article too.

Ciara is telling Guy that they are going to give it the feature treatment. This is noteworthy as it's not normally something they do (even a site as small as them gets bombarded with video links to feature every single day). She says that they think it could be the new *what colour is this dress* debate.

This is absolutely fantastic news because of the way the media cycle's content chain works: the big fish pick from, and link to, the smaller fish. The chain feeds upwards. If you can cause a stir at the bottom those sites are *always* scouring for hit content and even better, *weirdly.com* is maybe only a notch or two from being mid-level. If they feature the article or the video and they do big numbers? *Then* the big boys come calling. The article might end up with HuffPo anyway.

This a *great* head start. Guy looks at the shadow in his room and wonders if it is, in fact, cowering rather than remaining hidden.

No. He thinks that's a little optimistic... but even so. Something is changing, and it's not just the skin on Guy's body.

—I THINK THE PLAN IS WORKING NANCY, he texts. I THINK THE STUFF I'M TRYING TO EXPOSE THEM WITH IS RESONATING. THEY MIGHT BE WORRIED.

The trinket! The thought is an immediate cattle prod in his mind. *They sent Nancy a—*

—HOW DO YOU FEEL? he adds. HAS ANYTHING HAPPENED?

He hits send and immediately feels like a bonehead. That wasn't very subtle.

NO, she writes back. IS IT STILL THERE?

—NO, he lies. IT'S GONE.

IS IT REALLY? She replies.

—NO, he admits. He never was very good at lying to her.

CAN I CALL YOU?

Guy'd like her to. He really, really would.

—I'M NOT SURE THAT'S A GOOD IDEA IF THEY SENT YOU SOMETHING

He pauses, unsure how to finish the sentence. What is he worried about? If they sent her something... then what?

—I JUST DON'T WANT THIS THING TO HEAR YOUR VOICE, he writes. JUST HAVING YOUR VOICE IN THE ROOM EVEN. I DON'T WANT YOU ON THEIR RADAR AT ALL.

THAT'S STUPID, she says, with the usual Nancy bluntness. BUT YOU'RE THE ONE DOING ALL THIS SO I'M GOING TO TRUST THAT YOU KNOW WHAT YOU'RE TALKING ABOUT. CAN YOU STAY TEXTING AT LEAST?

—I THINK I'M SAFE NANCY. IT'S JUST STANDING THERE. GET YOURSELF TO SLEEP.

THERE'S NO WAY I'M GOING TO BE ABLE TO DO THAT NOW GUY. I'LL STAY UP WITH YOU.

—OKAY. IS YOUR MUM OKAY TOO?

Nancy feels close. Guy feels warmed and saddened. He's less frightened of the monster in his bedroom. He suddenly wants to talk about Larry's party, about that night. He wants to tell her yet again that he's sorry, that she was right, that she was always right. He nearly puts those thoughts into text. Instead, he makes a joke. A joke, a denial, or a distraction. Those things are always so much easier:

—SO WHAT ARE YOU WEARING, he sends.

A SCOWL, she writes back, IF YOU KEEP THAT SHIT UP.

They text about nothing, the length of time between messages slowly getting longer and longer and Guy knows she's fighting off sleep. Hours pass. Sam pops up now and then—EVERYTHING OKAY—and Guy tells him it is. Looks like Sam can't sleep either, although that might be due to the discomfort of a car seat.

The sky outside begins to lighten. So do the walls opposite the window. Guy looks for the thousandth time at the visible edge of the thing in his bedroom but still can't see it; he will soon. *A photo,* he thinks, holding up his phone, *be ready to take a photo when it's light enough, no flash needed.* A delirious thought hits him: he could put it on Instagram, a far bigger draw than Barkley Barley—

Realization suddenly smashes him between the eyes like a scaly fist, striking him so hard that he drops his phone in surprise. He stares at it as if it were a stick of unexploded dynamite. The idea is loose; he doesn't know how the woman in that terrible field fits into it, her response, the phone inside the boundary, what it meant... but he knows what she was responding *to.* It wasn't the one-eared dog, not Barkley Barley.

Wake up, the homeless man had said. Guy's own excitement at his video going viral. *We allowed this to happen,* Larry had said, *people like me...* but Guy now understands Larry hadn't just meant *ordinary* people. He'd meant, Guy realises with a chill, *specifically* people like him... and Guy as well.

Larry was right. They'd allowed this to happen.

Ask it, he thinks, and as he looks up at the monster just in time to finally make out the texture of its 'skin' in the growing sunlight—he'd expected to see scales, they would like that irony, sending one of his own future kind to visit him—he thinks *suede, its skin looks like suede* before it disappears.

He grabs the phone, mouth dry, and texts Nancy:

I THINK IT'S GONE. I WAS RIGHT ABOUT THE SUNLIGHT.

This time the text comes back immediately:

ARE YOU SURE? CAN YOU CALL ME NOW?

He does. Nancy's voice is cracked and she sounds exhausted.
"It's gone?"
"I think so," Guy says. "I'm gonna go check downstairs Nancy. Hang on."
He quickly texts Sam to say IT'S GONE and doesn't wait for a reply as he moves past the mirrors. In his haste to go and check the rest of the house, his attention slips and he unintentionally catches a glimpse of his reflected torso. He quickly turns away, putting a hand to his stomach to check: yes.

The scales have spread onto his stomach. Guy thinks they *are* speeding up.

He'd dared hope the existence of the video would somehow slow it down, calling their bluff to the point that they couldn't have him turn, but it appears to be having the opposite effect. *The woman who was turning said she was looking forward to it by the end,* Nowak had said.

"Nancy, I'm gonna put you on speaker with the phone in my pocket. I want my hands free."

"Okay," she says, sounding alert and fearful. "*Jesus,* okay. Okay."

He briefly pumps himself up and then throws the bedroom door open.

There's nothing there.

"... I think it's definitely gone, Nance."

"Thank God... are you going downstairs?"

He is. It's time to go and see what kind of message has been left for him, if it's still there at all.

But first...

"One sec, Nancy." He mutes his microphone. Before he does anything, he's having a massive piss.

***

Part Three

Waking Up

Chapter Seventeen
Communication
***

Eventually, Guy makes it downstairs. He checked all the rooms upstairs before he descended. The thing said the message was downstairs but Guy knows he can't trust them. Nancy has remained on the phone all the while.

The entrance hallway is clear. Only the living room left. Taking a deep breath, Guy kicks wide the partially-open living room door and actually jumps inside, bracing himself to see something terrible. There's nothing in there either. The kitchenette seems empty too... ridiculously, he checks all the cupboards and drawers to be on the safe side.

The back garden? Just because the thing said *downstairs*, that doesn't necessarily mean that the message is inside the house. That'd be bending the English language a little bit but Guy wouldn't put it past—

Goddamn. He's tying himself up in knots to try and stay one step ahead of them. He heads outside, checking the garden and the shed, and the front path too. Nothing.

"There's nothing here, Nancy," he says, pulling out his phone. "I think they were screwing with me, full stop."

"Okay," she says. "I'm gonna put my phone on charge a sec and use the bathroom myself. I'm on six percent. I'll call you back in five."

"Okay." She hangs up. "So what the fuck..." he mutters to himself, looking around. He *hopes* he's muttering to himself.

Wait. There's a piece of paper on the bookshelf.

It's folded in half, propped up like a birthday card. Guy sees it and that feeling returns in his stomach. He knows that paper is bad. He mustn't touch it. The thought of a creature that big neatly half-folding this piece of paper is bizarre. Maybe it was just the delivery boy.

Delivery monster.

Is he beginning to be less afraid? Certainly, by the time that thing had finally left, he'd gone from pants-shitting terror to nervousness and even annoyance.

He'd felt so sure it couldn't hurt him.

A quick root around in Sam's kitchen drawers and Guy finds what he's looking for: a pair of cooking tongs. If he never touches the letter, then he never accepts it, right?

He intends to read it, *then* call Nancy back, picking it up gingerly with the tongs, turning it over so he can see the insides as the outside is blank. The paper is yellowed and thick. It isn't parchment—like Guy had half expected—but it's textured and official looking, the way the deed to a Victorian country estate might look.

The words inside aren't in curling, ancient fountain pen or even quill writing. To Guy's astonishment, they are typewritten. Not computer-printed typewriting either; as he looks at the letters he can see the dents they've left in the thick paper:

> To Our Friend Mister Autumn,
>
> We understand that you are making your situation known to the world at large.
>
> We recommend that you abandon this behaviour.
>
> The path you are on has its own destination, and you do not yet know the intended outcome. All will be revealed in time, and this we swear by the Annot'Ai.
>
> Be patient. Do not force our hand.
>
> Regards,
>
> Mister Chair of the True Folk.

What the fuck? It reads like a threat and a reassurance. Is this because of the article, or the video, or because he's been corresponding with the emailer? And the *True Folk?* Is that another name for the *Other Folk?*

Or maybe there's another party involved

It's something that never occurred to him. Could there be divisions within their world? Different factions? Of *course* there could be. Mister Chair? What the hell kind of a name is that? Then Guy understands: it's the kind of name something that doesn't really understand human names would give itself.

Guy doesn't expect that Mister Chair is a man at all.

The address from the email, he thinks. *Check it on Google Street View.*

He fetches his laptop from the bedroom and returns to the kitchen, taking a moment to turn the kettle on. *Making cups of tea, about to make breakfast,* he thinks. *Already adjusting to life in the cursed world.* Google Street View tells him that 110 Appledore Avenue is not a church, or an old curiosity shoppe, or a burnt-out warehouse that used to hold satanic events. It's an ordinary detached house on a suburban street. Looks like a three-bedder, maybe. It has a small, neat lawn outside and even a garage at the end of a short driveway.

They'd told him in writing that they wouldn't harm him. That *means* something to them.

He jumps out of his skin as the front door opens.

"It's me, don't worry," Sam says. Guy breathes out. His phone rings, with lousy timing. It's Nancy.

"Did you find the message?" She asks.

"I did, it's just a written warning I think, but Sam just got back. I'll have to call you later, okay?"

"Okay. Okay."

He hangs up. Sam stands in the living room doorway as Rufus wheezes his way over to Guy for a stroke. Guy doesn't oblige; he's holding the piece of paper between his cooking tongs. Sam nods a greeting, eyes settling on the message Guy is holding.

"Before I get to this," Guy says, "I have to apologise for everything I said last night."

Sam shakes his head.

"It's fine," he says, sighing. "I said some things too. We're both strung out."

"No," Guy tells him. "I started it, this is your house, and I was drunk and being a dick. That's not making an excuse, if anything that makes it worse. I'm not blaming the curse or the booze, I was just being a straight up arsehole. I'm truly sorry. Also, I'm not going to drink again until... well, until this is over, either way."

Rufus gives up on fuss with a wet sniff and slowly pads his way over to his stinking basket.

"Water under the bridge," Sam says... but then pauses. "Guy, I lied to you when I told you why I wanted to help. Well, that's not strictly true either, I meant everything I said and every reason I gave you was real. But I didn't tell you the whole story. I was thinking while I was gone." He takes off his jacket and throws it onto the sofa. "I told you what I saw. In the past. And that I'd heard about dark goings-on. I didn't want to know. It was too much for me to handle; Melissa, at the time, she was..." He sits on the arm of the sofa. "It might be hard to understand, you not being a parent," he says, a deep sadness sinking into his face. "We'd tried everything, *everything*... the point was, Guy: I had, to use the modern parlance, *my own shit going on*, but isn't that always the one that everyone uses? It's too damn *good* an excuse, is the problem. And I criticised *you* for making excuses." He shakes his head. "Regardless: I let all the monstrous stuff slide, back then. I couldn't face it, so I can't judge you when I did nothing. Maybe if people like me had, things wouldn't have gone this far. Maybe Elias would still be alive. You remember when I told you—after the church, when we had our last little fall-out—that I wasn't angry with you?"

"I remember, Sam."

"Well I don't know who *you're* angry with Guy," Sam says, "but I know *I'm* angry with myself."

Silence.

"That makes two of us, Sam," Guy says.

"Huh?"

"I had a bit of a eureka moment earlier. While I was still checking my phone with a fucking monster *right there in the room.*"

"What about it?"

"The woman in the field," Guy says, holding up a finger and beginning to count off on his others. "The homeless man. Larry's last video; he was talking about this but he wasn't trying to *explain* it. He said we're to blame, and he's right. People like him and me."

Sam looks confused.

"... white males?"

"*No*, Jesus. I mean the people who make a profit from clickbait, social media... the *distraction economy.*"

"Go on."

"Remember what Nowak said about creating suffering? And that stuff about affecting an ecosystem?"

"Yes..." Sam sounds like he's starting to get it—he's the cop after all—but Guy keeps going, beginning to pace, still holding the tongs.

"So that would all be to do with our collective mindset, our, I don't know, *energy* as a whole right?" Guy says. "So what if, as well as suffering, there's other aspects to it? What if there's a threshold that other elements need to reach so they can move in?"

"Okay."

"What if..." Guy says, and then pulls out his phone, waving it and holding it up to make his point. "...what if they need us *distracted?*"

Silence.

"Did you notice it?" Guy says, wiping his face with his free hand and putting his phone away. "No-one in that field had a phone out. Not one. When was the last time you saw that? The mother—" He falters, remembering clearly for the first time in a while, then manages to put those feelings back in their iron box. "She didn't even panic when she saw the phone, either. And it wasn't Barkley fucking Barley that freaked her out. It was the method of delivery. No-one in that field had a phone for a *reason.* And the worst part is that those *things* don't even understand technology! They didn't plan this, we did it for them! They just took advantage!" He pokes himself in the chest, hard. "Me and Larry. *People like us.* Even fucking *weirdly.com.* We all helped this happen. We helped make it so they could get back in. For what? *Likes?!*"

"That might even be true," Sam says quietly, "but you can't—"

"Don't fucking tell me not to blame myself when you—*ah! Jesus, sorry...*" Guy holds up his hands.

"It's okay."

Silence again.

"We bicker a lot, don't we?" Guy says. Sam snorts in response, a small smile on his face.

"Stress," he says. "You especially. But more importantly: if what you're saying is true—if it is—then we're using the mediums you're talking about to get all this out there. Did you think about that? This might mean we're playing right into their hands."

"I did think about that," Guy says. "Without any better info, my only choice is to hope that I'm pulling a switcheroo here; the poison as cure. If I'm right about this, about the distractions, it only strengthens the reasoning behind our plan." He shrugs. "What's the opposite of distracting people away from something?"

"Drawing their attention to it."

"Exactly."

Sam sighs.

"It makes sense, and I hope you're right," he says. "It's done now either way. Can't change it." He pauses, then speaks to the floor. "I think that's the way you and I have to look at a lot of things Guy. We *can't* change the past. What matters now is what we *do* now, so let's make an agreement to not shit on each other while we're about this task. Okay?"

"... okay."

"Plus, I think we'd be a lot *less* stressed if we weren't up against the forces of darkness without a map," Sam says. "But speaking of which: your text said you have an address?" He points at the piece of paper clamped between the kitchen tongs.

"I do, but this isn't that," Guy says, eager to move on, crossing to the table and flattening the paper open so Sam can see inside without touching. "This is something else. Have a read."

"Where did you get this?" Sam asks, reading.

"The thing that came last night," Guy says, shivering a little as he says it. "It made a delivery." Sam stops reading and looks at Guy.

"And it didn't do anything to you?"

"Not a thing. It broke my weapons but didn't touch me at all."

"Hmm." Sam thinks for a moment. "By the way, I thought that, given the visit we received last night, I'd better look into some old school charms and spells for protecting the house. Soil across each of the entrances, that kind of thing."

"Jesus, I never thought of that. Do you think they'll work?"

"Who knows?" He looks back at the paper again. "*Mister Chair?*"

"Yeah."

"What do you think about it?" Sam asks.

"I think it shows that they're nervous."

Sam smiles again.

"Me too. Has your wife reported any...?"

"No. She's fine. Sam, I think they're bluffing with the thing they sent her."

"Interesting. Why so?"

"Well, we know they can't just curse people at will, right?" Guy moves away from the table and begins to pace. Despite this latest night of non-sleep it feels like his body is tapping into some turbocharged reserve of energy that is saved for emergencies. He feels wired. Excited, even. "We have to agree, or accept something, or touch something. So their ability to do that kind of shit *has* to be limited, yes?"

"Possibly," Sam says, taking a seat and letting Guy hold court.

"So what if they can only do so much of it? They cursed Larry. They cursed me. That's a lot of juice already spent on my social circle alone. What if they don't have enough left to curse Nancy too? What if that vase thing they sent her was just them shooting blanks to shit us up?"

"Again: possible," Sam says. "But I certainly wouldn't bank on it. Mister Chair seems to think that he has an ace up his sleeve."

"Or he wants us to think that," Guy says, holding up a finger. "An impotent monster in my bedroom? A *back off* note? These aren't the things you do if you're holding all the cards."

Sam strokes his top lip, considering this.

"So what are you saying we do?"

Guy pulls out his car keys.

"I think we push our luck," he says. "We tread carefully. We remove the words *yes* and *no* from our vocabulary. We know, after last night, that they can't just do what they want. Larry's house was different, that's their territory now, but I'm beginning to think that even if we're *in* their territory they couldn't do anything without our permission. *Rules,* Sam, *rules.* That's what they told me in the first place, and I don't think we need to know them all. We just have to be aware of the fundamental one, and we know what that is: compliance, and avoiding it."

"That's a lot of *I thinks,*" Sam says.

"Well here's another one," Guy tells him, grinning. "*I think* we jump in my car right now and drive to Nottingham. It's time for us to pay a visit of our own. It's risky, but..." How does he explain it? "I think I'll *know,* Sam. I'm becoming... I could feel the difference between Nowak and the old ladies in the church and the thing in my bedroom. I'll be able to tell if this is a trap or not, I think." He briefly considers that *this,* this becoming connected to this other plane, might also be the beginning of what Nowak referred to as *monstrous thoughts.*

"Again," Sam says. "You *think.*"

"Well can you *think* up any better ideas?"

"Nope."

Ten minutes later, they're on their way to Nottingham. Rufus stays at home, asleep in his heated outdoor kennel and as blissfully unaware as everyone around him.

***

Nancy is on the phone as Guy drives. He's told her what he and Sam are doing.

She takes the news surprisingly well. It isn't the raging are-you-crazy-it-could-be-a-trap discussion that Guy feared; in fact, she just sounds worried. She tries to be supportive, talking to him about other things—her new hire at work, a new campaign she's trying to book—but always back to the same question, revealing her nerves. She asks it again now for the twenty-sixth time:

"Where are you now?"

"I'm fifteen minutes away. Traffic is still crawling though."

Despite the early morning rush hour traffic, it's only taken them an hour and a half to get into Nottingham from Leicester, but Nancy and Guy have been on the phone all the way. Poor Sam hasn't even been able to listen to the radio, remaining patient and silent throughout, using his phone to do more of the protection spell research he was talking about.

Guy hasn't told Nancy how much the scales have spread over his body. They're now beginning to spread down his arms as well as his stomach—he checked before they left—and, finally, they're also beginning to creep up under his chin, nearly onto his face. He has a scarf wrapped all the way around his neck now; that much is needed to cover it. He's sure the vast majority of people can't see it anyway without some kind of video aspect being involved, but he doesn't want to take any risks.

He glances out of the window and freezes when he sees one of the little squat things again.

It's riding on the back of a young twenty-something woman's neck as she strolls along the pavement. She's pretty, blonde, slim, has the aesthetics going for her, and yet her eyes are haunted. The thing's hands are deep in her blonde locks. It's flickering in and out of Guy's sight, as if it can't fully materialise in the sun. Guy blinks and then he can't see it anymore. He doesn't say anything about it to Sam and Nancy. What would be the point?

He turns the car off the carriageway and onto the side streets, pleasant roads that suggest comfortable middle class living. How could anything supernatural be going on over here? He's two minutes away from his destination. They approach a short high street with a café, a small-scale Sainsburys, a butcher's, a salon. Totally ordinary. He takes a right, following the GPS. He wants to check the other reposted versions of his YouTube videos again. He'd read the comments just before they left and, yes, the majority are the don't-see-it-then-see-it crowd. The numbers—and Guy's life—are escalating.

"You're nearly there, aren't you?" Nancy asks. "You're there now."

She's right. Sam is squinting through the window, trying to see the house numbers. They may have seen the picture of the place on Google Street View but the houses are all so identical Guy can't spot it by the exterior alone.

"This one," Sam says. "110." Guy looks where Sam is pointing, glad to not be getting a vibe from the place; surely that means they're likely to be safe? No bats flying overhead, no ominous clouds gathering only above the one building. Sam, however—the expert—spots something before Guy does. "Look at the windows," he mutters.

The curtains are all drawn. So? No big deal.

What? Guy mouths to Sam, not wanting Nancy to think he's talking to her. Sam points to his eyes and back at the house. *Look.*

Then Guy sees it. The slight gap between each set of curtains reveals a *jet* black strip of darkness. It's so subtle you wouldn't notice unless you were really looking—or unless you have a trained eye, like Sam—but there should be some difference to the gloom from the light coming in—

Then Guy notices the way the curtains aren't just drawn, but pressed against the glass. Whoever is inside has drawn the curtains—to make it look normal to the outside world—but then also placed something behind them to make sure no one can see in. Blacked out boards, maybe. Now Guy feels nervous.

"Have you stopped?" Nancy asks.

The car pulls up on the kerb outside the house.

"Yeah. Nancy, I'm going to go and knock. Don't worry, okay?"

She doesn't argue.

"Okay."

"You're really taking this well."

"I have to," she says. "Like I said, if you're doing this... just promise me that you won't stop."

"I won't."

"Say *yes, I promise I won't stop.*"

"I promise," Guy says, a little annoyed. She already made him promise that once, for crying out loud—no. That isn't fair. "I promise I won't stop," he says, kindly this time.

"Good."

"Okay."

"Call me the second you're done."

"I will."

He hangs up. On a whim, he crosses himself. Sam nods and does the same.

"Hey," Sam says suddenly, making Guy jump. He's more tense than he realised. "Look at the front lawn." Guy does, and then he really notices what's lying in the long grass.

They hadn't been on the Google Street Maps image but God knows when that picture had been taken. Certainly not recently. He'd been paying such close attention to the house that he'd dismissed at a glance what he thought were lawn ornaments, thinking they were the kind of cheap tin and iron constructions street vendors sell to tourists in poorer countries. They're actually something far more sinister. More dangerous.

There are six of them set out on the grass; their position is too haphazard to be described as a line but it's obvious that they are progressing from the bottom of the garden towards the house, or vice versa. Each is maybe a foot high, the grass in the lawn now so overgrown that most are half-covered by it. Angular, rusting metal frames that hurt the eye when you look at them for too long. String tied around them in looping and intricate shapes, sticks knotted together. No two constructions look the same. Spread out like visible landmines. They're trinkets from the shanties, ornaments, totems, whatever you want to call them, and Guy is shocked to see so many in one place. Now he can feel their presence the way a Geiger counter senses radiation. His perception seems to be changing before his thoughts, at least. He thinks whatever is in those things is... low-level? They certainly have been here for a while—he feels that much for certain—their influence ebbing away like batteries left out in the cold.

He can only guess at the trinkets' purpose. *Landmines* is probably a misleading metaphor; if the spread was so dense that there was a chance someone might trip and touch them then it would be appropriate, but there are none on the driveway leading up to the house.

Speaking of which, there's a Prius sitting there.

"Look at the wiper space on the rear windscreen," Sam says. "The gap in the dust. That car has been recently driven."

"Come on," Guy tells him.

Once they're closer to the house Guy can just about see the painted-black wood in between the crack in the curtains. Someone doesn't want the outside world seeing inside. He knocks softly on the door.

There's a pause, and then Guy hears the soft thud of footsteps coming down the stairs from the other side of the white PVC door. Whoever it is in there, they don't sound big. And they only have two feet.

"Is that Guy?" The voice is muffled through the door but it's a woman, one perhaps younger than Guy. He goes to say *yes,* heart racing, but again Sam's hand shoots out, holding up a finger. That word has to be used *very* carefully when responding to questions now. Nowak got himself into trouble that way—

No. Nowak had to say out loud that he confirmed and that was in response to a question about his dead parents, wasn't it? No, it was a question that he thought was about his dead parents. They worded it very carefully. This isn't like letting something into your home either. Caution is good but Jesus, you have to be able to take a shit without thinking you're crapping your soul into Satan's back pocket—

He's tying himself up in knots again and she's only asked him his name.

"I... am Guy," he says, feeling like an idiot.

"Okay," she says. They can hear things being moved around. "Sorry. I can't find the key. I changed my jeans and I don't know where... hang on." She sounds sad. There's a rattling sound in the lock and the door opens.

In front of Guy is a woman who has to be in her early thirties at most. With the blocked windows he'd been expecting an old recluse, or maybe someone with unwashed hair, blinking in the light and scratching themselves at the sight of someone normal invading their little world. Instead this woman is wearing jeans and a blue blouse—both clean and ironed—as well as, he thinks, some light make-up. Her hair is drawn back. She could be going to work.

"Hello," she says.

"Hi," Guy says, thinking about offering his hand but not doing it for obvious reasons. Instead he points at Sam. "This is Sam. He's a friend." She squints at Sam slightly.

"You're involved too, aren't you?" she asks. Her tone is flat; not dismissive, yet not intrigued. "Not the same as Guy. But you're in it now. It's on you."

"I'm in it now," Sam echoes back, also avoiding the Y word.

"I didn't know if anyone would be in," Guy tells her. "Like you might be... at work..." He feels stupid saying it; someone who boards up their windows doesn't go to work. Then she proves him wrong:

"I normally would be," she says, "but I have the day off." Her face is totally expressionless.

"Are you..." Guy looks up and down the street. They're having this conversation in broad daylight. "... do you *work* for them?" A more likely situation occurs to him and he takes a slight step back. "Are you one *of* them?"

"No," she says, still with that blank face. "Not anymore, anyway."

"Uh... what do you—"

"Will you come inside?" she asks, stepping back, then catches herself, tutting. It's the first time she's shown even a hint of emotion. "Forget that question, that sounds loaded, right? You know what I mean. Uh..." She pauses, thinking. "Okay, I'm going to go inside my house and if you want to follow me you can. You don't have to say a confirmation out loud." She sighs. "Sorry. I imagine you're pretty worried about saying *yes* to anything right now. Especially with coming here. I know this will mean next to nothing in terms of reassurance but I can promise you I have no intention to harm you or trick you or anything like that. This will probably help you, in fact." She points at Guy's neck. "You're turning, right? Is that what the scarf is covering?"

"Are you alone in there?" Guy asks, ignoring her question and pointing beyond her into the house. The front entrance only reveals a porch area and a half-closed door to the left.

"Yes. Really, it's alright. Come in and have a seat and we can talk. I'm inviting you in, and that means something. You're safe."

Guy instinctively trusts her. This, however, actually makes him uncomfortable. She's clearly involved in this and yet he gets no vibe from her at *all*. How is that possible? If anything she only seems to be... faded? She's so pale, Guy notices, but otherwise seems to be so normal that its—

Then he has it.

She's beyond normal. She's lacking *presence*. It's almost as if Guy's brain has to keep reminding him that she's there, that he's talking to someone. If it wasn't for Sam standing right next to him, he would feel alone.

She isn't a threat, then. But he wants to know what's going on.

"Guy," he says, finally extending his hand. "I know you already know that but..." He thinks he should introduce himself before he enters. She nods, taking his hand—he almost flinches, not knowing what to expect—and that only confirms Guy's suspicions. There are limp grips, and then there are this woman's: so delicate, even for her small hand, that Guy has to grip harder to be sure that it's there. "Jesus," he says in surprise. "Okay. I'm just going to ask." Deep breath. "Are you a ghost or something?"

"No." She considers it further. "Well, maybe a little bit, in a way. Let's sit down and I'll tell you." She steps back again.

"I'm Erin," she says. "Erin Lafferty. I'm assuming you both won't accept any tea."

***

The living room is, of course, completely normal apart from the wooden boards placed over the windows. From this side Guy can see that they're MDF, the unpainted rear sides showing the true colours of the material. There's a big

- 230 -

flatscreen TV on a unit in the corner, two three-seater sofas with throws over them, a rug. There's a dog bed on the floor in the corner, but no dog or even a slight smell of a dog in the air. Guy and Sam sit on the couch, seated at either end. Erin sits in the sofa opposite, a mug of tea in her hand. Now she's turned the lights on it feels like evening. Erin looks more comfortable under the internal lighting.

"The scales on my body have spread a lot more since I made the video," Guy tells her. "Really fast. It's why I said I don't think I have much time."

"Yes, your video," she says. "They're not going to like that you put that footage out there. It'll be interesting to see how they respond."

"They already have," he says.

"With what?"

"So far, just a warning. Do you think they'll try to kill me?" The question comes straight out. Erin doesn't bat an eyelid.

"I'm pretty sure they can't just kill you, not without exceptional circumstances or specific things being agreed to, interference, all that. I think that's a *big* part of the rules. Have you met any of them yet?"

"Ye—I mean... I have."

"Mm. Did they look like old people, perhaps?"

Guy shudders.

"Ye—" Jesus Christ. "They did."

"If they were allowed to kill you they would have done so, instantly," she says. Guy suddenly pictures the old woman's long, sinewy limbs clambering up and over the back of the church pew with astonishing speed and hidden strength, that worm-smile turning into an eager grin as she pounces like a spider. Would she tear his throat out—

"I've been seeing things too, little things on people's shoulders," he says. "Sam saw one too."

"Yeah, that'll happen. What happened to you?" This last part is addressed to Sam.

"Cancer curse," he says, and then jabs a thumb towards the front garden. "I took one of those things into the house."

"You have a lot of them out there," Guy says, taking the opportunity.

"I do," she says. "Did you get some of them too?"

"I didn't, my story is different, but... you have so many. Are those outside all the ones you have?"

"No. There were two more, but they fell apart," she says. "It started with one. When I tried to move it the thing collapsed and formed this kind of...

anyway. It was freaky. Then I threw the bits of that one away. I didn't physically touch it though, I used tongs. Then a few days later *another* one arrived and I picked it up with a shovel to throw it in the bin. I didn't want to even go anywhere near it. Then..." She shifts awkwardly in her seat. When these little flashes of minor emotion appear in her they stand out dramatically against the rest of her cool demeanour. "A rat ran across my path. I've never seen rats in my garden, ever, by the way. But I hate them. I was so shocked that I just kind of jerked and I slipped and fell. I dropped the construction and when I landed it was under my hands. Both of them. It broke in half and each part ended up perfectly under my palms. I'm sure I don't need to convince you of that, no matter how unlikely it might sound."

"And that was it? That was enough to..." Guy begins to point at his neck, then changes tack. "Sorry, you said *not anymore*, that you weren't one of them. They turned you then? You *were* turning?"

"It was enough to start the process, yes. It began with these unbelievable nightmares," she says, nodding and sipping her tea. She looks up at the ceiling and Guy chances a glance at Sam, the practiced interrogator, who subtly holds up a hand to the younger man. *Let her talk,* the gesture says. *There's information here. We have time.* "I was thrashing around at night, every night," Erin continues. "Scubby—he was my dog—couldn't sleep in the bed with me anymore as he'd get kicked. It got so bad that I booked a few days off work. On the second day my skin started to become really dry, like flaking. I saw a doctor and he prescribed this steroid cream. Then on the third day I woke up to find that my face had *really* changed."

"To what?"

"It was so gaunt I looked like a corpse," she says, recounting the events with the detached but clinical tone of someone giving a witness statement to the police for the tenth time. "And my skin texture was thin. And I don't mean like old-person thin. I mean at certain points, like my cheekbones, it was almost see-through. Even Scubby backed away when he saw me, ran off into the garden. I was literally *running* to the phone to speak to the doctor again when the doorbell rang. I didn't dare open it—I was still in shock and couldn't let anyone see me—so I just said it wasn't a good time, trying not to cry, you know? And the person—well, I say *person*—on the other side of the door just said *how is your face?*"

Guy clenches his fists at his sides.

"They sounded happy about it," Erin says. "Not overly sinister, like this dark supervillain enjoyment of pain or whatever. They sounded like someone who has played a practical joke on you letting you know that it was them. They let the air out of your car tyres: *how's the car running today?*"

"What did you say?"

"I didn't say anything for about two minutes, I was so shocked. Neither did they. But I could feel that they were still standing there. I felt terrified... but I knew it was something to do with those first two things. The constructions. Whoever made them or sent them was whoever was standing on the other side of my front door. Eventually I said *how do you know about that?* And they said something like *Erin, you had probably better open the door, I think we have a lot to talk about.* I was scared out of my mind, but what choice did I have? I opened the door."

She looks at Guy for a moment before continuing, as if waiting to see if he judged her for her decision.

"There was a little man standing there," she says.

Now she shifts again, pulling her legs up tight beside her on the sofa. Guy thinks about the boards over the windows and he very much wants to know what she saw on her doorstep.

"He was very short and very thin," she says. "He looked like some kind of old bird. He wore a suit but not the kind that you would expect a businessman to wear. It was like someone had looked up the word *suit* and they'd dressed him in the closest thing to a suit they could find. It was like a military dress uniform almost but nothing like one I've ever seen. It looked old. It had these patterns on it... I had to keep tearing my eyes away from them. There were these things on the breast where medals would normally be but they weren't medals. They were... they looked like sea-shells but they were red and orange. His hair was slicked back, and it looked like a doll's hair. He had this big nose, like *really* big, but not in a way that would be funny or interesting. It was long with these big nostrils, like it had a *practical* purpose. Like he used it to smell hidden things out. Trust me, you would know what I mean if you ever saw him. And his forehead had so many lines in it while his cheeks and around his eyes were smooth as... his face was... " For a brief moment her own forehead creases, looking for a fraction of a second as if she were about to cry. Then it all relaxes, blank once more; the process almost looks inhuman. "I hope you never see him," she says. "I truly do. You know that thing, *one look at that person and I knew XYZ?* I looked at that man—looked at that smiling face, those eyes—and I knew about all of the evil things in the world. They *radiated* off him."

She looks at her mug, blinking and silent.

"Take your time," Sam says kindly. "It's alright."

"Oh, I'm okay," she says. "It's interesting actually, talking about this. I feel..." She thinks about it, cocking her head. "Sad. Angry, maybe. That's interesting. That's interesting."

Guy wants to ask why but needs her to finish her story.

"Anyway. He was holding another one of those things in his hands. Another construction. And he said *hello Erin. My name is Mister Chair.*"

Guy tries to keep a poker face but shifts nervously in his seat. There's no movement at all from Sam's end of the sofa.

"This is a present," quotes Erin, having no problem at all with her own poker face. *"You understand that we and our gifts are responsible for what has happened to you. This is the gift that will stop it, you will be glad to hear.* He talked like that, *you will* rather than *you'll*, never any contractions. *You just have to take it,* he said, like it was *nothing.* I couldn't believe it, even as I looked at his weird, too-perfect teeth. He was openly saying that they'd done this to me? I wanted to claw his eyes out but there was no way I'd do that. I was terrified of him. It felt like one of my nightmares—I've wondered since if that's exactly why I was having them, so I would assume this was another one and wouldn't think about it too much—and I said to him *why are you doing this to me?* And he shrugged, still smiling, and said *I do not make the rules. I am just helping my people.*

"*Who are you,* I asked him. *What did I do to deserve this,* that kind of thing. I was sobbing and the tears were burning my cheeks, and I mean *burning* like something had changed about my skin, which of course it had. And he shook his head, not as in *no* but as in *you silly sod, isn't it obvious,* which of course it wasn't. And he held out the little construction. *If you want this to stop,* he said, *you need to take this. Do you accept our gift?*"

She pauses again, looking at the wall. This was a key question, *the* question, and Guy already knows what her answer was.

"You have to understand, I was panicking and scared out of my mind," she says. "It might seem stupid to even consider taking it but I did. I was desperate. I tried to *snatch* it from him but he pulled it away. *This needs verbal confirmation,* he said, and now he just looked bored. *Do you accept our gift?*

She pauses again.

"*Yes,* I said. He handed the thing to me. I got this little electric shock—very mild, only like static—and the thing was heavy. He said *thank you Erin, I will be back in a few days.* And he started to walk away. *Wait,* I shouted, *why are you coming back? You don't need to come back!* And he didn't even turn around. *You will* want *me to come back,* he said. I screamed at him then. *You said this would stop!* Then he did turn around. *Oh yes,* he said. *What* was *happening* will stop. *Now you have agreed to something else. I told you, I do not make the rules.* And then I was hysterical and running towards him, not even thinking, and he vanished before my eyes. Literally vanished. And I was standing in the street holding this horrible thing and realizing that any of the neighbours could see my face. I threw the construction onto the grass, ran back inside and collapsed in the hallway. I had a panic attack. I'd never had one before. When it was over I went to the mirror to wash my face. It was back to normal."

"But that wasn't the end of it."

"No."

"Did you see him again?"

"No."

"Did you tell anyone?"

"No. I'd had some trouble in the past. Friends knew about it. I did a lot of drugs in my twenties, ended up in a dark place. I thought that if I told someone they'd think I'd relapsed or whatever, that I'd imagined everything. I couldn't take that. Plus even I wasn't sure if it *was* real. Even after the first night when my hair began to change. It felt strange, thicker, but not in the way I'd always wanted. It felt disgusting to touch." Erin looks up. "It felt like it was breathing."

"It…"

"I just locked all the doors and tried to ride it out, starting to think it really was all in my head and scared I'd end up contacting some old dealers and… you know."

Guy does. And it makes perfect sense. They don't do this stuff to just anyone—Nowak said so—unless they need to be silenced, like Larry, and even then they use a very different type of curse. In Erin's case they picked someone with a broken past who wouldn't trust their own judgement. And then they tricked her.

"My skin was changing again, but this time it was yellowing. The backs of my hands started to scab over. Then it spread up my arms. It was happening over the course of an hour and I *still didn't tell anyone.* In my head I was thinking that if I did, the man might not come back. He'd said it right: I *did* want him to come back. I looked out the window and saw another of one those things in the front garden. So they *had* been back, just like he said. They brought more over the next few days. I've never touched them. I don't think they needed me to, either; I think them just being there was accelerating what was happening. And I'd *agreed* to it, too. Scubby wouldn't come near me but he'd sit a few feet away, whining. My legs started…" She looks as if she's about to cry but instead she just cocks her head sideways, as if intrigued. Then she grunts a little and shrugs.

"They set you up to agree to a more severe curse," Sam says, helping her out. "And now perhaps you were turning into something worse than before?"

"That's putting it mildly. I had to take down all the mirrors. I couldn't look at myself. I think I was in here for maybe two days before—"

"Is that when you covered the windows?" Sam interrupts.

"Oh, no. That wasn't until after Kasie came. My friend."

"You called her?" Sam asks.

"I did, in the end. I couldn't take it anymore. If everyone thought I was crazy then it had to be better than living like that. And if I *was* crazy then they could help. By then my arms, my chest, everything... and my hair was... my *mind* was still there but that was starting to go too. I needed help."

"What did Kasie say?"

Erin pauses for a long time.

"We didn't get the chance to talk," she says eventually. "If I'd been more familiar with mythology I might have got it and I *never* would have called Kasie. It was Scubby that made me understand what I was becoming. By that point he wouldn't even sit in the same room as me. Then about five minutes before Kasie got here—I don't know why—he came to look at me. Maybe he couldn't help but check if I was alright. Who knows with dogs? I was curled up in a ball on the sofa and I heard the bell on his collar. I turned over to look at him. He made this little noise. And then he was gone."

She looks at her mug again, face relaxed and calm.

"He died?" Sam asks.

"Sort of, yes. Well, yes, in fact. I just sat there in total shock staring at him and then the next thing I knew Kasie was knocking on the door and I started yelling—" Here she closes her eyes, perhaps for her the equivalent of falling to her knees and hysterically pulling at her hair. "I should have said it *calmly*," she says quietly, "then she might have listened... but I didn't and so *she* didn't. I was telling her to get away, to go away, and of course Kasie had a spare key—she used to look after Scubby—and she was unlocking the door but I put it on the chain. She tried to talk me down and I kept yelling and suddenly she says *okay Erin, I'll leave you to it, but I want you to know you can call me.* And she left and I was just... just *fucked* at this point, Guy, and then I heard the back door opening and the clever bitch had gone around the back and let herself in. So I ran upstairs to the bedroom but she followed me, I was trying to hold the bedroom door shut but she was way stronger than me and she was pushing it open so I ran to the bed."

She puts her mug down on the side table and laces her fingers together, looking at them.

"*Erin, it's alright it's alright* she was saying, and I'd got the blanket over my face and I was holding it on top of me, gripping it as hard as I could. I don't know what she was thinking, I mean who handles a hysterical person like that? Chasing after them? That was Kasie though, she never took *no* for... hm." She shifts in her seat. "She was too strong. She got the blanket off my face. She saw what I looked like right before she died. The look on her face was captured in that moment."

Sam doesn't respond here, but Guy has to.

"She... died?" he asks.

"Yes. Same as Scubby."

Guy is amazed at both the story and at the fact that he's now accepting everything she's saying as truth, as a *reasonable* truth.

"What did the police say?" Sam asks.

"They never came, although I know they looked for her. She was a married woman, two children. I went to her funeral, you know. But I was never in the frame. Why would I be? I wasn't even her last phone call, apparently. She spoke to two other people she knew after me, and the records would show that we talked on the phone daily. Her car disappeared from outside my house the same day."

"Wait, how did you go to the funeral—" Guy realises he already knows half the answer. He and Sam are sitting here right now, talking to Erin, and *they're* not dying as a result. *Not anymore,* she'd said. Guy understands what this is.

Erin got turned back.

She's telling him that there is a potential way out.

This is what she's brought him here for.

"Yeah, you got it," she says, seeing him understand. "And I never told her family the truth about what happened, either. How could I?"

"So..." Guy feels callous talking about logistics when this woman is talking about the death of her dog and her best friend. "How did..."

"I didn't call anyone else, of course," Erin interrupts, ignoring him. "I didn't want any more risks. I could have covered my face but if they thought I was crazy then they might have pulled it off my face like Kasie. I wasn't thinking straight at all and I didn't think I could risk it. I remember covering the windows," she says, pointing at the MDF. "I waited until the first night—much less chance of the neighbours seeing in the dark—and pulled a pair of tights over my head and went out to the shed to get some of Richard's old boards and paint. He was the classic DIY guy that had all the kit but never actually did anything. I painted them black on the outside so they would look like darkness between the cracks in the curtains. Like I said, I wasn't thinking straight. I just didn't want to risk... the neighbours have kids, Guy."

"I understand. Why are the boards still up—*wait*, sorry," Guy says, holding his hands up. "Erin... I understand what you're telling me. But *how* did you turn back? They did it for you?" A glimmer of hope is in his belly, one he is frightened to let grow.

"Yes. Someone—the little man or one of his underlings—made another delivery. I can show you," she says, standing up. She crosses to some drawers on the opposite side of the room and then pauses, her hand hovering by the handle. "Actually... I'll show you this afternoon. That will be better. That's why I said that you had to come today; there's an event later and I wanted to vet you first. The next one isn't for a few weeks and I don't think, excuse me saying, that you have that long." She turns away from the drawer, to Guy's great disappointment—what was in there and why can't she just show him now?—and takes a post-it note off a stack by the phone. She writes something on it and hands it to Guy.

"Can you be here at two this afternoon? The drive is only about an hour from here so you might want to go and get a late breakfast to kill a bit of time." He looks at the note. It's an address for a community centre in Stoke-On-Trent. He catches the *yes* on the way out of his mouth. The habit is forming. She sees it. "Sorry, I mean there's a meeting going on this afternoon at two pm and it will probably be useful to you if you go there. You'll understand better."

"In the daytime?"

"Why do you think I took the day off? We prefer to meet in the daytime. Sunlight, and all that. We don't *need* it or anything but it's a preference."

"Well... obviously I'm more likely to go if I know what's going on..."

To Guy's surprise, she tells him.

"It's a support group," she says. "It's national but there's only about forty or so of us. There's probably others but this is the one we know about. We meet once a month."

"A support group for..."

"People like me, yes. People who were turned, and turned back."

"The *Other Folk*..." Guy asks. "That's the support group?"

The old lady-things in the church said—

"Yes. About a month after I was turned back this woman in the supermarket... one look at each other and we both knew. She came and told me about the group. I've been going for a while. It helps."

"But how *were* you turned back?"

"I made a deal. You can too. But you'll need to understand what that really means. It's my turn to lead the talk tonight so you'll hear it all later anyway; it'll be better hearing it then as it'll have context. That will be *very* important."

So this *is* all about leverage. There's a way out!

But at what cost?

Erin looks at Sam.

"You can come too," she says.

"Thank you," he says, "but with total respect to you, Erin, I don't think I'll be making any deals."

"Me neither," Guy hears himself say automatically.

"I understand," Erin says, "but you should come anyway."

Guy wants to say *just fucking tell me now* but doesn't. She's been very forthcoming about everything else and if she says he needs context, then he needs context.

"Okay."

"Good. And yes, the boards are still up. I just feel better with them there. I leave the house to go to work but I like coming home to this..." She gestures at the windows, trying to find the words. "This *cocoon,* I suppose. Every day at the office people look at me a little strangely when they talk to me—if they talk to me at all—and I like my safe space now."

Guy understands why her colleagues might struggle around her. There's something *off* about Erin, and it isn't the crazy stories or the garden full of cursed sculptures.

"The deal you made. I have to at least ask—"

"Was it for my soul? No. That was made clear in writing. But I gave something up, that was for certain."

"But *what—*"

"I don't honestly know the right words to explain it. This is why you need to see the group. Context. It's the best way to understand."

"... okay." He hesitates, but Sam asks the question for him.

"Erin," Sam says carefully. "How do you think all of this is even happening? Why now?"

She shrugs.

"We talk, those of us at the support group. We think a watershed has been reached. What's happening with the three of us... it wouldn't have been possible in the past. Starting with the homeless, they bent the rules, spread their influence. Made the hole wider. There's only so much energy in the world, Guy, so much power in nature that's taken up by humans, and only so much for our minds and our awareness and we're using that for cat memes. *Things slip through.* What used to just be superstition *now works.* And those things got clever and they're mobilising and they can't believe they're getting away with it because like I said... their weapons work."

"But I don't understand how there's people like... I met this man who was cursed to be unlucky, and he's not turning into anything." Guy pauses, remembering Nowak's purpose. "He said he thought his suffering was the point..."

"I've heard that," Erin says. "And for some their suffering is a tool to force them into spreading the curses like a chain letter, doing things like making the constructions. A lot of them end up homeless and the cycle continues. Then there are people like me, and this is my theory. People that have changes put on them that are so monstrous, so extreme, that those people's only purpose is to *exist.* To be a foothold in the world, and whether we get turned back or not the result is still the same. A win for *them.*"

She doesn't mean the cursed people.

"You just said something about a watershed," Guy asks, "how is that—"

"Imagine the world's energy as being like an ecosystem, Guy," Erin says. "If you place enough of a certain type of related organism into an environment—like releasing spores into the air—after a while, provided you release enough of them, soon their very presence means that environment is more suitable for *another* species, one that previously couldn't exist there. Now imagine that, while *that's* going on, you have a side project where you blackmail the dominant species to do your work for you by infecting them too and offering them the promise of healing..." She shrugs. "It's a very smart two-pronged attack. This at least is definitely true: they've seeded. They're getting bold, they're starting to be seen, and they don't seem hugely worried about that. I think that means soon they won't need to stay secret and once that happens... well, I think eventually we'll cease to be the dominant species. I don't think that will happen in our lifetimes, fortunately." She sounds as concerned as she would talking about an episode of *Downton Abbey*.

"If you're the *Other Folk*," Sam asks, "then who are the *True Folk?*"

"Who do you think?" she asks, crossing back to her chair and picking up her mug. "I really don't want to be rude gentlemen, I really don't," she says, "but I do still have a strange thing about having people in my home. It's not you, I just... would you mind leaving me to it until I see you at the group?"

"Oh, of course—" Guy says hurriedly, standing up. So does Sam. Neither of them had any intention of sticking around for the next few hours until it was time to drive to Stoke.

"Do you need to use the bathroom or anything before you go?"

"Actually, I do," says Guy.

"Upstairs, on the right."

"Thanks."

He glances at Sam, checking he doesn't mind being left alone with Erin; Sam gives an almost imperceptible nod of the head. Guy turns to head up the stairs—he doesn't want to be going there but he has to—and looks at the two partially open doors on the right, head spinning. He just needs to use the toilet and get out of here, then process—

There's a person standing inside the leftmost doorway.

He can see someone's leg, backward-trailing hand, and their backside. They're bent over, not moving. *Hiding?* Guy freezes before realizing that the person's colour is uniform; their hand, jeans, even their shoes, Guy now notices, all the same dark grey.

And he realises that he never asked what happened to Kasie's body.

Feeling strangely calm he crosses to the door and pushes it open. It's a bedroom. Kasie is standing against the wall, bent at the waist, both hands reaching out, the moment perfectly captured: *Erin, Erin it's alright, look at me,* bent and trying to take the blanket from her friend. Even seen from the side, Kasie's wide, bulging eyes show the terror of the moment of her death.

Kasie—and her clothes—have been turned completely to stone.

If Guy picked the Kasie-statue up and moved it over to the bed the mattress would line up perfectly with Kasie's bent-over form, a terrifying art installation.

Guy uses the bathroom quickly and heads downstairs.

***

Chapter Eighteen
Witnesses
✳✳✳

Guy is going to appear on TV.

They've left Erin's place and, at Sam's suggestion, they've driven to a cafe. Neither of them have spoken—he and Sam being silent in the car seems to be their thing, and it's not like they're actually friends, Guy supposes—and as they're walking inside Guy unlocks his phone. Larry's article's page on *weirdly.com* is still onscreen; he refreshes it and checks the comments. It's the usual polarising debate: *why don't these shanty people get a job/those poor homeless people, they need help.* And away they go, accomplishing nothing.

But then Guy checks his emails. Three letters immediately jump out:

BBC

That's interesting. It's from one Anna Souton, an assistant producer for BBC Midlands Today. That's an evening news show. It's regional but might still have viewers in the low millions. This is *exactly* what he's looking for, maybe even better than he'd dared to hope.

"Go on in Sam, I'll join you in a second," Guy says. Sam does. There's a contact number in the email; they've been doing a series of short featurettes on Midlands people that are internet famous and yada yada yada *they want to put him on fucking TV with this.* They've had a cancellation for *tomorrow night* and they want him on. If TV people are paying attention, certain other parties will be too—but then the letter from his dear penpal Mister Chair seems to have rather confirmed *that* already. He calls Anna Souton's number and gets her voicemail. He leaves her a message telling her to give him a call anytime, and that yes, he'd love to do the show tomorrow.

That's if the *Other Folk* don't make him into a ritual sacrifice first. Erin *feels* safe, but it won't hurt to keep their wits about them when they go to the meeting. *If* they go to the meeting. He needs to discuss it with Sam. He walks into the cafe, sending Nancy a quick text to tell her he's okay and that he'll explain once he's got Sam's assessment too. He also asks if she's still feeling okay but he's less worried about that now. He thinks her delivery *was* just more intimidation. Sam is sitting at a table. Guy joins him. The place is nice, if trying a little too hard to be bohemian in the middle of suburban Nottingham. Guy tells Sam about the TV offer.

"Good," he says. "That's going to reach a whole audience that YouTube might not."

"Do you think its a good idea?"

Sam looks surprised.

"Of course," he says. "Isn't this all about exposing you-know-what?"

"Of course, of course." Sam stares at Guy for a second. "Speaking of good or bad ideas," Guy says, quickly changing the subject, "the more immediate question is: are we going to actually go to this meeting today?"

"Well I know we're saying these two words a lot right now," Sam says, "but *of course*... you want information don't you? Are you worried about safety?"

"I think we'd be silly not to."

"Do you think it's a trap or something?"

"...no."

"Me neither," Sam says, picking up a slim and laminated menu. Guy is amazed Sam has an appetite. "Sometimes, when you're trying to get answers, you have to fall back on instinct. I trust her."

"I do too, but she wouldn't tell us what the deal was, remember?"

"She couldn't explain it without us seeing the..." Sam pauses for a moment. "You seem rather fixated on this deal business."

"Again: *of course* I am, Sam," Guy says. "You might not be but—" His phone buzzes. It's the BBC number. Anna Souton, calling back. "It's the TV people," he says.

"Tell them you'll do it," Sam says, his tone light, but his eyes don't leave Guy's. Guy doesn't respond and instead stands, walking outside.

"Hello?"

"Guy? Anna Souton, sorry for missing your call."

She sounds nice, young, the exact same bubbly media type Guy has spoken to a few times in his career. He's never sure if it's a false front or not, but at least they like to get on with things.

"No problem at all Anna," he tells her, "thanks for getting in touch. What did you guys have in mind then?"

She tells him, yet throughout her explanation her tone makes him unsure if she thinks he's crazy. He can't blame her; to her he's some dude on the internet claiming to have a Magic Neck. He has to go in first thing tomorrow morning for a pre-interview—presumably so they can check he's not mental and to give them time to find a replacement if it turns out that he is—and then Guy will be live tomorrow night. The thought is suddenly terrifying—the thought that *they* will be watching—but Guy hears himself agreeing and Anna gives him the details. They're providing a hotel stay for tonight so Guy can be nearby in the morning. He'll have to pack all his mirrors...

They hang up. The appearance is booked.

Nancy rings.

"Hi," he says, dazed.

"Sorry, I know you're with Sam," she says. "But you can spare me five bloody minutes, okay? Sorry, but Jesus, *what happened in the house?*"

He tells her.

"If you think it's safe," she says, "if she sounds legit, then I say do it."

"Yeah, I agree. So, no... news?" he asks.

"*No*, Guy. I'd tell you if there was. Don't change things around. I'm worrying about *you*, remember?"

They hang up and he heads back inside. Sam is engrossed in his phone.

"Just seeing if there's anyone locally who does spiritual guidance," he says. "Or protection spells."

"If you'd said that to me a few weeks ago..."

"Indeed."

"Sam, I have to be in Birmingham first thing tomorrow morning, so they're putting me in a hotel tonight. I know Birmingham's not too far from Leicester but it saves me having to get up crazy early and battle with the M6. I can just roll out of bed in the morning." Sam nods, and to his great credit he doesn't point out that which they both know: after last night's encounter Guy doesn't want to stay at Sam's house again.

"Okay. Which hotel?"

"Why?"

"I'll get a room as well."

"Oh... what about Rufus?"

"I have a sitter I use sometimes."

"Ah, right. Why are you checking into the hotel, though?"

"We're a team, aren't we?"

For a brief moment, Guy is touched… and then he gets it.

"I'm not taking any deals, Sam."

"I didn't say you were."

"I haven't even been offered one."

"Just as well then, right?"

He goes back to his menu.

The waitress comes over and they order. Guy checks YouTube repeatedly. One of the reuploaded videos—some of the other new ones have been taken down but more have sprung up since—is somehow at 576,937 views. If he goes on the news can he expect a visit from a little man with a strange outfit? But Guy can't deny it: he's feeling hopeful. Erin was cured, and she's even gone back to work. Yes, she's a little weird, but Guy didn't know what she was like before.

The food comes. Sam breaks off halfway through his ham and eggs to speak to someone who is apparently returning his enquiry. After he finishes:

"We have some holy water and some crystals and things to collect near here. Cheap. Can't hurt, right?"

"No."

"I don't mean to sound like I'm judging you, Guy," Sam suddenly says. "I know how badly you must want a way out of this. But we have to stick to the plan. We draw them out. We make it so they don't have a choice but to turn you back, maybe even me too, and more importantly we scale back some of that *threshold* in the process. It's not about us."

"I know," Guy says hurriedly. "Don't worry. We're sticking to the plan."

"Okay. Good. Good."

Guy looks at his watch. It's gone ten thirty. They have plenty of time to eat, collect the tools Sam is talking about, and make the meeting. Guy tries to relax.

He can't. He's desperate to leave and to see what the *Other Folk* have to say. He tries to keep his legs from jiggling in anticipation. He doesn't want Sam to see.

***

It's two pm and Guy and Sam are in a village hall in Stoke on Trent, sitting on plastic chairs arranged in a circle. They've picked up the charms Sam sourced in Nottingham. Their pockets are full of things like bones, precious stones, and small pieces of wood engraved with runes. Guy doesn't really put much faith in any of them, but he doesn't think they're needed here.

Of the forty or so other people present, only Sam, Guy, and two of the older Other Folk are sitting down. The rest are standing around in clusters, quietly chatting; no, *quietly* doesn't do it justice. The conversation Guy can make out is robotic, polite to the point of strangeness. He already understands some of what Erin meant about context.

They're all like her.

All of them.

The group is a mix of various ages and races. There's a tea urn and most people are holding little plastic cups. The ceiling is high with strip lights in it, the floor has various markings on it for things like indoor five-a-side football and netball, and one end of the room is filled by an old stage with shabby-looking brown curtains. It couldn't be more ordinary. No-one has spoken to him and Sam other than Erin since they arrived, and even she only spoke to tell them it'd start in ten minutes. Erin is pale but *all* of the people here are the same. There are three black people present and even their dark skin has a more... *washed out* look.

Not light-skinned. Drained.

Guy did need context to see what they've given up; he needed so many of them under one roof to feel it, as now it's palpable.

They're all missing a little piece of themselves. Not their souls, apparently, but... what *is* it...

"What do you think?" he murmurs to Sam.

"It's safe," he says. "Let's just leave it at that." Sam is tense though.

Guy remembers the last time he was in a room like this; for that group Nancy made him go to. It was bollocks, of course, but he had to at least try it as she'd said she'd leave him otherwise. Everyone there had major issues; it was totally inappropriate for Guy to go, he was nowhere *near* as bad as them. Actual alcoholics, drug addicts, people that were a fucking mess. Guy made excuses not to go back and eventually Nancy stopped asking.

Guy notices someone else enter the room, a tall man in his fifties, and sees a lady of a similar age spot him and approach. The tall man smiles when he sees her, but it doesn't reach his eyes. They hesitate as they draw closer to one another, and their arms almost spasm awkwardly up and down as they weigh up whether or not to hug. The smiles are now gone from their faces. Now they embrace, slowly, gingerly, and Guy sees the man's chin rest on the woman's shoulder; he doesn't look sad. He just looks confused. Their arms are around each other yet it isn't a true hug. Guy sees that what they are trying to do is beyond them, and for some reason he can't tear his eyes away but now someone is approaching from his left. It's a woman around Erin's age, mid-thirties maybe, wearing a blazer with a T-shirt and jeans.

"Hello," she says, her demeanour, her *delivery* exactly the same as Erin's. "Just thought I'd say hello. You're new, aren't you? Both of you?"

"Uh, that's correct," Guy says, wooly-mouthed after watching the two non-huggers. "I'm Guy, this is Sam."

"Nice to meet you both," the woman says. "I'm Zara Culpepper. I just wanted to put you at ease. There's nothing to worry about here." Its sincere yet somehow also a rote performance. She *wants* to welcome them, to reassure them, and it could be argued that the intention is enough... but somehow it isn't. Then Guy has it: there's no connection. He can't feel her humanity. The plug is in the socket, the switch has been flicked, everything is lined up as it should be, yet the lights aren't coming on.

But she's trying anyway—

Suddenly Guy's vision is going and he realises that he's about to cry. What the hell? He blinks quickly, trying to wipe his eyes without Zara Culpepper—without *Sam*—seeing.

"Thank... thank you, Zara..."

What the fuck is wrong with him?

Erin blessedly saves the day, clapping her hands gently. Zara Culpepper moves away and takes a seat, as does everyone else.

"I think we're all here," Erin says. "We have two new visitors tonight who... well, they are at the start of their journey," she says, gesturing to Guy and Sam. Everyone looks towards the newcomers. None of them make actual eye contact apart from an old man with thinning hair.

"You had your contract then?" he asks. He sounds a little suspicious.

A contract?

"No," Guy says, aware of everyone watching. "I mean... I had a warning letter, but..."

"That's not a contract," the old man says. "That's different."

"Well, Terry, that's true, but it doesn't matter," Erin replies. "Though you do bring up a good point, everyone, let's..." She gestures with her hand rather than finish her sentence, but everyone seems to understand. All of them either reach into a back pocket or handbag or under their seats and produce pieces of paper. Guy recognizes them as being made of the same material as the one he found in his living room this morning. Erin waits until they're all done.

"Okay," she says, holding her own paper, and then holds it up in the air. It's folded in half, as is everyone else's. They follow her lead and do the same, holding up their papers. Contracts, then? So the deal is in *writing?* He'd thought it was just a turn of phrase when Erin mentioned it. But what did they agree to? Erin didn't seem to know, other than that her soul itself was safe. Was the contract the thing she had in her living room drawer?

"*For myself,*" she says softly.

"*For myself,*" everyone else echoes. It isn't an affirmation or a battle cry. They sound like schoolkids responding to the register... and with that, Guy understands.

"*For my loved ones.*"

"*For my loved ones.*"

The flatness.

The lack of energy.

"*For the good I can do.*"

"*For the good I can do.*"

The little pockets of defeat, little holes that can be filled by something else. Little handholds and footholds in the world.

"*This sacrifice we have made.*"

"*This sacrifice we have made.*"

Those things out there in the darkness don't need souls, that isn't their problem. Guy wouldn't have understood it if he hadn't been in this room where the air is so thick with defeat that he can taste it. It's anti-energy, a hungry vacuum.

They just need people to surrender.

"Thank you everyone," Erin says, and there's more rustling as everyone puts their pieces of paper away. "It's my turn to share this month. If it's alright I'd like to start my story with the *parley* rather than the constructions arriving. For most of us that part's the same and I've told it here many times anyway. Is that alright?" Murmurs of agreement. Erin begins. She skips through it, glossing over the contract signing and how she turned back. That's not the important part to her, of course. She gets onto her life *now,* and what she's achieved recently; how she got a promotion at work, and the hobbies she's doing. She's learning to paint. She's doing Sudoku. She's involved in an online political discussion forum. She's telling a version of her life that lets all the people around her know that *it was worth it.* She doesn't mention about being diminished; everyone listening already knows it. They're the same. Guy watches them; he wonders how they can even get anything out of it, being the way they are, but their attention never wanders. They don't look sad or miserable. They're just... there.

But they're alive, the voice in his head whispers. *They're not monsters. Some of them are even still wearing wedding rings, and* look—

He sees a man and a woman holding hands on the opposite side of the circle.

Isn't that all that matters? It's still a life... just lessened.

And Guy realises that this is how they want him to think. To see the way out and take it.

Be another brick in the wall—

But what if that's what it takes to save Nancy?

She might not need—

The room sways a little. Guy looks at Sam... and sees he is furious. Red-faced, covering his mouth with his hand. Guy catches his eye for a moment and then Sam turns away, listening.

"I don't regret it," Erin is saying. "I'd make the same choice all over again. And I have to say, I know a few of us have taken Sally's advice recently." Erin gestures to a woman opposite. "Dancing has made a big difference. I go twice a week now, Lindy Hop and Salsa. It's hard and I have to force myself, but I think its worth it. I really recommend it. Carl, you too...?" A skinny guy in his fifties gives her a thumbs up, nodding.

See? They're still living.

But Guy is finding it hard to breathe. He needs to leave. The air, the energy... Erin was right. He had to experience this. His own anger flares as he thinks how his enemy—the *True Folk*, he reminds himself—would *want* him to know... because that makes the surrender that much more important.

It's nothing, they would say. *Give it to us and you can go back to normal.*

And what scares him to death is that maybe he could.

"Brenda?" Erin asks, speaking to a chubby woman in a yellow T-shirt and blue jeans. "You wanted to share?"

"Thanks Erin," Brenda says, standing. "Taking your lead, I'll start with the *parley* too. I like that idea." She describes the visitor and the contract, not mentioning Mister Chair by name, although from her description Guy thinks it has to be 'him'. *Parley* has been mentioned twice now; is that the phrase for conversation about the contracts? He knows *parley* is an old word for talking or having a meeting. Brenda doesn't talk about what her curse was, but she does briefly talk about clothes not fitting, or realising that she was looking up to talk to people that she used to be on eye-level with. Were they shrinking her? Like

Erin, her story focuses on what she does to keep her head above water: bingo and recently the WI. She hasn't made up her mind about that yet, but talks about the various members and what she thinks of them. She seems to like them all. Eventually, Brenda sits.

"Siobhan?" Erin asks, addressing a woman who can't be more than twenty-five. "You wanted to speak, I think?"

"Thank you, Erin," Siobhan says, standing up. She looks shy, quiet even for the Other Folk, but she's talking anyway. She's wearing a baggy black knitted sweater and a gypsy dancer's skirt, her hair scraped back in a bun. "I..." She pauses for a second, anxious, and Guy sees she would be turning red if she could. "I don't really have any advice to give or experiences to share this month. You all know that I don't normally share."

"That's okay Siobhan," someone says. A murmured chorus of genteel agreement goes up.

"But I thought I should say something this time," Siobhan continues. "I just want to say that I think... I think you're all really brave. You made a sacrifice to... you know, to stop you becoming something worse. Something that could hurt others. I just... I just want to say..." Her fingers dance around one another and she looks at her hands. "You're heroes that will never be recognized. I wanted to let you all know that. I think you *needed* to hear that."

She sits down quickly without another word and someone starts gently clapping. Everyone quickly joins, a round of quiet cricket applause that for this crowd is the equivalent of a screaming standing ovation.

Suddenly Sam makes a *psssssshhhht* noise with his lips. He stands up.

"I'll see you outside," he mutters to Guy, and turns away to leave.

"Sam?" Erin asks.

"Thanks for the invite, Erin," he says, "but I'm leaving." Guy is stunned; *Sam* is doing a dramatic flounce-out?

"Is something wrong?" she asks. Sam pauses, torn over responding.

"Sam—" Guy begins, embarrassed and confused.

"No disrespect to the young lady there," Sam says, wagging a finger at Siobhan, "but I'm amazed to hear the way you people talk about yourselves. You'd endorse that word? *Heroes?* Is that really how you see yourselves?"

No-one says anything.

"What's the purpose of this group?" Sam continues, throwing his hands up. "A little monthly groupthink conniving session? To tell yourselves that your lives are worthwhile after the decision, that the alternative was far worse? And who were you hurting, selling your little plots of psychic land, right? *No one,* that's what you told yourselves. *Except you know that isn't true.* You pat yourselves on the back for *talking* but you've *done nothing*, in fact you've done *worse than nothing."*

Guy looks at the faces around the room. Every single one is placid, as if they were watching a river flow by.

"You won't understand," Brenda says gently. "You're not in the same situation. We can tell. Give your friend a week," she adds, meaning Guy, "and ask him how *he* feels about it." Guy reddens too, and Sam looks at him, mouth frozen open. Guy remembers what Sam's issue is: he's angry with himself. Guy has to stop this.

"Come on Sam," he says, moving towards Sam, but Sam backs up a step, pointing a finger at the watching faces.

"I'm not like *them*," he says to Guy, "but you think I'd take their lead to stop what's coming to me? They're *already dead.* Better dead than *this,"* he says, but he lets Guy put a hand on his shoulder. Guy doesn't mention how he doesn't think his curse gives him the option of death. He thinks he'd be a lot less frightened if it did. Brenda was right; Sam isn't like them.

As Guy's right hand touches Sam's shoulder they both notice how the scales have now reached Guy's wrist.

They've progressed in just the last few hours.

The blood drains from Sam's face. He looks up at Guy.

"Can we leave?" Sam asks quietly. Guy nods, patting Sam gently on the shoulder.

"Sure." He turns to Erin. "I think we'd better go." She nods. Her face is completely unsurprised. She expected him to be angry—*these people are selling out the human race*—but he isn't. Half of him understands their choice completely.

"You don't understand yet," she says. "But you will. This way we have something left."

"Whatever works for you, Erin," he tells her. He begins to turn away, but her voice stops him.

"What about you, though?" she asks.

"What?"

"What do *you* have?" she asks. Of course, her face is inscrutable. "We can all sense it on you. That's part of our situation. 'No filter', you could say. We see things as they are." The eyes in the circle stare at him, heads nodding in agreement without a trace of malice. "I'm not saying this to shame you, Guy. I'm saying it to help you. You're struggling and hurting and you don't even know why. For you, life in the *Other Folk*..." She closes her eyes for a moment, concentrating. Her brow furrows in sadness. "...it would be a blessing." Her eyes open, so pale they are almost grey. "You know I'm right."

Now it's Sam's turn to put his hand on Guy's shoulder.

"Let's go," he says quietly. "There's nothing here for us."

"Whatever you *do* have left," Guy says to Erin, his voice flat. "Whatever you *can* feel; I hope you can live with it. I really do. Because I don't think you have anything at all."

He's amazed to see her head drop slightly. He turns and leaves, feeling the collective gaze of the room on him, knowing he wouldn't stay long. Maybe all newbies arrive and react the same way. Maybe they think he'll be at the next session himself, contract in his back pocket, looking a little more pale than he does right now. His ears are ringing and his heartbeat is up as he and Sam walk outside. What did she mean? He thinks of the gentle tone of her words and something inside him responds with rage. He looks at the scales on his wrist and he has to stop himself from turning back inside, from storming up to Erin and putting his hands around her throat—

"*Goddamnit!*" he screams, and it feels *good* to get this fucking shit out. Sam doesn't even turn around at the noise, walking ahead with his shoulders hunched and his fists clenched at his sides. They're in the car park now, the village hall fortunately on a quiet street with only a few houses and little passing traffic. *The perfect place to lose your shit,* Guy thinks, gleefully letting it come, and then his fingers are tearing at the disguise dressing on his neck and tearing it free, screwing the fabric up into a ball and hurling it towards his car. And it's not enough, something is pouring out of him as he thinks *fuck it* and now his jacket is coming off and following the same arc as the bandages. It hits the side of his car with a rustling *flop* sound and now Sam turns round but then Guy can't see him as now his shirt is being yanked off over his head, buttons popping as he can't be out of it quick enough, and all he sees is sky as he bares his torso to the world and screams to the heavens *because he needs to be seen.* The sound is good and frightening all at the same time, hurt and rage, so much *rage* as his terrible secret is gloriously exposed for all to see. He screams so hard that his vision whitens for a second and as he straightens back up he sees Sam, standing frozen by the car now, his own anger evaporated. He's seeing the full extent of Guy's scales' progress for the first time.

Guy looks down at himself. His shirt is held clutched in his left fist like the scalp of a defeated foe. His palms hurt from his nails digging into them. His left arm is now covered down to the elbow with white scales, as is the entire length of his right, all the way up to his wrist. Half of his stomach is now covered too. Guy looks up at Sam and yes, *of course*, waits for him to say something.

Guy sees Sam's gaze move sharply, spotting something behind him.

Guy spins around—he thought they were alone—and sees a dog walker standing near the car park entrance. He's an old man, wearing a long brown coat and a small hat over a sweater and jeans; he's stopped dead in his tracks. For a second Guy thinks *he's one of them* but he knows that's not true. The dog—a Staffie, Guy notices—has its tail tucked between its legs. He sees the nervous expression on the old man's face. This stranger who was minding his own business is seeing a screaming, shirtless man.

Nancy, Guy thinks. *I'm so sorry.*

Their eyes meet, but the dog walker quickly turns away, embarrassed, frightened even, and Guy begins to babble.

"I'm sorry," Guy says, the moment reminding him of that most awful of truths: sorry only goes so far. "I... I just came from a support group in there," he says, desperate for something to say and pointing at the village hall. The old man stops walking, waving away Guy's concerns with a timid flick of his hand, but he doesn't make eye contact.

"Don't worry," he says, eyes darting around. "Been to a support group myself. For the wife." He pauses for a second before adding: "It does get better."

"Oh... no," Guy says, not thinking. "It's not for..."

"Oh, right, yes," the old guy says, beginning to walk away and looking even more embarrassed. "Sorry. Something to do with the, the..." He begins to point at Guy's body without looking, but then catches himself, reddening. "None of my business, sorry, sorry, couldn't help but notice with the shirt off there, I, uh... good luck," he finishes awkwardly, but then the importance of what he just said finally hits Guy:

He could see Guy's scales with his bare eyes.

Unless this old man has watched Guy's YouTube video or one of the copies, that shouldn't be possible. Guy spins to look at Sam, who is already hurrying towards the old man.

"Excuse me!" Sam calls, Guy running after him, but the old guy keeps on walking. Guy can't blame him. "It's alright, don't worry, I just need to ask you something!" The old man hesitates, then turns around.

"Yes?" he asks nervously.

"Yes, we're sorry to bother you," Guy says, trying to sound calm, normal. The old man fumbles the dog's lead in his fingers, uncertain. Guy supposes this man isn't used to talking to strangers with white scales all over their shirtless bodies. He hurriedly begins to put his shirt back on. "The scales," he says. "You can see them? I'm asking because... I'm just checking that, uh, that this shows up in, uh... daylight. It's..."

"It's make-up," Sam says, his poker face back and stronger than ever. "For a fancy-dress contest. It's supposed to be glow-in-the-dark but we wanted to see if it looks good in the daytime. We do monster make up on Youtube. Sorry about the screaming, we're filming a promo."

"Yeah," Guy says, relieved by and amazed at Sam's quickness. "You... don't use YouTube, do you?"

"No, not really," the old man says. "I mean me sister does sometimes for recipes and cross stitch stuff, and me grandkids are never off it, but I never use it meself. I have to say, the makeup is *very* good."

"So you've never seen him before?" Sam asks breathlessly, pointing at Guy.

"No, sorry. Should I have?" The old man breaks into a smile. "Are you famous, then?"

"Not really, not yet," Guy says... but he's starting to think that maybe he's famous *enough.*

That maybe there's another way out of this after all.

He needs to talk to Sam *right now.*

"Sorry if I scared you," Guy says, wrapping it up.

"Oh, I'm hard to scare, me," lies the old man, smiling and giving a thumbs-up as he walks away. Sam and Guy return it. Once the man is a few feet away Guy eagerly turns to Sam.

"Sam—" he hisses, but Sam's plastered-on smile and watchful eyes never waver from the old man's direction.

"Hold... on... a second..." he says through gritted-smile-teeth, waiting. Guy follows his gaze and there's an awkward moment where the dog walker turns around again to see Guy and Sam grinning after him like a couple of idiots. They both wave. This time the old man just nods and quietly fucks off.

As soon as the dog walker rounds the corner, Guy spins back to Sam.

"*Sam—*"

"I know," he says, breathing out. "He could see it. And he doesn't watch YouTube."

"Exactly!" Guy says, beginning to hop from foot to foot. "You remember what Erin said at her house? About thresholds being reached? This whole thing is about *awareness,* right? Some kind of universal distraction? So what if all the YouTube stuff has meant that a point is reached where enough people know—"

"Uh-huh," Sam says, looking thoughtful. "This could be *extremely* useful."

"No shit, it could," Guy says with a grin, because he's already forming a plan. "I have an idea." Now Sam starts to smile.

"I think I might be one step ahead of you," he says, "but hit me with it anyway."

Guy does. As they talk, both of their smiles slowly turn into looks of concern. The plan makes sense, but it's high-risk. Not quite a Hail Mary, but close. One thing's for sure: coming to this meeting today has given them some *very* useful information.

"Yeah..." Sam says solemnly once Guy's finished. "But I really, really don't like the first part."

"Me neither," Guy tells him, but points under his chin, feeling along his throat until his fingertip touches skin again. He can feel the scales just beginning to creep around the underside of his jawline. Maybe two or three days left. "But if I'm not going to make a deal, and I want to have any chance of saving myself—of saving *us*—while not pussying out on this thing, then I'm all out of any other ideas." Sam nods, but it turns into a head shake as he sighs heavily.

"Let's go do it now," he says. "Before I change my mind." He looks at his watch. *"Fuck,"* he says, another rare F-bomb. That shows how worried he is. "Why couldn't this all be happening in the summer? Sun's going to be down by the time we get there."

"No choice, Sam," Guy tells him, and it's the truth. Today is their only window, because tomorrow, Guy is going on TV.

They have work to do first.

***

Chapter Nineteen
Pressure
✳✳✳

The room is quiet except for Sam's nose-breathing. He's trying to stay calm. So is Guy. It's not working.

They're standing in the dark, facing one another. Guy's entire body is as tense as a tightrope and he knows Sam is the same. The charms in their pockets, the holy water and the like, feel utterly useless.

Outside, the sun has set. It's gone 4pm, the November nights drawing in early, too damn early. The air in here is thick and heavy, as expected.

All they can do is wait. It's interminable.

Sam's chin suddenly shoots upwards.

"What was that?" he whispers. Guy listens, straining his ears. There's nothing.

"Nothing," he hisses back. "We'll know when it happens. Just listen."

Someone had changed the locks, they discovered, but that was to be expected; so much so that they came here via Sam's house to get his lock-picking kit. Knowledge of latin, fine cigars, and lock-picking skills; Sam is only a few career choices away from being a gentleman thief, Guy thinks, he and his expert team hitting the casinos in Monte Carlo—

He tries to halt the silly thoughts he's desperately using to take himself away from what they're—

Wait. What *was* that? Something outside maybe?

Just as Guy realises he's beginning to smell ammonia, he hears a horribly familiar sound:

Skri. Skri-skri. Skri-skri, skri.

Sam's whole body tenses and his breathing accelerates. Guy puts a trembling hand on Sam's shoulder to reassure him in the dark but the older man is already nodding quickly, letting Guy know he's alright. Guy isn't.

Their escape route to the right is blocked; whoever changed the locks, presumably the police or someone in Larry's family, has also boarded over both of the patio doors. The only way back out is through the kitchen door. The feeling of being trapped like easy prey is the only thing thicker than the soupy air in this place that once was Larry's home. They're in its lair now, and they need to make sure they don't end up in the actual belly of the beast.

What the hell were you thinking, Guy's mind babbles, *what the—*

Skri-skri-skri-skri—

The tiny rodent skittering begins in earnest above them, and goddammit if it isn't happening *faster* as it swells almost immediately, sounding as if it were covering the left hand side of the ceiling over their heads and then already it's switching from mouse teeth on sticks to giant claws on planks.

"Oh shit, it's different, *listen,*" Sam hisses, trembling as he echoes Guy's thoughts, but Guy closes his eyes and grips Sam's shoulder more tightly. He wishes he could have told Sam to stay away, but he didn't know if the presence of them both was needed to draw the thing out, to be detected—

"I know Sam," Guy whispers back, voice shaking. "Just hold on. Hold on."

"Yes, yes, but—are you going to do it—"

Skri-skri, ski-skri-skri, ski, ski-ski-skri-skri—

It's coming fast. It knows it missed them last time and it *wants* them, Guy can feel it.

"Not yet... wait... just hold on a little..."

The myriad scratches become one just like before, forming that steady, awful, tearing rhythm.

SKRIIIIIIIII— SKRIIIIIIIII— SKRIIIIIIIII—

"*Jesus,*" Sam whispers, and Guy can feel the older man's pulse under his hand. "*It's nearly here. Now, do it now—*"

"*Wait,*" Guy hisses, clamping his feet to the floor, everything in his subconscious screaming that time is nearly up, the window's closing, and the noise is at a deafening crescendo now—

SKRIIIIIIIII— SKRIIIIIIIII— SKRIIIIIIIII—

"*It's here!*" Sam says. "*Now, do it now!*"

"*Wait!*"

SKRIIIIIIIIIIIIIIIIIIIIIIIIIT.

THUD.

That's what Guy was waiting for. The sliding sound begins, it's quicker—

Slumph—thud, slumph—thud, slumph—thud—

"*NOW!*

This time Guy agrees.

He opens his mouth to scream... and nothing comes out. He's frozen.

He thinks of Nancy.

"PARLEY!" he screams, so loud that his throat burns. "I, GUY AUTUMN, REQUEST PARLEY!"

He'd looked up the word the *Other Folk* had used at their support group to be doubly sure. His interpretation—that it was an old word for a meeting—was only half right. It means a conference—a *protected* conference—between two opposing sides. It's the protected side of it that Guy is gambling on, if these fuckers are as obsessed and empowered and bound by rules as he thinks they are

Even if it's a word that has its origins in war.

"*It's not working,*" Sam says, eyes darting around the ceiling. He's right. The sliding is continuing as eagerly as ever, more so in fact. A great worm hungrily charging towards its meal.

Slumphthudslumphthudslumphthud—

Did it not hear him!? The noise it's making—

"PARLEEYYYYYY!" Guy screams again, screwing up his fists as he does so. "I, GUY Autumn, REQUEST PARLEY!"

Slumphthudslumphthudslumphthud—

It *isn't* working! They have to—

"*Mister Chair!*" Sam suddenly hisses. Guy uses it.

"WITH MISTER CHAIR!" Guy bellows. "I WANT PARLEY WITH MISTER CHAIR!"

Thud.

Silence.

Neither Sam nor Guy dare breathe. Nothing happens for a full minute that feels like a week. They don't move. It doesn't move.

Who the fuck is Mister Chair that his name—

Creak.

That's the floorboards. It's shifting its weight.

A slow, wet snort comes from upstairs. It sounds like a pig mixed with a jet engine. Both Sam and Guy flinch.

SKRIIIIIIIIII— SKRIIIIIIIIII— SKRIIIIIIIIII—

The sound is suddenly everywhere again, and they both crouch as they wait for Mister Chair to suddenly burst through the wall and murder them. The rhythm begins to fall apart almost as quickly as it arrived, breaking off into the individual mouse scratches and then rapidly becoming less audible. There's a final handful of tiny *ski-skri-skri* sounds and then the floorboards above them make a soft *pup-pup-pup-pup* noise as they settle quickly back into their usual position. A great weight has been lifted from them.

It's gone. Even Sam can feel it.

"Goodness..." he breathes, falling forward and putting his hands on his knees. "Oh my goodness. It... that worked. I can't believe that worked." Guy breathes out too and pats Sam's shoulder, trying to let his own heart rate slow.

"Well..." Guy gasps, trying to catch air too. "We only know... it got the message... we don't know... if it will mean anything."

"Do we... wait here?" Sam asks, straightening up. "What do you think?"

"I don't think we have to," Guy says, but also meaning *I absolutely am not bloody waiting in here.* "I get the impression that when Mister Chair wants to see you, he comes to you wherever you are."

"Then let's get *out* of here," Sam says, already heading for the front door. "We can check into the hotel now and I suddenly feel the need to be around people."

Guy follows, wanting only to be in a well-lit hotel room away from public view; the attendant at the petrol station on the way here, the customer on the forecourt; both of them saw his neck, goggling at the still-uncovered scales. His theory about the old dog walker was right; most people, if not everyone, can see the scales now, and the glimpse Guy unwittingly caught in the rearview mirror showed him the whiteness was well onto the bottom part of his face now. He doesn't want to sit in a public bar with a fresh but uncomfortable dressing going up to his mouth. Besides, Guy doesn't think that would be the right place to wait.

He's going to sit in his hotel room and wait for the pre-interview in the morning.

That, and Mister Chair.

***

"Say it, Guy."

"No. I've promised twice already, Nancy. That should be good enough. It's starting to get annoying."

"Well third time's the charm, then." She's trying to be light hearted but quickly abandons it. "Just promise. I know I'm on you about this but I need to be sure—"

She sounds tense. Guy gives in.

"Fine. I promise I won't stop. No matter what."

"Do you give me your word?"

"I do."

Nancy's ball busting is really making Guy wish that Sam would hurry up and get back from the bar with the drinks. He's constantly watching the corners of the room so that Mister Chair can't suddenly appear from the periphery. Guy pictures his arrival like a horror movie jump scare: you glimpse the bathroom cabinet mirror as you open it to get the toothpaste, the glass reflecting the *empty* room behind you, but when you close it again...

"And there's nothing I can do to help you?"

"Not since you took a trinket into the house, Nancy," he tells her. "That was the deal: I won't stop if you do your best to stay off their radar. It seems like they forgot about you. Some little monster in scary admin forgot to press the button marked *activate curse*. I'd like to keep it that way."

"If we knew for sure that I was cursed though, you'd let me help, right?"

"In a heartbeat." It's true.

There's a thud-knock on the door.

That'll be Sam, unable to knock properly because his hands are full. Guy had mentioned his own promise to stay off the booze, but Sam had said *after today, I think you're allowed.* Guy wasn't sure but didn't disagree. They aren't sharing a room, though. Sam is on another floor. He'd checked in for them both while Guy hurried into the elevator, covering his neck as best he could. He'd kept his eyes closed for the ride up. The elevator's internal walls were all mirrors.

Maybe, uh... his mind suggests, *you could sleep on the floor in his room...?*

Jesus. Try and save *some* dignity.

Sam brought protective mirrors up. They're piled up against the wall, yet to be arranged around the bed.

"What time's your interview tomorrow?" Nancy asks, changing the subject.

"Well the pre-interview is first thing in the morning," he says, standing to open the door. "It's why I'm staying so close—" He pauses, trying to remember what time the bloody interview actually *airs*—

"I'm glad Sam's there with you," she says. "Have you been managing to... uh..."

"We've been getting on, don't worry," Guy lies, old bristles coming up at the question. It's time to end this conversation.

The thud-knock comes at the door again.

"That's Sam," he says. "I'd better go."

"Call me before you go to bed."

"I will, I will." It's almost like they're together again, and then in the words of Frank and, ironically, Nancy Sinatra, Guy goes and spoils it all by saying something stupid. "I miss you."

There's a pause down the phone line.

"I'll talk to you later Guy," she says. "Please be careful."

She hangs up.

The thud-knock comes again, harder this time.

"*Jesus,*" Guy snaps, annoyed and of *course* not with Sam but Sam is the one who is here. Guy yanks open the door.

Sam is standing there with a bottle of red and two glasses.

"Sorry to bother you," he sniffs, seeing the look on Guy's face.

"Well..." Guy begins as Sam shuffles past, the words *I heard you the first time* on his tongue but he's *trying* goddammit, he's trying. "*Aah,* I was just on the phone to Nancy, I didn't mean to—"

"Let's just drink this and shut up, eh?" Sam says as the door clicks shut. "If we're drinking, we're not arguing." Guy chuckles a little at this, glad of it, and then another knock comes on the now-closed hotel room door.

The two men look at each other.

"*Did you order anything?*" Guy mouths. Sam shakes his head quickly.

Guy feels the hairs on the back of his head begin to stand up. Not the hairs on the back of his neck; he doesn't have any anymore. The new scales there have seen to that.

He wants to tell himself it's just a member of staff knocking but he knows—he *knows*—that it isn't.

"No... thanks," Guy calls, dimly hoping that it's because he didn't put the *Do Not Disturb* sign on the door, that somehow it's a cleaner doing a late visit even though the room was perfectly turned down when he checked in.

There's no sound of footsteps walking away.

"Hello?" he calls. "Who is it?"

No reply. To his amazement, Sam takes a step towards the door. Guy stops him.

"Who's—" he begins, before the sentence is cut off:

"Open the door, Guy."

The voice is deep, Johnny Cash deep, with an unusual accent that Guy can't place. His body seems to recognize something in it, though; a violent shiver passes through him. Poor Sam backs up a step; he may be a grizzled veteran in the world of men, but Guy thinks Sam's missing something that he needs to deal with these close encounters. The man is trying but he's not doing well.

Silence.

Say something, Guy thinks.

"Who is it?" he repeats.

The spyhole in the door stares like an unblinking eye; if Guy looks through it, he'll see—

"You know who it is."

Each word vibrates in Guy's spine.

Holy shit. This is the real deal.

They've come to parley.

Guy suddenly breaks and rushes past Sam to the spyhole, taking large soft steps so he doesn't make any noise. He breathes in, looks through. No-one—

The voice speaks again, unseen, and so close to the door now that Guy jumps back. The speaker must have his mouth right up against the wood.

"You asked for *parley,* and I have come to engage in it," the voice says, and Guy can hear a smile in it. He still can't place the accent. The twang is almost from the American south but the *Ts* and the *Ss* have a soft Scandinavian sound, like a European raised in Texas. "Was there some kind of *misunderstanding?*" The speaker enjoyed saying that last part. "You do not have to ask me to come in. But you can open the door. I have something to give you. Some information, too. I give you my word, formally and recognizable under the sun and above the earth, that neither I nor my people will harm you if I enter."

Guy opens the latch and yanks the door open, bracing himself for what he's about to see.

The visitor stands a lot shorter than most men. Not dwarfism short, but close. One look and Guy understands what Erin meant.

It's not just the strange suit; she was right when she described it as *military style.* It's collarless and buttoned up all the way to the neck. It has epaulettes on each shoulder, and seems to be made of something like tweed but not. The fibres are almost as thick as wool in a knitted sweater. The damn thing is weird, and yes, there are the seashells on the breast where medals should be. Guy doesn't remember what colour Erin said they were but these particular seashells are iridescent blue, orange, green, and blue again, four of them. His shoes are too large for his height. But even with all that it isn't the outfit that gives him away.

It's not the hair, even though it *is* like that of a doll, but you could mistake that for a bad transplant.

It's not the teeth, even though they *are* too white and too even and too numerous, but you could mistake them for a bad false set.

It's not that his nose *is* way too big, but you could mistake that for unfortunate genes.

It *is* his skin. His godawful skin. It looks like it's made of rubber.

It *is* his eyes. They're huge—far too big for any human—so much so that Guy is amazed that the visitor made it up here without anyone freaking out. Maybe people can't see the visitor the way Guy can. Even with their size—and the way the visitor hasn't blinked once in the twenty speechless seconds Guy has been standing here—one look into them shows that something profound is missing. Guy finds its absence as horrifying as the sight of blood flowing from a loved one's artery. Malice *radiates* from the visitor as much as his smell; he *stinks*. Mould. Age. Damp. Clothes left soaking wet in a pile.

Mister Chair has come to pay them a visit.

He's holding something. A piece of paper. Of course he is.

"I will try to keep this brief," Mister Chair says, holding the paper up and grinning more wildly than is physically possible for a human face. "You know what this is. What it means. I am here to offer it to you and to answer any questions that you might have."

He doesn't say the rest of the sentence: *and to accept your signature.*

Steady yourself, Guy thinks. *This is the start of a dance.*

Guy *wants* to show Mister Chair that he isn't scared, although Mister Chair's huge bent nose—Erin Lafferty really wasn't wrong—certainly looks capable of smelling fear. Guy steps back out of the doorway—if his legs are unsteady he doesn't think it shows— and slowly sweeps his arm back, displaying the room. Unfortunately, the gesture passes across Sam as if Guy were presenting him. Poor Sam, frozen and not knowing what to do, uncertainly raises a hand in a little wave. He realises what he's doing and snaps his hand down.

"This isn't me inviting you in," Guy says, his voice sounding steady. "I know your people like to keep things official. Like with your little contracts." He mentally pats himself on the back for the word *little* there. "But I don't own this hotel room, and there is nothing stopping you from entering. But this is *not* an invitation," Guy hurriedly adds the last part, repeating himself.

Mister Chair cocks his head to the left slightly, unmoved from the doorway. He looks at Sam.

"Hello, Sam," he says.

"No," Sam says, and it's enough.

That's something. Attaboy.

Guy turns his back on Mister Chair, every muscle in his body resisting, screaming that it's a bad idea. He crosses the room and sits on the edge of the bed, facing the small chair in the corner. The implication is obvious. It occurs to him that all the lights are on in the room. Can this thing even *be* in light like that? But then Erin said Mister Chair came to her in daylight; he's different to the thing that came to Sam's house, then?

A few seconds pass and Guy hasn't heard a thing. He can't stop himself; he turns around and when he sees that Mister Chair has moved to the foot of the bed, that he's *inside the room now and didn't make a sound getting there,* Guy manages to catch his scream of fright. Those big, wide eyes and that plastered-on, grotesque smile stare at Guy, and damnit if Mister Chair doesn't look pleased as punch. This was payback for the *little* comment.

Okay then. One point each.

Sam has backed up a step or two, his hand to his mouth. However Mister Chair moves, it clearly wasn't nice to see.

"Shall I sit down, Guy?" Mister Chair asks, cocking his head to the right this time. His head movements look like someone taught a chicken how to relax.

"It's up to you." Mister Chair chuckles a little and moves to the chair Guy's facing. *Now* Guy sees him walk. It's grotesque, like watching a marionette made of flesh, the head bobbing slightly with each step, no, each *lurch.* His eyes watch Guy all the way and the fucker doesn't blink once. Mister Chair may be small, but it feels like being trapped in a room with a rabid chimp; one wrong move and it will tear off your jaw. Guy tries to find his anger and to his surprise it's *there.* For once, that's wonderful news. Mister Chair sits, his stench wafting towards Guy. It's even more intense in the smaller space. They are four feet away from each other.

"Are you comfortable discussing this in front of your friend?" he asks.

"You don't have a contract for me?" Sam says, forcing a scowl. Mister Chair turns his unblinking gaze towards Sam.

"Oh, *no,*" Mister Chair says. "Of course not. You are unimportant, Sam. We do not do deals with people we have put in *your* situation. You are merely bricks and mortar."

With that, he turns back to Guy, dismissing Sam. Sam's confused eyes find Guy's.

"You... don't have to stay if you don't want to, Sam," Guy says. "It's alright." Sam blinks a few times and then looks at the piece of paper in Mister Chair's hand. He takes a deep breath.

"I'll stay, if that's alright," he says quietly.

"Sure."

Sam quietly backs up to the wall, sweating, and leans on it, watching Mister Chair. Guy turns back to Chair and sees those big eyes are back on him, shining a little under the electric light. Guy imagines those huge round teeth suddenly opening wide and fastening around his neck, too fast to even see—

Mister Chair holds the piece of paper up.

"Would you like to read it?" he asks.

"Open it up and show me," Guy says, not wanting to risk touching Chair's hand, who does as he's asked. There's less writing than Guy expected; two paragraphs. One latin, one english with the words ENGLISH TRANSLATION OF THIS DOCUMENT above it just to be clear. Anyone but Guy would think that a pointlessly obvious explanation but Chair knows *Guy* knows how they operate: the words in latin could be something completely different, actually saying THE BIT IN ENGLISH BELOW ISN'T PART OF THIS CONTRACT AND DOESN'T MEAN A THING, SUCKER. The words *English Translation* clarifies it *in writing*. Erin didn't get that treatment; she was ignorant of the True Folk.

The English section says:

> I, GUY AUTUMN, RETAIN MY SOUL, MY CHARACTER, MY PHYSICAL HUMAN FORM AND MY FREE WILL, AND SHALL HENCEFORTH REMAIN IMMUNE FROM ALL HARM OR INTERFERENCE BY THE PARTY KNOWN AS THE TRUE FOLK OR THEIR ASSOCIATES EXCEPT UNDER CONDITION OF DIRECT INTERFERENCE WITH THE TRUE FOLK OR THEIR ENDEAVOURS. IN RETURN, I, GUY AUTUMN, CONCEDE DEFEAT TO THE TRUE FOLK, AND RECOGNISE THEIR SOVEREIGNITY IN THE HUMAN REALM, ALTHOUGH I SHALL REMAIN FREE FROM THEIR INFLUENCE AND WILL NOT BE SUBJECT TO THEIR LAWS OR BOUNDARIES. I WILL ALSO DENY ANY INVOLVEMENT WITH THE TRUE FOLK DURING MY UPCOMING TELEVISION APPEARANCE AND CONFESS MY MEDIA CLAIMS TO BE LIES.

"Direct interference?" Guy asks.

"Yes," Mister Chair says. "You live your life. You leave us alone." He shrugs, a movement that makes his whole body undulate. "We did not intend to discuss this with you until your transformation completes, but you asked for parley. There is an honour code within such a request. Plus, we did not anticipate you going *so* public with your situation. That never happens. Nothing we could not discredit or deal with, but when parley was requested it seemed opportune to get this signed." Nothing they couldn't discredit? Another bluff? "There was, I should add," Mister Chair continues, "no need for you to *exacerbate* things in the manner you have chosen. This contract would always arrive eventually, albeit in our own time."

Guy can't look at that smile any longer so he stares at the paper instead. He thinks of the support group. Of Erin's face as he left. Then the scales and the thoughts come screaming back to him, the ones he's been wrestling with ever since he set foot in Erin's house, the ones he lied to Sam and Nancy about because of *course* he's considering taking this route, the scales are all over him now, they've reached past his hip bones:

Erin didn't have anyone.

There's Nancy for support, at least.

Those two Other Folk holding hands. They had each other—

"Can I ask you something?" Guy says.

"Within reason."

"Why the *True Folk?* Why that name?"

"My folk are older than yours. Much older."

"But..." *You're so powerful.* Guy doesn't say it. "Why aren't you running the show? Running *us?*"

"It is complicated," Mister Chair says, lifting his chin upwards while keeping his eyes on Guy's. His head continues backwards until a normal man would be unable to see anything but ceiling. His eyes, though, are more than capable of staying on Guy's, angling sharply downwards in their large sockets. He grins all the while. "We were few, very few, and you were so many. It has taken a long, long time for us to arrive at this point. But I do not wish to be here long, Guy, in this room with you. I can bear the light but that does not mean it is pleasant. I am sure you understand."

"One more question," Guy says quickly, even as his mind spins at the concept of beings older than the human race, of one sitting before him. The keys to some of the biggest answers in existence are in this room. Wonder trumps even fear, it seems. "You said about... my soul. You even specified it in writing it would be safe. That you have to do that suggest... the soul is a real thing. So we..." Can he even trust anything this thing says, even if the question has nothing to do with his situation. "... we go on? Beyond? Is that where the True Folk live?"

Mister Chair's chin slowly comes back down. Do his eyes seem darker? He leans backward a little, saying nothing, still smiling.

"Is it just more mind games?" Guy asks, leaning forward on instinct. "Is that just in there to screw with me?" Still nothing. Whatever the truth is, Guy doesn't think Chair likes it... and then, of course, *Sam* figures it out.

"*Oh my God...*" he breathes. "Don't you get it, Guy?" He points at Mister Chair, addressing him, although Mister Chair's eyes never leave Guy's. "That's the *difference*, isn't it? The soul. That's the difference between you and us. You *can't* ever go beyond."

Mister Chair says nothing. Instead he slowly lowers the contract and leans towards Guy. Guy doesn't move. The smile *is* still there, but yes, his eyes—so shiny before—are now almost grey where the white should be. The visitor raises his free hand and extends a finger towards the ceiling. To the heavens. He cocks his head the other way and opens his mouth.

He begins make a *haaaaaaaaa* sound that reminds Guy of a coffee machine starting up. Fetid breath wafts from Mister Chair's throat, engulfing Guy's face, so unpleasant that it makes his moldy odour smell like the finest cologne. Guy gags and throws his hand up, eyes watering, his other hand stopping him falling onto the bed. He gags, trying to find clean air, but refuses to get up off the bed and move away. He won't do it. Sam has dragged the corner of his jacket over his face in time.

"Guy!" Sam barks, his voice muffled. "Are you okay?"

"I'm fine," Guy coughs, but realises with grim delight that Mister Chair's trick is the monstrous equivalent of a child's insult. He's screwing with Guy for one reason and one reason only.

Sam was fucking *right.*

"That's ok," Guy coughs, once the smell has died down enough to breathe easily. Mister Chair's eyes are bright again now. He's pleased with himself. "You don't have to answer that... but I think you just did." If Chair's eyes dim slightly, it's only brief, but that one landed. Two points on the board each, then... but he's beginning to feel better. Steadier. He can unsettle Mister Chair, it seems.

And Guy knows he hasn't even played his best card yet.

"So," he says, wiping the last of the moisture out of his eyes. "I sign this and you lift my curse? I'm asking for an official *statement.*"

Mister Chair's head nods, a lolloping, loose movement like the Scarecrow in *The Wizard of Oz.*

"You understand a lot, Guy. And yes, that is what I am saying. You will return to normal. You may have noticed—of course you have—that the process is accelerating now? I think your face—as well as the rest of you—will be covered by the end of the week, certainly, and then you will begin the final transformation." *The rest of you.* Guy thinks it will be onto his thighs by the end of the day. He thinks his face and groin will be the last parts to go. The final insult. It would match their MO. "It is not," Mister Chair says, "as your people like to say, *an exact science.*"

"What am I becoming?" Guy whispers. Anger, again. "*What have you done to me?*"

"There is no exact name for it in your mythology," Mister Chair says quietly. "Your kind of transformation is usually very secret. Your final form is... not well known in your stories."

"The contract talks about free will," Guy says, suppressing a shudder. "Peter Now—" Guy thinks better of mentioning Nowak's name. "I was told about people's minds changing. *Monstrous thoughts,* was the description. When does that begin? Has it begun?" Guy wants to punch the visitor so, so badly, but he wants answers and doesn't know what will happen when his knuckles meet Chair's face. It isn't made of bone and flesh, after all. Would it flatten? Would something worse be revealed underneath?

"Different thoughts, certainly," it says. "Has it already begun? You tell me. *Monstrous*, I cannot say. My perspective, the True Folk's perspective, is certainly different to yours. Eventually you will see for yourself. Unless you sign, of course. Then the progress will halt and I believe the scales should disappear within a few hours."

"But why stop me turning at all, then?" Guy cries, exasperated. "It's better to, to what, make enough people *surrender* than to swell your ranks—"

"How does one win wars, Guy?" Guy doesn't say the answer he knows: you win wars by gaining and holding land. "You felt it at that meeting when enough of the Other Folk—our Allies—were together. The atmosphere is turning our way, Guy. And our numbers are great enough now. We have enough servants. Situations like yours are now about leverage."

Leverage. Holy, holy shit... Sam was right about everything. Guy looks at Sam to see him staring back, gently shaking his head; guilt stabs Guy as he understands why:

Please, Guy. Don't do it.

Enough servants, Chair said. The threshold really is being reached.

It's a deliberately tiny movement—so small that even Chair's enormous eyes won't see it—but Guy shakes his head in return.

They have a plan, after all. *And now it's time to call the True Folk's bluff*

Guy takes a breath, then immediately honks it out again quickly as he realises he doesn't know what the hell this arsehole has just puffed out into the room.

"So that's all this about then,' Guy says, trying to sound casual. "Me becoming another foothold? Another surrender?"

"You may put it that way if you wish," Chair says. "You have seen Erin Lafferty and others like her, and understand what is being asked of you. Her group is not, of course, all of our signees. Why, before you met them all together, I wager that you would have seen at least one signee every day of the last few decades. Riding on your public transportation. In your gathering places. You may have even worked with them. Perhaps you noticed that they were a little different, detached. Defeated. But again, as in war: *surrender* is not the end. It is simply a change of state. Life can still be lived. It is, we think, a very little thing in the grander scheme."

That's always the excuse, isn't it?

"So it's not about anything else, then?"

"No."

"Are you sure about that?"

The clown-from-hell smile doesn't falter... but Chair hesitates before responding and Guy knows *he has the bastard.*

"Yes," Mister Chair says.

"You didn't seem too certain there."

"It sounds as if you are implying something. Can you explain?"

"Yes. I'm happy to."

Guy is nervous again so he stands, forcing his limbs to move. Mister Chair's eyes track Guy as he begins to pace by the foot of the bed. Sam is trying to catch Guy's eye, but Guy ignores him.

"Did you—you personally—see my video?" Guy asks. Mister Chair doesn't answer, of course. "I know your *Folk* aren't apparently *au fait* with tech but you must at least know about the one I put up, because I think you had it taken down. You have to operate under your *own* rules, but you still have a little bit of influence in certain circles. Right?" Silence. "I'll take that as a yes," Guy says, trying to sound confident. "And I've been thinking: why hasn't anyone done something similar in the past? After I went and met with the *Other Folk,* I figured it out. Most of your signees had to have been *very* carefully picked, right? Like Nowak, who you picked for his conscience... and his shyness. I bet that's important: picking people who would rather die than come under the public microscope, people with only a small number of friends and family. People who, like you, prefer to stay in the dark." Mister Chair's enormous eyes don't blink. "And even on the outside chance that they *did* put anything out there," Guy continues, "you probably got that taken down too, but that would have been easier to do because it never had a chance to go viral. Not enough people knew about it before you intervened. But then, like any organization that grows too fast, or too big... keeping tight quality control gets harder. Especially when someone like Larry threatens to maybe cause a little, tiny problem by writing an unintentional expose on the shantytowns and the trinkets being made there. And you were overconfident. You didn't cross the Ts. And I got involved, and *that* didn't matter either because I tripped the wrong triggers and ended up on the inside myself. No problem, eh? The transformation will make me keep my mouth shut and then you offer me a surrender deal. Or maybe my curse was intentional and you just got sloppy and picked badly, but either way, I was a little different. I wasn't your usual victim—"

Guy freezes; he's caught sight of Mister Chair's reflection in the hotel room's mirror. For a split second he thinks he's seeing a true form, something bigger, darker... no. There's just the little man's grinning head and his stupid suit with his seashells.

And he's reflected in the mirror.

Guy crosses to the nightstand, making it look like it's part of his pacing. There's a heavy-looking hotel ornament sitting next to Sam's bottle of red, a stylized, abstract, mass-produced statuette of two people embracing. It's black.

"Something happened that maybe you didn't expect," Guy says. "*My* video got a little traction, and quickly. That probably wouldn't have happened with anyone else, but I was lucky. I had a little help from a few industry buddies that got me kickstarted, cut me through the noise. And then it took on a life of its own. You got it taken down but you couldn't keep taking all the *new* versions of it down without that drawing too much attention."

Guy picks up the sculpture, turning it over, hoping it looks like a whimsical examination. Columbo admiring objects in the millionaire murderer's study as he delivers his denouement. Guy could fling it at the reflection in the mirror from here; he couldn't miss. The bed is between the two of them. Mister Chair is still holding the contract.

"I met a fella today," Guy says, talking to the ornament in his hand. *Ornaments.* If there's one thing Guy's learned since all of this started, they're *always* potential weapons. "Old guy. He hadn't seen my video. Barely even used YouTube at all, in fact." Guy taps his neck with his free hand. "He saw my scales. Saw them from thirty feet away, in fact. Wasn't like that at the start. No-one could see it. Cameras made a difference because, I think, they only work with light. Not just because they're mechanical and our eyes aren't," Guy says, wagging a finger briefly at Sam, "But because they *only* work with light. All the light the human eyes sees also gets run through *perception*, which I imagine is *your* side of things, the mind. You know how to fiddle with that, mess us up. Cameras show things as they really are. And once we see something through that middle man of a digital lens, our brains seem to be unable to un-see it. Except the old guy hadn't done any of that."

Guy turns and begins to pace along the short alleyway between the side of the bed and the wall, keeping his eyes on the sculpture in his hand. Is Mister Chair buying the false whimsey?

"How could that be, then?" Guy says. "I mean he could be psychic or something, able to *see beyond the veil* or whatever... but he didn't seem the type. He certainly didn't seem to know anything about what he was seeing." Guy turns to pace back towards the nightstand. "It all makes me think maybe something has changed with me. People suffering under you, people surrendering... it's all about energy, isn't it? What did you say earlier? *Atmosphere?* Vibe, something in the air... that's important to your lot. And I think I know why."

Guy reaches the nightstand again and stops.

"The more of it you control, the easier it is for you to operate," he says. "Or rather, easier to operate in secret. But I'm changing it. The old guy showed me that. Enough people have seen the video that it's having its own effect on that energy. It's crossed some sort of threshold of awareness in the public consciousness, one you like to stay below. I wonder what happens when I add some primetime TV exposure to that? This thing will *explode.*"

Guy faces Mister Chair, points at him with the ornament, and takes his biggest shot yet.

"So if all that's the case," Guy tells him, "I think you're going to *want* to turn me back."

Mister Chair's face doesn't change. Okay. Guy looks back at the ornament in his hand and continues.

"I'm pretty sure you can't just kill me to take me out of the picture," he says. "That's apparently in the rules. And *then* what do you do? What happens when everyone in the street can see me, *touch* me, and it can't be kept secret? Hell, what happens when I fully turn and *people can still see me because of what I've done?* Do you even know? Has this ever even happened before?"

Sam cries out suddenly—*Ah!*—and Guy spins to look at Mister Chair.

He's gone.

He's on Guy's right, standing at the end of the bed, blocking the path. He never made a sound. He's still smiling but his eyes are now black as beads.

Guy steps back, but then reminds himself that this is more mind games.

"I'm fucking right, aren't I?" Guy says, forcing himself to take a step forward. *Make. A. Stand.* "You're *nervous*," he says. "Maybe you don't know for sure... but you don't like it. And you'd really like it if I signed..." Where is the contract? It's lying on Mister Chair's chair. Guy realises that he's looked away from his visitor and panics for a moment, expecting to turn and find the visitor within a foot of him, but Mister Chair hasn't moved. "... that thing," Guy finishes. "And you'd *really* like me to believe I'm just another sucker to you. But I think I'm more important than that. So why don't we cut the bullshit and begin the *real* negotiation?"

He's done. The only sound in the room is Guy and Sam's breathing, noisier and heavier than Guy would like. Still Mister Chair hasn't replied. And Guy understands that Chair is *losing* and he's not used to it. They always chose their marks so well in the past, didn't they? *Your organisation grew too big, too fast, buddy.*

"Okay, I'll start us off then," Guy says, starting to feel the edges of something that might be victory. "Go get me a *new* contract. One that not only ends what is happening to me and Sam—*without* surrender—but one that still says we can't be screwed with. As long as I don't mess with the True Folk, yada yada. And you give protection to my wife as well, but I think you were bluffing there anyway, right? In return I'll renounce it all as a hoax. I'll go on the TV today and claim it was all nonsense. It'll be easy. There'll be the conspiracy people that won't buy it, but the masses are cynical. You know that. I can say it was a magic trick, cutting-edge perception trickery, something like that. I'll refuse to say how it was done. Whatever. You know that would work. Then we go our separate ways and you can move onto whatever's next in your delightful machinations."

Guy feels lightheaded as he says this last part. This could be over. It looks like it's *about* to be over.

So why doesn't he feel like he's winning?

Even Sam had agreed: Guy can denounce this but the people that believed his video won't accept that as the truth. He'll have sown the seeds for others to pursue, neither he or Sam surrender and become another part of the problem, and they'll have given the True Folk—Sam's words—a bloody nose in the process. It's not perfect by a long stretch but it's *something*, a small win stolen from a no-win situation.

So again: why doesn't Guy feel like he's winning?

You have a chance here, a voice says inside him. *You hold cards that maybe no-one else ever has.*

Then Guy sees Mister Chair's smile is a little wider, though his eyes are still black. Why is he smiling? Guy has him and Chair knows it—

"Do you think we were bluffing about your wife?"

Guy becomes cold.

"We *never* waste our gifts when we send them," Mister Chair says, black eyes watching Guy, sharklike. "They take a huge amount of effort to prepare, you know. The gift for your wife was particularly special."

Guy's mind is blasted into silence, even as he yanks his arm back to hurl the statue at Mister Chair's reflection as hard as he can.

"You can save her," Mister Chair says, voice calm and low, *pleased,* and Guy freezes. He knows he read Chair wrong; there's a difference between anger at insolence and being pissed off because you're losing. He freezes mid-throw, whole body shaking.

"What..." Guy begins, and then *no.* He spoke to Nancy five minutes ago. She's had the vase for days. This is bullshit. She would have said—

An awful, awful thought occurs to him:

Was that even Nancy?

It had to have been. They aren't good with tech, how would they—

"What did you do to my wife!" Guy screams. *"Where is she—"*

Mister Chair holds up a hand, or rather his arm raises with its hand hanging down like a puppet's.

"At her house, of course," he says. "You spoke to her yourself, didn't you?"

"Don't listen to him Guy," Sam says, voice shaking but stepping forward."

Yes. Yes, he *did* speak to her. He's been speaking to her constantly.

... and she kept asking him to promise things.

To say *yes.*

"You're... lying..." Guy suddenly dives towards his visitor, dropping the statue as he grabs the shoulders of Mister Chair's jacket in his fists. Something awful and invisible immediately washes over him and he can't breathe, dropping to his knees and falling sideways. As soon as he lets go of Mister Chair the feeling passes and Guy is already clambering back to his feet.

"Please do not touch me, Guy. I am not touching you," Chair says, cocking his head again. It seems to be something they just *do*, perhaps struggling to balance human-shaped skulls on such thin necks.

"What have you *done?!*" Guy yells.

"She is under Obligation, just as you are," Mister Chair says. "She accepted our gift, after all."

"She took the vase from her mother!"

"Even so, acceptance is acceptance and like I said, our gifts are extremely difficult to construct," Mister Chair says. "Not their physical form, but that which they are imbued with in order for a mere acceptance, a *touch* by their intended, to count. You could not understand how much each of us must give—" He stops himself. "It does not matter. But your wife is indeed *blessed* by us."

"That's bullshit. *Bullshit,*" Guy babbles, looking frantically for the statue. He dropped it when he grabbed Mister Chair, where is it? Did it fall under the bed? *Does it even matter,* his mind screams. *He says they've done something to Nancy. Mister Chair is in the driving seat.*

"In the name of Hamareth and under the Free Oath I can assure you that I am telling the truth," the visitor says. "But you seem to think that we have replaced your wife. We have not. That would be extremely difficult. Not impossible, but difficult."

Wait... what? So Nancy was just asking him to promise because she wanted him to promise... is Chair lying? Guy can't think straight—

"Do you think we are stupid, Guy?" Mister Chair asks. "You were going *public.* You actually managed to get your message to a wider audience in an impactful way. Did you think that we would blindly turn your wife into a living, changing piece of *additional* proof for you?"

Guy blinks rapidly, trying to clear his head—*of course,* call her, *see* her, and his phone is in his hand and he's dialing. He steps back in case Mister Chair tries to stop him but the visitor doesn't move an inch. He looks as if he *wants* Guy to call Nancy. Guy stands with his phone on in front of him on speaker mode, holding it up between himself and Mister Chair like a priest warding off a vampire with a crucifix. *Like trying to ward off a vampire with a vial of fresh blood,* Guy's battered mind thinks as, the drone of a video call tone fills the room.

"Guy…" Sam says quietly. "I don't think you should do that. Look at him." Guy lets the call continue but does as Sam asks: Mister Chair is staring and yes, he looks very pleased. Guy sees his face framed onscreen and even now he can barely look at it as the scales are even closer to his mouth. The image mercifully shrinks to an inset window as Nancy's confused eyes fill the screen.

"Hello?"

She's lying on the bed, her head framed by her hair where it lies against the pillow.

"Nancy!"

She looks completely normal.

"Guy… is that you?" she asks. "The picture isn't—"

"Are you okay? Are you *okay?*"

Wait, she said *is that you?* His name would come up on-screen when he called—

"I'm fine, everything's fine," she says. "What's happened? You sound—"

"You're sure? Nothing's happening to you?"

"What? Sorry, the signal's really bad, I can barely hear you."

A faint chuckle comes from the visitor.

"She is very good," he says.

"Shut the fuck up!" Guy screams at him.

"Guy, what's *happening?* Who's there?"

"One of *them,* Nancy, he has a contract for me, just like he did for the others—"

"In your room? In the hotel?"

He turns the phone around to show her the visitor. Mister Chair doesn't look at it. His eyes remain on Guy.

"Ask her to describe me," Mister Chair says softly.

"What?"

"What's it saying, Guy?"

It? The thing in the room looks roughly like a man. Guy knows it's not human but Nancy doesn't, not for sure. Why would Nancy say *it* if she was seeing a man onscreen?

Did you think that we would just blindly turn your wife into a living, changing piece of additional proof for you? That's what Mister Chair had asked.

Oh my God.

"Nancy…"

"Guy? Are you there?"

She is very good, Chair had said, when Nancy had talked about the signal being bad. When Nancy said about not being able to hear Guy.

"Nancy..." Guy says. "What can you see...wait—"

He won't ask her to describe Mister Chair. He looks around frantically, seeing the black and white wall photo of New York at night. He turns the camera to it, the phone shaking in his hand. Even pixelated over a shitty signal she would be able to see it, or at least spot a skyscraper-filled blur and guess at New York or Chicago or *anywhere*—

"What's this a picture of, Nancy?"

Silence.

Oh Jesus.

"Come on baby," Guy begs, the word that he hasn't used in so long coming out as a sob. "Please. Tell me what it is."

When she replies, she's sobbing too.

"I can't..."

Guy whips the phone around, looking into his wife's eyes and realising that they aren't even staring down into the screen the way everyone on a video call does. They're slightly off to the left.

She's looking where she thinks her phone screen is.

"Can you see me, Nancy?"

She bites her lip, her eyes filling with tears.

"... no. I'm *so sorry... it keeps getting worse and worse...*"

"Why... didn't you tell..."

"I can't hear you, I'm trying, I dropped my headphones and I can't find them and without them..." she sobs, covering her mouth with her hands.

"*Why didn't you tell me?*" Guy shouts, sitting backwards onto the bed and covering his mouth with his trembling hand. It isn't a cry of anger. It's one of despair.

"*You would have stopped!*" she cries, dropping the phone as her face crumples into full tears, and now all Guy sees is a shot of the ceiling. He glances at the visitor and understands how perfect this curse is. The crazy man that claims monsters are after him decides that his wife's encroaching deafness and blindness are their work too. Guy would bet everything he has that if Nancy were to have an MRI scan the causes would seem perfectly normal in her brain, too.

"*GUY! NO!*"

Sam yells this as Guy drops the phone and charges towards Mister Chair. He begins punching the visitor's fake face as hard as he can and as his knuckles connect he feels the nature of Mister Chair's skull. It feels like fried egg wrapped around high-density foam but every time Guy makes contact that same feeling washes over him and he sinks a little more to his knees. Chair doesn't even try and move as Guy hits him, that disgusting grinning head rocking loosely back and forth, expression unchanged. Guy staggers backwards, trying to regain his equilibrium.

Guy grabs the phone again. The screen is still showing that shot of the ceiling, her phone still lying on her bed. He can hear Nancy crying.

"Nancy, Nancy—" Guy coos, trying to sound reassuring as he dies inside.

Then he realises she can't hear him.

"Nancy!"

"... hold on..." she sniffs. He hears her clear her throat. He looks at the visitor.

"How long?" he gasps. "How long until she's fully... how *long?*"

"Only a few more days," Mister Chair says happily. "Three at most, I would think. She still has some sight, some sound. Like I said, Guy: leverage. Sometimes we like to make doubly sure of these things. In your case, it certainly looks like it paid off, no?"

Nancy's face reappears onscreen. Her eyes are red, but her tears are gone.

"I'm so sorry," she whispers. "But this *is* bigger than both of us, Guy."

She always was the stronger of the two of them.

"I can't let this happen Nance, there's no fucking way, no fucking *way*—"

"No!" she yells, startling him. "Don't you fucking *dare*, Guy! Think of Larry and Marianne! You *promised me three times!* You go on TV and you tell the fucking *truth!*"

"I can't! Not like this! I can't let them do this to you!"

"Then they'll do it to everybody else!"

Guy stares at Nancy and she stares into nothing.

"Oh, *Nancy...*" he says, stroking the screen. "Oh, baby..."

"It's alright... I'll be okay." *She's* trying to reassure *Guy* right now, even when being forced to imagine a life trapped in a void without light or sound. He suddenly understands that *this* is why the True Folk will always win: because those who stand against them have people they care about.

"I have to deal with the visitor, Nancy," he tells her, certainty coming to him. It puts something solid in his voice. "I'll..." *Call you back?* That sounds ridiculous when his little world is ending.

"Don't fucking sign it, Guy," she says, partially-seeing eyes blazing. *"Do you understand me?"*

"Yes. I love you," he tells her, the words leaping unbidden from his mouth. He hangs up before she can respond and puts his phone on airplane mode.

He looks at Mister Chair

"Give me the contract," Guy says.

"G—" Sam begins, then stops. Even he understands. Guy can't look at him now. Without a word, Mister Chair collects the contract and hands it to Guy. Is that smile even wider?

"It will not be as bad you think," he says.

Guy feels the unpleasant texture of the contract as he reads the words. Mister Chair might be telling the truth; it won't be as bad as he thinks. It can't be.

Nancy.

He won't sign it in front of Mister Chair. He won't give them that.

"I... want you to leave."

"That is fine, Guy. Take your time," Mister Chair says softly. "You know what to do. And what to say on television." He crosses the room and pauses by the door. "So if we had agreed to your deal, removed your transformation, and you then denounced your video as a lie; you believe that those who previously thought your neck was real would continue to do so? In our experience, Guy, that thinking is flawed at the core. You were planning on belief being enough to affect things, and it is not. Your kind..." Guy hears him sigh softly. "You need such momentum to elicit real change. You face extinction and you just blink."

He's right about everything. Momentum, as Larry would have said, is always what's needed, but that doesn't matter now.

It's over.

"Good evening, gentlemen," Mister Chair says, and leaves. The door clicks shut behind him. Silence again descends on the room. Guy sits slowly back down on the bed.

"I don't know what to say," Sam says eventually.

"Can you leave me for a bit, Sam?" Guy asks. He hears how weak he sounds. How broken.

Sam hesitates.

"Are you... going to..."

"Can you leave me for a bit?" Guy repeats. Sam hesitates, but then nods quickly. He moves to the door—checking through the spy hole first—and leaves. Guy notices that he lets the door slam shut behind him.

He stares at the contract. He wants to crush it and throw it out of the window, but he doesn't. He sees the way he's holding it, so gently, so *respectfully*. It says everything.

He's beaten.

For Nancy, he surrenders.

***

Chapter Twenty
Surrender
✳✳✳

Guy has signed the True Folk's contract and the live TV interview is over.

It's done.

The producers didn't like it, that's for sure. They wanted him to talk about the video and his story behind it, about rapid internet fame. They wanted to have a talk piece that could go on their own YouTube channel; of course, they couldn't be seen to be indulging someone who was mentally ill, so they'd selected their questions on the basis of false respect, covering their backsides but still letting the potential lunatic dance for the people wanting to tour Bedlam remotely.

Guy lightly strokes his neck, face and chest—he's shirtless, letting the breeze from the fan blow over him—enjoying the feel of ordinary human flesh under his fingers. The scales are gone. He will say this for the True Folk; as much as they have to live by the rules—for there is power in that, for them—they do keep their word. Nancy's eyesight and hearing have come back too.

Nancy, he thinks. *I love you.*

He feels... different. But that's to be expected, isn't it?

He surrendered, after all.

He looks at the clock. It's nearly midnight. That's okay. He's lying on the bed, appreciating the sensation of the fan's air on his skin while he can.

He realises that maybe he can watch the video of Larry's party now. That feels possible. He fetches his laptop, opens the folder and presses play on the clip without hesitation. He sees old faces, old friends that slowly had enough and went away. That he *drove* away. His old life. He sets the footage to play at double speed, looking out for a glimpse of himself and Nancy.

He knows what he'll see. He remembers the moment Larry drunkenly approached them in the garden with the camera, how embarrassed Nancy was, how he became even angrier that she would be more concerned over being seen than with what Guy was saying; feeling that *tipping point* moment when the shock of being caught on film could have jolted him back to sanity... and choosing, somehow, to double down. As always.

The people zip in and out of shot before his eyes. Guy lets them. He's waiting.

2:47:04, the video timecode says. *2:47:06. 2:47:08.*

As it ticks away, Guy thinks back to the TV interview once more.

Poor Debbie Starley. She didn't know what was going on.

***

"... that was the video from the West Midlands' very own Guy Autumn, one which, if you haven't already seen it, you certainly won't forget in a hurry, and Guy is here with us in the studio now."

"Thanks, Debbie."

Everyone in the office—and on the way *int*o the office— had stared when Guy had turned up in the morning for the pre-interview. What happened with the old man really was happening to everyone. When Anna Souton shook his hand she looked uneasy. Guy wasn't surprised. He knew it wasn't just the scales that were still on his face then; he'd lost quite a lot of weight after all; his eyes were sunken. She'd had a showrunner or whatever you call them go through some trial questions in a back room with him—*how did this happen, what is it you think is going on, what do you think is happening with your neck, what do you want people to know.* He'd managed to make himself sound as lucid and rational as possible with his answers. No mention of *monsters* or anything else of that nature.

He talked about how the YouTube video 'effect' was achieved by using secret trickery that he'd invented. The makeup was cutting-edge stuff. The showrunner/assistant/gopher looked extremely happy. Now they weren't putting on someone with a mental illness, but an unknown who just might be a star in the making.

"The makeup looks *amazing,*" the showrunner said, staring at Guy's face. "We were hoping you'd be wearing it when you came in."

"Well, I thought about not wearing it," Guy lied, "because I'm coming clean, after all, but then I thought this would be a better visual, right?"

"Oh, absolutely!"

He still had to talk briefly with their psychologist, though, just to be sure.

Later. Makeup. There had been the weirdest professional courtesy while Sheila, the makeup artist, tried making small talk; she'd tried to hide the way her eyes kept darting to Guy's scales as she tried to figure out if it really was a monster makeup job or not. Professional curiosity. Guy knew she was *dying* to ask.

There was more time-killing, and Guy's part in a brief rehearsal, until eventually he found himself sitting on-set, live and trying not to look at the camera. It was true what he'd heard about studio lights. They were *very* bright, and hot, and the darkness behind them—the very air in the studio—was thick and oppressive, reminding him of Larry's now-tainted house. *Everything* felt dark and oppressive, for obvious reasons.

"I think it's worth saying that, no matter what anyone might believe, it's an amazing video," Debbie the presenter said, in her early 40s and possessing that perfect British TV combo: a good smile and a particular brand of attractive appearance that isn't *too* attractive. She seemed nice though; they'd had a little chat while his video was playing and she'd told him not to worry. She said this *after* warning viewers with young children that they might want to take them out of the room. "When I saw it, I really *couldn't* believe it," Debbie said. "There was nothing there at first and then slowly your neck changed, but when I rewound it... just amazing." She was squinting a little; the scales were shining brightly under the lights and Guy hadn't allowed Sheila in makeup to actually touch them. "But you originally claimed in the video, as we just heard, that..." She gave a nervous laugh. "Well, that creatures or supernatural creatures did this, correct?" She turned to address the camera directly as she added: "And I should stress that we have had Guy evaluated by our psychologist, we wouldn't want to take advantage of anyone, and Guy is perfectly fine, but what you're *saying* is... *supernatural*, that word? How do you think that sounds to people?" She was teeing Guy up for the confession that she knew was coming; he'd given it to the showrunner, and he'd made it in rehearsal. Now he was expected to deliver it to the world.

Guy looked into the camera, the red light on top glaring at him like a laser sight aimed right at his soul. There would be no going back after this.

"I think it probably sounds like a load of nonsense, Debbie, and there's a very good reason for that," he told her, as a new way of phrasing what he was about to say suddenly occurred to him. "All the stuff about monsters... that's all lies."

"Well that's a relief," Debbie said, chuckling. "I'm assuming you can't tell us how you did it? Like a magician—"

"Sorry, Debbie," Guy said, interrupting. His hands and voice were shaking a little. "That didn't come out right, I didn't think the words through prop—I mean it's been an emotional... look. I'm not being clear. When I say *the stuff about monsters is all lies,* I'm not talking about my video. That's real." He pointed at his neck. "*This* is real."

Debbie blinked, confused.

"But I mean everything we were told as children by adults," Guy continues. "That monsters don't exist, there's no such thing, they can't hurt you." *You've started in this vein so you may as well continue,* he thought, head spinning. "They're lies, and they aren't the only ones; everything *around* us now, every little piece of constant popcorn information—even when they're true—are essentially lies too because their real purpose is hidden. It's white noise." He rested his hands on his legs, beginning to feel a sense of calm as he talked to the floor.

"Well Guy, I think—"

"Have you ever noticed in horror films how," Guy interrupts, "for the first two acts at least, the spooky goings-on disappear when a secondary character walks into the room and turns the lights on? The supernatural forces only *tease* the protagonist, brief glimpses of something scary but nothing concrete, nothing to let other people know anything is going on until it's too late; nothing *openly* monstrous happens until the third act. It's stupid. If the supernatural movie antagonist has that kind of power, why would they wait until the third act to use it, when the protagonist has almost figured out how to stop them? Turns out real life is only a little different." He was delaying, knowing he shouldn't; the production team would be nervous and someone would be talking in Debbie's ear. She was used to thinking about timings, asking questions and waiting for the answer to finish—rather than really listening— so she can get to the next one. This meant she was only a little confused, and Guy knew she and her handlers would be cutting this short. He had to get to the point.

"Sorry Debbie, what I'm saying is *this:* there's a *reason* they held off, rules that meant they had to stay out of sight. The problem is that our side is finally starting to come to the end of the *first* act. And the monsters really want to get to that third act and make it so we're all living in it, all the time."

He looked into the camera again and—even though he knew there would be a heavy, heavy price to pay—he took no small amount of glee in what he said next, a big fat verbal middle finger to the True Folk and that little bastard that dared to hurt his fucking wife.

"Monsters are real. One hundred percent real. And if I may, Debbie, I'm going to prove it right now."

***

Something had happened earlier. Not long after Mister Chair left, leaving his contract behind.

Guy had turned his phone on, only to receive a call, and it wasn't from Nancy. She'd been leaving frantic voicemails while his phone was off—using Siri to call, Guy had assumed—and he'd sent her a voice text to tell her that he needed some time to think. She knew he was thinking of signing. He couldn't have her lobbying at him. She'd kept calling. When his phone had buzzed at him for the umpteenth time he went to put it on airplane mode and saw a different number was now calling. He'd answered.

The conversation that followed had been a lightbulb moment.

Maybe there was a way to save himself and Nancy after all. An absolute Hail Mary move.

Yes, he'd thought. *The True Folk have everything sewn up. They knew that your video would cause a problem but also that it alone wouldn't be enough. Not enough dominos, not enough—Mister Chair was right—momentum. Not enough to cause change, even with the TV interview.* And as his blood thrummed in his scalp and the phone call continued, Guy began to believe that Hail Mary move might actually be that all important last domino.

Bullshit, the Critical Voice in his head said. *It wouldn't save the day any more than* not *signing would. It might also lead to Nancy spending the rest of her life blind and deaf if it doesn't work.*

But it might *work—*

He'd had until the live interview to prepare, but he'd still needed help; he couldn't miss the pre-interviews and rehearsals or they would just boot him off the show. He'd flung open his hotel room door and began running down the hallway to the elevator, hoping that Sam hadn't decided to leave.

If he wanted momentum, he would have to go nuclear.

***

So there he was, new plan in place, sitting in the TV studio with Debbie. She was looking at him with a mix of curiosity, eagerness and fear. She had no idea what Guy was about to do but even though it was live he knew there was a five second delay on the broadcast. If he did anything too suddenly, they could maybe stop it going out before the viewers got to see. He had to time this out perfectly.

"Debbie, we had my friend here earlier in rehearsal," he told her. "And actually, I think they're feeling a little better now so I'd really like to bring them in as originally planned if that's possible, their input on this will be..,?"

"Oh, uh, yes, I think we can..." Debbie said, looking off-camera to the floor manager who was giving a rapid thumbs up; they didn't *want* to be doing this but it will only be a quick addition, one that checked out earlier, and they're on the spot. Plus, this was organic TV. Producers love this shit. "Can we get a microphone for..."

Sam walked out from behind the camera, eyes locked on Guy as he headed over. He was leading an excited but wheezing Rufus along by his lead.

"Well firstly this is Rufus, everyone..." Debbie said, smiling. "He was getting a lot of fuss and attention earlier and I think he was enjoying every minute of it." Guy patted his legs and, after a long, painful warm-up, Rufus jumped up into his lap, still on the lead. Guy could feel the old, skinny dog's ribs vibrating against his chest. Sam paused to quickly ruffle the dog's head—paused a little too long—before he handed Guy the lead. He made eye contact for a brief moment and then walked away. Sam's eyes were wet.

Then a woman approached the set.

"And this is Erin," Debbie said. "Hi Erin."

Erin, white-faced, nodded in response but didn't reply as a floor hand got her a chair and Debbie forced a chuckle. "Erin," Debbie said, "take, uh, take a seat. We should explain," Debbie said to the camera, "that Rufus is here because Erin has some, uh, anxiety issues and Rufus helps with that. Erin is really being brave by being here." Emotional support animals weren't a common thing in the UK yet but there were enough media types in the building familiar with the term and, of course, keen to show just how progressive they were, so they just let Rufus' presence go.

Erin silently sat next to Guy as the floor hand quickly attached a microphone to her. Guy had brought her into the studio earlier claiming that she was his co-creator in all this and that she deserved the credit. Live, she was shaking like a leaf, her lips tightly pressed together. Of course she was. Guy tried to find his own steel as he watched Sam's departing back. *He said it himself,* Guy thought, *this is a war. He knows that.*

"Glad you could join us," Debbie said, relaxing again. She addressed the camera once more. "Erin here was going to be part of the interview too but wasn't feeling too well in rehearsal, but it looks like she's ok now. We were hoping you'd recover," Debbie added, forcing another chuckle. Guy hadn't wanted to show Erin onscreen from the start of the interview. If the True Folk's people had seen them both live on TV they would have instantly known that something was up. Did they have the connections to get the plug pulled in time? Guy didn't know, but he wasn't going to risk it. The *Erin's feeling sick* trick was so they could wheel her out mid-segment 'on the night' without too many questions.

Live in front of the Midlands, Guy stared at Erin and wanted to hold her, to thank her, to comfort her, but there was no time. He had to be staggeringly brutal for the next few minutes. He *was* in a war, and she'd volunteered to make a stand.

There are always casualties.

"Erin was trapped into something she didn't want," Guy told Debbie, speaking for the silent Erin. He was sweating, the studio unreal, too bright, too hot, but he had to get his shit together for Erin. "She's being..." He had to let her know, to publicly recognize it. "You're right, Debbie. Erin is being *unbelievably brave* by coming here today."

Erin was the one who called him earlier.

At the support group, you and your friend... she'd said, pausing in her reluctance to admit the next part. She'd been making choking sounds as she talked, as if she were trying to cry but couldn't remember how. *He had this energy.... his passion, his anger... it was like he was full of light in a room full of grey people. I know I can't be grey anymore. I'd rather die.*

"Thank you Erin," Debbie said pointlessly as Guy nervously stroked Rufus' head, who was wheezing away, eyelids already beginning to droop. As usual, Rufus' excitement could only last so long against the protests of his aged and aching body. He began to settle in Guy's lap. Guy felt beyond sick, but tried to tell himself that this was kinder for Rufus.

Plus, this had meaning. At least that's what Guy told himself.

I'd thought you were done? he'd asked Erin on the phone. *Surrendered?*

I was, she'd said. *I am. You asked me at the meeting what I actually had left, said you didn't think I had anything. I knew I had something but I couldn't think of the answer. I couldn't stop thinking about that afterwards... until I realised what it was.*

"So, Guy—" Debbie began, but Erin suddenly stood and moved in front of Guy's chair and to his left, her back to the camera. She was in between Guy and Debbie but not blocking he and Rufus from the cameras' sight. "Erin, sorry, we need you to—"

"One second, sorry Debbie," interrupted Guy, trying to buy valuable seconds. They could pull the segment at any moment. "She just needs to help me settle Rufus here, trust me, you're gonna love this," Guy lied. "I promise this isn't a political stunt or anything," Debbie looked out into the studio at someone, presumably a producer. This had suddenly turned into messy, amateur-hour TV, and if they were about to pull the plug he had to keep the tease dangling; if they could get viral footage out of this then this could mean promotions for some of them. He was walking a live TV tightrope. "This is going to make my video look like a kids' party magician." He watched Erin's eyes as he was talking, seeing how fast her chest was rising and falling. He raised his eyebrows, asking her for confirmation. She nodded. He glanced at Sam, standing by the camera once more. Sam nodded too, his face like stone, and showed Guy that he had his phone surreptitiously held in hand.

Filming. Just in case.

Live might well be one thousand percent better, but at the very least Guy wanted footage of this. Erin's actions could not be wasted. Erin pulled a piece of paper from her pocket and opened it, her fingers quickly finding its centre. They were shaking violently. She didn't surrender her fear, then. Guy glanced around at the layout of the cameras, the angles at which they were filming her. Was it safe?

"Okay Guy," Debbie said, "well we have a lot of things to get to—"

It *was* safe. No one could see Erin's face directly except Guy. Everyone else was at an angle. Even the camera could only see the back of her head. Erin's eyes, as always, were locked on Guy's.

What I have left, she'd said on the phone, *is that little part of me that can change my mind. And take the consequences.*

Erin blinked. Then she froze.

Guy made the terrible mistake of looking into her eyes right before she made her move. He's been seeing them ever since.

"*Don't waste this,*" she said, and even though this whole thing was planned and Guy knew *exactly* what was going to happen, he finally understood what Nancy had been trying to tell him all along.

"You... you can do it, Erin," unable to respond to her words, stunted and lost as ever, but forcing a smile, wanting her to see kindness, but her eyes, the terrified bravery—

And if I can't live with being grey anymore, she'd said, *then I want those consequences to mean something.*

"I think we'd better wrap—" Debbie began, but Erin suddenly screamed.

She tore her contract in half.

Guy screwed his eyes up tight.

He heard a *slap* as Erin's hand's flew to either side of her face, shielding it from view.

He immediately began to hear the hissing of snakes.

He heard screams erupt around the studio and prayed that what they were seeing was so shocking, so unbelievable—even when seen only from the rear, a woman's hair becoming a mass of writhing snakes is still unbelievable even if you can't see her monstrous face—would mean that even the most seasoned of cameramen or producers sitting in the booth would be too stunned to react straightaway, too beyond shocked to kill the live feed.

"*If anyone can see her face, close your eyes* now," Guy yelled, just to be sure, but in that moment the only creatures who could look directly at Erin's face were himself and poor Rufus.

Rufus, whose breathing was quickly stopping.

Guy held the dog tight, stroking Rufus uselessly as his furry body suddenly became very still and heavy in Guy's lap. Guy felt Rufus' soft fur change into textured stone. There was pandemonium in the studio and now they surely would have cut away or *something* but Guy was praying it was too late for that, that the viewing public saw a dog turn to stone before their eyes on prime time TV. He felt a weight drop to the floor near his feet and knew it was Erin, moaning as she fought the transition going on inside her mind. He knew she was about to carry out the next part of the plan. Guy pushed Rufus cruelly off his lap and the dog's stone corpse fell to the side of him, Rufus' unwitting sacrifice complete, and Guy knew he should show more respect given what he'd just done but there wasn't time. Eyes still shut tight, he reached down to feel blindly for Erin. He could hear people running towards him, but he had to check that it was safe for people to be near; yes, she'd pulled her top up over her head to cover her face and he heard a gagging sound as, under her clothes, Erin jammed the plastic box cutter she'd brought with her—plastic to get through the studio metal detectors—into her throat.

I won't be one of them, she'd said on the phone. *I think I'll have time to take care of myself before it's too late.*

He could feel the snakes writhing under the material, becoming weaker and weaker, and something stung his hand—one of them biting him, perhaps—as he frantically tried to tell her that, at the very least, she'd completed her part of their task successfully.

They'd showed the world. There was no way *this* wasn't going truly viral.

"You did it Erin! You did it—" The movement of the snakes fell still and, as Guy's hand pressed against them, he felt them becoming thinner, thinner...

I don't think they can let me stay transformed, Erin had said. *They couldn't let evidence like that exist, right?*

Right. And if they'd been watching—if they'd had more time or if they'd known she would be there—they maybe would have stopped her turning on regional TV. All she'd needed was a few seconds after all, and she got it.

He opened his eyes, rapidly scanning the room. No one had been turned to stone. Debbie was sobbing hysterically into the shoulder of a woman wearing a headset mic and two burly security men were rushing towards him.

He looked at Erin on the floor, her body curled up at his feet as blood spread outwards from it, spilled by her own hand. For some reason he squatted down, feeling a sense of almost awe, his hand at his mouth. There was so *much.* He wanted to uncover her head, to give her dignity, but he never wanted to see those terrified eyes again... no. He couldn't do it.

He looked away.

He looked at Rufus' stone body lying away to his left. The dog was on his side, one of his legs lying separate to his body, snapped off. His stone eyes were open in a relaxed expression. It was instant for him, then.

He looked at Sam, who gave him gave him a shaking thumbs-up, eyes watery, his face a perfect example of sorrow. Sam then slipped his phone back into his pocket, ignored in the chaos. *Good,* Guy thought. *We got it.*

He looked at the cameras facing him. All of their red lights were off. Had he created momentum?

He better have, or Erin died for nothing, never mind the dog, and that had been their best shot. He'd called what he thought was a bluff and now he would see what cards the True Folk really had..

Turn me now, motherfuckers, he thought, trying to feel victorious. *Let me complete How are you going to hide me now?*

He felt cold, though. Small. Humbled.

As the security guards grabbed him and hustled him off, Guy saw Sam slip away through the exit.

If this was a victory, he thought, *it's the strangest one ever.*

And it couldn't be wasted.

***

All of that happened yesterday.

Of course, Guy didn't sign the first contract the True Folk gave him, the one Mister Chair brought while Sam was in the room. Even when the police turned up at the studio he was still thinking that his plan *hadn't* been a complete and utter failure.

Everything changed when he realised his stunt had achieved nothing.

The contract he ended up signing—the one that made all of his scales vanish—was the *second* one the True Folk gave him.

After he'd been to the police station. After he'd heard the news.

***

Chapter Twenty-One
You See the Monster
✳✳✳

After the cops picked him up from the studio, Guy found himself once again in a police interview room. He wasn't worried about the cops. He knew this was just a formality, same as before. Worst case he was going to jail for animal cruelty. He accepted that. They were asking him about Erin, but he knew they couldn't get him for murder; even if the studio had killed the feed after Rufus died there were enough witnesses present to testify it was suicide. Besides, he didn't care about the law. They could put him in jail for the rest of his days. As Nancy had so very rightly said, this was all so much bigger and about more than his own frightened life.

He'd asked to speak to Nancy and Sam but wasn't allowed to do so. He hoped Nancy at least thought that he'd done the right thing. He couldn't stop thinking about her. Had he doomed her to an existence in darkness? No, they'd *have* to turn her back now—and him—as all eyes would be on them, unable to be kept secret. They'd irretrievably exposed the True Folk to boot; the stunt he and Erin and Sam and poor Rufus all pulled off would make Guy's video look like a parlour trick. The TV plan was far bigger than a bloody nose. Surely this was a broken arm. The world had just seen something supernatural happen on live TV. How's that for changing the energy in the world? How much of their work will *that* undo as well?

Enough of the broadcast had gone out. Enough to see Rufus turned to stone. The five second delay was triggered but it was too late; Guy had been right about the people in the booth being too stunned to do anything.

Erin—

She'd died on her own terms. A good soldier.

No. A comrade. Guy suddenly understood that he was prepared to do the same if need be. He didn't think that would be necessary but the idea brought a strange sensation of peace with it.

Detective Munsen—him again, Birmingham was only a twenty-five minute drive away from Cov and Guy guessed he was in the system with this cop already—tapped his pen on his thigh, shaking his head, probably wondering what the hell he did to deserve this. The police were called the second Guy'd been frogmarched off-set. He hadn't resisted. There was no way they weren't coming to get him anyway. Munsen's eyes looked at Guy's neck for the hundredth time. He sighed.

"Okay," he said, and it was déjà vu when Munsen added: "You're free to go for now, but we'll need to talk to you. To be honest, in your shoes I'd be asking to stay in custody tonight. Lot of people out there very angry with you, Guy." Guy nodded. *Rufus.* Guy had just had a dog killed on national TV. There would be a huge amount of people that considered that the same as killing a human being. Guy almost agreed. If killing one human would save, say, five humans, could he do it even in those circumstances? If not, then how could he simply kill a dog, even one who was days from the needle and sixteen years old (87 in human years for a dog of his size, but still no excuse.) He'd been charged with an act of animal cruelty. He'd thought he'd end up in court for that. The True Folk couldn't fix it so he ducked that one, the crime was too public. "We'll drive you home," Munsen continues, "or wherever you're staying. For your own safety."

"I appreciate that."

"Okay. Interview concludes at ten seventeen." He stopped the audio recorder and looked at Guy, who expected the detective to ask *is this real?* To look scared, maybe. The scales were on Guy's face and neck, after all—they were still there at that point, Guy hadn't signed yet—and Munsen had seen the footage of the dog. He didn't look unnerved in the slightest, though. He just looked... angry?

That was when a horrible, sneaking suspicion began to creep over Guy. Munsen spoke, confirming Guy's worst fears:

"What was the point of it?" Munsen asked, looking genuinely disgusted. "What does your wife think of this?"

"You saw it with your own eyes, Detective," Guy said, sitting up, still trying to deny the ugly cogs beginning to turn in his mind. "You can see *this.* This isn't makeup. You even had a good look yourself. I can scrub at it if you like."

"Autumn, you have a skin condition," Munsen said, shaking his head. "You know what I think? I think you've developed *that* right in the middle of a mid-life crisis and—with lousy timing—after the violent death of your best friend. It's sent you over the edge. And the only way you can make it all make sense is to latch on to some crazy shit that you found in the last thing your best friend wrote. And here we are."

Guy stared at him, stunned. Munsen, it seemed, was convinced.

And if *Munsen* didn't believe it then Erin—

"You saw the dog!" Guy snapped, suddenly livid and *fuck it,* why the hell not? "You *saw* it! You saw the back of Erin's head *turn into fucking snakes on live TV!*"

"Snakes that, rather conveniently, were gone when the body was recovered—"

"Do you have *any idea* how ignorant you're being—"

"Okay, I'm ignorant then, Guy," Munsen said. "But I've been online during the last few hours. You made headline news, certainly. But it looks like people are thinking the same as me."

Guy's stomach dropped into his feet.

"...*what?*"

Munsen leaned back in his chair, but his gaze was on Guy like white scales on skin.

"Concern for a missing dog after a sick magic trick on live TV," he said. "That's the general narrative. It doesn't help that the BBC are covering their backsides and already having magicians and visual effects people theorise as to how it could have been done. If you were hoping to convince the majority of the public into seeing things your way, then it doesn't look like it worked. The media narrative is that you are one sick bastard." He leaned forward over the desk, staring into Guy's gaping, disbelieving face. "This is what I don't get. You tried to save one of our boys in your friend's house. He really vouched for you, before he died. I don't think—I *didn't* think—that you were a sicko. But I'm a dog lover, Autumn. You're going to go to jail for a little while once the courts are done with you, but I'm glad the animal nuts will tear you to pieces *long* before that happens. Nothing like a good old-fashioned mob frenzy in the golden age of social media, eh? Ironic, given your line of work." He stood. All Guy could do was continue to sit with his jaw hanging open as if he were simple.

How could it not have worked? They all saw it.

Then it comes to him. Mister Chair had even said so himself, warned Guy of how much it takes for humans.

Just how *much* momentum is needed. *You face extinction and you just blink.* Guy saw it then: he was a teardrop trying to put out an inferno. It was all a waste of time.

And no matter what Nancy had said, he knew that he couldn't let her live in darkness and silence.

When the escort arrived, Guy turned his phone off. He didn't want to speak to anyone. He asked to be taken to his hotel rather than his house. Not because he'd been staying at Sam's, or because he was worried about a mob that might have already gathered outside his house. It was because he knew who would be waiting for him. He didn't want to tarnish Sam's home any more than he already had by having that visitor enter it.

He couldn't have his final surrender be inside either of their houses.

***

Mister Chair was already seated in Guy's hotel room.

He hadn't invited Mister Chair inside, so that probably meant Guy couldn't be hurt for what he'd done on TV. That smile, those eyes, looked pleased regardless. The contract was lying on the small table nearby.

"It was a nice try," Mister Chair said. "We thought you might do *something* given that you hadn't yet signed, but Lafferty was a surprise. We had written her off a long time ago." He shrugged. "We were slightly concerned about you going on television, as I mentioned. But, as expected... you know." He held up his limp hands, gesturing around himself. *People.* "The offer still stands, although the contract is now, of course, a standard one." He opened the paper—it turned out to be two pages this time—and showed it to Guy. "It is non-specific," Mister Chair said. "The same contract as everyone else. Nothing in there about television announcements or anything like that."

The writing was different; more of it for starters and it was all in latin with no translation. Standard contract, as Mister Chair said. At the top of the first page there was a space where Guy's name was handwritten in an almost childlike scrawl: GUY AUTUMN. The second page had another name at the top: NANCY AUTUMN. They looked exactly the same as Erin's surrender contract. She'd shown Guy before they went on TV.

"I sign for my wife? I can surrender *for* her?"

"Signing yes, surrender no," Mister Chair said. He was clearly enjoying this, but this time Guy had no anger left. He now knew he'd been beaten before he even started. "The standard contract here means that *your* surrender will return your wife to her original state, as said surrender covers any Obligations that may have put upon your spouse. Hers was a secondary Obligation to yours and there is a knock-on effect..." Mister Chair shook his lolling head. "It is complicated, but essentially: she will be restored, and live entirely and woefully *normally.*"

That word again, *Obligation.* He meant *curse.* Guy tried one last bluff—out of principle alone—but it was weak.

"You still... can't risk me turning," Guy murmured. "Even if the TV stunt didn't work, people see what's happening to me even without seeing me on camera now. If I become something—"

"We feel confident that we can still hide you, Guy," Mister Chair said. "And even if we cannot, has today not told you we might not even *need* to anymore? Regardless: your wife. Are you happy to let her suffer for your failures?"

"She... she said..."

"I know what she said, Guy," Mister Chair cooed. "I was there. But you are the one that will have to live with that choice—"

"Why do you care?" Guy whimpered, hating himself for how he sounded, his failures, all of it. "Why is my surrender so fucking important?"

"Oh, Guy," Mister Chair said, sounding genuinely surprised. "Do you not understand? *Every surrender we offer is important.* The amount of our resources it takes to create the circumstances for each primary Obligation... why do you think we do not just put them upon everyone? If we were to *cancel* one, why, we may as well let our whole system collapse."

He stood up to leave.

"That's it?" Guy asked, confused. "Just a standard contract and we're done?"

"The situation has not changed, Guy. We are not vindictive. We just want that which is our right." That sickening, wobbling gait carried him towards the door where Guy stood. His big eyes and horrible smile never changed focus. The smell was unbearable.

"We do admire your tenacity, Guy," Mister Chair said, resting a hand on the door handle. "The softness in which your people live means they so rarely resist us. If it is any comfort, you fared better than most." He opened the door. "Once you have signed, the scales will leave very quickly. Our effects are very difficult to put on but very easy to take off, as Lafferty's deal breaking would have shown you... your Obligation will then activate at midnight. A little theatrical perhaps, but somewhat of a holdover from the old days. An indulgence, on our part. I would not leave it longer than another day or two to sign though, Guy, for the sake of you and your wife. Both of your completions would be unpleasant. Be well, Guy Autumn." Mister Chair walked silently through the doorway and Guy didn't say another word. His surrender was already complete, then.

He didn't call Nancy. He should have, but she would have told him not to sign it. He did text Sam, though; Guy took his phone off airplane mode and ignored the avalanche of info—as well as Nancy's many, many missed calls and messages—that fell into it. For all he knew, Sam was downstairs in his room, waiting.

I'M BACK AT THE HOTEL, Guy wrote. He decided to be blunt: I'M SIGNING, AND I DON'T WANT TO ARGUE ABOUT IT.

A small idea struck him; an ending was required here. He didn't know if Sam and he ever truly became friends—he liked to think so, and he hoped Sam did too—but if nothing else, Guy wanted to show his respect. He and Sam would go their separate ways now, he knew that much.

I WOULD LIKE TO HAVE BREAKFAST WITH YOU, THOUGH, he wrote. IF YOU'RE HERE, OR BACK IN LEICESTER, I WOULD REALLY LIKE IT IF YOU COULD MEET ME AT THE HOTEL AT 9AM. LET ME KNOW IF YOU CAN. EITHER WAY: THANK YOU FOR EVERYTHING, SAM. WE DID OUR BEST.

He couldn't talk to Nancy. He just couldn't. Once he'd signed and her hearing and sight came back, she'd know what he'd done. He'd deal with that later. Fortunately, she didn't know where he was. He ignored his phone for the rest of the evening, setting it to Do Not Disturb and only checking the message feed with Sam for a response. Eventually, one came:

SEE YOU AT 9.

Guy browsed the internet. At that point, fuck it: why not?

He let his imagination take him wherever he wanted to go, deliberately choosing websites he'd never visited before. He went down a few rabbit holes and felt no shame whatsoever, satisfying any curiosities that took him. He remembered a quote by Samuel Johnson that he'd once lived by: *curiosity is, in great and generous minds, the first passion and the last.* He had to give them that, as a race: for good or ill, humans are curious.

After a while, strangely, he felt ready to sleep in a way that he hadn't in days. He passed out. When he awoke in the morning—this morning—he didn't even read or listen to any of the new messages that Nancy had dictated. When he met Sam, the older man looked tired and beaten.

"How'd you sleep?" Sam asked, or at least that's what Guy thought he said. He couldn't tell if the *how'd* in Sam's sentence meant *how did you* or *how do you* sleep. Big difference. They didn't talk about monsters and curses. They talked about football—Guy had no idea what had happened in the Premier League since Larry died—TV, politics. They didn't mention Rufus, and Guy didn't bring the subject up. It hurt him, so he couldn't imagine what Sam was going through. Given that the scales had reached so far up on Guy's face—he could feel them moving on his cheeks as he chewed his food—and half the people in the hotel dining room seemed to recognize him from his TV appearance and the subsequent news stories, seeing not just a scaly-faced man, but a notorious one—he and Sam were certainly ignoring the impossibly large pachyderm in the chamber. It should have been awkward, but it wasn't. It was good. Guy expected Sam to shake his hand and leave as soon as they'd eaten, but Sam didn't.

"Want to stretch your legs?" he asked. "There's a park near here, saw it on the way in. Might be nice to enjoy some scenery while you can still..." He trailed off, leaving *enjoy it* unspoken. Guy could tell by Sam's face that it was a genuine mistake, not a dig. It was a good idea though.

"Let's go," Guy told him.

They went to the nearby park and walked in silence until they reached a small metal bench. Guy remembered sitting on a similar bench with Nancy in a similar park. He missed her—he *missed* her—so much that it was almost a physical pain. The bench was uncomfortable but Guy enjoyed the *real* feeling of the hard, unyielding metal against his scaly body.

"Are you going to see a doctor?" Guy asked Sam. "To get an update about the cancer?"

"Yes. I don't think it'll make any difference at all, but it would be good to clarify the timescale some more. I doubt our shenanigans will have helped with that." Guy didn't respond. "It's alright, Guy," Sam says. "I've made my peace with it even before I met you. Technically, all I have left is Melissa and she hasn't returned my calls in years. I tried lots of times this week. I couldn't reach her when she was a teenager and I can't reach her now. You know, I sometimes wonder if there really was any other way I could have..." He sniffed, then shook his head. "Rufus didn't suffer. That was important, very important. It was instant, with him knowing nothing about it. *Much* better than a vet's surgery. He hated going to the vet, *hated* it. He'd have been scared to death, and soon I'd have had to take him there. It's alright."

But his voice is full of pain as he says it. He sniffs again.

"Anyway," Sam coughs. "I don't really have anything to say, Guy, about the, you know, your choice... *ah* that's not true, that's not true. Listen... you probably already know what I think of your decision but I also know it's very easy for me to *have* an opinion. I'm not in your shoes, or Nancy's. But I have to tell you: over this last week I've been scared out of my mind, furious, confused, and facing the abyss. Hell of a week. But you know what?"

Sam smiled.

"I've felt more alive than I have in a long time," he said. "It's nice to have had that before the end. So: thank you."

"Well... Jesus," Guy said, surprised. "You're welcome, I think."

Sam nodded and went back to staring ahead. "How do you feel?" he asked.

Beaten. But Guy didn't say that.

"Don't really have much other choice but to try and be in the moment, Sam. Focusing on getting to the next minute. That's it."

"Yes. Being present."

"Well," Guy said, chuckling bitterly. "If that isn't ironic."

"Ha."

"Sam? I think I need to sit by myself. Do you mind? You haven't said anything wrong or anything, but... I need to think."

"No offence taken at all." Sam offered Guy his hand and Guy took it. "Take care of yourself, Guy. I hope it's... okay for you."

"Thank you, Sam. Try and make the most of the time you have."

"I will." Sam began to stand, but hesitated, brow furrowed as if he wanted to add something... but then forced a smile instead and straightened up. "Good luck, my friend," he said. Sam walked away.

Guy watched him leave. About a hundred feet or so from the bench, Sam turned, still walking, and looked back. He held up a hand. Guy did the same.

Guy sat on the bench a little longer and then headed back to the hotel. He ordered room service all day, somehow finding a huge appetite and wanting to enjoy food the way only a free man can.

In the early evening, he video-called Nancy. She could barely hear him. They both cried.

"I love you," he told her. She didn't say it back. She couldn't; when Guy said it, she put her face in her hands, wracked by fresh sobs. Guy didn't know if that was sadness because of his fate or because she couldn't lie to him. It didn't change the way he felt about her, either way.

At 10:34pm, Guy finally signed the second contract.

***

And now here he is, Mister Chair surprisingly as good as his word; shortly after signing the scales began to fade. Nancy had texted to say *it's working*. He now has just a little more time to enjoy the fan's breeze some more before the clock strikes midnight, signaling the end of the ball for Cinderella. He lies on his hotel bed, scanning through Larry's video at double speed. Waiting for a shot of the garden, where Larry found he and Nancy.

26:30:06, the timecode says. *26:30:08. 26:30:10—*

There.

Guy puts the playback onto normal speed and forces himself to watch.

Finally forces himself to see.

Larry's back garden is in shot, the one that will be covered in broken glass only a few years later; patio doors will be fitted after this video is filmed, and a barstool will be then thrown through them, flung by a desperate man running away from a monster.

The garden onscreen is empty, of course, apart from Guy and Nancy. He's managed to clear it out by causing a scene.

They're only on camera for a moment; even drunk, Larry the cameraman knows that you don't walk up to an arguing couple and start filming them. The image drops and turns upside down, showing the house, inverted. Larry's let the camera drop to his side, held in his hand but still unintentionally filming, but just before that the image shows a glimpse of what was going on: Guy, all clenched fists and flailing arms, chest to chin with Nancy, towering over her, toes touching hers. He's physically squaring up to her, *over* her. In his hotel room, Guy wants to look away—he needs to—but this is what he has to see. It's time.

Nancy's back is up against the fence.

Hotel-Guy barely has time to see Nancy's face before the camera drops but he knows what he would see if he had the balls to press pause. He remembers it as clear as day, no matter how many lies he's told himself and believed: Nancy, backed up against the wood, eyes closed, jaw set, breathing hard. Not moving away from him, but not cowering either. Her lips are tight but she looks quietly furious. The face of a woman realizing that she is finally passing her breaking point. Moving past fear.

Her back is against the fence. How did he see that and not back down?

Why is everyone else at the party so cowardly that they aren't doing anything? Why is it down to drunk Larry to deal with it?

Who is he kidding—Guy's the worst coward of all. He can hear himself.

Guys, Video Larry slurs. *Come on guys.*

Fuck off, Larry, Guy tells him. *Not now.*

It's... it's my party, Guy. Come on.

Nancy mumbles something.

What? Video Guy barks at her.

Can we do this at home, she repeats. Her voice is steady. *This is embarrassing.*

You, you're fucking telling me, Video Guy yells, *that you, you're actually more concerned with what these fucking cunts think than what I'm saying to you? You don't give a fuck about Ray, as long as you get your little fucking albatross, right? You'd give a shit when* something happens to them *though, won't you, you selfish bitch?*

The inverted camera shows the upside-down guests mingling nearby now, watching, doing nothing. Hotel Guy knows what's coming. He hears his video voice rise up a notch in pitch.

You don't—

Bang.

That's him punching the fence with a closed fist. Right next to Nancy's head.

Give a FUCK—

Bang.

Say something! Video Guy barks. *Fucking say something, you're always starting SHIT!*

The camera doesn't show it, but Guy remembers what happened next.

Nancy had opened her eyes and looked at him.

His pumping fist had frozen. There'd been tears in her eyes, but she'd stood up straight. Guy remembers the instant blind panic, how he'd known on some level that this was it, that *this was the breaking point.* She'd believed in Guy's own smoke and mirrors even though she'd seen flashes of the truth. Now she finally perceived it all. Her voice in his memory mingles with disgusting audio onscreen.

Guy, Nancy says. *We're done—*

Slap.

Both of them had gasped in disbelief and horror, neither of them able to believe what had happened. In the hotel room, Guy hears that slap and his now-human fingers grip deeply into his eye sockets.

Fuck... you... She says, the *you* audibly disintegrating as the hurt and angry tears come.

Oh... oh Jesus, Nancy, Jesus, I'm sorry, I didn't—

GUY! That's Larry.

The image onscreen fills with a mix of blurred green and grey as the camera falls to the grass. The mic is muffled too, but the sound of Larry and Guy arguing can be dimly heard. Video Guy is yelling and swearing—*screaming*—and trying to get past Larry so he can pursue the fleeing Nancy, desperate to fix the unfixable and now, sitting in his hotel room, Guy turns the video off. That's enough. He's finally seen it. He saw it.

He crosses the room and looks at his bare torso in the mirror. The scales may be gone now, but Guy knows that's just more smoke and mirrors. They're not truly gone. They're just covered up.

Guy typed out an email to Nancy a little while ago, scheduled to send later on courtesy of Mailchimp. He doesn't want it to go to her yet, but he needs to know it's done. His phone is off again, of course. He doesn't trust himself to go near it right now. He lies on the bed, stares at the ceiling, and breathes, finding strange enjoyment in the silence.

After a while, he looks at the wall clock again. Jesus. It's three minutes to midnight, when the contract will activate. He nearly missed it. He's amazed at how extremely relaxed he's feeling, but then remembers how he is, in fact, dosed up to the eyeballs. It's finally kicking in. So much so that he'd forgotten he'd taken anything. He's amazed it's even working because he's been drugged up every night ever since Larry's death. If he were clearheaded, he would be scared out of his mind. All the histrionics were earlier, after Sam left. As it is, he's just sitting here waiting. He wants to be out of it when the last true version of Guy Autumn ends. He wishes Nancy were here, but knows she shouldn't be.

His thoughts tick away with the minutes.

11:58. *I'm so sorry, Nancy.*

11:59. *This wasn't a choice. It was an obligation.*

12:00.

He tries to tense for it as he sees the numbers turn digitally over but now the drugs are working so hard that all he can physically do is shift slightly on top of the mattress and linen. His thoughts are hazy. That's good.

He blinks and there's a monster at the foot of his bed.

It's huge.

It's lit by lamplight—he's taken the mirrors away now, there's no point in them—and it looks comfortable, not even trying to hide.

That's because it's the same monster that killed Larry, after all.

He sees the monster. It's smiling.

Here's what it looks like: a distorted, bulbous, giant toad, black and knobbly. It's having to sit in a squatting position at the foot of the bed in order to fit into the space there, it's knees and elbows up around its ears. Its arms are long and thick, with a span almost as wide as the room. Its eyes are blue slits in its head and its pinkish, thick-lipped mouth is filled with foot-long teeth. Its immense back, its ribcage if it has one, expands and contracts with each breath.

Guy rocks uselessly back and forth on the bed, instinct trying to get him to run, but the cocktail of drugs are industrial strength and he's taken way too high a dose. And where could he run that they couldn't find him?

"Guyyyyyyy," it says, that deep, ragged voice cooing the name. *"I've been waiting for this, you know."*

"Hwww…." Guy says, trying to say *how*. He manages to get his mouth to open. "Contract… surr..runder. Deal. Nd." He can't get the words out. *"End."* he manages.

"The last part is right," it says, chuckling. *"This is the end."* It reaches out with its long, long arms, resting them either side of Guy on the bed. The section of mattress that he's lying on bulges upwards slightly, bowing under their weight. *"You hurt me, you know. That isn't something I'm used to. Some people get lucky with the mirror thing sometimes but that one was a doozy. I've only just healed up. Darn! You know, all this time I've been thinking about what I was going to do to you should I get the chance."* It leans towards Guy, filling his line of sight, that *eager* grin filling its face. *"You aren't running… that's interesting."* It inhales sharply, the snakelike, elongated holes in the centre of its face—presumably nostrils—contracting and puckering like a spasming anus. *"Medicine for sleep?"* it asks, smelling the chemicals in Guy's sweat. *Not that there's any point running anyway. I could just—"* It raises one of its long arms off the bed and holds a huge clawed hand in front of Guy's face. Then it grips it into a fist so fast that the breeze from its swishing fingers wafts across Guy's face. The talons don't touch him. "—snatch *you. A long time ago—centuries,*

really—that's what we used to do to kids whenever we could. Snatch them. No messing, no trickery, no bloody deals. *Before we started making rules, changing things. Worth it in the long run—there's* power *in dem rules, boy—but I don't know. I miss the old days."*

Guy shakes his head as much as he can, his eyes screwed tight.

"Dll," he manages. "*Dll. Deal!*"

"*Yes, yes,*" the monster says, shifting its chin onto the bed, settling its full weight down. Guy's end of the bed rises up into the air. "*You really should check what you're signing. I know it was in the old language—your* latin—*but you creatures and your beloved technology... you didn't even* try *to translate it?*"

Guy's eyes bulge in his now-elevated head, his end of the bed now seesawed a clear two feet off the floor.

"*What did they tell you Guy? That it was the* standard contract? *That we weren't* vindictive?*" That low chuckle comes again. "*You committed the greatest crime. You tried to expose us. We even* gave *you an out and you still didn't take it the first time.*" A red tongue, thick as a side of beef, leaves its mouth and slides across its enormous lips almost absent-mindedly. "*You were right. Full disclosure: we couldn't let you turn. We just didn't know what your... presence in the world would mean for you in your new form. Too visible. Maybe too rebellious even in your surrendered form too. Soon they'll all be visible, I think. But by then it won't matter. The world is changing.*"

Even with the drugs, Guy's fear is turning his trembling into spasms. He begins to bounce on the bed like a fish dragged from a river.

"*You should have kept calling our bluff, but then I guess your wife would be screwed. Your lot are always so damn vulnerable as soon as you've got something to lose. Well, I hope you're happy; your wife's part of the contract* was *as described. You know how* hard *it would be to actually put a* permanent *secondary Obligation via their husband? We* had *to turn her back if you were signing yours, idiot. But maybe you're only thinking about yourself right now, though?*" The throaty chuckle becomes louder, more resonant, as the thing's grin becomes dark redness before Guy's eyes, filling the world as its awful mouth is beginning to open wide. The tongue disappears away into a gaping hole at the back of its throat. "*Love only goes so far, surely? I wouldn't know, but, hey.*"

Its clawed hands wrap themselves around Guy's arms.

It begins to slowly drag Guy's spasming, helpless body down the bed into its gaping pit of a mouth. It's drawing the moment out as much as possible.

Guy tries to think of Nancy, but for some reason all he can think about in his final moments is what he saw this afternoon in the park. The last revelation.

He doesn't know if it's the drugs. He doesn't know if it's the desperate physical effort flooding him with endorphins. He doesn't know if blessed, blessed madness is *finally* kicking in—here, right at the very end to give him some sort of solace—but even as he remembers that horrible image from this morning he is wrapped up in a sense of deep, blessed peace.

Job done, he thinks.

***

Earlier. In the park. Sam had just left.

He'd continued to sit on the bench and watch the parents play with their kids, feeling the dim British winter sun on the still-human parts of his face. He wondered if he would still appreciate such things once he'd signed the contract and it kicked in at midnight.

Over in the playground area a woman was playing with her two young children, a trio that particularly stood out because of their matching mops of curly blonde hair. He pushed away the awful, connected memory of the children in the field. Maybe that, at least, would no longer torment him once his surrender was complete? The kids ran off to the swings and Mum took a brief moment to check her phone... no. To take a picture. Guy relaxed a tiny bit.

He checked his email, ever the hypocrite.

Ah yes; the email he sent the night before while in his Samuel Johnson-quoting mode, going down online rabbit holes. He'd emailed that company out of that magical human trait, curiosity; their website said a super-fast turnaround and he'd assumed that they farmed their work out to much poorer countries in other timezones. As Guy sat on the park bench it was still early in the UK, but maybe they'd come back to him already? It wouldn't make any difference either way, but, hey: curiosity.

Guy took his phone off airplane mode and waited calmly while his phone finished pinging. He wasn't going to read Nancy's messages. Only his emails. To his surprise, there was a reply headed *Here You Are!* with the little attachment paperclip in the preview. They really did have a fast turnaround. He listened to the kids laughing as he opened the attachment.

He read it.

His entire body turned icy cold.

Would he have signed the contract at all had the next thing not happened? The fact he saw it at all almost confirmed something he'd quietly wondered about since all of this began: if there are bad things hiding in the darkness, then surely there were good things hiding in the light. Both have influence. The timing of the email arriving and the sight before him... it couldn't be anything else.

As his last few patches of his still-human skin turned white with fear, his eyes—spots beginning to dance in front of them—fell on the little curly blonde-haired boy. The kid had come over to the low fence between them and looked at Guy over the top of it. He had to stand up on his tiptoes, but smiled cheekily and gave a little wave. He had to be six at most. Of course, he was staring at Guy's neck and face, but didn't seem scared. His mother, a few feet to the boy's left, looked up from playing with the sister.

"Alfie," she said, "come here, play with Kelly." She turned her back on Guy for a moment and—despite everything Guy had seen and heard and what he'd just fucking *read*—his breath still caught when he saw the thing on the mother's shoulders. As always, the moment was brief, but this time Guy saw the influencer more clearly than ever. One of the little figures was hunched up behind her neck, riding it. Guy could make out the edges of its dark clothing now, what looked like a shirt and leggings made out of rough material, topped off by a tight hood around its skull. Guy realised that what he'd previously thought was it sitting in a crouch was actually its horrifically hunched back, the spine dramatically bent so that its head appeared to be growing out of its chest. Its knees were up around its chin and its hands were out of sight in the woman's hair. Its head was bent eagerly forward and its face was wrinkled and blackened like a turnip left to rot in the sun. It was only a quick, there-and-gone sight, but Guy could have sworn that the godawful thing was smiling. Its mouth wasn't by the woman's ear, not yet anyway. The woman beckoned to her son, enjoying her morning with her children, but she looked troubled. The thing disappeared from view, as if Guy had looked at a Magic Eye picture and blinked the image away. "Alfie..." the mother said, irritated that her son was ignoring her and still looking at the stranger on the bench. If the mother had looked up and seen Guy properly, she surely would have been unnerved, not only because of Guy's scale-infused face but because he was *staring* at her, wanting to be wrong but trying to bring the vision back.

The boy at the fence pointed at Guy.

"That man," he said. "What's wrong with his face?"

The mother looked now, instantly turning red at the filter-free comments of her son.

"Leave the man alone Alfie, come on," the mother said. The boy turned away. As he did so, Guy let out an audible moan.

The boy had an unseen rider of his own on his shoulders, a matching dark figure squatting hunched on his neck.

Guy only saw it for a moment before it too vanished before his eyes. The mother heard the horrified noise he made and looked his way again, saw Guy with his hand over his mouth.

"Is everything okay?" the mother asked. There was an open challenge in her voice and understandably so. It said *you're being rather weird for a man sitting here without children, staring at mine, and I want you to know that I know.*

Guy understood more than ever why parents are so suspicious. There were monsters everywhere, after all.

"Yes. Sorry," he gasped. "I'm not..." His brain was trying to say *I'm not a pedo* while reeling from the terrible realisation of what he'd just read and the fact that *they're* on *the children now, they're actually on the goddamn* kids and trying to figure out an excuse. Guy chose sincerity. "Sorry. I've just had some... very, very bad news. I was miles away. I didn't mean to make you... nervous..." Guy stood up, his brain now numbed by shock, but the vision of the creature on a child's back was burned into his retinas, hanging there like the aftereffects of a camera flash.

The kids—

Why are you surprised, his mind fired back, *you knew that ever since that field—*

And with that thought, something clicked. He had it again—that sense of the light, of a counteracting force at work, *in* him this time—as the double revelation came.

The kind that brings peace and shows you your path.

Guy began to turn away, his entire body shaking. Was *this* how Nancy had been wanting him to feel all along? He thought he understood it after he'd looked into Erin's face at the end, but *this...* he'd had unspeakable news and yet every hair on him was standing up, brain going a million miles an hour.

Larry had been right for years. *Years.* It works the same way comedy works, he'd said. How could he forget *exactly how to create momentum?*

He needed to sign today, before his transformation completed, and that meant he had until midnight. A plan was forming and he thought he had time to implement it; time to get hold of Frank Beckwith. He was sure he could. He always could. They might not have been true friends anymore but Frank was always quick to arrive when he could make money, and he owed Guy some big favours—

"Sorry," the mother said, interrupting Guy's rabid thoughts. Tenderness had crept into her voice, seeing that Guy meant what he'd said. Her sincerity tipped him over the edge in his moment of dark and delighted delirium. The tears began to come as she asked him: "Are you alright? There's sometimes weirdos around here and I'm always a little..."

Guy barely heard her over the thoughts in his brain yammering away. A great weight left him. He should have been terrified beyond measure and he *was* and yet *purpose* made him feel superhuman, raw, electrically untouchable even in the face of his certain doom.

Was this what it was to be without fear?

Guy smiled apologetically as he wiped away his tears, standing and backing away. He had to *move* if he had a chance of pulling this off.

"It's alright," he told her, grinning and knowing exactly how he must look but being far, *far* beyond such small things. "I understand. You always have to keep your eyes open." He broke into a run, hoping he could catch Sam once again.

The poor man is probably sick of the fucking sight of me, he thought.

***

She comes to him in his mind now, here at the end of his life.

Nancy, he thinks. *I love you.*

Already he can feel the meaning of those words dying within him. The contract is taking effect.

He screws up his eyes and, with his last true breath, he releases his final scream into the atmosphere. In doing so, he changes his own small piece of it.

"WAKE UP!!"

He even smiles just before he disappears into the creature's throat.

***

Chapter Twenty-Two
Here We Are
***

From: rapidtranslate.org
To: guyAutumn31@hotmail.com
Subject: Here You Are!

Hello Mr Autumn,

Attached is the English version of your document. Thank you very much for your business and we hope you use rapidtranslate.org for your future translation requirements!

On a personal note, we don't normally comment on documents or make editorials, but I was wondering if you wouldn't mind settling a debate in the office as this has really got people talking, LOL.

Is this part of a prank? The part about being eaten raised a few eyebrows, ha ha!

Regards,
Nadia Beaker

***

From: frankbeckwith@hotmail.com
To: guyAutumn31@hotmail.com
Subject: Re:

Re: what we discussed on the phone. I can get it by early afternoon but then we're square mate. This has to be the last urgent one, okay? I'll give you the correct dosage in its oral form but you take it at your own risk, it's serious stuff. I wish you'd go to hospital but I owe you big time so I'm gonna hook you up here and then we're all good. Whatever you need it for, I promise you that after taking this stuff you'll feel next to nothing. I hope you're okay bud. When you're better, bring Nancy round and we'll have another game night. I miss that stuff, it's been years.

F.

***

From: guyAutumn31@hotmail.com
To: nancyrobbo@hotmail.com
Subject: I Love You.

Nancy,

This was set to email to you after midnight so maybe you'll still be awake. Maybe you'll read this in the morning.

I'm sorry that I had to keep this part secret. My resolve feels like it's unbreakable right now but the one thing that could make me waver would be your sadness.

I don't know whether to begin with the apology for the past or the explanation for the present, so here's both in a sentence: I will always be sorry for the former, and I am sorry for keeping the latter from you too.

You told me to do whatever it takes, and I think this is just that. I know what is going to happen to me and I've been dosing myself up with morphine in preparation thanks to our old friend Frank Beckwith. I'm not afraid. Strangely, I've never felt such a sense of purpose in my entire life. It turns out that Viktor Frankl, yet again, was right: *those who have the 'why' to live can endure almost any 'how'*. It took me a while, but I found the *why*, even though the *how* will be very short-lived.

But don't forget this: *you* were the biggest *why* of my entire life, even though you deserved so much better.

At least I get to go with my dignity intact, and I've discovered just how much that means. I signed a piece of paper saying I surrendered, but the things I set up before that— both the tech and the people involved—mean I haven't surrendered at all. All I have to do now is to lie here, drugged out of my mind. The most passive of resistance.

I keep thinking about all those times I rolled my eyes at Larry banging on about his marketing theories... I didn't even get it when Mister Chair told me exactly what I needed! Momentum. Larry had always told me exactly *how* you create it. The three act structure. The three stage joke. The goddamn 3x Rule.

People need to hear a message three times before they act on it; comedy works the same way, coming in threes. If you want the biggest momentum, then the third time has to be the punchline. My first video, the TV appearance... and now the kicker. How did I ever think two would be enough? Momentum is harder than ever to create amongst the hurricane of messages.

But if you can do it, you can change the nature of the air, the atmosphere, more than anything else can.

Promise me this, Nancy: please don't ever watch the video.

I love you, Nancy Autumn. Even before all of this, I came close to being a monster—maybe I was one for a while—and I didn't protect you then. For once, I'm protecting you now, whether you like it or not.

I'm sorry for everything I ever did to you, and you were always right.

I hope that, as I leave this world, I'm giving it real information for once.

Guy

***

Chapter Twenty-Three
Reply All
✳✳✳

Sam sits and stares at his phone.

The only sound in the room is the dull buffeting of the wind against his living room window. He remembers Rufus; storms always made the old dog antsy, but right now even painful thoughts of his pet can't penetrate his thoughts.

After a few minutes, he finally puts the gadget down and turns his attention back to his laptop screen.

The email is still sitting there, unsent.

He looks back at his phone.

Send the email.

He doesn't. Not yet.

His mind actually starts to wander, playing out the chain of events—the ones that he is about to set into motion—in his head.

✳✳✳

Charlie Heisman—known to the wider world by his online persona as Duckbuggerer—would have been sitting with his hands over his mouth for ten minutes, unmoving. The events onscreen ended about five minutes ago.

As a video game streamer, he didn't have a large following by any means, less than two hundred. He didn't know that this was the exact reason that Sam Heinrich had contacted him under instruction from Guy Autumn. Easy to contact, likely to respond, and a number of eyes on his channel but not so many that it may draw the wrong kind of attention.

Less likely to be shut down before the job was finished.

The camera angle onscreen seemed to imply that the webcam was attached to the ceiling. Is that a second webcam tucked away in the opposite ceiling corner? A feed going to another streamer perhaps? He didn't know. What he did know was that Sam Heinrich, a man claiming to know Guy Autumn—the man who was now famous thanks to his YouTube video and explosive TV appearance—had just handed him the biggest break possible. In that moment, sadly, Charlie Heisman didn't care.

He'd just watched a monster eat a man alive.

He hadn't been prepared for it. The comments in his video game streaming channel's chat window were pure astonishment. There were only about five people watching at the time.

The people, *he thought dimly.* You know what you're supposed to do.

"Uh... uh, guys," he said, voice shaking as he spoke into his headset mic, catching a glimpse of himself in the onscreen window, embedded in the shot of Guy's now empty bedroom. "The, uh... I don't know, I mean... uh..." His stomach turned over. "Sorry—" he managed to say before jerking sideways at his desk and throwing up onto the carpet. He coughed out the last of it and returned to camera. "What I need you to do," he groaned, trying to remember what he'd been told to say. "Is upload your screen captures of this to, uh... Guy Autumn, uh, in the video there... he asked us to..." He glanced at the comments in the chat window again:

—WHAT THE FUUUUUUUUUUCK

—Was that shit real? The other stuff looked real but that looked real real

—It fucking ate him what the fuck that wasn't CGI

"Yeah, I don't know what to, uh..." The website, *he thought.* Give them the link to the website that Sam gave you. *What else was he supposed to do?* Put the screen grabbed video recording in the Dropbox folder. Sync it. Put the link on the website. Tell them to download the video and upload it to YouTube themselves. *"When you upload to YouTube, uh, make sure you put the website address in the description."*

The web address Sam had sent him, along with the Squarespace login details. This is all as real as it gets, I can assure you, *Sam had written. Charlie leaned forward and dropped his elbows onto his desk, seeing himself onscreen again and looking at the carefully curated, anime-filled backdrop he'd created for his streaming room. For the first time it seemed foolish, trivial. The comments continued to scream. He didn't know what to say. Then he did. Of course he did.*

"Make sure you tag duckbuggerer in those YouTube uploads too, please."

He typed out the web address for them to go and get the file.

***

Zara Culpepper would have sat in her quiet, darkened living room, watching the same footage yet again, the one Duckbuggerer and people like him had spread. The one she would have watched and watched for days. She wouldn't have been crying—she couldn't and hadn't been able to for some time—but an infinitesimal part of her remembered how that felt, certainly. It was thrumming away deep inside her, encased inside whatever held it prisoner. It didn't stop rational logic. She understood a watershed moment when she saw it. Being a part of it would be more important than continuing to live this way. She understood this in her bones. Such knowledge was deeply uncommon to her.

She couldn't know that, all across the country—across the world—people like her would be thinking the exact same thing. People for whom the word inspired *was inaccurate—they weren't capable of true inspiration anymore—but this was something close.*

She clicked off the video and opened up Zoom. She found the contact she wanted and pressed the Call icon. Neil picked up quickly. He was at work after all and spent a lot of his time sitting at his computer not doing very much, Zara knew. He was a work colleague and certainly not a friend. She'd taken the day off to do this.

"Okayyy," Neil said as his image appeared onscreen. She could see the office behind him, an environment so normal that Zara—lost in the most intense moment of her life—thought it suddenly alien. "What's up Zara? Something so important that you're calling into the office on your fucking day off..." He was fiddling with something on his phone while talking to her, distracted. Maybe even watching the video that Zara herself had just finished watching. It had over nine million views already, so it was certainly possible. She'd lied and told Neil it would be good for his career.

Neil was a weasel, and that was one reason why she'd picked him.

He could potentially profit from what she was about to do, which was the other reason. That way she didn't feel too bad about it as there might be money involved, but she still hadn't wanted to do this to anyone decent. It would be traumatizing.

"Thanks for taking the call Neil," she said, her voice steady. "Did you download the software I asked you to?"

"Yeah, but I went to the link and it's some kind of video capture stuff? You gonna do a striptease for me?" He looked up and smirked as if this was some silly, flirty banter between two friends, but Zara knew that the prick was only half-joking. She was thirty-four years old and still in good shape somehow despite never going to the gym for the last two years—finding motivation for people like her was almost impossible—and turned heads even though she had no interest in doing so. Neil had grabbed her ass at the office Christmas party last year. He'd done it three times despite her asking him not to. If she had been her old self she would have clawed his eyes out for it. As it was, the current Zara hadn't reported it to HR, and Neil had pretended it never happened.

"I'm afraid not," she said. "Can you start screen recording now?"

"Sure, sure," Neil said, sounding bored. "Can I just leave this recording while I take care of other stuff?"

Zara began to say yes... but then changed her mind.

"Actually Neil, I think you should watch this," she said. "You remember what to do with it?"

"Yep. Upload the recording to youtube—"

"Good. Put this web address in the YouTube video description, please?"

"Which web address—"

"I'm emailing it to you now."

She hit send.

She didn't know why she waited until she heard the ping on his end. Waited for him to open up the email and see the web address she'd sent him. She watched him fiddle with his mouse, saw his confusion turn to—yes—mild fear as he recognized the URL.

It was the perfect start.

She held her contract up to the camera and tore it in half.

She had time to see the realization hit him—he'd seen the footage of Guy Autumn's TV appearance, had heard the growing claims about the footage on the already-infamous website—before the transformation began. Even as her human awareness quickly dimmed, she registered Neil's screams.

Quickly, quickly, quickly, the knife, *quickly*—

The change was coming upon her so fast, and as her hands began to change shape she fumbled for the blade she'd prepared. Her thoughts began to turn into dark shapes and terrible desires, colliding in her mind like thunderbolts in a storm, and she struggled to remember what she had to do. She had only seconds, she knew. Just having the beginning of the change on film begin would be enough, but she couldn't allow it to complete.

STAY IN... SEAT, her dimming thoughts told her. HAS TO SEE

Her hands found the knife's handle. Immediately—and just in time, for this was the last human action left in her—Zara plunged the blade into what was still a vaguely human-shaped throat and dragged it sideways, opening up her neck. Before she died she realised two things, and both were blessings: there was no pain, and that she briefly felt her old self before that self vanished forever. The thing that had once been Zara Culpepper completed its transformation as its dead weight fell forwards, its increased mass smashing through Zara Culpepper's home desk.

Neil sat silently at his desk in an industrial estate seventeen miles away. He had his hands over his mouth, unaware of his colleagues staring at him, white faced, so disturbed by his screams that none of them had moved. Eventually Michelle Daggett quietly got up from her seat and approached him. All eyes watched her.

"Neil..."

He looked up. The sight of someone within viewing distance of his screen— even though it only now showed the ceiling of Zara Culpepper's living room— made his hand shoot out and close the Zoom window.

"Sorry," he babbled, his brain instinctively working on a lie even as the sweat continued to run down his back. "Someone... uh, sent me this horrible email attachment. Really sick video."

Michelle looked at the rest of the office. Some were already turning back to their machines. It was all people ever needed; something ordinary to hang their hats of complacency on, something that allowed them to say I don't need to worry then.

"Jesus, that must have been something pretty bad," she said. "You were really screaming." Michelle had her own experiences with Neil. Her concern was genuine but she couldn't pass up the opportunity to make him squirm a little.

"Yeah. Yeah it was," he said. "Really horrible."

Michelle patted his shoulder and went back to her desk. Neil reopened Zara's prior email and reread the instructions within, words that had seemed batshit crazy earlier. He'd always known Zara had a little thing for him; he'd thought that going along with her bullshit would take him one step closer to banging her. Oh God, he wished he'd ignored her. What should he do now? Call the police?

Yes, *a voice in his head told him, before adding something so loud and clear that he had no doubt that it was the right thing to do. It almost felt like a voice from above.* But upload that video. Do what she asked you.

His mind was fog and he blinked like a simpleton as he tried to follow the emails instructions. He couldn't seem to grasp it just yet.

It's alright, Neil. Take your time. Soon equilibrium will be restored.

There was a web address in the email. That, he understood. He copied and pasted into his web browser.

He wouldn't have been alone. He could see that already; the Dropbox cloud folder was full of files, some of them with titles like jessybowker3rdreupload *and* guyautumn15thupload. *Was this happening everywhere?*

He stared at the web address. It was a sentence, it had meaning.

ibelieveguy.com

***

Yes, Sam thinks, thoughts of Zara Culpepper leaving his mind as his attention comes back to his living room. *That's how it would happen. Dominos, like that.*

His fingers hover above his laptop's trackpad.

The email to Charlie Heisman, AKA Duckbuggerer, stares at him from the screen, still unsent. The one written for him by Guy. All Sam has to do is click *send.*

Once again, he imagines the scene playing out.

This time he doesn't picture Zara Culpepper in the lead. This time he imagines that younger woman from the Other Folk meeting. What had been her name , the one that had tried to lead them all in a backslapping exercise? *Siobhan,* that was it.

Sam pictures Siobhan renouncing her surrender and paying the price. He imagines it happening all over the world with people just like her.

Then send the email, he thinks.

He looks at his phone again. It's not necessary; the message he received hours earlier is now completely burned into his memory, but he looks at it anyway.

DAD, it says. I TOLD YOU BEFORE. DO NOT CONTACT ME. I RECEIVED YOUR WEIRD PARCEL AND I THREW IT IN THE BIN. I AM NOT SAYING THIS TO HURT YOU. I AM SAYING THIS TO BE CLEAR: YOU ARE NOT A PART OF MY LIFE AND YOU

ARE NOT MY FATHER ANYMORE. DO NOT RESPOND TO THIS.
LEAVE US ALONE.

Sam, of course, hasn't sent Melissa anything at all.

He twitches for a moment, thinking he hears a sound coming up the driveway. He doesn't know for certain, but Sam thinks that he will have a visitor soon. The sun is still up, but he knows that the visitor he's expecting can handle that.

This is bigger than you, Sam thinks. *She said it herself: you aren't her father. Send the email. Start the chain.*

But blood is *different* to a marriage contract, isn't it? It doesn't matter what Melissa says, at least not as far as the concerned party sees it.

The pointer onscreen is right above the *Send* button. Sam's eyes lock onto it, his gaze frozen.

Blood is different. On every level.

Sam keeps staring at the *Send* button.

Trying to focus.

***

Author's Afterword

Current list of Smithereens with Titles—and your name if you left a review of THE EMPTY MEN— are all after the afterword, along with a sample chapter from the beginning of the first book in Luke Smitherd's bestselling THE STONE MAN series...

BEFORE WE GET TO THE AUTHOR'S AFTERWORD: IF YOU ENJOYED THIS BOOK, PLEASE LEAVE A STAR RATING ON AMAZON; THEY MAKE ALL THE DIFFERENCE TO WHETHER OR NOT A BOOK SELLS... IF YOU WOULD LIKE *A WHOLE DELETED CHAPTER FROM* YOU SEE THE MONSTER THEN VISIT WWW.LUKESMITHERD.COM AND SIGN UP FOR THE *SPAM-FREE BOOK RELEASE NEWSLETTER*, AFTER WHICH YOU'LL IMMEDIATELY BE SENT THE CHAPTER AND A FREE SHORT STORY TOO.

About twenty years ago (*shiiiiiiiiiiiiiiiiii—*) long before I ever wrote a whole novel, I wrote a very, very short story about a man who was walking down the street and happened to pass an alleyway. Inside the alleyway he saw an enormous monster accosting another, terrified man, and giving him what appeared to be a gleeful telling-off for breaking the rules; its victim was terrified but seemed to know what the monster was talking about. The monster then picked up the man (not the observer, the other dude) and slowly lowered him into its throat, the man screaming all the while. I'm reliably informed that, nowadays, this would fall under the sexual fetish category of 'Vore', apparently, but I've checked and I'm pretty sure this doesn't do anything for me. If you got your kicks out of this element of the story though, then hey, that's a nice bonus for you and you're very welcome. Regardless, I suppose the idea must have never left me, because not only did I remember it about halfway through writing this book (and *after* I'd written the book, actually) but it also featured the same accidental (or was it?) glimpse of a larger supernatural world, something that I realise that I really, really like to write and have been doing for entire 'career.'

Hello to you, and if this is the first book of mine that you have read, and I really hope that you enjoyed YSTM. If you did, then maybe check out some of my other books and welcome to the Smithereen collective. I didn't come up with the name, and anyone that says I did is definitely a Smithereen; it's exactly the kind of filthy lie they *would* say. Also, check your pockets or bag before you finish talking to them, they've probably switched your phone with a piece of hand-finished, phone-shaped wood that has *IT ALWAYS LOOKED LIKE THIS* written on it. Those guys, waddya gonna do, eh? (Speaking of which, the updated list of Smithereen titles is at the start of this book.)

If you didn't enjoy the story, then sincere thanks for trying my stuff and I'm sorry it disappointed.

To be clear, I'm *not* anti-social media. I think it can be a genuine force for positive real-world change. It can also be great for keeping connections with distant people you know or knew; I use it myself for that reason and also to promote my work and connect with readers (you'll see the plug for my socials below.) I think it can inspire and genuinely help people. I *do* have concerns about the manipulative elements of it, and it should be treated like any kind of vice: it's great in small doses, and a little goes a long way. I'm addicted to my phone to the point that I have a second phone that I use during my work day— one without Whatsapp or Instagram or anything like that—so I don't disappear down rabbit holes and lose hours that could be spent working or doing something I *really* enjoy. I do think it's disastrous for young kids, and I think that the following phrase should be plastered in an unmoving bar along the top of the screen over ever single thing you interact with: *comparison is the thief of joy.* So make of all that what you will.

If there are elements of Guy's story that resonated with you, I strongly recommend you check out the non-fiction books *Self Compassion, King Warrior Magician Lover,* and *Iron John.*

There were a few elements that, sadly, couldn't make it into the story; the scene with poor Scubby the Stone Dog (now there's a series title) was originally a courtroom scene, and Erin's house was originally a hut in the Arizona desert. She looked *very* different, too. The latter sequence was quite long and I have it as a deleted chapter, along with all my development notes in the text; if all this *inside baseball* talk is interesting to you, I'll be shortly sending out this deleted scene, along with an intro from me, exclusively to my mailing list subscribers as a thank you. If you're not already on the LUKE

SMITHERD SPAM-FREE MAILING LIST (go to lukesmitherd.com), then if you sign up you not only get a free copy of my short story THE JESUS LOOPHOLE but, from the release date of this book, you will also get that deleted chapter. Getting on the mailing list means you find out about new stuff before anybody else, and the good news is I only send it out a few times a year, so you won't get bombarded with nonsense. I save that for the books.

My good friend Matt Leeming was on hand to generously help me with police-related questions; if there are errors in here, they are mine, not his. Thanks Matt. Big thanks also to Barnett Brettler, whose early input on the first draft made a big change to the story. Originally, Guy and Nancy were happily married, and Barnett's suggestion that they be separated added in whole new elements that vastly improved the book. In fact, along with THE EMPTY MEN, this is another book that changed massively from the first draft to the last. Originally the book was mostly in America (but don't worry, Cov too) and Guy was motly alone. Sam Boyce, my favourite hired gun/goon, gave the excellent suggestion that Guy needed someone with him throughout the story; in the original draft, Sam Heinrich was only in the initial coffee shop meeting, but I loved the character. As soon as it was suggested that Guy needed a sidekick, I knew exactly who that would be. She also, however, pointed out that the book needed to be in the third person (*why do you always do this to me Sammmmm*) for the very good reason that we had the main character, effectively, narrating his own death at the end. In my defence, I read a wonderful book as a kid called SLUBBER (the book was called SLUBBER, not me, it wasn't some cruel nickname my parents gave me.) in which the main character, a boy, narrates his own death at the end, so I always took that as being acceptable. (Hmm...I just looked it up to get the writer's name and Google says it doesn't exist. Is this the Mandela Effect in action or does anyone else recognise this title?) So the whole bastard book had to be completely switched over, *again,* into the third person. I have to add that, *scandalously,* I don't think I thanked Sam for her help on THE EMPTY MEN; she was *vital* to that process, as she was with this project. Thanks also to Ryan Lewis, Kristin Nelson, my good friend and mentor, Carole Dutra—I don't know how I would have made it through the last year without you—and my early readers Pete Robinson, Mike Hands, and Mark Iddon.

The biggest thanks of all goes to my regulars. If you weren't out there, this book wouldn't exist. Thank you from the bottom of my heart. Your emails and facebook messages always make my day, even when you're nagging me about the next STONE MAN book (as with any healthily abusive relationship, I know it's really your way of showing you care... right?)

Note: sorry about killing both of the named dogs in this story. As you should know from A HEAD FULL OF KNIVES, I love dogs.

Note: I also don't think we've seen the last of Sam Heinrich, either.

Okay. Okay. Let's get the rest of the plugs in. If you enjoyed this book, please leave a star rating on the Amazon website. It not only massively helps protect the book's overall rating from those devastating one-star ratings (heyyyy, you don't wanna do that to ol' Red Eyes here, do ya? To your Second Favourite Author?) but it also helps other, new readers to find it. Technically, I still haven't been traditionally published in the English language; Audible have produced a few of mine, but if you go into any UK bookstore at the time of writing, you won't find any my books on the shelves (although you will in Germany now, and, soon... Finland! I just saw the finnish language cover for THE STONE MAN yesterday, and it looks genuinely great. German ones are pretty too.) Therefore, anything that helps my reach is a... help. I long for the day when I don't have to tap-dance for star ratings like this as its rather embarrassing, but frankly the reviews I've received over the years have got me this far, so until that day comes, I'll keep doing the old soft shoe and buck-and-wingin' it like this on the streetcorner for every star rating that gets slung into my cold, rusty cup (no, not like that.) And if you leave an actual review too, I'll put your Amazon reviewer name into the beginning of the next book ☺ Kindle readers, however: the 'rate this book' feature on your Kindle doesn't put those ratings on the actual website... so, if you felt like helping a pasty white brother out, please click on the link HERE. Paperback readers of this afterword, you will only see the word HERE in capitals, and if you press it, it won't do anything. If it does, however, seriously: let me know. I think it would mean that you were *on the inside* and you would be facing much bigger problems than you know. And if you *did* enjoy this book, I would perhaps recommend IN THE DARKNESS and THE MAN WITH ALL THE ANSWERS as others of mine that you may like.

So, as always: what's the next project? Well, many of my existing readers have politely asked what's happening with UNTITLED: THE STONE MAN, BOOK THREE, and how it's coming along. For once, I can say: it's already written (and it has a full title too, but I'm saving that for now.) It's on its third redraft and only needs a few minor tweaks, so depending on what Audible have to say about a release date, I anticipate it being out towards the end of 2021. Ideally, I'd like it to come out in November. Actually, I have to say a big thank you to the reviewers of that one; I asked you nicely to avoid spoilers and *everyone* did. I was chuffed!

And after TSM 3? I have an idea for a book that I'm going to be working on first, and then once *that's* written, the next book will be... SECRET TITLE: THE STONE MAN, BOOK FOUR, ending the story arc that began in THE EMPTY MEN: THE STONE MAN, BOOK TWO. I wasn't going to tell anyone that there would be a following book, as I did with TSM2, leaving the reader to discover it at the end, but I thought that this time I didn't want everyone to expect it to end as a trilogy. So there you go; a little bit of news for you, and that's a nice point to leave it. For new readers that haven't read any of the STONE MAN books yet, there's a sample of the opening chapter following now; maybe a good point to get on at the ground floor?

Stay Hungry folks.

Luke Smitherd

Nottingham

26th May 2021

Facebook.com/smitherdbooks

Instagram.com/lukesmitherdyall

Twitter.com/lukesmitherd

www.lukesmitherd.com

And we're all going to hell.

And now for the opening chapter from THE STONE MAN, shortlisted for Audible UK's Book of the Year 2015 and available now in all formats on Amazon and Audible.

Chapter One
Andy at the End, The Stone Man Arrives, A Long Journey Begins On Foot, And the Eyes of the World Fall Upon England
✱✱✱

The TV is on in the room next door; the volume is up, the news is on, and I can hear some Scottish reporter saying that it's about to happen all over again. I already knew that, of course, just like everyone watching already knows that 'The Lottery Question' is being asked by people up and down the country, and around the world. Who will it be this time?

That was my job, of course, although I won't be doing it anymore. That's why I'm recording this, into the handheld digi-dicta-doodad that Paul sent me after the first lot of business that we dealt with. To get it all out if you need to, he'd said (he knows I find it hard to talk to people. He thought talking to the machine might be easier. Plus, getting it all out now gives me an excuse to use it after all; feels strange holding one again, as if my newspaper days were decades ago instead of just a year or so).

I didn't really know what he was talking about, back then. It had hit him a lot harder than me, so I didn't really understand why I'd need to talk about it. Eventually I got it, of course ... after the second time.

That was worse. Much worse.

This room is nice anyway, better than the outside of the hotel would suggest. I actually feel guilty about smoking in here, but at this stage I can be forgiven, I'm sure. Helps me relax, and naturally, I've got the entire contents of the mini bar spread out in front of me. I haven't actually touched any of it yet, but rest assured, I expect I shall have consumed most of it by the time I finish talking.

I just thought that I should get the real version down while I still have time. Not the only-partially-true, Home Office approved version that made me a household name around the world. I'm not really recording this for anyone else to hear, as daft as that may sound. I just think that doing so will help me put it all in perspective. I might delete it afterwards, I might not ... I think I will. Too dangerous for it to get out, for now at least.

I'd obviously had to come here in disguise (amazing how much a pair of subtle sunglasses and a baseball cap let you get away with in summer) and it's a good job that I did. They'd already be up here, banging on the door, screaming about the news and telling me what I already know. Thanks to my disguise, I can sit quietly in this designer-upholstered, soft-glow, up-lit, beige yuppie hidey-hole, with Steely Dan playing in the background on my phone's speakers (sorry if you aren't a fan) and remain undisturbed, until ... well, until I'm done. And it's time.

This is for you as well, Paul; for you more than anyone. You were there for all of it, and you're a key player, not that you'll ever actually get to hear this.

Well, actually, you weren't there at the start, were you? I often forget that. Which, of course, would be the best place to begin. Heh, would you look at that; I just did an automatic segue. Still got all the old newsman moves. Slick ...

Sorry, I was miles away for a moment there. Remembering the first day. How excited those people were. Everybody knew it was something big.

Nobody was frightened. Not at first.

***

It was summer. Summer meant more people out shopping, eyeing up the opposite sex, browsing, meeting friends, having outdoor coffees and watered-down beer. In Coventry, the chance to do this (with the sun out, and not a single cloud visible in the sky on a weekend no less) was as rare as rocking-horse shit, and so there were more people out and about in the city centre than at pretty much any other time of the year. I sometimes wonder if this was the reason that particular day was picked; attracted to the mass of people perhaps? Or maybe it was just sheer chance.

I was stuck indoors for the earlier part of that day, and that was just fine by me. One, because I've never been a person who enjoys being out in harsh sunlight (makes me squint, I sweat easily, I burn easily, I can't stand it when my clothes stick to me ... need I go on? Sun worshippers doing nothing but sitting in sunlight; I'll never understand them) and two, because I was interviewing a local girl group ('Heroine Chic'; I shit you not) who were just about to release their debut piece-of-crap single. And it was awful, truly awful (I don't mean to come across as someone's dad, but it really was an assault on the ear drums. Middle-class white girls talking in urban patois. Exactly as bad as it sounds) but, at the time, I was still just on the right side of thirty-five, and so considered myself in with a chance of charming at least one of the trio; a stunning-looking blonde, brunette and redhead combo in their early twenties whose management were clearly banking on their looks to get them by, rather than their output. None of us knew it back then, but even that wouldn't be enough to help 'Get Into Me' (again, I shit you not) crack the top forty. Two more non-charting efforts later, Heroine Chic would find themselves back in obscurity before fame had found them; of the six of us in that room, including their enormous security guard and their wet-behind-the-ears looking manager, only one of us was destined to be known worldwide. None of us could have ever guessed that it would be me.

Not that I didn't have high hopes of my own in those days, lazy—but earnest—dreams of a glorious career in my chosen field. Obviously, the likes of Charli, Kel and Suze weren't going to land me a job at Rolling Stone, but I was starting to get good feedback on freelance pieces that I'd written for the Observer and the Times, and was listed as a contributor at the Guardian; I'd finally started to believe that in a year or two, I'd leave behind the features department at the local rag and then make my way to London to start shaking things up. I actually said that to colleagues as well: I'm gonna shake things up. That's how I often find myself talking to people, using sound bites and stagey lines to make an impression. As the interview drew to a close, and their manager started making 'wrap it up' signals while looking nervously at his smartphone, the girls and I posed together for a brief photo by the office window. They pouted, and I grinned honestly, enjoying the moment despite receiving zero interest from any of them. I made myself feel better by putting it down to the age gap.

They left with an all-too-casual goodbye, their bouncer blocking them all from view as they made their way to the escalator. I was done for the day—I'd only come in for the late afternoon interview, with it being a weekend—and it was approaching five, so the temperature would soon be dropping nicely into that relaxing summer evening feel that I actually like. I had no plans, and flatmate Phil had his brother over for the weekend. He was a good guy, and his brother a good guest, but I didn't particularly want to be stuck at home listening to the two of them endlessly discussing rugby. I decided that I'd maybe find a beer garden and have a read for an hour or so. In my twenties, this would have been that magical exciting hour where you'd text around and find out who was available for an impromptu session. No one was anymore.

I grabbed my bag and headed out of the building, thinking about possibly getting a bite to eat as well—although I intended to have something healthy, as lately the gym hadn't really been graced with my presence, and it was starting to show—and for some reason, I decided to stroll towards Millennium Place.

It used to be a big open-air space, a modern plaza designed for concerts and shows of all kinds. None of it's there anymore, of course; after the Second Arrival they dug it all up and put a small lake in its place, to see if it made any difference.

For some reason I was in a good mood and—in the words of the song—having 'no particular place to go', I thought I'd take a look at the summer crowds at Millennium Place, and then decide my destination from there, giving me time to work up an appetite. I people-watched as I went, passing barely dressed young couples who made me feel old and think about past opportunities of my own. I realised that the tune I'd been humming was 'Get Into Me'. I laughed out loud—I remember that distinctly—as I turned the corner and saw Millennium Place fully. When I saw what was going on, the laughter trailed off in my throat.

I suppose that I must have heard the commotion as I'd drawn closer; I'd been so lost in thought that somehow it didn't really register, or possibly I just subconsciously wrote it off as the usual summer crowd sound. But this was different. Around two hundred people were gathered in a cluster near the centre of Millennium Place, and there was an excited, confused buzz coming from them, their mobiles held out and snapping away at something in their midst. Other people were hanging back from them, getting footage of the crowd itself. That was the other reason I wanted to get into the big leagues, of course; everyone was a reporter in the digital age, and local print was shrinking fast.

I couldn't make out what was in the centre of the crowd, standing at a distance as I was, but I could see other people on the outskirts of the plaza having the same response as me; what's going on, whatever it is I want to see it. Don't misunderstand me, at this stage it was surprising and intriguing, but nothing really more than that; a chance for hopeful people to capture some footage that might go viral. You have to remember, none of us knew what it really was at that point. I assumed that it was somebody maybe doing some kind of street art, or perhaps a performance piece. That in itself was rare in Coventry, so in my mind I already had one hand on my phone to give Rich Bell—the staff photographer—a call, to see if he was available to get some proper photos if this turned out to be worth it. Either way, I walked towards the hubbub. As I got closer I could hear two people shouting frantically, almost hysterically, sounding as though they were trying to explain something.

The voices belonged to a man and a woman, and while I couldn't yet make out what they were saying, I could hear laughter from some listeners and questions from others; my vision was still mainly blocked by the medium-sized mass of bodies, but I could see that there was something fairly large in the middle of them all, rising just slightly above the heads of the gathered crowd and standing perfectly still.

I reached the cluster of people, now large enough to make it difficult to get through (to the point where I had to go on tiptoe to get a clear view) and that was the moment that I became one of the first few hundred people on Earth to get a look at the Stone Man.

Of course, it didn't have a name then. I'd like to tell you that I was the one who came up with it, but I'm afraid that would be a lie. As you may know, I was one of the people who really brought it into the common parlance worldwide, but I'd actually overheard it being used on a random local radio station as Paul and I raced through Sheffield later on (obviously, more on that to come) and thought it perfect, but I'd never actually intended to rip it off. By the point I was in front of the cameras, I'd used it so often that I'd forgotten that it wasn't a common term at the time.

It stood at around eight feet tall (to my eyes at least; the Home Office can give you the exact measurements) and it made me think then, as it does now, of the 'Man' logo on a toilet door, if someone were to make one out of rough, dark, greyish-brown stone and then mutate it so the arms were too long, and the head were more of an oval than a circle. The top half of its body was bent slightly forward as well, but the biggest departure from the toilet picture was that this figure had hands, of a sort; its arms tapered out at the ends, reminding me of the tip of a lipstick.

The most intriguing thing was, there was also an extremely quiet sound emanating from it. The best way I can describe it is as a bass note so low as to be almost inaudible. They still haven't figured that one out.

Now that I was closer, I could hear what one of the ranting people was saying. It was the woman, stood about ten feet away from me on the inside of the circle of gathered people. Based on the distance between the crowd, herself, and the Stone Man, it looked to me as if she was the reason they were hanging back from the hulking figure, and not swarming forward to touch and prod it.

She was patrolling back and forth in front of the Stone Man, wide-eyed and breathing heavily. If she wasn't keeping the people around her at bay deliberately, she was still doing a damn good job of it.

***

T H E
STONE
M A N

A
SCIENCE
FICTION
THRILLER
NOVEL

THE #1 AMAZON HORROR BESTSELLER
BY THE AUTHOR OF *THE BLACK ROOM*

LUKE SMITHERD

Continued in THE STONE MAN *by Luke Smitherd, the first volume in the* STONE MAN *series, available on Amazon and Audible now.*

The Stone Man
The #1 Amazon Bestseller

Two-bit reporter Andy Pointer had always been unsuccessful (and antisocial) until he got the scoop of his career; the day a man made of stone appeared in the middle of his city.

This is his account of everything that came afterwards and what it all cost him, along with the rest of his country.

The destruction, the visions ...the dying.

Available in both paperback and Kindle formats on Amazon and as an audiobook on Audible.

Also by Luke Smitherd:
THE EMPTY MEN
THE STONE MAN, BOOK TWO

The long-awaited sequel to the #1 Amazon and Audible
bestseller The Stone Man, shortlisted for Audible Book of the
Year 2015

On a quiet seafront in the middle of the afternoon the sun sets, the clouds part, and something like a pale, elongated human figure appears on the horizon.

For Maria, watching from the beach, it's proof that she should never have dared to return. Five years earlier, her life shattered by the arrival of the Stone Man, she'd fled the country. But now she can't escape: suddenly, there are news reports of 'Empty Men' materialising all around the coast, and the roads are gridlocked. The Empty Men are killers, and they're heading inland.

A hundred miles from the sea, lonely, grieving Eric obsessively keeps watch in the ruins of Coventry, never straying far from Ground Zero, the site of the Stone Man's first appearance. For five years, Eric has known there was a massive government cover-up of the circumstances surrounding the Stone Man and its disappearance, and he's determined to find the truth.

As Maria battles the Empty Men in a desperate chase for survival, and Eric is caught in a terrifying transformation at Ground Zero, both find themselves on a path leading straight to the heart of the Stone Man mystery.Chilling, fast-paced and full of stunning twists, this science fiction thriller is the highly-anticipated second book in Luke Smitherd's outstanding *Stone Man* series.

Available in both paperback and Kindle formats on Amazon
and as audiobook on Audible

Also by Luke Smitherd:

THE MAN WITH ALL THE ANSWERS

From the author of Audible #1 bestsellers In The Darkness, That's Where I'll Know You, The Physics of the Dead, and The Stone Man (shortlisted for the Audible Audiobook of the Year award 2015)

He seems to know everything you want before you do.
He's insightful, kind, and understands you in ways you don't even understand yourself.
He's everything you ever dreamed of. *But there's always a catch, and now it's time for The Man with All The Answers to tell you the truth about his incredible, impossible gift.*

About the friends that died in its creation.
About the terrible price he's had to pay.

Audible Book of the Year Nominee Luke Smitherd returns for the first time in over three years with a tale of speculative fiction and psychic romance.
What would you do if the Man with All the Answers fell in love with you?

Praise for KILL SOMEONE:

"For a jaded reader, there is no greater thrill than to experience a story that takes you down an unexpected, unexplored path... Smitherd once again proves himself a master at his craft."
—Ain't It Cool News

Available in both paperback and Kindle formats on Amazon and as audiobook on Audible

Also by Luke Smitherd:
WEIRD. DARK.

PRAISE FOR WEIRD. DARK.:

"WEIRD and DARK, yes, but more importantly ... exciting and imaginative. Whether you've read his novels and are already a fan or these short stories are your first introduction to Smitherd's work, you'll be blown away by the abundance of ideas that can be expressed in a small number of pages." - Ain't It Cool News.com

Luke Smitherd is bringing his unique brand of strange storytelling once again, delivered here in an omnibus edition that collects four of his weirdest and darkest tales:

MY NAME IS MISTER GRIEF: what if you could get rid of your pain immediately? What price would you be prepared to pay?

HOLD ON UNTIL YOUR FINGERS BREAK: a hangover, a forgotten night out, old men screaming in the street, and a mystery with a terrible, terrible answer ...

THE MAN ON TABLE TEN: he has a story to tell you. One that he has kept secret for decades. But now, the man on table ten can take no more, and the knowledge - as well as the burden - is now yours.

EXCLUSIVE story, THE CRASH: if you put a dent in someone's car, the consequences can be far greater - and more strange - than you expect.

Available in both paperback and Kindle formats on Amazon and as an audiobook on Audible.

Also by Luke Smitherd:

IN THE DARKNESS, THAT'S WHERE I'LL KNOW YOU
What Is The Black Room?

There are hangovers, there are bad hangovers, and then there's waking up someone else's head. Thirty-something bartender Charlie Wilkes is faced with this exact dilemma when he wakes to find finds himself trapped inside The Black Room; a space consisting of impenetrable darkness and a huge, ethereal screen floating in its centre. Through this screen he is shown the world of his female host, Minnie.

How did he get there? What has happened to his life? And how can he exist inside the mind of a troubled, fragile, but beautiful woman with secrets of her own? Uncertain whether he's even real or if he is just a figment of his host's imagination, Charlie must enlist Minnie's help if he is to find a way out of The Black Room, a place where even the light of the screen goes out every time Minnie closes her eyes...

Previously released in four parts as, "The Black Room" series, all four parts are combined in this edition. In The Darkness, That's Where I'll Know You starts with a bang and doesn't let go. Each answer only leads to another mystery in a story guaranteed to keep the reader on the edge of their seat.

THE BLACK ROOM SERIES, FOUR SERIAL NOVELLAS THAT UNRAVEL THE PUZZLE PIECE BY PIECE, NOW AVAILABLE IN ONE COLLECTED EDITION:

Available in both paperback and Kindle formats on Amazon and as an audiobook on Audible.

Also by Luke Smitherd:
A HEAD FULL OF KNIVES

Martin Hogan is being watched all the time. He just doesn't know it yet. It started a long time ago too, even before his wife died. Before he started walking every day.

Before the walks became an attempt to find a release from the whirlwind that his brain has become. He never walks alone, of course, although his 18-month old son and his faithful dog, Scoffer, aren't the greatest conversationalists.
Then the walks become longer. Then the *other* dog starts showing up. The big white one, with the funny looking head. The one that sits and watches Martin and his family as they walk away.

All over the world, the first attacks begin. The Brotherhood of the Raid make their existence known; a leaderless group who randomly and inexplicably assault both strangers and loved ones without explanation.

Martin and the surviving members of his family are about to find that these events are connected. Caught at the center of the world as it changes beyond recognition, Martin will be faced with a series of impossible choices ... but how can an ordinary and broken man figure out the unthinkable? What can he possibly do with a head full of knives?

Luke Smitherd (author of the Amazon bestseller THE STONE MAN and IN THE DARKNESS, THAT'S WHERE I'LL KNOW YOU) asks you once again to consider what you would do in his unusual and original novel. A HEAD FULL OF KNIVES is a supernatural mystery that will not only change the way you look at your pets forever, but will force you to decide the fate of the world when it lies in your hands.

Available in both paperback and Kindle formats on Amazon and as an audiobook on Audible

Also by Luke Smitherd:
How to be a Vigilante: A Diary

In the late 1990s, a laptop was found in a service station just outside of Manchester. It contained a digital journal entitled 'TO THE FINDER: OPEN NOW TO CHANGE YOUR LIFE!' Now, for the first time, that infamous diary is being published in its entirety.

It's 1998. The internet age is still in its infancy. Google has just been founded.
Eighteen-year-old supermarket shelf-stacker Nigel Carmelite has decided that he's going to become a vigilante.

There are a few problems: how is he going to even find crime to fight on the streets of Derbyshire? How will he create a superhero costume - and an arsenal of crime-fighting weaponry - on a shoestring budget? And will his history of blackouts and crippling social inadequacy affect his chances?

This is Nigel's account of his journey; part diary, part deluded self-help manual, tragically comic and slowly descending into what is arguably Luke Smitherd's darkest and most violent novel.

What do you believe in? And more importantly ...should you?

Available in both paperback and Kindle formats on Amazon and as an audiobook on Audible.

Current list of Smithereens with Titles

Emil: King of the Macedonian Smithereens; Neil Novita: Chief Smithereen of Brooklyn; Jay McTyier: Derby City Smithereen; Ashfaq Jilani: Nawab of the South East London Smithereens; Jason Jones: Archduke of lower Alabama; Betty Morgan: President of Massachusetts Smithereens; Malinda Quartel Qoupe: Queen of the Sandbox (Saudi Arabia); Marty Brastow: Grand Poobah of the LA Smithereens; John Osmond: Captain Toronto; Nita Jester Franz: Goddess of the Olympian Smithereens; Angie Hackett: Keeper of Du; Colleen Cassidy: The Tax Queen Smithereen; Jo Cranford: The Cajun Queen Smithereen; Gary Johnayak: Captain of the Yellow Smithereen; Matt Bryant: the High Lord Dominator of South Southeast San Jose; Rich Gill: Chief Executive Smithereen - Plymouth Branch; Sheryl: Shish the Completely Sane Cat Lady of Silver Lake; Charlie Gold: Smithereen In Chief Of Barnet; Gord Parlee: Prime Transcendent Smithereen, Vancouver Island Division; Erik Hundstad: King Smithereen of Norway(a greedy title but I've allowed it this once); Sarah Hirst: Official Smithereen Knitter of Nottingham; Christine Jones: Molehunter Smithereen Extraordinaire, Marcie Carole Spencer: Princess Smithereen of Elmet, Angela Wallis: Chief Smithereen of Strathblanefield, Melissa Weinberger: Cali Girl Smithereen, Maria Batista: Honorable One and Only Marchioness Smithereen of Her House, Bash Badawi: Lead Smithereen of Tampa, Fl, Bully: Chief Smithereen of Special Stone Masonry Projects, Mani: Colonel Smithereen of London, Drewboy of the Millwall Smithereens, Empress Smithereen of Ushaw Moor, Cate1965: Queen Smithereen of her kitchen, Amy Harrison: High Priestess Smithereen of Providence County (RI), and Neil Stephens: Head of the Woolwellian Sheep Herding Smithereens, Chief Retired British Smithereen Living in Canada, L and M Smith - Lord Smithereen of Gray Court, SC, Jude, Lady Smithereen of Wellesbourne, Joan, the Completely Inappropriate Grandma of Spring Hill, Vaughan Harris - Archbishop of Badass, Rebekah Jones Viceroy Smithereen of Weedon Bec, Avon Perry - Duchess of Heartbreak and Woe, Dawnie, Lady cock knocker of whangarei land, Renee - Caffeinated Queen of the Texas Desert, Carly - Desk Speaker Fake Plant Monitor AirPods Glass of Vimto, John Bate - Infringeur Smithereen of Blackpool, Stephen Stewart - Smithereen of Outer Space, DWFG "Abbess of the Craggy Island Smithereen High Order, Dave Carver - Chief Smithereen of Big Orange Country, Drucilla Buckley - Queen Mawmaw Smithereen, Adele - Mistress of her house and all within it (even the cat) Spanish chapter, David Coykendall – Twixton - A Necessary Evil, and Tracey Galloway-Lindsey - Joffers the bastard a spaceworm in the Shire Smithereen

Made in the USA
Monee, IL
19 September 2024

66159776R00204